MW00803091

THE SHIVER TREE

HOLLY SEARCY

THE SHIVER TREE

BLACK STONE

PUBLISHING

Printed in the United States of America

First edition: 2024
ISBN 979-8-212-43772-1
Fiction / Fantasy / Action & Adventure

Version 1

Blackstone Publishing
31 Mistletoe Rd.
Ashland, OR 97520

www.BlackstonePublishing.com

To Ben, my constant source of inspiration

Old Home

Gold Bay

Solacru

Coral

Hangman's Watch

Rovenia

Tribali

Highmane

Battle Tree

Dulin

Thessia

Bo

Devil's Trident

Stormfront

Harrian

Estlin

Akkra

Massing

Northland

Storm Lake

Camisierra

Southland

Mooreland

Garrison

Haven

High Crag

Eastdale

Marago

Sea of Glass

Byre

Teal

Amarra

CHAPTER ONE

Lights danced above the treetops, filling the late-afternoon sky with pops of burgundy and indigo, a smattering of purest white outlined in gold. Below, the mages that conjured them twirled in time with the lute music drifting through the air, accompanied by the sweet refrain of summer carols. The revelers celebrated the opening of the annual Druid Conclave in the city of Corval, home to the High Druid and all but a few of Tribali's coastal elves. Over the next few days, the merriment would merge with a fall equinox fete as the lands bid farewell to summer in anticipation of the cooler autumn and winter months.

While the jollity continued all around the town square, druids from all over the continent of Amarra gathered in a secluded courtyard half a mile to the east, sitting in a large circle surrounding a white stone pedestal. Atop the platform, five symbols glittered in the sunlight, emblems of each of the founding Druid Orders: Sky, Ice, Jade, Spirit, and Sun. Though the Orders had long since scattered, drifting and mingling for centuries until the distinction between them had faded to legend, High Druid Ozmand Paletine still kept the old traditions alive, honoring the memory of things lost. A memory his daughter Kiana very much hoped to bring back to life.

Kiana stood at the back of the courtyard, waiting for a few others to sit before she took her place beside her father. Her thumbs tapped a steady rhythm against her fingers. For ten years she'd attended these conclaves, watched the endless declarations of achievements, the glad-handing, the recitation of druidic lore, always to be honored but never acted upon, as best Kiana could tell. When she was fifteen, the gathering fascinated her. At twenty, she began to question the status quo, mostly in the safety of her own rooms but occasionally at dinner with her father. Now, at twenty-five, weariness crept into the deepest corners of her soul.

"Lady Paletine, a pleasure to see you again." A blond gnome appeared from behind a statue, startling Kiana from her thoughts.

"Waylyn, hello." She dipped her head, strands of her deep-auburn hair falling over her shoulders. "How are matters in Teal?"

"Most excellent, thank you for asking. Late spring we were able to rid the west shore of a terrible wheat blight. Spared thousands of crops. Many likely would have gone hungry, suffered through a meager winter."

"That's wonderful." A smile found itself to her lips by rote. "Praise Nelami." The nature goddess's name slipped out perfunctorily as well. While Kiana held the Lady of the Wilds in the highest esteem, the young druid often felt that the Conclave turned her into an inanity, her name tossed about like every other platitude or banality.

"Praise Nelami indeed." Waylyn bowed and moved off to find his seat, skirting around the taller attendees with practiced care.

Two half-elf brothers strode past, barely sparing Kiana a glance, wearing their resentment like a summer sash. As daughter of the High Druid, Kiana enjoyed elevated status among their kind by proxy, and some felt it lent her an unfair advantage in the bid to ascend once Ozmand's position of leadership ended its fifty-year term a decade from now. He himself made no secret of the fact that he wished her to follow in his footsteps. No one had yet asked Kiana whether she intended to take that path. If she did, she'd be the youngest High Druid on record.

"Lusha, Arneth," she said, her greeting bouncing off the siblings' backs.

"Ignore them," a low voice said just over her shoulder. "Manners in Old Home are not what they used to be."

Kiana turned to face the raven-haired elf wearing robes of pale green, the shade a near match to his irises.

"And what of Tiresh? Have the Southland elves managed to maintain their decorum?"

One side of his mouth quirked up. "A matter I'd be happy to discuss after the Regent Ceremony this evening. Let you decide for yourself." With a flourish of the hand and a sparkle of mint-colored magic, he produced a jasmine blossom, Kiana's favorite. He tucked the flower behind her ear.

Kiana pasted on a polite smile. "A tempting offer, Elin. But I'm afraid I already have plans for tonight."

"Mmm. With Ari, no doubt. Is she here?" He glanced around.

Kiana's stomach wobbled. Apparently she hadn't been as clever as she thought. She relied on her best friend, Aravel, to provide her with an excuse to bow out of social interactions she found too tedious or awkward. She'd pulled the scheme on Elin the last two years running to ward off his affections. Though also a druid, Aravel had chosen to skip the Conclave's opening ceremony, partly because she loathed the self-important back-patting even more than Kiana did, but also in case Kiana decided to make up some mysterious condition for her that required Kiana's assistance. Her father had grown wise to this deception, and it seemed Elin was doing the same. Fortunately, the two druids did, in fact, have plans that evening.

Kiana felt a distinct pang of envy at Aravel's ability to simply opt out of such an event, despite more or less being raised by Ozmand after her parents were killed nearly twenty years before. The same night Kiana's own mother died.

"Yes, as a matter of fact. A belated birthday dinner for her. And no, she isn't here tonight. She'll join the festivities tomorrow, though."

Elin's gaze roamed her face, perhaps searching for a lie, maybe an invitation. Kiana kept the latter trapped behind clenched teeth.

After a lengthy pause, he said, "Right, well, give her my best wishes."

"Of course."

"One of these days I'll get you to Tiresh. Have you still never been to Southland at all?"

"Haven't yet had the pleasure, no."

"The invitation stands. Anytime you feel like gracing our humble mountains with your presence, you are welcome."

"That's very kind."

He looked like he wanted to say more, perhaps press the issue, but fortunately Ozmand chose that moment to call the meeting to order, a small clap of thunder reverberating through the room. The hedges surrounding the courtyard filled out and suddenly doubled in height, topping twelve feet. Though nondruid residents of Corval knew to avoid this area while the Conclave was in session, the added privacy ensured curious eyes found nothing of interest.

"Welcome, druids of Amarra!" Ozmand's voice filled the space, warm like the late-summer air. "Please, everyone take your seats."

Shifting bodies maneuvered around the circle, approximately eighty in all. Fewer every year. Four chairs remained unoccupied, in homage to the lost representatives of the Ice and Sky Druids, the first of the Orders to vanish from the annals of druidic history. Honoring their memory became a fixed tradition during the Conclave even after the remaining Orders also ceased to be, albeit under less extreme circumstances. While the Sky Druids were believed to have secluded themselves in their impenetrable home at the center of Storm Lake, the Ice Druids had simply disappeared. So much history had been erased around that time, buried, forgotten, stolen by tragedy. Over the years, Kiana had thrown herself into the study of the Orders, yet she still knew very little about them.

Sliding into the cushioned seat to her father's right, Kiana scanned the gathering, eyes skipping over Elin to avoid a rush of guilt. She suffered that emotion enough already. Most of the visiting faces looked familiar. All were elven, gnomish, or half-elven, the only races known to have innate druidic magic. Far from all members of these races were born with the gift; in fact, fewer and fewer druids were born every year. Their numbers had dwindled to hundreds rather than the thousands once filling the different lands of Amarra.

Three faces on the far side of the circle stood out as first-time attendees—two elves, one gnome. Their gazes darted from place to place, taking it all in. They would be the initiates, those receiving the mark of the Regent Tree this evening to become full-fledged druids. All those with druidic potential were born with the outline of a seed on their left forearm. After completing the appropriate training, each was invited to the following Druidic Conclave to fulfill their rite of passage in the Regent Ceremony.

Kiana ran her fingers down her left forearm along her own mark, a five-limbed tree with sparse foliage and an empty circle in the trunk's middle. At rest, the mark was a pale sienna only a few shades darker than her skin. When a druid used magic, the tree darkened, taking on hues of their innate magic. Kiana's adopted shades of purple. She wondered what colors would decorate these newcomers in a few hours' time.

Once everyone settled, Ozmand raised his hands. "Let us begin with the Druids' Hymn."

Together, the druids cast their voices to the sky.

> *Blessed Nelami, Lady of the Wilds,*
> *our hearts seek communion with thee.*
> *We call on your grace for aged and for child,*
> *the power of nature and sea.*

A moment of silence followed before Ozmand stood, hands lifting as though raising an invisible tome on upturned palms. A dais of vines sprouted from the stones at his feet. Kiana caught the faint darkening of his Regent Tree to a gentle teal as the podium reached his chest.

"Now we come to order," the High Druid said. "And I fear our first matter of discussion is a grave one indeed."

Whispers rose and then faded as Ozmand raised one hand for silence.

"All of you are already aware that Tribali has suffered continued attacks at the hands of the pirates. Though an all-out raid has not occurred in more than a year, the theft of Crucian metal continues to desecrate our shores."

Sudden rage boiled beneath Kiana's skin, an unfamiliar sensation. Crucian metal was a rare material whose ore was found deep in the waters around Tribali. The country's blacksmiths used it to craft weapons that held a divine magic particularly well suited to slaying fiends, like the demons and devils who had repeatedly tried to invade and enslave Amarra over the millennia. Kiana's people also believed the metal absorbed some of its bearer's soul, making it sacred. Those weapons not buried with their owners passed to trusted family members. Pirates had been sporadically pillaging the metal from Tribali's shores and burial grounds for centuries, an act both unthinkable and unforgivable.

The issue hit especially hard for Kiana, whose mother was slain during one of the pirate raids nineteen years ago.

"Our Tide Hunters continue to track pirate movements, seeking an opportunity to strike," Ozmand continued, "but the brigands have become more furtive of late. They're keeping off the main waterways, further out to sea. We will continue to do what we can to stop them. In the meantime, *stelirian*."

He waved a hand in time with the incantation, a broad stroke across the front of his body. Starlight bloomed in the air before him. The constellations coalesced into a map, its contours denoting the eastern edge of Northland, near Rovenia.

"A different problem persists. In recent months, there have been six werewolf sightings outside the Northland borders. Their violence within that territory has grown untenable, refugees fleeing wherever they can get out. The druids there are fighting an unwinnable war, their numbers insufficient to stem the tide of the werewolf blight. They've sent just one representative to give us a full briefing while the others continue the fight." He indicated an elf to his left, who nodded acknowledgment. "We cannot allow the curse to spread. These blights, greater abominations of the natural order, must not continue."

"Then we need to reestablish the Orders." The words were out of Kiana's mouth before the thought had finished forming in her mind. Her cheeks burned.

Murmurs wisped around the circle, Kiana's elven ears having no trouble picking up various comments along the "this again" vein. Ozmand's lips flattened in a tight line.

"While I do not disagree," he said, "we have more pressing matters to deal with. If the werewolf numbers continue to grow while our own drop like stones in a well, the people of Amarra will suffer greatly. The moon-turned beasts are not like our own wild shapes. They lack control, killing indiscriminately wherever they go. Likewise, the pirates *must* be found and stopped. The diseases wiping out crops across the continent *must* be stopped."

The familiar argument heightened the weariness gnawing at the center of Kiana's being. She'd tried for years, futilely, to get her father to see the importance of reestablishing the Orders. She'd had enough. She stood.

"How can you not see it? As druids, it is our duty to maintain balance in the world, between elements, between nature and those who inhabit it. That balance cannot be *maintained* because it no longer *exists*! Ever since the Druid Orders fell, Amarra's equilibrium has deteriorated. These blights, as we're so fond of calling them, have to be a direct result of that. Without balance among ourselves, how can we supply it for everyone and everything else?"

Silence met her outburst. Most of those seated around her averted their eyes, the rest keeping their gazes fixed on Ozmand, awaiting his response. Elin turned his eyes to his lap, expression unreadable. The first-timers stared straight ahead uncomfortably.

"You"—Kiana pointed at Waylyn, too fired up to stop just yet—"you say the druids of Teal stopped a wheat blight, but do you know what caused it in the first place? This is your fifth crop blight in three years. When the Jade Druids lived, they didn't have five blights in three *centuries*." She turned to Arneth. "And Old Home. Two plagues this year alone. How many have died needlessly in the absence of the Spirit Druids' influence?"

The half-elf glared before lowering his gaze.

At last, Kiana turned to her father. "Even here, druidic power wanes. Our forests were once a guarding force against invasion. How many pirates have pierced our borders because the greater balance has been lost?" Unshed tears glittered at the corners of her eyes, the power of her emotions and the pain of her memories colliding in a suffocating wave.

The shutters fell over Ozmand's expression. "I admire your passion and agree that the Orders must be revived. But"—her father's crisp pronunciation of the word deflated Kiana's spirit—"it must wait until we can put the threats in check."

Giving a nod of resignation, Kiana sank back into her chair. For the next two hours, she barely listened as the visiting druids updated the others on what they'd accomplished in the year past, what councils and rulers they'd advised on matters of nature and medicine. Even talk of plans to reinforce the border at Rovenia fell on ears muddled by despair and frustration.

She had her own plans to make.

CHAPTER TWO

In the stretch of forest that lay between Kiana's cottage and Ozmand's home, a lone elm dwelled among the redwoods, pines, and firs. Half again as tall and four times the width of a normal mature elm, this Tree shed a peculiar light into the coming dusk. Motes of glowing yellow drifted like fireflies in a ten-foot radius around the sprawling branches. Each flickered into nothing before touching the ground.

This was the Monarch Tree, the key to druidic magic. By its power, a druid was granted abilities beyond basic spells like lighting a campfire or moving sticks and rocks from their path. It was here the Regent Seed would become the Regent Tree, the mark of a full druid.

Members of the Conclave gathered near the base of the massive elm, the three initiates shuffling their feet at the edge of the group. Ozmand took his place directly beside the tree, hands folded before him.

"It is my great honor to guide our newest initiates into the next stage of their magical growth." He placed a hand reverently on the rough bark. "The Monarch Tree has ever bestowed Nelami's gifts upon our people, and we give thanks for continued blessings." He swept a hand in a wide arc. "Alura, step forward."

The female elf stepped toward her destiny, gait measured but confident. When she came within two feet of the trunk, she knelt.

Ozmand moved to stand before her. "By the grace of Nelami, may the Monarch Tree welcome you to the fold. Rise and accept your gift."

Alura did as instructed, taking the final few steps forward. Her hand reached out and caressed the bark, coming to rest with palm flat against the trunk.

Nothing happened.

Kiana knew from witnessing dozens of these ceremonies—and experiencing one of her own—that light *should* have engulfed the initiate's arm, filled the air with its comforting glow as the tree infused her with new levels of magic. Hundreds of motes of yellow *should* have exploded into the night. And finally, the seed mark on Alura's arm *should* have grown into a tree, sprouting but a few leaves to signify experience and ability. Not a single one of those things occurred.

Ozmand cleared his throat and motioned for Alura to step back. She did so, and Ozmand repeated the recitation. He again had her approach the tree, placing her hand firmly on the trunk.

Again nothing happened.

Unease clenched Kiana's insides, tightened her chest. The others around her looked about for some kind of explanation. Her eyes found her father's, the confusion in his turning to something else entirely when he took note of the emerald blaze of accusation in her own. She didn't need to say the words out loud.

I told you so.

Never before had the Monarch Tree failed to grant a Regent Tree to a properly trained druid. Kiana watched with mounting dread as the remaining two initiates went through the motions of the ceremony only to suffer the same result.

The power of the druids hung over a dangerous precipice. Kiana spun on her heel and marched into the falling night.

Nestled into her favorite beach cove, Kiana watched the sun complete its descent behind the far edges of the sea, this day of would-be celebration

melting into an unsettled twilight. Her keen eyes drifted restlessly across
the waves. Behind her, evergreens stretched toward the darkening sky,
immovable guardians of the coast. For all the good they did now.

Kiana breathed in the salty air, the brine of the sea tickling her
nose. The tide was gentle this time of year, yet every lap of the waves
against her bare toes increased the sense of dread building in the pit of
her stomach. She picked up a small, smooth stone from the sand and
rubbed it between her fingers.

"How did we let it come so far?" she whispered to the horizon.

The soft slap of water against wet sand and the gentle roar of distant waves were the only response. She tossed the stone out into the
water and picked up another, digging the cool, rounded edge into
her thumb before sending it, too, out into the sea. Though still holding some warmth from the summer sun, the night air grew heavy,
mirroring the weight pressing ever more firmly on Kiana's chest.
The tide rushed over her feet, and she felt something brush against
her. Absentmindedly, she reached down and picked it up, expecting another stone. Instead her hand clenched around metal, cold
and sharp.

In her palm lay a piece of metal perfectly crafted into a jasmine blossom, an exact replica of the flower Elin had gifted her this very night,
the bloom still adorning her hair. A symbol of good fortune. Kiana cast
her gaze back out to the water, searching.

"Where did you come from?" she muttered.

Firelight flickered into existence behind her, averting her intense
curiosity for the moment.

Without looking back, Kiana tucked the flower into the satin belt
of her slit green dress.

"You found me," she said, a twinge of irritation turning the words
bitter in her mouth.

Ozmand settled into the pebble-strewn sand beside her, a spurt of
flame hovering above one palm. As always, he smelled of jasmine and fir.
Despite herself, Kiana found the scent acting as a balm on her nerves,
even with everything hanging between them.

"You've loved coming out here to think since you were small. Some things don't change."

Change.

The word hit Kiana's rawest nerve, and she bit the inside of her cheek to keep her emotions level.

"But maybe others should," she said, her words barely above a whisper.

Her father shifted beside her. He exhaled a long, slow breath through his nose, a sign he was searching for the right thing to say. Always the diplomat.

"I know you tire of hearing the same old arguments. I want you to know that I hear you about the Orders. I do. But being High Druid is a complicated balancing act. There are many factors, many peoples, to consider."

Kiana bit off a laugh at his choice of words. "Perhaps there should be more balancing in such an act."

Ozmand swallowed a sigh. "There are political factors to consider as well."

Kiana sat up straighter. At last, she turned her piercing green eyes on her father, their former blaze reduced to embers but not extinguished.

"When did the honor of leading as High Druid become only about politics?"

He pulled in a deep breath, gaze moving to the water. Moonlight danced through his hair, silver since his birth. "The world isn't what it once was. With our numbers dropping rapidly, responsibilities have shifted."

"Exactly my point! We have to rebuild the Orders. By letting the in-dividual elements weaken, we've sabotaged our own strength as a whole. The hourglass tipped the moment the bonds between Orders were sev-ered. If we don't act fast, the sands will run out." A hopeful entreaty glittered behind her eyes.

A cloud passed over the moon, wisping shadows across Ozmand's face. He stayed quiet for a moment; then with a sigh he brushed a hand over his hair.

"It's not that simple."

"Why not?"

"I   "

"High Druid!"

Both father and daughter turned toward the anxious voice. From the tree line farther up the beach emerged a lanky elf with shoulder-length brown hair pulled into a bun, his deeply sun-kissed skin taking on a bluish tinge from the brilliant moon above.

"Sir!" he called again. Swift feet unencumbered by the shifting sand carried the messenger closer. "Your presence is requested at the manor immediately."

"What's this about?" Ozmand's fatherly tone evaporated as he effortlessly slid back into the role of Tribali's leader.

"Lord Ilirian arrived via teleportation rune not ten minutes ago. He has come seeking your help. Urgently." The messenger's typically calm demeanor struggled behind the hint of panic clouding his features.

Spikes of anxiety shot through Kiana. She had no time to dwell on the possible implications, however, as her father had taken off at a dead run the moment the messenger finished speaking. Kiana was quick on his heels, the messenger bringing up the rear. Pine boughs arched up and away of their own accord as they raced back through the woods, easing their way through the forest. Kiana barely noticed, the beauty of the night drowned out by the worry of what they would find when they arrived at her father's estate.

Please let Tash be okay, she thought, sending a silent prayer to Nelami.

The trees opened up on the outskirts of Corval. Straight ahead, the town square still glowed like a beacon to the lost and weary, orbs of magical light dancing tranquil circles around a lone, majestic elm, a smaller version of the Monarch Tree. They hurried past shops and cottages, catching concerned glances along the way.

At last, the High Druid's home emerged from the shadows ahead. Though known affectionately as "the manor," the house wasn't much larger than the others in the area, the coastal elves having little taste for extravagance—unlike certain city elves, Ozmand's unexpected guest among them.

A glance told Kiana the other druids had also dispersed from the Monarch Tree, but she spared it no further thought as she ran.

Outside the front door stood an elf in black leather armor, longsword drawn and held at his side. The deep-brown skin of his face drew back tightly, concern flashing behind the cool blue of his eyes. He nodded to Ozmand as they approached but said nothing, his only communication silent.

Hurry.

Kiana burst through the door behind her father, mind now racing wildly through a host of distressing what-ifs. The scene that lay before her was not one she'd considered.

Lord Kellen Ilirian stood rigid by the fireplace, long black hair falling around his shoulders. Shadows flickered across his pale features. His eldest son, Tem, hunched over the sofa, hands worrying over an inert figure. Behind the sofa stood another visitor. Kiana's breath caught.

"Tash," she said, the name slipping past her lips involuntarily in a breathy hush. Relief poured through her.

The tall, elegant elf pushed himself up from where he'd been resting his hands against the back of the sofa. A soft smile crept up his face, reaching all the way to his amber eyes, which were perfectly complemented by the deep blue of his silk shirt. His thick shock of dark hair, the rich brown hue of Tribalian black walnut wood, caught the firelight.

"Lady Kiana," he said with a respectful nod. Despite the smile, worry laced the gorgeous features of his face.

Ignoring the exchange, Ozmand moved quickly to the sofa after offering the briefest of greetings to Kellen.

"What's happened?" He knelt beside the limp figure on the couch.

Kiana noted, with alarm, that the figure was that of a young girl, one she'd met before. Tem's daughter, Laera. Tash's niece. The girl's shallow breath came in ragged gasps. Beads of sweat dotted her ashen brow, the skin far paler than the last time Kiana had seen her—saved her. She seemed to have shrunk in upon herself, bones protruding where they should not, visible beneath her thin nightdress. Kiana hurried to her, crouching between Tem and her father. Gently, she dabbed at the perspiration drifting down one cheek.

"Tem?" Tash prompted when his brother made no reply.

The distraught father choked out a sob and pressed his forehead to his daughter's, seemingly unaware of Ozmand's careful examination of the child. Behind him, Kellen lowered his head.

"She fell ill two weeks ago," Tash said, stepping in to fill the silence. "At first, her symptoms seemed minor. Slight fever, memory lapses, loss of appetite. After a week, she started talking to herself, muttering nonsense for hours on end. Then, three days ago, she collapsed in the garden." He gazed fondly at his niece, concern knitting his brows together. "She hasn't woken since. We've had healers from all over come to see her." He looked at Ozmand. "No one can figure out what's wrong with her. As High Druid, we're hoping you can do what others apparently cannot."

The whole time Tash spoke, Ozmand remained focused on the girl, doing his best to work around Tem, whose face was now pressed into the cushions, hands clasped around his daughter's frail arm. Kiana stood and moved back to the edge of the room to give him space.

Despite the High Druid's lack of acknowledgment during Tash's explanation, Kiana knew he'd heard every word, soaking in the information as he worked to determine the source of the ailment. He placed a hand on the girl's ashen, glistening cheek.

"Revelerme incante."

Motes of silver sparked across Ozmand's stormy blue irises. On his left forearm, the Regent Tree, lush with foliage, darkened against his skin, changing from its usual sienna to a deep ocean blue. A small whimper escaped the girl, causing Tem's head to jolt off the couch.

"What did you do to her?" he yelled, finally taking notice of the others in the room.

"I did nothing," Ozmand replied calmly. Something in his expression sent a tickle of disquiet shivering down Kiana's spine. "There is strong magic at work here, something I've never encountered before."

"Can you fix it?" Kellen asked, more a demand than a question. As a member of the Elven Council in Highmane, he was used to getting his way, though Corval hadn't fallen under the Council's sway for some time.

A frown creased Ozmand's brow. "Not until I know more." He held up a hand as Tem's chin dropped onto his chest. "But I can at least buy us time to find answers."

Tem raised a tearstained face to the healer. "Do it," he said, throat raw, ravaged by grief.

Immediately Ozmand lifted the shivering child's head between his palms.

"*Ivocar majese popeli mea . . .*" His eyes flashed silver as green spectral runes flared up before him. He continued the incantation, the runes shifting and reshaping with his words. The Regent Tree's magical ink turned nearly black on his arm, hundreds of tattooed leaves fluttering.

Kiana watched her father weave the spell into the girl, felt its power, and self-consciously rubbed a finger over her own tattoo, the leaves of which she could count on two hands. Her father's effortless command of Nelami's magic sent a helpless pang of inadequacy through her, compounded by the presence of the Ilirian family. The family she'd failed. She shook the feeling off. There was no time for that now.

As the glow from the runes intensified, Tash moved from behind the sofa and joined Kiana. She felt his warmth beside her and suppressed the urge to lean into him. Heat prickled her belly, want and guilt at war within her.

A full minute later, Ozmand finished the spell. The spectral runes slammed together, forming a single shape, then vanished from the air, reappearing as a sigil on the girl's forehead. A sharp intake of breath preceded a small bit of color returning to her cheeks. She remained still, though her breath came easier. She seemed at peace.

"What happened? What is that?" Tem asked, voice trembling. He pointed at the symbol, which glowed a faint blue.

"The Mark of Alsäm. I've placed her in stasis sleep. Whatever magic has a hold on her should be held at bay until we can find answers."

"How long will it last?" Kellen asked.

Ozmand turned to the noble, who fiddled restlessly with a small rectangle of carved jade: the teleportation rune, one of the rarer and more expensive magical items on Amarra. Few were privileged enough to acquire such a thing.

"Up to a year, if need be. But my hope is we learn what ails her long before that."

Kellen nodded. "Thank you."

"Let me see what I can learn tonight," Ozmand said, standing. "The Conclave has concluded business for the day. You're welcome to spend the night in our guest cottages, or even right here. We have plenty of bedrooms. Your teleportation rune will be of no use to you until tomorrow, anyway."

Kellen nodded. Most magical runes took up to a day to refresh their infused enchantment once spent, though a few could be used multiple times a day.

"Again, thank you," the elder noble said. Tem remained glued to his daughter's side, hovering over her like a shroud. Kiana shook the image away.

"I'll have some food brought out," Ozmand said. "Make yourselves at home." He started toward his study but paused, head pivoting back to the room. His eyes found Kellen. "Pedigree will not help her here. Prayers for healing would not go amiss." He disappeared down the hall.

CHAPTER THREE

Kiana stood frozen, unsure how to address the anxiety-ridden room, desperate to offer Laera comfort but not wanting to disrupt a father's grief. Tash's nearness redoubled the knots around her tongue. Conflicting emotions throttled her typical verbal proficiency when speaking to the man who had unwittingly captured her heart. The man she could not have.

"Would you like to go for a walk?" Tash said softly in her ear. "I think it best we leave Tem to his prayers for the time being."

His sudden closeness, the warmth of his breath, sparked her nerve endings.

He motioned to the door. "I haven't seen you in nearly two months and thought we could catch up."

Kiana held her hands out to him, a telltale flush tingling along her cheekbones. She wondered to what extent her face betrayed her. "I'd love to." She looked to Laera one last time, safe beneath Tem's watchful eye, and headed to the door.

Outside, starlight glittered through the canopy of trees like a million tiny diamonds. Kiana breathed in the coastal forest air, savoring the familiar woodsy scents of her home. She felt tension melt from her shoulders. For a minute, neither elf spoke, strolling leisurely toward the center of town. Tash reached out a finger and touched the jasmine blossom Elin had tucked behind her ear. She'd forgotten it was there.

He spoke. "I remember when I was quite young, a druid passing through Highmane on her way back here stopped to aid a horse that had been spooked by a cart. I'd been to the Crystalline Waterfalls with Tem and was returning home by myself. The druid was so gentle, so kind, that I couldn't help but stand and watch as she soothed the animal, speaking to it like it was the most natural thing in the world. Afterward, she caught me looking and gave me a wink. Just like that, a dozen jasmine blossoms bloomed along the stick I was carrying, easy as anything. That was the first time I ever witnessed druidic magic at work."

Kiana smiled and pulled the flower from her hair. "I didn't know that." She placed the bloom atop the low wall along the road, praying they didn't cross paths with Elin. More than likely, he was with the rest of the druids in the Treetop Grove, finishing the evening with somber reflection on the day's events.

"Sometimes it amazes me how isolated we in Highmane tend to keep ourselves from the rest of Tribali. A shame, really." Another beat passed before Tash said, "I apologize for disrupting your evening like this. I wish I could have come under different circumstances. I've been meaning to come for another visit, since our time touring the Kalia Groves got cut short during my last sojourn, but life has a way of putting duty before pleasure." The young noble dipped his head, hands folded behind his back.

The movement instantly reminded Kiana of Kellen, a habit no doubt passed from father to son through mere exposure. Aside from noble bloodline and proficiency with arcane magic, that was about where the similarity of the two Highmane elves ended. Kellen's preoccupation with wealth, status, and power set him vastly apart from his kind, unpretentious offspring.

"I'm so sorry about Laera." She clutched at the amethyst pendant she wore around her neck, a gift from her mother. "I wish I could've been of help."

Tash turned his body slightly toward her, head cocked.

"Considering how much you've already assisted our family, I wouldn't worry about it."

Her head snapped in his direction, eyes searching his face for sincerity, fearing she'd find the opposite. All she saw was kindness.

Does he mean it?

Awkward silence stretched between them. Every word Kiana knew exited her brain as the lull in the conversation lengthened.

Anything, she thought desperately. *Say anything.*

Finally, she came to her senses, squashing the nagging accusations, the memories of *that day*, scattering her thoughts like seeds on the wind. The crunch of a leaf beneath her sandal spurred her on.

"Do you plan to attend the Festival of Tamai again this year?" She knew the celebration of autumn's return was one of Highmane's biggest events, one she'd been keen to attend in years past but failed to make the journey for. Had she done so before, perhaps she would have met Tash under better circumstances. Perhaps she could have closed the distance between them without fear of unrelenting guilt tearing them back apart.

"Indeed. Perhaps you could come up to Highmane for a few days and enjoy the festivities?"

Yes, please, Kiana's brain urged her to say. Instead, her mind drifted to the evening's Regent Ceremony, the failure of the Monarch Tree.

"That sounds lovely, truly. Unfortunately, I have somewhere else I have to be."

"Oh?"

Kiana sighed. "This year's Druid Conclave got . . . complicated."

"Complicated how?"

Nature's magic as we know it hanging in the balance, she thought. "There's a problem with the Monarch Tree. It didn't . . ." Her head drifted from side to side, disbelief overtaking her as the next words came out of her mouth. "It didn't work."

Tash tilted his head. "I'm sorry, I'm not particularly familiar with druidic rites. What does that mean?"

As a sorcerer, an arcane caster, Tash drew power from his bloodline. Sorcerers could use any type of arcane magic, from evocation or illusion to necromancy. They didn't have ceremonies to come into power. They simply harnessed energy from within themselves, usually beginning at puberty.

Druids, by contrast, were gifted magic by the goddess Nelami, allowing them to work in harmony with nature. They became healers, grove tenders, advisers on environmental matters. They could even shift forms into animals. While bloodline made innate druidic ability more likely, it was never a guarantee.

Kiana held out her arm, showing her Regent Tree. "The ceremony at the Monarch Tree is how we get these, how we become fully endowed with nature's power. This year, the marks didn't come."

"Has that ever happened before?"

"Not as far as I know."

They circled around a group of mages enchanting a trio of flutes to play as they danced.

Kiana shook her head. "Everything has become so politicized. There was a time when being High Druid meant more than saving wheat crops and corralling werewolves."

Tash pursed his lips. "From what I've seen, your father has been far more active in his duties than the previous High Druids I've heard about."

A hint of shame sent a burning sensation along Kiana's hairline.

"You're right, of course. I don't mean to sound disrespectful. I'm just so frustrated. All my life I've been taught to do good, help others, promote peace and balance—like my father—but none of that means anything if there's no balance to promote. For years I've been studying the Druid Orders, and I am fully convinced that they existed for a reason. But instead of hearing me out, my father redirects his attention to the symptoms of the issue rather than the cause. All the while, he keeps me sheltered in our little corner of the world, tasking me with mentorship here or grove tending there."

"Why do you think that is? Him sheltering you, I mean."

"I imagine it has something to do with his disapproval of my sister's life choices. And probably my mother's death when I was small. He thinks he can protect me by keeping me close. All this training to be High Druid . . . sometimes I fear it's his way of keeping me here with him."

"So, is that where you having somewhere else to be comes in?"

From somewhere inside her, Kiana felt a nudge. The mysterious sensation pressed harder the longer she focused on it.

You must go.

"Yes. I think the time for talk has ended. I need to get out in the world and see what I can actually *do*. My father would be furious, though."

Tash's mouth curved in a strange half smile. "It's not his life. It's yours."

The shift in his tone caught Kiana's attention. She wondered if he spoke from personal experience. Family ties ran strong in elven culture, but sometimes conflicting personalities led to unbridgeable rifts between parent and child. Kiana had witnessed too many such fissures crack foundations in her own childhood home. It was why her sister no longer lived in Corval.

"You're right. I've been living the life he wants for me without standing up for what my heart tells me to do. It's time for that to change."

"That's the spirit." Tash nudged her with his elbow, grinning.

They found a bench in the center of town and settled onto it, gazes drawn to the swirling lights hovering about the elm. The magical orbs cast their bright-white glow along the boughs, which reached out welcomingly to all who passed.

Something wistful came over Tash's expression, a bit of his worry finally drifting away. "I've missed this."

Kiana followed his gaze. "The lights?"

He chuckled. "No. Our conversations." He tilted his face to look at her. "Every time I'm with you, I'm surprised anew at how easy it is to simply . . . talk."

At least it is for one of us, Kiana thought, swallowing the words in favor of a smile. She leaned into the compliment, savored it.

"I've missed it too."

The moment slipped away into the ensuing silence. Tash lifted a hand, palm up.

"*Tanslk ogna*," he whispered.

A spark of amber magic crackled in his palm, forming into six glowing orbs that floated one by one into the air. As they rose, the lights morphed into six small prancing foxes.

A delighted grin stretched Kiana's mouth wide.

"I noticed your furry companion is nowhere to be found tonight, thought maybe these could make up for his absence."

Their eyes met, and Kiana couldn't suppress another smile.

"Thank you," she said. Admiring the luminous foxes, she added, "Snow spent the day with Aravel, blackberry hunting, while I was trapped at"—she cleared her throat—"*attending* the Conclave. We're all going to meet up later for some mead." Her eyes widened. "I mean, Snow doesn't drink, just Aravel and I . . ." She let the words die on her tongue.

Tash graced her with an amused quirk of the lips.

"You're welcome to join us," Kiana added. Her thoughts slipped again to Elin, and she prayed he'd stick to the Conclave.

"On any other night, I would readily accept such an invitation. Unfortunately, I should get back to Laera and my brother, make sure everything is okay."

"Of course. I'll check in on her later as well. Let me know if you need anything."

"I shall, thank you." He stood, then reached out and took her hand, pressing his lips into it. "Thank you for the company." With a bow, the sorcerer took his leave.

Kiana watched him saunter back across the square. She could still feel where his lips had pressed into the back of her hand, warm and soft.

Tomorrow suddenly felt heavy with possibility. She didn't relish the thought of telling her father of her new plans, but she was well past the age of needing permission to live her life.

Heaving herself off the bench, Kiana set off toward her best friend's cottage. All thoughts of what her journey might bring would have to wait.

CHAPTER FOUR

Old Home.

The morning sun was shining high and bright by the time those two words, spoken somewhere far in the back of her mind, pulled Kiana from a deep and dreamless slumber. Four hours of sleep seemed enough to wipe away the roughest edges of the previous night's revels, but her final shot of rum—insisted on by Aravel—knocked lightly at the back of her skull. She hadn't even bothered to strip off her clothes when she'd fallen into bed the night before.

Her thoughts took a moment to focus, and she fought through the morning cobwebs to find a reason she'd be thinking about the city of Old Home upon waking. The events of last evening came crashing back to her. She knew what she had to do.

But first, a more pressing matter. Touching her palms together in front of her chest, she closed her eyes and focused her attention on the dull ache in her head. Magic surged through her, gentle but insistent.

"*Sanye dolim.*" Streaks of magical energy formed intricate patterns of luminous, tessellating leaves in her mind's eye. A single leaf twitched on her Regent Tree, deepening to lilac before resuming its resting hue. Fortunately, minor spells could be cast without tapping into one's well of magic, which would replenish with enough rest or the breaking of a new dawn. The most powerful nature mages, those with fully mature Regent Trees—like the High Druid—could cast any spell without losing a leaf, though at a certain point, physical exhaustion would win out.

Spell complete, the throbbing in Kiana's skull dissipated like an early-morning fog lifting with the rising sun.

She smiled. "Much better." She glanced down at the red fox sleeping soundly at the foot of the bed and ruffled his creamy belly fur. "How about you, Snow? Any regrets from last night?"

A snort and soft whine met the question. The druid pressed a kiss to his snout and left him to sleep away the morning. As usual.

At her dresser, she grabbed her hairbrush and felt something slip over her hip before hitting the floor. She bent down and picked up the metal flower she'd found on the beach the night before. She'd forgotten to remove the item from where she'd tucked it in her belt. She held it to the light, examining the craftsmanship: simple but elegant, slightly warped on one side, giving the illusion of movement. She rubbed her thumb over the curve of the petals.

"Let's hope you really are a sign of good fortune. I may need it."

Carefully, she placed the flower in a small trinket box carved to look like a book. The new bauble lay beside a single jade earring of her mother's, one of Snow's baby teeth, a shard of wood etched with the druidic symbol for integrity from her father's old staff, and a shiny brass button. She closed the lid softly, then picked up her mother's silver circlet, which she braided her hair around to secure it atop her head.

After throwing on her favorite purple dress, which highlighted the subtle plum tint in her hair, she headed to her father's house, knowing today's Conclave events wouldn't begin for another couple of hours.

Stepping through the manor's side door, she found Ozmand and Tash enjoying their morning repast at the dining room table. Both men stood as Kiana entered.

"Kiana," Ozmand said with a smile, moving to kiss her on each cheek.

"Father." She looked across the table. "Good morning, Tash."

"Good morning, milady."

"Please, just Kiana is fine," she said, feeling oddly embarrassed at the honorific. She was, after all, speaking with a future lord of Highmane. The elves in the northern reaches of Tribali held tighter to status than those anywhere else on Amarra, though Tash often treated his nobility as more of a triviality than anything. "No need for such formalities here."

Tash smiled. "Of course. My apologies. Old habits."

Ozmand pulled out the chair next to him. "Join us, please."

Kiana obliged, snagging a honey bun from the platter at the center of the table as she sat. She plucked a chunk from the pastry. "How is Laera?"

Tash's easy smile remained in place, but something dark, a mere shadow of a shadow, passed briefly across his brow.

"The same. The stasis spell seems to be keeping her comfortable."

"That's good."

Old Home.

The words that had woken her earlier echoed unbidden in her thoughts. The moment of truth had arrived, and if she didn't speak now, Kiana wasn't sure she would. She cleared her throat.

"Father, I'm afraid I'm not going to be able to make it to the Conclave later." She felt his eyes burn into the side of her face. She forced her gaze to meet his. "Or the rest of the week."

"I beg your pardon?"

"I'm going to see Ravaini in Old Home. After what happened last night, I cannot continue to sit idly by. It's time I experience more of the world, figure out a way to mend the Orders, and Ravaini is always game for an adventure."

Storm clouds gathered across the High Druid's brow at the mention of his eldest daughter's name. Something dark blazed behind his deep-blue eyes.

Kiana's sister had left Tribali seven years earlier after a long and none-too-quiet fight with their father, the last in an extended series of arguments that had spanned most of Ravaini's life. She hadn't been back since, and neither would talk to Kiana about that night. They didn't need to. Born with the seed mark of a druid, Ravaini had turned her back on Nelami's gift, opting instead to throw herself into the Tide

Hunters—Tribali's elite fighting force—and the pursuit of pirates, their mother's killers. Furious at the betrayal of her birthright, Ozmand never let her live it down, and eventually Ravaini abandoned Tribali entirely.

The morning Ravaini left, Kiana woke to find her sister's cottage empty but for a beautiful dagger with the words "Sisters in life, sisters in death" etched into the blade. For Ravaini, it was a touching farewell. Kiana kept the weapon, a family heirloom, secured in a leather strap around her thigh.

Ozmand kept his voice steady. "Your duty is here."

Kiana held firm. "Eventually, maybe. But being your daughter doesn't guarantee anything, and how will I know if I'm the right choice to lead all of our kind if I don't experience their trials firsthand? Besides, I have plenty of time to become High Druid. Most don't gain the proper experience to be accepted by Nelami until after their first century. And you still have ten whole years remaining."

Ozmand swept aside her reasoning. "Old Home is nothing like Tribali. You have no idea what lurks in the shadows there, the iniquity that spreads through its core." His jaw set. "And I won't lose another daughter to darkness."

This time Kiana flinched, taken aback. "You speak as though Revy has given herself to the devils, sold her soul for power and glory."

"Has she not?"

Mouth agape, Kiana sat frozen.

Ozmand rubbed his hands down his face and through his hair, then put them out in supplication.

"I'm sorry," he said. "I shouldn't have said that."

Kiana lifted her chin, though doubt niggled at her. Lacking specifics, she did realize that her sister's chosen line of work put her in the company of dangerous folk. "You will never lose me, Father. And this is something I have to do. Besides, I'm twenty-five. Most elves have gone out on at least one adventure by this age." She held up a preemptive hand. "And I don't count diplomatic assemblies as adventures."

Though twenty-five was considered quite young for an elf, beings who lived for centuries or even millennia, most started exploring the

world and their potential callings by twenty. For Kiana, the grooming
to take her father's place had begun at fifteen and shoved all other experiences to the periphery. Her studious nature helped ensure that she
remained focused on this primary goal, staying home with her nose
wedged in a book while her friends hitched rides on passing ships destined for distant cities or roamed the wilds at Tribali's northern border.

Resignation softened Ozmand's features. Weariness etched itself in
the faint wrinkles around his eyes. After a few moments, he let out a
long sigh.

"I'll make you proud," Kiana promised, squeezing his hand.

As Ozmand's resigned smile faded, Kellen appeared in the doorway.

"Forgive the intrusion," he said, though his tone lacked any apparent apology.

"Not at all," Ozmand said, standing. "Would you care for some
breakfast?" He motioned to the spread of pastries, cheeses, and fruits
set atop the table.

Lord Ilirian gave the table a perfunctory glance. "No," he said. "We
would like to be on our way soon and were hoping you could attend
to Laera one last time, make sure everything is in order before we go."
He added, almost reluctantly, "After you've finished here, of course."

"Of course," Ozmand said pleasantly.

Kellen nodded once and turned to Tash. "Be ready to depart in two
hours." He didn't wait for a response, vanishing out the door as swiftly
as he'd come.

Tash cleared his throat and shot a quick rueful glance at the two
druids. "I apologize for his abrupt manner. He's been distracted of late."

"Indeed," Ozmand agreed, studying the younger mage, who casually avoided his gaze.

Tash finished the last bite of his scone and scooted back from the
table. "If you'll excuse me, it seems I will be departing shortly, and I
have something I must attend to."

A thought struck Kiana, and she spoke before her nerves could dis-
suade her.

"I know you have duties back home, but if you feel like throwing

off the Ilirian mantle for a bit in favor of an adventure, I was thinking maybe you and Aravel could join Ravaini and me, at least for
a while."

Tash cocked his head, a smile wiping away the crease in his pensive
brow. "Of course. I'd be honored to accompany you." The pleasure in
his voice thrilled Kiana's heart. He straightened the cuffs of his coat.
"I'll make the arrangements."

A grin flashed across Kiana's face, and she breathed a sigh of relief
when he hurried out of the room before the blush of her cheeks could
betray her again.

A familiar pang of guilt quickly tempered the joy spreading through
her, and she felt her face start to fall.

"It's been a year," Ozmand said softly beside her. Sometimes his in-
tuition could be maddening.

Her stomach clenched, and Kiana shut her eyes tight against a wave
of shame and sadness, hope and despair.

"I know," she whispered. She sensed the small intake of breath she
feared would lead further down this worn lane of memories, a path
choked with the weeds of regret. Before he could speak, she said, "If
you don't mind, I think I'll finish eating while I pack. I have a lot to
consider for this journey."

A look of knowing passed over Ozmand's face, unspoken disappointment weighting his half smile until it barely tugged at his lip. He nodded.

Grabbing some extra pastries for herself and a slice of cheese for
Snow, which she knew would be a mistake, she gave her father a brief
kiss on the cheek and executed a hasty retreat.

"This is so exciting!"

A beautifully tanned elf, golden hair woven into a gorgeous fusion
of braids, stood with her back against one of Kiana's porch columns,
one booted foot pressed against the carved wood.

"Our first big quest! I've dreamed of the day we set out to face the world, planting enchanted groves and fighting off blights and deranged woodland creatures." Aravel's lavender eyes sparkled.

Kiana laughed as she finished fastening Snow's collar. "If that's what you want to do, I'm sure we can make it happen." She propped her staff against the wall, its druidic runes standing out against the dark wood, a large chunk of amethyst glimmering inside a woven sphere at the top. The gem helped channel magic through the staff to heighten the effect of certain spells. "Once I get settled and have some sister time with Revy, I'll send word of where I'm staying, and you and Tash can join me in a few days." She looked at her father, who walked up to the porch holding a cup of tea. "That is, if you don't mind sending them on their way after me, of course."

Ozmand looked at Aravel, who was practically vibrating with pent-up excitement.

"I honestly don't think I could keep this one from going if I tried." He shook his head with a chuckle. "She may even learn to treewalk herself in that time through sheer force of will."

"By the tides, that would be something, wouldn't it? Bypassing *years* of study and practice in a matter of days?" Aravel's eyes lit up like she thought she might actually be able to achieve this remarkable feat.

In truth, teleportation magic was an incredibly rare gift. Most druids never mastered it, and those that did were often centuries old. As High Druid, Ozmand was blessed with the ability through Nelami's grace.

A flicker of gold rippled across Aravel's purple irises as she held out a hand and muttered the druidic words she'd heard Ozmand recite for a treewalk the previous week. Her Regent Tree, sparser than Kiana's, became saturated to a hue reminiscent of burnt butterscotch.

Thirty feet away, a massive redwood tree creaked, and several needles fell to the ground. A startled squirrel leaped to a different tree. Aravel dropped her hand to her side.

"Drat."

From the opposite direction, a voice said, "Impressive. I think you really showed that squirrel what for."

Tash climbed onto the porch, taking in Aravel's look of defeat before handing a small wooden box to Kiana. She took it slowly, shooting the sorcerer a questioning glance.

"I was planning to give you this for your birthday, but I think perhaps now is a better time." He smiled.

Kiana grinned back as she opened the box. Nestled inside was a bracelet of amber and amethyst, the latter a near-perfect match to the pendant her mother had given her. The stones were strung together with bronze wire.

Stunned, Kiana struggled for words, finally settling on a simple and wildly insufficient, "It's beautiful."

Aravel came to look, a sly smile creeping onto her lips. "Beautiful indeed."

Tash reached for the box but stopped short of taking it.

"May I?" he asked.

"Certainly," Kiana said, handing him the box.

He removed the bracelet and fastened it to her wrist. A slight tingle, like a tiny electric shock, ran along her arm. She looked up in surprise, not used to the feel of arcane magic. It was wilder, less rooted in balance. Kiana's innate connection to nature and its forces momentarily clashed against Tash's hereditary gift before settling into a rhythmic hum throughout her body.

The sorcerer smiled. "It's more than just a pretty thing, I admit. After your invitation to join you on your adventure, I infused the stones with a homing spell. Thought it might come in handy while traveling together. Should you ever need to find me, this will point you in my general direction. The closer you get, the stronger the pull."

Kiana ran her fingers along the stones. "I don't know what to say. It's perfect." She looked up. "Shouldn't you have one too? So you can find me as well?"

Tash's smile shifted to one side in a charming smirk. He pulled a black leather cuff from a pouch on his belt. From one end dangled an amethyst bead; from the other, amber. "I made a set. I can anchor this one to you; then it works both ways." His eyes briefly drifted to Ozmand, who still stood nearby, sipping on his tea.

Aravel pressed a hand to her mouth, hiding a smile.

Kiana ignored her. "Perfect."

Tash stepped forward and placed the cuff in Kiana's hands, then wrapped his own hands around hers. He locked his warm, honey-colored eyes on hers and began an incantation. Little sparks of electricity crackled where their hands touched, and an amber glow emanated out from their grasp.

This apparently displeased Snow, who started barking frantically.

"Shhh," Kiana soothed, opening her mind to him. "He means no harm."

The fox sank to the porch with a final yip.

Words spilled forth from Tash's lips, a torrent of hushed arcane syllables tethering Kiana to the cuff as the amber glow grew brighter. As the final word of the spell echoed into silence, Kiana felt a tug in her mind.

"I think it worked," she said. As a test of her own bracelet, she closed her eyes, calling Tash's face to her mind. A powerful mental shove hit her so suddenly that she actually lost her balance, falling toward Tash. He grabbed her arm to steady her.

"Whoa, there. This is meant to work across leagues, not within swinging distance." He released her arm as she righted herself.

"Wow, yes, I can see that now." She rubbed the stones. "How far away can these sense you?"

Tash bobbed his head from side to side, pondering. "Mmm, I'd say no more than five miles, so you'd need to be reasonably close to start with. Although, with the pair intact, that might extend the reach to about seven miles." He shrugged one shoulder casually. "I can work on the spell, see if I can't increase that over time."

Kiana nodded, impressed with the power of the enchantment, though the tethering spell paled in comparison to the one Ozmand had infused into Snow's collar. The fox could blink himself back to Tribali at will from anywhere on Amarra, reappearing at Kiana's cottage in a flash.

Kiana had made decent strides in her own spell casting of late, watching leaves sprout from her Regent Tree at an agonizing pace, but her skill had yet to reach even Tash's level. Reasonable, considering he had several years on her and could sling magic all day without drying up his proverbial magical well, certainly a benefit of a sorcerous bloodline. On the other hand, overtaxing one's magical ability as a sorcerer could come at a much greater cost than the physical exhaustion a druid experienced.

"I'm sure this will do fine." She stepped forward and wrapped her arms around Tash. He immediately reciprocated the hug, squeezing tightly for a few seconds before letting go. Turning back, Kiana admired the bracelet one last time and tied the empty box into the front pocket of her pack.

Aravel's hand still rested on her lips, and she watched the exchange before her with open interest. Only after both Kiana and Tash looked at her curiously did she drop her arms, revealing an enigmatic smile.

Kiana cleared her throat. "So, I'll see you two in a few days?"

"If that works for you." Tash regarded her warmly. "I don't want to rush your reunion with Ravaini. I know you haven't seen her for a couple years."

"I appreciate it, but we'll still have plenty of time to catch up during our travels, wherever they may take us."

She turned her attention to her pack and sundry pouches, which Snow proceeded to give a thorough sniffing. She hesitated at her trinket box, picking it up and putting it back down several times before finally tucking it securely between her green traveling dress and her most comfortable pants. Books lay scattered around her, each having been agonized over before being placed reluctantly in the "nonessential" pile. The only two books she packed were *The Book of Nelami* and her treasured copy of *Nature of Druids, Druids of Nature*. While the title needed work, the book's contents had always proved informative. She spent the next several minutes putting on her gear—including, at her father's urging, armor consisting of a leather corset and bracers, which she secured before donning her gray hooded travel cloak. At last, she picked up her staff.

"Well, that's everything." She looked herself over, then turned to her father and friends.

Aravel flew into her, making Kiana momentarily grateful for the armor.

"I'm going to miss you so much." Aravel squeezed her tight, cheek pressed against Kiana's chin.

Kiana wheezed out a laugh. "I'm going to see you in a few days, remember?"

Stepping back, Aravel said, "Yes. Don't do anything too fun until we get there, okay?"

"Ha, you got it."

Next, Tash pulled her into a warm embrace.

"Take care of yourself, Kiana. Let us know if plans change."

She nodded into his chest, inhaling the scent of fresh pine and waterfalls he carried with him from Highmane.

Lastly, Kiana turned to her father.

His internal struggle showed on his face. For a moment, Kiana thought he might try to make her stay. Instead, he finally said, "I'm so proud of you. Your mother would—" His voice caught. He pulled her toward him and kissed her forehead. Before letting her go, he whispered into her hair.

Kiana felt familiar druidic energy pulse through her in a powerful wave. She closed her eyes and let it wash over her, heightening her senses and deepening her connection to nature, to the Lady of the Wilds. The effect would be temporary, but she'd use it as long as she could.

"I love you, my dear Kiana. Nelami be with you, always."

The four elves made their way to the large redwood tree. Ozmand laid his palms flat against his forearms and in a swift, practiced gesture rotated them up and out, pressing his palms out from his sides.

"Aperata ent arberia Rovist."

Silver energy shimmered to life around the tree. Like a bolt of lightning, some of the energy shot up the middle of the trunk and arced, separating the wood into an arched, glowing doorway.

Kiana approached, Snow at her heels. Lifting her chin, she turned back one more time.

"See you soon."

Aravel stood at attention and gave her a two-fingered salute. Tash tilted his head up in a nod, his face tense. Sunlight danced through the top of his hair, which seemed to burn with the same amber intensity as his eyes.

"Be safe, Kiana." Ozmand nodded for her to proceed.

The sudden, icy grip of apprehension and self-doubt stretched down the back of Kiana's neck. With an effort of will, she shoved it aside and stepped through the doorway.

CHAPTER FIVE

Silver light faded behind her as Kiana stepped out of the trunk of a large oak tree on the edge of a low hill. The air smelled different here, the tangy salt of the sea replaced by the oddly sweet mustiness of dry leaves and parched grasses. Deciduous trees of various types spread out behind her. Up ahead the land dipped, and beyond the slope of the hill lay vast stretches of lush farmland scattered with houses. The farmland abruptly stopped at a ravine, which wrapped around another hill. On that hill rested Kiana's destination: the city of Old Home. She'd never visited but had read its history more than once.

Made up of concentric circles, the city was originally built as a fortress, gradually spreading out and down the hillside with fewer and fewer defensive measures. At the top of the hill, behind a wall, sat the Noble Ring, comprising beautiful neighborhoods where the city's most rich and powerful dwelled. Below that, the narrower Temple Ring accommodated dozens of houses of worship: stunning, ornate structures worthy of the gods to whom they paid homage. Next was the Merchant Ring, which would be bustling with activity even this early in the day, and lastly the Blue Ring, home to the workers that kept the city going.

To the east of the hill where Kiana stood, the harbor nestled up

against Old Home. Though she'd never seen it herself, Kiana had bid
farewell to her fair share of ships destined for that harbor.

Below Old Home sprawled the Hollows, a ring of the town built
into the sides of the ravine that bordered the city proper. There dwelled
the unwanted, those too poor or immoral to have a place in the city
itself. While criminal activity did occur in the Rings, most who were
caught got shunted below.

When last Kiana heard, the Hollows was the latest slum Ravaini had
decided to put her burgeoning fighting prowess to work in, meting out
whatever passed as justice in a morally bankrupt pit of iniquity and despair. Kiana refused to spend too much time dwelling on the particulars
of Ravaini's chosen profession. Still, she had a place to start her search.

"Well, Snow"—the fox's ears perked up—"here we go."

Descending the hill, Kiana noted the position of the sun, marveling that she could be hundreds of miles from home after taking only a
few steps. Now, though, she was on her own.

"Guess the first order of business will be to find a place to stay tonight, eh, buddy?" she said.

Snow tilted his face up at her, tongue lolling out the side of his
mouth, and let out a squeak of agreement.

Over the next hour, the two companions strolled along narrow dusty
roads that ran through the farmlands, taking in the smells of crops rip-
ening for the harvest. The closer they got to the Hollows, the larger Old
Home loomed above them, a monolithic beacon of hope and uncertainty. Along their path, Snow scavenged for fruits and vegetables fallen
from farm carts. He offered each of his finds to Kiana, who refused, so
he chewed them noisily but contentedly as he walked along beside her.

When at last they reached the edge of the ravine, Kiana stared
down in wonder. Buildings had been carved directly into the side of
the chasm, others erected on outcroppings or held in place by support
beams jutting out at all angles. Dilapidated shacks sprinkled the steep
walls, unsightly blemishes on an already marred face. A haphazard series
of rope and wooden bridges connected the two sides of the ravine, allowing for people to travel around as they pleased—and to avoid the

ravine's bottom, where Old Home's sewage flowed like a lazy, putrid river. Even now dozens of people moved back and forth, some with sacks thrown over their shoulders or pushing small, one-wheeled carts in front of them. Kiana had never seen anything like it. More importantly, she'd never *smelled* anything like it. The stench that hit her nostrils as she peered into the shabby chasm triggered a gag reflex she was only just able to suppress. The scent of waste, unwashed bodies, and lonely desperation threatened to overwhelm her.

Staircases placed at strategic points along the rim led down into the ravine, easy access to busier areas. The steps terminated at narrow wooden pathways that edged along the ravine wall, makeshift roads that came to sudden ends and then popped up again farther along the cliff face. Locating the nearest staircase, about fifty yards to her left, Kiana tightened the straps of her pack, suddenly nervous about her father's warning regarding the city's mysterious threats.

"Here goes nothing," she said, sucking in a deep breath through her nose, instantly regretting it, and letting it out quickly through her mouth. With a grimace, she added, "Let's go find Revy." She whispered a prayer to Nelami and headed left.

Massive metal bolts secured this staircase to the ravine wall. About twenty feet down, a landing hovered over a tangle of treacherous-looking rope bridges and more shacks and landings. Two hundred feet below flowed the thick sludge Kiana deemed responsible for the worst of the horrendous smells assaulting her nostrils.

Once at the landing, Kiana leaned down to Snow.

"Stay close," she whispered.

Unlike in other regions of Amarra, where the populations tended toward race uniformity despite amicable relationships among most peoples—the elves of Tribali, the gnomes of High Crag, the humans of Massing, and so forth—the Hollows bustled with many races, from half-orc to human and practically everything in between. Though, strangely, no other elves that Kiana could see. Most of the people looked as though they'd just as soon push her off the walkway as give her directions to an inn or tavern. Nevertheless, she stepped into the path of a passing human pushing a small cart that appeared to be full of potato sacks. The wooden footpath barely stretched wide enough to accommodate his barrow.

"Excuse me, sir. So sorry to bother you, but I was hoping you might point me in the direction of the nearest inn."

The man stopped, hands still on his cart handles, and looked her over carefully. His eyes lingered on Snow, whom Kiana moved to block from view.

"What type of establishment interests ye?" he asked, mouth opening to reveal yellowed teeth and breath rivaling the river of sewage for stench.

"Anything with a clean room for a few nights should do." Somehow Kiana managed to keep the queasiness she suddenly felt off her face.

"Just passing through, then, are ye?" Again his eyes passed over her. The question held a note of interest reeking of devilish intent.

Uncomfortable under the man's gaze but annoyed at his manner, Kiana suppressed the urge to wrap her cloak tightly around her to obscure her body. Instead she called forth every ounce of training she'd received for how to behave in diplomatic scenarios. Putting on her best friendly-neutral expression, she straightened her posture as much as she could and planted her staff next to her with one hand, a nonthreatening, stately gesture.

"Yes, you could say that."

"The Hollows ain't exactly known for its cleanliness." The man continued to leer. "Perhaps you should take yer fancy pants elsewhere and let a man get back to his business."

He started to wheel around her, a move that would force the druid dangerously close to the edge of the path, but Kiana stood firm. The man's lips pulled back in a half snarl.

"What d'you—"

Kiana held up a silver coin. "Would this make the information worth your time?"

The man considered her only a moment before snatching the coin from her hand. He ceased his ogling long enough to toss his head back over his right shoulder. "Try the Half Moon, just down the way. It'll be on yer left." This last bit he said with a hint of snarky condescension, and his lip curled as he snorted at his own cleverness.

Kiana dipped her head, ignoring the joke. "Thank you."

"Don't suppose yer lookin' fer some company while yer here?" A grotesque smile split the man's lips.

Kiana's breakfast made a sudden lurching motion in her gut.

"Um, no, thank you."

He lifted a hand in dismissal and continued on his way, forcing druid and fox to press closely against the ravine wall to make room.

Once he was out of hearing range, Kiana let out a slow breath.

"Not exactly the type of negotiation I was trained for, but I think I made it work."

Snow looked up at her and released a gentle whine.

"Thank you."

She shook off the unpleasant encounter and took in her surroundings, filled with the faces of other potential antagonists. Beside her, a post leaned tiredly against the weight of age and rot. The words "Be Vigilant" were carved into the chipped wood.

"You don't have to tell me," she muttered, adjusting the strap of her pack and stepping back onto the worn, semirotting planks.

The Half Moon Inn was a small but relatively tidy tavern right where the foul-breathed potato man said it would be. The wooden sign out front, a half circle painted white with only the word "Inn" written on it in slanted gold script, hung crookedly over windows trimmed with peeling dark-yellow paint that looked in on a dimly lit interior.

Stepping inside, Kiana winced at the scents of ale mixing with cabbage and a hint of cooked meat. Not her favorite odors, but it could have been worse considering some of the less-than-frequently-bathed clientele. Not to mention the ambient aromas outside. Snow licked at his snout to contain his drool.

Ahead and to the right, a burly dwarf with a thick black beard and hair to match stood behind the bar. Using a rag, he wiped down a tankard while chatting up a young gnome in black, her corset undone perhaps two laces too many for polite company given her surprisingly sizable bust. A flute dangled from a loop at her waist. To the left sat a dozen round tables, half of which were currently occupied. Up against the wall, six cozy booths with brown leather seats sat vacant. Kiana picked the booth in the deepest corner, with the best view of the door, and wound her way through the tables, keeping an eye on Snow to make sure he didn't sneak any treats from unsuspecting patrons.

While most people remained absorbed in their day drinking and conversations, a couple took note of the new arrivals and spent a few moments appraising them before returning to their grog. One of the servers, a human woman, scowled at an inebriated man trying clumsily to pluck at the laces of her corset. She slapped his hand away, throwing him further off balance as he wobbled atop his stool. As she turned to go, she caught sight of Snow and pressed her hands to her cheeks.

"Ooooooh, he's so cute!" she exclaimed, scowl fading. She followed Kiana to the back booth. "What's his name?"

Kiana dropped her pack on the bench and pulled back the hood of her cloak.

"Snow," she said.

"Snoooow," the girl repeated. She crouched down and held out a hand, which Snow inspected for treats. Finding none, he snorted and looked at Kiana.

"Sorry, he's always on the lookout for goodies, and sometimes he can be rude when he doesn't find what he wants." Kiana scolded the fox with a raise of her eyebrows. Turning her attention back to the human, now scratching the thick fur beneath Snow's collar, she asked, "Do you have any water?" She leaned her staff against the wall inside the booth, amethyst gleaming in the torchlight from the sconce above it. "And I was hoping to speak with someone about renting a room for a few nights."

"Of course!" The woman popped up. Her long brown hair, knotted into a braid, fell over her shoulder. She tossed her head, flipping the braid back. "Can I get you anything, maybe an ale, some food? We've an ox-meat stew on for tonight that's most excellent. Could pour a couple bowls for your lunch."

Kiana's stomach turned a little. Despite her abbreviated breakfast, she found her appetite curbed after the march through sewage land. Plus, her food interests fell on the more vegetable-oriented side of the scale.

"I'm okay for now. Just water is fine."

The woman shrugged and disappeared into the back. Within a few minutes, she returned. She set a full mug of water in front of Kiana, then knelt on the floor. With a quick, "Hope you don't mind," she placed a bowl of water and a heaping plate of meat scraps in front of Snow. The fox wasted no time devouring the offering.

Kiana bit the inside of her cheek as her gluttonous fox slurped and grunted through his meal.

"Thank you. That's very kind of you . . ."

Catching her intention, the server said, "Jessa."

"Ah. Thank you, Jessa."

She shrugged. "So, Ryndl, the innkeeper, says he can give you a room upstairs for as long as you need for three silver per night."

Kiana looked away from Snow's mortifying display of poor manners. "Wonderful, thanks."

"No problem. You let me know if I can get you that ale."

Flashes from the night before, the flowing mead and rum as she and Aravel worked to drown out thoughts of the failing Monarch Tree, rolled through her mind, and she held up a hand.

"I'm sure I'll be fine."

"Suit yourself." Jessa shrugged again. "Where you here from, anyway?"

"Tribali."

"No kidding! Our best-selling rum is from down in those parts."

The mention of the rum sent acid burbling up Kiana's throat. She swallowed hard.

Jessa eyed Kiana, no doubt taking in her clean clothes and freshly bathed skin. "What brings you all the way up here, to the Hollows, no less?"

"Just visiting a friend."

Suddenly feeling the burn of someone's gaze, she glanced behind Jessa. One of the tables previously deep in conversation now sat quiet. Four pairs of eyes, all human, rested on Kiana. One of the men sported a long, unkempt beard with beads braided into it. A trident tattoo adorned his cheek. Living where she did, on an oft-traveled coast pillaged by scum, Kiana knew a pirate when she saw one. The dread that had been building within her since the night before sprang to life, clawing at Kiana's insides. Panic rose in her chest. Images of a grisly ship—bones jutting from bow to stern, black sails catching the winter winds—crashed through her mind, stirring up memories she wished desperately to forget. Blood. Terror. Death. Grief-filled nights spent curled at the foot of a marble memorial.

She fought back the memories and tried to take in details of the rest of the table. Two of the other three men were bald, and Kiana could see spiderweb tattoos on the backs of their necks, the ink stretching about two inches in diameter. The taller of the two tugged idly at a patch over his left eye. The fourth man was plain as butter pudding but had a greataxe propped against the table next to him, which he stroked almost lovingly. The downward movement revealed the same spiderweb tattoo as the others but on the back of his hand.

When Kiana looked their direction, the men slowly returned to their business.

"Well, I hope you enjoy your stay here in the Hollows," Jessa said, pulling Kiana's attention back. Her forehead crinkled. "As much as one can enjoy a stay in the armpit of Old Home." With that, the server returned to the kitchen.

Doing her best to appear fully absorbed in enjoying her water, Kiana kept one eye on the table of men, who appeared to be doing the same to her. She noted that the pirate and the two bald men wore scabbards sheathing short swords.

Kiana quickly scanned herself to see if she wore anything these men might be considering stealing. Aside from her amethyst pendant, which would hardly seem worth the effort to anyone else, she came up with nothing. Opting not to let her mind explore a different possibility, she instead focused on picking up anything she could from their conversation.

Though they spoke in hushed tones, Kiana's keen elven ears caught the occasional word or phrase.

". . . they're still looking . . ."

"... gone tomorrow ..."

"Shh!"

Kiana nursed her beverage until the pirate and one bald man got up and bid their companions farewell. The two that remained, Great-axe and Eyepatch, shifted so they could see both Kiana and the exit.

The dwarf previously tending bar approached Kiana's booth.

"Hear ya want a room," he said.

"That's right," Kiana said, attention still half on the men watching her. "Just for a few nights. Maybe less." *Please let Ravaini have better accommodations.*

He dropped a brass key on the table. "Three silver a night."

"You must be Ryndl." Kiana pulled a gold coin out of a leather pouch and let it fall into the dwarf's palm. "That should be enough to cover a few nights and my friend's meal just now, yes?"

The dwarf grunted his agreement and turned to leave. "Second floor, third door on the right," he said in parting.

Kiana scrunched her face in displeasure. No way her eavesdroppers hadn't overheard that. She gathered her belongings and picked up her room key. As she stood to go, surreptitious glances darted her way. She turned and faced the men head on.

"I'm sorry, is there something I can help you with?"

They straightened slowly in their seats, looks of mild amusement on their faces.

"That an offer?" Greataxe said, leering.

Kiana's stomach did a flip. She tamped down the unwelcome sense of fear.

"Hardly," she said. "You just seem to have taken an interest in me, and I've no idea why."

"Don't flatter yourself, missy," Eyepatch said, his voice hoarse. "We take an interest in all newcomers. Never can tell who means trouble."

"Well, I assure you I mean no one any harm. I'm just here to see a friend, and then I'll be on my merry way."

"Then I guess we ain't got nothin' to worry about," said Greataxe. "Enjoy yer afternoon."

"Gentlemen." She dipped her head and made her way to the door.

As she stepped out, she heard a hoarse voice say, "Hear that, Rudge? She called us gentlemen," followed by an unfriendly snicker.

Once outside, she took a deep breath. Confrontation ranked among the lowest of her talents. Her diplomatic training fell short of preparing her for hostile encounters with common criminals.

Navigating her way back to the top of the ravine, she found a quiet spot near a copse of birches and sat cross-legged on a large rock while Snow explored a nearby bank of blackberry bushes. Closing her eyes, she reached out with her senses.

"*Averum venicht acepa verbus.*" She spoke the words aloud, then sat quietly as they echoed over and over in her mind.

Two minutes later, a peregrine falcon soared overhead, circling in a lazy arc before descending to Kiana's arm, which she held aloft in welcome.

She sat with the bird for a while, working to establish a connection. Eventually she was able to communicate what she wished the bird to do, ensuring at least the words "Half Moon Inn" would be communicated to Aravel upon the bird's arrival in Corval. The falcon launched herself from Kiana's arm, headed south.

"There," Kiana said to Snow, who wandered back to her, face smeared with berry juice. "By the time Aravel and Tash get that message and make it up here, we should be able to get some quality time with Ravaini and then be ready to leave this place behind, don't you think?"

Snow cocked his head to the side.

"I'll take that as a yes."

Rest did not come easily to Kiana that night. She'd wandered rather aimlessly through the nearest taverns and shops all afternoon, hoping to catch a glimpse of fiery red hair, but the hundredth unfriendly proposition had finally sent her slogging back to the Half Moon Inn to regroup and come up with a better plan of attack. Though the men were gone when she'd returned, her unease at their unwanted attention now kept her mind racing. Unfamiliar sounds—carts bumping over stone, drunken shouts that turned to brawls, the clanking of a dozen pots and pans as the kitchen served well into the night—set her further on edge. She longed for the peaceful serenity of Tribali.

She'd tried to rig up a protection spell Tash had attempted to teach her several months ago as an experiment, one that would alert her to any intruders, but the arcane nature of the enchantment fought with her magic. Rather than dwelling on the failure, she let the moment pass, reminding herself that not everyone could do all things. Her father and Aravel had drilled this mantra into her since the day she met Tash. The day she failed him in the worst possible way.

No, Kiana commanded herself. *Do not dwell on that. Not tonight.*

Eventually, the gentle sound of fox snores lulled Kiana into much-needed sleep. Snow had no trouble drowning out the sounds of the Hollows. Belly full of meat and berries, he'd fallen asleep within five minutes of Kiana settling into bed. She'd considered setting him on sentry duty but figured he'd wake her instinctively if anyone entered the room.

Much too soon, the sun's morning rays poked needles into Kiana's eyelids. Weariness draped heavily upon her shoulders. Hoping for a boost of energy, she pulled out two leftover scones from her pack and munched on them while she considered her options for the day.

"What do you think, Snow? Try our luck with the innkeeper, surly as he may be?"

The fox stared hungrily at her scone.

Kiana sighed. "You're no help, you big fluffy piglet." She tossed him a carrot she'd picked from her garden the day before.

The tavern below stayed quiet as Kiana descended the stairs, but the air was thick with the smell of bacon grease. Ryndl stood at a small desk at the end of a hallway, keys hanging on wooden pegs behind him. He looked to be sorting receipts.

"Good morning," Kiana said as she approached.

"Mm-mmm," he mumbled in response, not looking up from his work.

Scanning the room to make sure she hadn't missed anyone, she lowered her voice a little. "Out of curiosity, do you know where one might go if they were seeking . . . less-than-reputable work?"

At last Ryndl lifted his head to look her in the eyes. He planted one forearm on the desk and leaned forward.

"This here's the Hollows, missy. Everyone and their great-aunt Mildred is doing less-than-reputable work. And I don't want no part of any o' yer shady dealings. Got enough on my plate as it is." He straightened and picked up another stack of receipts.

Embarrassment warmed Kiana's palms and cheeks. She waved her hands in front of her as if trying to erase the mix-up from existence.

"No, no, you misunderstand me. I'm not looking for work. I'm trying to track someone down."

The dwarf raised an eyebrow and looked her up and down.

"Ya certainly don't seem like the mischievous sort," he said.

"You are very perceptive."

Seemingly satisfied with her response, he relented. "There're a number of places in the Hollows to find any type of unsavory character you might be lookin' for, but I'd say the Plank is a good place to start if you want the 'professionals.' That is what yer after, ain't it?"

Kiana coughed out a vague affirmative response, then asked, "The plank?"

Ryndl nodded, offering no further clarification. He went back to his receipts, the parchment crinkling between his stubby fingers.

After a few moments, Kiana said, "Forgive me, I'm not familiar with the area. Is that a specific piece of wood, a spot at the docks, maybe, or . . ." She shrugged with a small shake of her head.

Ryndl narrowed his eyes at her. "It's a bar. Hung a sign ages ago, never put anything on it. So folks jus' call it the Plank."

"Ah."

Another moment passed. This time Ryndl maintained eye contact, receipts still clutched in one hand.

Kiana blinked first.

"So, any chance you could tell me where I might find this place, the Plank?"

"Sure." He tapped the receipts against the desk, setting them in a neat pile.

For a second Kiana thought she was going to have to prompt him to speak again. Exasperation eased into the muscles of her face, widening her eyes.

"Fastest way from here is north, then east round the back of Old Home, by the harbor. If ya get to the docks, you've gone too far."

The druid relaxed. "Thank you so much."

Eager to be on her way, Kiana didn't stay long enough to see if Ryndl would even acknowledge her gratitude. She guessed no.

The Hollows buzzed with renewed vigor this morning, alive with denizens conducting their daily business, if day drinking and plotting crimes could be considered business. As Kiana moved along the west side of the ravine, she couldn't help but stare up at the city towering above her. From her position, she couldn't make out much, thanks to buildings jutting out over the edge of the ravine, but she found herself wishing Ravaini had settled a little higher up than where Kiana now found herself. But here was where the wicked dwelled.

Passage through the Hollows presented more than a few problems. With no clear path from one end to the other, the series of poorly constructed bridges forced Kiana to zigzag from side to side almost randomly to discover the best way forward. Having Snow with her prevented her from shifting into a bird form and simply bypassing the whole bridge-web of terror.

Finally nearing the bend in the ravine that led around the hill to the harbor, Kiana stepped out onto a foot-wide piece of wood that would qualify as a road only here in the Hollows. As she did, her cloak caught on a cart exiting a bridge, its sole wheel equipped with clamps to keep it steadier on the swaying ropes and planks. A trigger on the front end of the clamp released the mechanism when it hit the solid surface of the lane.

"Oh, I'm so sorry," she said, turning to untangle herself.

"That's quite all right, lass. Wasn't looking where I was going meself." The cart pusher tipped his threadbare hat and continued on, adjusting a few cabbages that had fallen askew. One rolled over the edge into the chasm below, but he barely spared it a glance before moving along.

Kiana smiled after him, something back across the bridge catching her eye. She thought she saw someone dodge behind a wooden post supporting a partially caved-in awning. Senses once again going into high alert, she waited where she stood for a couple of minutes, eyes glued to the post. When no further movement occurred, she turned back to where she was headed.

"And now you're starting to see things," she muttered to herself.

Another quick glance back revealed nothing suspicious. She continued on her way.

A seemingly endless maze of ups and downs and back-and-forths later, Kiana could smell the salty brine of the bay over the refuse and filth around her. A welcome, familiar scent. Having not asked which side of the ravine the Plank was on, she stopped and scanned the vicinity, seeking the least threatening person to ask. A young gnome wearing little more than rags rooted through a barrel of old food a short ways ahead.

"Excuse me," Kiana said, approaching cautiously.

The gnome's head shot up, eyes wide. Stringy blond hair matted with dirt stuck to her washed-out cheeks. She started to bolt.

"Wait, please, I mean you no harm." Kiana held one hand up, palm out. The other hand hugged her staff to her side.

Casting a glance behind her, the gnome slowed, curious.

"I just wanted to ask you a question. I'm looking for a tavern, the Plank, and I'm not sure where to look." Kiana kept her hand outstretched.

The waif flicked her gaze to the right, perhaps subconsciously. Across the way, a few buildings up, Kiana saw a decent-sized establishment with a plain plank of wood hung above the entrance. Its front end protruded out over the chasm and the river of sludge sixty feet below, and dozens of support poles angled every which way held the building precariously aloft. A rounded porch wrapped around from one side of the tavern to the other, offering access to the front entrance.

"Aha," she said. Then, turning back to the gnome, she added, "Thank you."

The young girl looked at the ground and kicked at some loose rocks with her scuffed boots. Dust already coated her from head to toe. Kiana couldn't tell if the sickly hue of the girl's skin was from the grime or malnutrition. Likely a bit of both, given the location.

Bending down on one knee, Kiana pulled open a side pocket of her pack and produced a wrapped bun. She held it out to the girl.

"A token of my gratitude," she said.

The girl hesitated but eventually closed the gap between them. She reached out tentatively for the bun. Her eyes met Kiana's as if to confirm permission to take the pastry. Finding the answer in the affirmative, she plucked the bun from Kiana's grasp. She unwrapped it quickly and began to inhale it, barely taking the time to chew between bites.

"Whoa, it's okay. No one is going to take it from you." Kiana placed a soothing hand on the girl's shoulder.

The gnome paused in her feasting and smiled at the druid. Crumbs fell from her stretched, cracked lips.

Kiana grabbed her pendant with one hand and with the other twisted her wrist in a practiced series of movements. From her palm sprouted a small purple flower. This, too, she offered to the girl.

Eyes wide with wonder, the girl accepted the gift, looking from it to Kiana and back again. Without a word, she skipped away, cupping the flower gently between two grimy hands sticky with honey.

Brushing dust from her dress as she stood, Kiana sought a bridge leading to the Plank, or at least somewhere nearby. Nelami blessed her this time. The bridge right beside her ended one hundred feet from her destination. Before crossing, she spent a few minutes watching the bar, gauging the activity. No one went in or out. Dark crevices, almost like alleys, ran down either side of the bar, carved deep into the ravine walls, and she wondered if other entrances lurked in the shadows.

On the lookout for any of her "friends" from the night before, Kiana made her way across the bridge, a rickety old thing missing several slats. Snow stuck close. Standing in front of the bar at last, she peered in the door's tiny window, noting a bustle of activity within. Booths spilled over with patrons, despite the early hour. Some ate from plates heaped with eggs and sausage; others clearly preferred a liquid breakfast.

A thick, dark curtain at the back of the room parted and revealed a gaunt man dressed all in black. He fixed her with a menacing stare.

She jumped aside, nearly colliding with Snow.

"Yikes," she whispered. "Wasn't expecting the place to be quite so busy this time of day."

Anxious from the gaunt man's glare, Kiana paced to the side of the building in hopes of finding another entrance. As she passed by the mouth of the western alley on her right, something large and solid slammed into her from the left, sending her flying to the ground in the darkened passage, out of sight from the main walkway. Despite the surprise, she recovered her feet quickly and turned to face her assailant.

A large, plain man holding a greataxe, whom she now knew as Rudge, blocked her path out of the alley.

"Sorry, didn't see ya there," he said with a sneer, two gold teeth gleaming out from his upper jaw.

Snow flew into a snarling frenzy and leaped toward the attacker, but a large pair of hands threw a heavy wooden crate over him from behind, trapping him. Muted barks and growls rumbled from within the makeshift cage.

"I thought we weren't going to have us a problem," a familiar hoarse voice said.

Anger flared in Kiana's chest, winning out over her fear. A tingle crept along her forearm as color seeped into her Regent Tree. "As far as I know, we don't"—she gestured toward the crate—"assuming you let the fox out of there right now."

The one-eyed man chuckled. "No, I don't think I'm gonna be doin' that. Need meself a new winter scarf." He drew his short sword. "Besides, *you're* the problem."

Snow's crazed yips awakened something in Kiana she hadn't felt in a good long while. All thoughts beyond saving her companion evaporated.

She narrowed her eyes at Eyepatch. "I am now."

She slammed the end of her staff into the ground, tapping into the magic roiling through her, eyes lighting up with concentrated energy. The mark on her arm shifted fully to lilac. Everything brightened, edges sharpened. Green, leafy vines sprouted from the point of impact and snaked up the staff, weaving intricate patterns until the wood was fully engulfed.

"*Vinai assseqi,*" the druid whispered, sending more vines racing along the ground toward Rudge. A leaf from her Regent Tree detached and fell, fading to nothing as it reached her elbow.

"What the . . ."

His confusion slowed his reaction, and the magical vines snared his legs before he could head them off with his axe. They continued to move up his body as he struggled to break free, twisting around his torso and arms.

Less surprised than his companion, Eyepatch launched himself toward the druid, sword raised.

Expecting the attack, Kiana dodged nimbly out of the way as he swung, but she teetered off balance as he brought the butt of his sword back toward her face. The hilt connected with her cheek, eliciting a grunt of pain as she stumbled back a step.

"You should have just let the fox go." Kiana summoned another pulse of magic through her, channeling it into her staff. Spinning the weapon into a horizontal position, she shouted, "*Tona vat!*" and shoved it forward, hands gripping tightly.

A gust of intense wind rippled out from her. The spell collided with Eyepatch, hurtling him a few yards down the alley, toward the main path. He barely stayed upright. Rudge held his ground, still grappled by vines, but roared with fury as the gale hit him like a wall of bricks, whipping his head back.

"You're gonna regret that, druid," Rudge growled.

He freed one arm enough to swing his axe, slashing through the magical plants. He was nearly free.

Keeping one eye on the rabid thug about to break free of her trap, Kiana saw Eyepatch start to move back toward her from the mouth of the alley, but not before he kicked the crate containing an infuriated Snow.

More anger burned through Kiana, and she flung a hand outward.

"Lamilia glaciré."

Two shards of ice the size of arrow tips appeared in midair halfway between Kiana and the thug. She channeled more magic into the spell until the shards grew to the length of her dagger. They flew into Eyepatch's chest. He gurgled something unintelligible and collapsed beside the rocking crate.

With a depraved bellow, Rudge finally broke free of the vines and charged the druid, slamming her back against the wall of the Plank. He pressed his forearm to her throat, his face inches from hers. A hateful smile spread across his lips as Kiana struggled for breath.

"You're gonna regret that too," he snarled.

Moments away from losing the ability to speak, Kiana grabbed Rudge's shoulder and rasped, *"Infurian vulneri."*

Purple lines spread out from each of Kiana's fingers along the exposed skin of the brute's shoulder, sparking with electrical current as they opened into bloody gashes. Surprise and more than a little pain caused Rudge to jerk his arm away from Kiana's throat. She sucked in air, noting the fall of two more leaves.

Rudge backed up a step, looking at Kiana as if she'd just sprouted antlers. He raised his axe.

"I'm going to ki—"

Before Rudge could finish his threat, Kiana thrust her hand up and forward, and radiant light shimmered into existence above his head, rolling down over him like molten moonlight. Silvery smoke wafted out from his body as he shrieked in pain, falling to his knees. The shrieking stopped with the thud of his body against the ground.

"Nelami, forgive me."

Kiana's focus quickly shifted from the fact that she'd just killed two people when a barely audible scraping sound drew her attention to the mouth of the alley. Another man—spiderweb tattoo stretched across his bared bicep—stood beside his fallen comrade, mace in hand.

"Well, well. What do we have here?" Dark chest hair sprouted from his open leather vest. Two skull tattoos leered out from beneath the material. The man's tall, bulky frame blocked most of the view out of the alley.

Great, Kiana thought. She tightened her grip on her staff. Four leaves still fluttered along the plum-colored branches of her Regent Tree, probably enough to contain this threat but likely little else.

"A little pale-faced nature mage who thinks she's pretty tough shit, eh?" He spun the mace around in his hand. "We'll see about that."

He drew his elbow back and leaned slightly forward, getting ready to charge. Kiana readied herself, druidic energy already pouring back through her, awakening her nerves, heightening her senses. Then a blade appeared through the center of the man's chest, metal glistening with slick red blood. His eyes went wide.

In a flash, the blade withdrew back through the man's body with a sickening slurp and he collapsed to the ground, revealing his attacker: a figure perhaps a few inches shorter than Kiana wearing a cloak of black feathers, a crow mask adorning the head and face. A sword dripping with blood hung from one gloved hand. Behind the figure, a woman wandered by with a towel-covered basket. Her eyes flicked briefly to the corpse mere feet away, then the bloody blade. An arch of her brow suggested more curiosity than alarm or surprise at the sight of a daylight murder. She continued on her way.

Unsure if this new arrival was friend or foe, Kiana maintained her readied stance, waiting for some signal one way or the other. The crow face, pointy and menacing regardless of the daylight filtering in behind it, sent a slight chill through her.

"I'll be damned," the crow person said in a low voice.

Something in the voice made Kiana relax her grip on her staff. Blood returned to her knuckles in a rush of warmth.

The figure took a few measured steps forward and pulled back its hood. The cloak's feathers vanished, the fabric assuming the look of an everyday garment. The mask fell away to reveal scarlet hair framing a fair-skinned face with fierce green eyes that glistened in the dim light of the alley.

Kiana stared, shock nudging her mouth open even before she found her voice.

"Ravaini?"

CHAPTER SIX

"You know, you were probably the last person I expected to find in that alley today."

The Paletine sisters sat at a booth in a private back room of the Plank, a little away from the raucous chatter and clanking tankards of the patrons out front. Black leather covered the bench seats, torn in places to reveal hints of the flattened, downy padding within. The six dark wood tables throughout the room absorbed what little light illuminated the space, their stained and chipped surfaces dulled by years of use and abuse. Despite these blemishes, the tavern appeared clean and well cared for, the floors swept and mopped, the dust and grime minimal.

Ravaini had rushed Kiana inside through a hidden entrance before pouring them each some calming tea and shedding her feathered cloak in a different back room, behind the dark-green curtain Kiana had noted previously. Snow, still sulking from being trapped in the crate, lay on Kiana's folded cloak.

"Surprise," Kiana said half-heartedly. Bile burned at the back of her throat, nausea having hit her as soon as the shock of seeing Ravaini behind the crow mask had faded. She sipped her tea.

"Understatement." Ravaini twirled her cup between her hands, watchful eyes on Kiana.

"Don't suppose you want to tell me how you happened to be in that alley dressed like something from one of our childhood bedtime stories."

"I think the bigger question would be how *you* happened to be in that alley. I work here."

"At a tavern? Dressed like that?" Kiana nodded toward the other room where Ravaini's cloak had been deposited.

"From the tavern, not at. And consider the crow getup my uniform." She grinned. "Creepy as all hells in the dark."

And the daylight, Kiana thought.

"Do all of your, uh, associates dress that way?"

Her sister hesitated. "No. It's sort of my"—she coughed—"signature."

Ravaini didn't offer further information, and Kiana didn't ask. She was pretty sure she didn't want to know what that entailed. Ravaini had killed before, as a novice Tide Hunter defending Tribali's shores, but this was something else. There was a reason communication between the sisters had waned over the years, despite their bond and deep love of each other. The image of the blade protruding from the alley man's chest crowded into Kiana's mind.

Who dresses like a crow, carries a sword, and works out of the back room of a tavern in a neighborhood full of criminals?

Ravaini smiled, a fleeting motion. "I don't mean this to sound rude, because you know I'm always happy to see you, but what *are* you doing here?"

Kiana tapped the side of her teacup with one fingernail, chewing on the inside of her cheek and wondering what her sister would think of her impulsive, rebellious departure from Tribali. She sensed a rush of impending pride.

"What is it?" Ravaini prompted.

"I told Father I can't do the political posturing nonsense to become High Druid anymore."

Surprise skittered across Ravaini's face. She sat back in the booth slowly, her red hair extra vibrant against the dark leather behind her.

"I decided I needed to get out of Tribali and try to make a difference in the world. If I'm to have the position, I want to earn it the right way, like in the old days. Prove I can be the leader the druids need."

The elder sister smirked. "I'm sure he took that real well."

Kiana frowned down into her mug. "Not at first, but he came around." She met her sister's gaze. "I know you two don't see eye to eye, but he's always been supportive of me."

"Yes, of *you*," Ravaini said wryly. "You chose the 'right' path."

Kiana sighed.

Ravaini sensed the mood and dropped it.

"Okay, so you shrugged off the mantle of Perfect Daughter and came here because . . ."

Kiana winced. "I was hoping you'd be up for an adventure."

Ravaini's smirk wavered. "Oh. Uh . . ."

"Unless you're busy, of course. I know this is last minute. I just—I miss my sister."

Ravaini looked pained. "I'm so sorry, Kiana. I wanted to come visit, was planning to soon, actually, but things here are . . . complicated. Even more so now."

"What do you mean?" Kiana pressed the tip of one finger against her mug, cooling the liquid inside to a more appropriate drinking temperature. She reveled in these minor bits of magic she could use without affecting the sparse branches adorning her left arm. And that reveling had a much-needed calming effect for her at that moment.

Ravaini added some more hot water to her own steeping leaves. She sighed.

"Those guys you killed—" She paused when Kiana drew a tense breath. "In self-defense, by the way, so don't even try to feel guilty about it—anyway, they're part of a group called the Obsidian Web."

Kiana shifted in her seat. "Okay."

Ravaini's next sigh seemed to pull the air from Kiana's lungs as well.

"They're bad news. They've been skulking around for about a month now, and they've tortured and killed at least half a dozen souls in the sewers." She glanced at her hands briefly before meeting Kiana's eyes again. "All druids."

The blood in Kiana's veins cooled. "What? Why?"

Ravaini sat forward, elbows pressed into the table, hands wrapped around her steaming mug. Some sort of mental battle waged inside her, resulting in an irregular tug at the corner of her mouth. The face Kiana had known so well looked almost foreign now. Whatever burdens, physical or moral, her line of work had visited upon Ravaini were carved in the tight set of her mouth, the distant coolness her eyes took on when she looked away.

"They seem to be working for the Deep Ones."

A current of fear, deeply instilled from childhood, shivered through Kiana.

The Deep Ones recurred as villains in children's tales across the continent, thanks to their terrifying powers of mind control and nightmare-inducing appearance. Lacking the capacity for kindness or empathy, Deep Ones dwelled in the continent's underbelly, the Shadow Core, though their true origins were rooted in another plane of existence entirely: the Realm of Eventide. Their faces were nearly devoid of features, save for two solid black eyes and rivers of black veins that crisscrossed their nearly translucent skin. Legend held that they communicated by pouring their will into the minds of their prey.

"They're . . . they're back?"

Ravaini nodded solemnly. "The Web serves them willingly—idiots—but I've come across a number of their thralls as well."

"How can you tell?"

Ravaini pointed two fingers at her face. "It's the eyes. When a Deep One takes over someone's mind, fully possesses them, their eyes become glazed over with a weird silver film. That's the point of no return. If they've been fully taken, there's no helping them. As soon as you kill them"—Ravaini watched her sister shift in her seat and hesitated briefly before continuing—"their eyes go back to normal. Didn't know what was happening the first time I saw it, but . . ." She averted her eyes.

"What?"

"But then I saw one of the telepathic bastards enthrall an associate of mine while we were clearing the sewers. He grabbed her head, and this smoke poured into her face. Her scream was . . . Let's just say I still hear it at night sometimes. The Deep One fled while the rest of my team and I were busy dispatching our friend." Her mouth set in a grim line.

"Gods," Kiana gasped. "And they've been killing druids? Why?"

Ravaini ticked her head to the side. "Don't know for sure, but we found the bodies after our encounter in the sewers. Didn't recognize any of the faces, don't think they were local. Then, during a job, I managed to infiltrate one of the Web hideouts and overheard a couple of their thugs talking about some magic ice crystal the Deep Ones have been experimenting with. Think I saw it hanging from the bastard's neck when he mind-fucked my friend. Possessing an elemental magic artifact and torturing druids is more than a coincidence, I'd say."

Kiana's head shot up from the sip of tea she'd started to take. Ravaini regarded her curiously.

"You wouldn't know anything about such things, would you? We both know magic falls outside my purview."

"Freya's Crystal," Kiana whispered, eyes unfocused on a point near Ravaini's ear. "It has to be." She shook her head, trying to bring her thoughts into focus. "It's an old druid legend. Centuries ago, before the Druid Orders scattered, an Ice Druid bearing the Crystal was attacked by a water jinn while at a festival in Corval. The Crystal was lost, and the jinn put a curse on the druid that transformed her into a forsaken jinn, binding her to the waters off the coast of Tribali. The curse wore away at her sanity, and—" Memories of a ship exploding from within flashed through her mind, and she stopped midsentence. "*No.*"

"What?"

People screaming. Bodies in the water. A lone figure striding across the water's surface. Kiana lived with these memories every day. And not just because it was when she'd first met Tash. She could not banish them from her thoughts, no matter how much she wished to. Now she considered what had happened in a new light.

Kiana said shakily, "They say she's the reason for some of the ships mysteriously sinking off the Tribali coast. I thought it was just a ghost story."

Ravaini peered closely at her sister for a moment. "Okay, so, what? This Crystal controls the crazy jinn, this Freya lady?"

Kiana shook her head. "No. The Crystal was a source of power to the druids. Ice magic, not mind control. And Freya isn't the druid who was cursed to be a jinn. She was the leader of the Ice Druids centuries ago. The Crystal kept her name long after she was gone."

Ravaini rubbed her temples. "Sorry, this magic stuff is your domain, so I'm not quite sure what to make of this. Why was a water jinn on our plane attacking druids? And why would the Deep Ones want a crystal that controls ice magic? Aren't they more the fire-and-lightning types?"

Slowly, Kiana shook her head again, racking her brain for some kind of hint within what she knew of the legend. "I can understand the water jinn wanting it. Water, ice . . . It makes sense, though I don't know what would drive them to steal it from the druids. Druids and jinn have always felt a kinship toward one another, given their elemental nature. They don't venture to the Primary Plane often, but they've always been welcome at druidic festivals." She drummed a finger on the table, thinking. "And you're right. The Deep Ones should have no desire for such a thing."

"Well, apparently they have it, and they're trying to do *something* with it."

Kiana shivered. "Maybe they can't, and that's why they're taking druids. To wield the Crystal for them, under their sway."

"Maybe," Ravaini murmured, watching her sister carefully. "Whatever the case, them having it can't be good. The Deep Ones don't show their ugly-ass faces unless they're ready to act. Whatever their endgame is could be happening soon."

What are the odds that the day I leave with hopes of reuniting the Orders, I stumble upon ties to the long-lost Ice Druids?

Kiana stared into her nearly empty mug of tea. Something had urged her to come here. Even now, she felt a push, some internal force pressing against her mind.

Find them! Save them!

The words whispered across her mind. She started.

"We have to stop them."

"Yes. Unfortunately, they up and left last night."

"What?"

Ravaini dipped a spoonful of honey into her tea. "My informant network has kept an ear to the ground, tracking the Web and trying their best to follow the Deep Ones' movements. Seeing as how they mostly travel through the Shadow Core, that's not easy to begin with. But then, yesterday, *poof.*" She flicked her fingers in an outward motion to illustrate. "All signs of them being in the area vanished as of last night."

"Maybe they ran out of druids," Kiana offered sardonically.

"Until *you* arrived," Ravaini said, the warning in her voice subtle but undoubtedly clear.

"Oh." Fear quickened Kiana's pulse.

"Which is why you can't stay here," Ravaini went on. "Even if the Deep Ones *are* gone, it seems the Web is still staying diligent in its duty to track down druids. Hence your little adventure in the alley."

Kiana swallowed. "Well, we have an adventure to go on anyway." She took in Ravaini's grave expression and added tentatively, "Maybe we could track the Deep Ones together?"

Ravaini lowered her eyes to the table. "I'm so sorry." She lifted her face. "I can't leave the city right now. The Deep Ones aren't the only assholes causing problems in Old Home."

Disappointment slumped Kiana's shoulders. "I understand."

Ravaini shook her head. "No, I don't think you do. It's the pirates."

CHAPTER SEVEN

The marble memorial decorating Tribali's Gardens of Bluethorn loomed large in Kiana's mind. She held her sister's gaze.

"The pirates. They're here, and they're importing Crucian metal—loads of it—for someone with enough influence, and deep enough pockets, to remain anonymous, even to my spying eyes."

Rage bloomed anew in Kiana's chest. The idea that pirates were desecrating Tribali's shores, despoiling family graves in order to steal precious Crucian metal, never failed to awaken the darkest parts of Kiana's soul—parts she refused to explore.

Ravaini ground her teeth. "It's gotta end. Which is why I don't have time to go chasing after under-dwelling psy-monsters. My fight is here. I've been gathering intel from the docks for months, intercepting communications and bills of lading wherever I can. Even kil—" She coughed. "Eliminated a few high-priority targets in the process. But I still don't have answers as to who's at the top of the heap. As much as I'd love to accompany you on your first adventure, it's not in the cards."

Kiana flashed back to the night of the Regent Ceremony, the looks of confusion, even fear, creasing the faces of her fellow druids. She thought of her outburst during the Conclave's opening session, her accusations. This was why she'd left, why she'd demanded action. A legendary Ice

Druid artifact in the hands of the Deep Ones could be disastrous. Who knew what they had planned?

She placed one hand on the table, palm pressed flat to the surface. "I'll still do it."

"I'm sorry?"

Chin up, Kiana repeated, "I'll go after them, the Deep Ones. The Crystal is important to the druids, and I'm not going to sit by while more of them are put in danger by these Eventide monsters. This actually aligns perfectly with my desire to reestablish the clans."

"Kiana, the Deep Ones are targeting druids. You'd be walking right into their plan. Not to mention the fact that they are *fucking dangerous.*"

"I'll be careful."

Ravaini scoffed. "So you're going to single-handedly take on the Deep Ones?"

Kiana smiled. "No, of course not. That would be foolish, trying to take on the world by myself." She arched an eyebrow meaningfully. As a child, Ravaini refused to ask for help. Even as part of the Tide Hunters, she was known for going rogue and taking on assignments better suited to two or three fighters.

"Whoa, hey. I may work alone at times, but I never bite off more than I can chew." She shrugged.

Kiana narrowed her eyes.

"Well, almost never," Ravaini amended. "Okay, not every week. Besides, I have a crew for backup when I need it."

"So do I."

The elder Paletine sister cocked an eyebrow. "Oh?"

"Yes. I mean, of sorts."

Ravaini crossed her arms, leaning back. "Don't you dare say the fox." She glanced at Snow out of the corner of her eye. He looked back at her with his eyes at half mast.

"No, not just Snow." Kiana squirmed. "I may have neglected to mention something."

"What, that you started a ragtag band of monster-slaying druids?"

Kiana rolled her eyes. "No."

"What then?"

"I met a guy." Kiana winced, unsure how that would land.

Ravaini pondered this a moment. "You met a guy."

"Yes."

"Is he a dragon? Or an army? Because if he's not, I don't see how that helps here."

Kiana scowled.

"I'm kidding," Ravaini said. Then she half shrugged. "Sort of. When did this happen?"

"About a year ago. His name's Tash."

Ravaini sat forward. "My sister has been seeing a guy for a year and didn't tell me?"

"First of all, we're not actually . . . together. Second of all, you're not exactly around enough to be able to tell."

"Whoa, whoa, whoa. Wait," Ravaini said, waving her hands in front of her face. "You're not seeing him? Your big news was that you literally just met a guy?" She leaned back again, recrossing her arms. "I can see why the news could wait."

Discomfort roiled within Kiana's belly. She stared at the table, focused on a scuff in the rough shape of a heart.

"It's complicated."

"What does that mean?"

Guilt started to swell within the young druid's chest. Picking up her tea, she inhaled the soothing steam.

"We didn't meet under the greatest of circumstances." She set down her cup without taking a sip. Her fingers tapped against the ceramic.

"What happened?"

Explosion. Screaming. Death.

Kiana screwed her eyes shut tight, willing the sounds and images to leave her in peace, just this once. When they didn't, she sighed.

"Last summer, I was walking on the beach past Hunter's Cove when I heard an explosion. A ship about half a mile off the coast just blew apart from the inside. I grabbed a boat and tried to get out there, but it was sinking fast." She pressed her palms into her eyes. "I heard people

screaming for help, but I couldn't get there fast enough. I'd been practicing spells with Aravel all morning, and my magic was all but sapped."
She rubbed the mark on her arm self-consciously.

*Maybe if I'd spent more time building up my magic and less time shak-
ing people's hands . . .*

She halted that line of thought. With a deep breath, she continued. "There were bodies in the water. Everywhere. I was having a hard
time telling who could still be saved, so I jumped into the water to start
checking. Two were within saving distance, a woman and a young girl,
both alive, both unconscious and sinking. I knew I'd only be able to get
to one. I chose the girl. Tash's niece, as it turned out."

"I'm sure he appreciated it," Ravaini said.

Kiana fixed her with a gloomy stare. "Yeah, well, the woman . . . she
died. We didn't even find her body until the next day."

Ravaini nodded, encouragement to continue.

Kiana sighed. "It was Tash's fiancée." The threat of tears burned extra
hot, the guilt almost overwhelming.

Slowly, Ravaini rested her elbows on the table and steepled her fingers under her chin, understanding dawning.

"I got the girl back to shore and stabilized her. That's when I met
Tash. He'd pulled a couple others to safety, despite his own injuries. After
that, we tried to save as many as we could, but the force of the explosion
had done a lot of damage. Of the thirty people on board, only eleven
survived." Taking a moment to sip her tea, now cool, Kiana pushed
down the tears stinging her eyes.

Ravaini took all of this in thoughtfully, her gaze intent on her sister.

"Ships don't just explode. What caused it?"

The scene flooded back to her: a gaping hole in the side of the ship,
debris scattered across the surface of the water, intermingling with the
bodies of Tash's friends and family. And then that figure.

"They never determined that."

Keen insight ran strong in the Paletines, perhaps the only consistent family trait.

"Buuuut . . ." Ravaini prompted.

A rippling silhouette. Mist rolling out to sea.

"I saw someone." She paused. "A figure, walking on the water."

Her sister's sharp mind made the leap back to their earlier conversation. "And you think it might have been the forsaken jinn."

Kiana shrugged. "I didn't have any explanation for it until now. In fact, I thought I was imagining things when no one else mentioned seeing it. Still, it's just a theory."

Blowing out a strong puff of breath, Ravaini rubbed her hands along her thighs.

"Okay, let me see if I have this straight. Something, maybe a cursed Ice Druid turned wild water jinn, ripped apart a ship, killing nearly twenty people. You hustled out there to save as many as you could, helping bring passengers to safety and offering them medical treatment."

"More or less, yes."

"So, what is it you think . . . Tash?"

"Tash Ilirian."

Ravaini stopped, hands pressed to her legs, brow furrowed. "Ilirian?"

"Yes."

"Why does that name sound familiar?"

"They're one of the most prominent families in Highmane."

Ravaini pursed her lips to the side. "Hm. 'Kay. Anyway, what is it you believe Tash Ilirian of Highmane thinks when he's with you?"

"His fiancée died, Revy. I let her die."

"Bullshit. You made a tough call and saved a little girl's life."

Kiana shrugged, dejected.

"You may be wise, but you can be pretty dumb sometimes." Ravaini swiped their teacups to the side. "This Tash, you've stayed in touch with him, yes?"

Kiana nodded. "He comes to visit once a month or so."

"Well, there you go. If he held you in any way responsible for what happened—which would make him a moron and not worth your time, by the way—I highly doubt he'd keep coming back." She placed one hand over her sister's. "And lost loves . . . People can heal from those things. You're beating yourself up for nothing, Kiwi."

The old nickname drew a wry smile from the younger sibling.

"I thought that nickname died when I finally agreed to wear colors other than green."

"Pff. Not a chance."

More than a year's worth of guilt and anxiety had formed into a tremendous weight bearing down on Kiana's shoulders. For the first time since that tragic day, some of that weight started to lift.

"I don't understand. Father and Aravel have been hounding me with confidence-inspiring mantras for a year. Why is it that the first time I talk to you about it, everything seems just a little bit better?"

"It's possible I know a thing or two about a guilty conscience. And you, darling sister, have not warranted that burden quite yet."

Kiana swung around so she was sharing a bench with Ravaini. She pulled her into a hug.

"Thanks, Revy."

Ravaini squeezed back.

"Wait here," she said, scooting them both off the bench.

While Ravaini disappeared into the mysterious other room to rummage around, Kiana returned to her seat and gave Snow a few good scratches behind the ears.

Less than half a minute later, Ravaini set a box wrapped with a purple satin ribbon in front of Kiana.

"What's this?" Kiana slid the box closer and loosened the ribbon.

"Like I said, I was planning to come visit soon. I was going to bring this up for your birthday in a few months. Had it commissioned just last week." She planted herself in the booth across from her sister. "And it sounds like this might be a better time for it."

Kiana smiled at this second early birthday surprise, biting down on her lower lip to suppress some of her childlike glee as she slipped the ribbon off the box and opened the lid.

Inside, a small card sat atop a pile of folded dark-green fabric. The words "Lars & Hoot" gleamed in metallic gold ink from the card's surface.

"A local clothier," Ravaini explained. "A little eccentric, but absolutely magic with fabric."

This only enhanced Kiana's excitement. She pulled the green cloth from the box and watched it unfurl into a gorgeous cloak trimmed in silver. At the neckline shone an amethyst clasp.

"Ravaini," Kiana gasped. "It's . . . it's . . ."

"Perfect? I know." Ravaini threw the cloak around her sister's shoulders. "And it's enchanted with what I like to call a comfort spell. It'll adapt to your temperature, so it will help keep you cool if it's hot or warm if it's cold."

"I don't know what to say." Kiana snuggled into the cloak, immediately feeling the cooling effect in the stuffy tavern.

"Words are overrated. Maybe just forgive me for not being able to come with you?"

Kiana smiled. "Already forgiven and forgotten."

Ravaini smiled back. "Good."

CHAPTER EIGHT

Two hours later, the Paletine sisters climbed the embedded staircase up to Old Home. Having agreed Kiana should leave quickly—both to minimize the Deep Ones' head start and to escape the reach of the Obsidian Web—they decided only to make a perfunctory stop at the Merchant Ring to stock up on any additional supplies Kiana might need and hadn't brought. While she'd packed for several weeks of travel and adventure, her plan had been a mission of peace and unification. She hadn't exactly planned for hunting down a group of frighteningly intelligent, mind-controlling fiends.

After tapping back into Ravaini's network of thieves, spies, and other rogue elements, the sisters deduced that the Deep Ones were likely headed west, but their subterranean travel through the vast, murky Shadow Core made their movements hard to track. Before she had any hope of stopping the Deep Ones, however, Kiana needed to figure out why they'd stolen Freya's Crystal and where the Ice Druids had ended up. No one had heard from their Order in centuries, since they had presumably abandoned their home at the east edge of Northland to escape a brewing war. As to what happened to them after that, none of the books in Kiana's vast library gave any hint.

With the plan set, Kiana had Snow teleport back to Corval with a note for Aravel and Tash attached to his collar. For now, she kept the details vague.

> *Ari & Tash,*
>
> *Change of plans. I found an adventure that aligns with our goal, but Revy is tied up, and time is of the essence. I will return to the oak Father treewalked me through outside Old Home around midday today. Meet me there. Give Father my love.*
>
> *Ki*

So, in the time leading up to the rendezvous, Kiana shopped.

Potions, weapons, trinkets, snacks—the items for sale in the Merchant Ring ran the gamut. Stalls packed with rows of little jars and vials beckoned with promises of titans' strength, greater speed, and renewed vitality; vendors selling enchanted blades called out the attributes of their wares; and artisan mages displayed shelves of shimmering crystals, glowing pendants, and finely crafted rings.

"I don't even know where to begin," Kiana said.

"Well"—Ravaini planted her hands on her hips and looked around—"considering your targets, I'd say protection against mind control would be in order."

"So, what, some sort of potion or charm?"

"Seems reasonable." She hooked her arm through her sister's, and they stepped off in the direction of a half-elf selling jewelry.

"Ah, welcome to my shop," the vendor said when they approached, spreading his arms wide. The sleeves of his crimson robe gaped open at the wrists. "I am Orwell, purveyor of finely crafted goods both beautiful and useful. What is it I can do for you lovely ladies today?"

"Good day, sir," Kiana said, stepping closer to a small display case filled with rings. "Are any of your items enchanted?"

"Some are, yes. The rest can be, though you'd have to come back in a few days to allow time for the enchantment to be completed, depending on what you require."

A delicate ring with vibrant orange stones flecked with gold fashioned into the shape of a small owl drew Kiana's eye. Sunstone, she guessed.

"What's that one?" she asked, pointing to the owl.

"Ah, excellent choice. The Ring of Owl's Wisdom. That is a relatively rare find that will heighten your mental senses, open your awareness." Orwell opened the case and slipped out the ring, handing it to Kiana.

Rotating the ring between her fingers, she asked, "Would it guard against mind control?"

"It would certainly act as a layer of protection against such things but wouldn't stop it outright. The level of enchantment needed to do that would be tremendous." Orwell gave her a concerned look. "I take it you have a rather perilous adventure ahead of you?"

"You might say that," Kiana said vaguely, still examining the stones. They tingled in her fingers, humming in tune with her own magic. "How much for the ring?"

"Three hundred gold."

"What?" both Paletine women cried in unison.

Orwell pulled back, surprised at their surprise.

"This is a powerful item that is rather uncommon. That is a fair price."

Kiana bowed her head and proffered the ring back to Orwell.

"I'm sorry, I don't have that kind of coin to spend," she said.

Before the half-elf could retrieve the ring, Ravaini said, "Hold up." She glanced back and forth between her sister and the ring a few times. Apparently making whatever decision she'd been pondering, she pulled out a coin pouch. "We'll take it," she said.

"We will?" Kiana said incredulously.

"Excellent," Orwell exclaimed, clapping his hands together once.

Ravaini started to count out the gold. "I can't do three hundred, but how about two fifty?"

"Well—"

"Wait, Revy, no," Kiana said, placing her hand over her sister's. "I can't ask you to spend that much gold for me."

"And I can't let you fall under the sway of a shadow-dwelling mind-fucker." She cast a half-hearted apologetic glance at Orwell, though if he was offended by the profanity, he didn't show it.

Ravaini pulled Kiana several feet away from the vendor, causing Orwell to put out his hands in protest, probably afraid he was about to be robbed. Ravaini waved him off and held up a finger for him to wait.

She bent her head toward Kiana and whispered, "Look, I've had some decent-paying jobs lately." She bobbed her head. "Okay, I make a *killing*, if you get my point."

Kiana grimaced.

"And rent in the Hollows isn't exactly a king's ransom. If this will help keep you safe while I can't, it's worth it."

"But two hundred fifty gold, that's—"

"Far less than your life is worth, I agree. Glad we got that settled." Ravaini tugged Kiana back to Orwell before she could object further. "So, two fifty, where'd we land on that?"

"I'm afraid that's quite impossible," Orwell said, crossing his arms.

Such bartering games rarely happened in Tribali, where a more communal spirit reigned, but Kiana decided to throw her circlet into the ring.

"I have ten gold," she said meekly, pulling out the coins. "Would that help?"

The half-elf seemed about to protest, but seeing the hopeful looks on the two beautiful, entreating faces in front of him apparently had the intended effect.

He sighed. "Fine. Two hundred and sixty gold it is."

Transaction complete, Orwell tucked the coins into a large brown leather pouch. Kiana slipped the small but intricately carved ring onto her left index finger.

"Now, this ring is no chintzy cantrip caster," Orwell said. "When dealing with magic that enhances the mind, it takes time to acclimatize yourself to its power to gain the full benefits of its effects."

"How long?" Ravaini asked, leaning on the pedestal housing the ring's display case.

With exaggerated movements, Orwell wobbled his hands back and forth in a facsimile of weighing something, his head matching the movement of his hands while his eyes blindly scanned the sky above their heads.

"Mmm, hmmm, it varies from person to person. If you have innate magic and are already endowed with at least fair mental acuity, could be a few hours. Those blessed with neither magic nor brains tend to take a few days."

He hadn't immediately identified Kiana as a druid, which boded well. She'd left her staff at the Plank and kept her tattoo out of sight. She also pulled her new cloak's hood low to avoid recognition by any Obsidian Web thugs who might be wandering about. So far, so good.

Exchanging a glance, both sisters shrugged.

"I can work with that," Kiana said. She could already feel the magic inside her stirring with the presence of the ring, vibrating across her cells to harmonize with the new flow of power.

"Good luck on your journey," Orwell said with a half bow before returning to the back of his stall.

As they walked away, Kiana elbowed Ravaini gently. "I can't believe you did that for me. First the cloak and now this?" She held up her hand to admire the ring.

"And this," Ravaini said, slipping a silver ring onto Kiana's middle finger, next to the other. The ring covered most of the space between her two knuckles and branched out into the shape of a tree.

"Wha—" Kiana halted. "Did you steal this from him?"

"What?" Ravaini leaned back, an exaggerated look of indignation on her face. "That doesn't sound like something I would do." She adjusted the ring on her sister's finger. "Looks like it was made for you." She turned and kept walking along the stalls.

Unable to come up with an appropriate response, Kiana followed, mouth frozen open in shock. She had to repeatedly tamp down the urge to return the ring to the vendor with profuse apologies. That would only draw attention to Ravaini.

Another two hours passed as the sisters wound their way through the Merchant Ring, forgetting their mission to keep the visit brief and instead catching up on everything they hadn't told each other since they'd last spoken, nearly two years before. Ravaini talked about her work in vague terms, for which Kiana was grateful. She adored her sister but had no desire to ground any of the horrific deeds she imagined happened in the Hollows in unavoidable fact. Especially if her sister played a starring role. She was perfectly happy in the sweet bliss of ignorance.

Aside from a few indulgent food items she almost certainly wouldn't be able to obtain once on the road, Kiana made no further acquisitions—legal or otherwise—for the journey. After snacking on a couple of bags of hon-eyed peanuts and three kinds of cheese breads, she glanced up at the sky.

"Oh, salt it all. I told Aravel and Tash midday. If I want to make it to the rendezvous in time, I have to go now." Kiana pulled Ravaini into a tight hug. Two years' worth of missed embraces poured into her grip. "I can't believe I have to say goodbye to you already."

"When all this is over, we'll have ourselves a little holiday together, yeah?"

Kiana nodded as a tear rolled down her cheek. Ravaini wiped it away.

Saying goodbye again after such a short time together felt cruel, but both sisters knew letting the Deep Ones get further ahead of them could only end in disaster. At least Kiana had accomplished part of what she'd come to Old Home to do: ensure her sister was okay. How long that would stay true, Kiana didn't dare ponder. Ravaini walked a peril-ous road not exactly bursting with sunshine and daffodils. Then again, Kiana herself now followed a dangerous path.

As the druid turned back toward the Hollows, Ravaini called to her. "This Tash, you like him, yeah?"

A familiar emptiness screamed within Kiana to be filled, an ache she'd tried to ignore. She didn't know if she should smile or cry.

"Very much so," she managed to say through the crush of conflict-ing emotions.

A tenderness Ravaini's face had not shown in some time softened her features.

"Then don't be so quick to count yourself out."

A group of shoppers moved between them. When they passed, Ra-vaini was gone.

Back at the Half Moon Inn, after retrieving her staff, Kiana found Ryndl flirting with the same flutist from the previous night. She'd traded her black outfit for an even more revealing blue one.

To each her own, Kiana thought with a smile and small shrug.

"May I borrow you for but a moment?" she asked Ryndl politely as she approached the bar, eyes averted from the impressive display of cleavage.

Clearly not pleased with the disruption of his clumsy wooing, the dwarf flashed Kiana a vaguely hostile scowl. Still, he moved around the bar with a grunt and an apologetic head tilt to the gnome.

Once tucked back in the hallway leading to the small wooden desk, Kiana held out her room key.

"Turns out I won't be needing it for as many nights as I thought."

Ryndl looked at the dangling key for a moment before snatching it from her hand. He tossed it down the hall to the desk, where it landed fleetingly before clattering to the floor on the other side. Then he looked at the ground on either side of Kiana.

"Didn't you have a dog with you?"

Finding it unnecessary to correct him, she simply said, "Yes, I did."

With an indifferent shrug, he started walking back to the bar.

Kiana cleared her throat pointedly.

Ryndl stopped and turned reluctantly back.

"I believe I paid for a few nights in advance," the elf said.

"And?"

Kiana took a step toward him, keeping her expression friendly. "And I'm going to need some of that silver back, please."

At first he made no move to comply, perhaps testing her resolve. She didn't waver.

Finally, with a harrumph, he pulled a coin purse from his belt and removed a few coins.

"Thank you."

"Harrumph," he said again, at last making his way back to the bar and his waiting quarry.

Stepping into the quasi-fresh air, Kiana took in her final glimpse of the Hollows. She wouldn't miss this place. Where leaving Ravaini behind ripped at Kiana's heart, bidding farewell to the Hollows inspired only relief. No more grumpy tavern keepers. No more unwashed street vendors and their leering gazes, hocking rotten or misbegotten wares. No more toxic river of waste. Yes, leaving the Hollows offered sweet relief indeed.

Despite already being late for her rendezvous, Kiana pulled out her canteen and took a long pull, washing down the last vestiges of peanuts and cheese bread. As she tucked the container back into her bag, she felt a gentle prickle around her left index finger. A thought tugged at the back of her mind, but she couldn't focus it. Believing it to be part of the new ring's attunement process, she ignored the sensation—until hurried movement stirred in her peripheral vision. A cold-hot sensation flared beneath the ring, ensuring her attention.

To her left, across a decaying rope bridge, she saw three men running toward her, swords drawn. Another moved at a less rapid pace a little ways behind them, a green hood pulled low over his face. One of the men sent a jolt of recognition through Kiana: Rudge and Eyepatch's companion from the Half Moon. Murderous hate painted all of their features into ugly sneers.

"Uh-oh." Kiana considered her options. She looked at her Regent Tree. She'd drawn heavily upon her magical resources already that day and had only rested enough to recuperate a couple leaves, which meant a mere six grew among the branches. Four against one didn't seem like odds she wanted to try in this state. She intensely longed for the day when she mastered every discipline and didn't have to ration her magic.

With any luck, Aravel and Tash were already through the oak tree, allies Kiana knew she could count on. She decided to run, and she would need speed on her side.

Securing her staff to the straps of her pack as fast as her hasty movements allowed, she put her arms down by her sides, palms flat and facing forward. She tilted her head back. Ripples of magic coursed through her as her form shifted from woman to bird. The next thing her pursuers saw was a peregrine falcon rocketing out of the ravine.

Cresting the edge of the Hollows, Kiana felt adrenaline rush through her feathered body. She could do this.

Thwack.

A bolt of force came out of nowhere, knocking Kiana from the sky. She hit the ground hard, skidding across dirt and gravel, the force of the impact shifting her back to her elven form. At least she was out of the Hollows.

"So they have a mage," she grumbled. Unlike druids, who were chosen for their worthiness, or clerics and paladins, who called on their deities for magical assistance when needed, arcane mages like sorcerers were not held accountable by a higher power. Some used their powers for good; others chose a more nefarious path.

Kiana lay still for a second, making sure nothing was broken. Then she carefully picked herself and her staff up out of the dirt before turning and running down the country road, only chancing a brief look behind her.

So far, no visible pursuers.

As soon as she began to sweat from exertion and the heat of the early-autumn sun, Kiana felt a wave of coolness wash over her, starting at the amethyst clasp at her throat.

Thanks, Revy.

Seconds later, Kiana heard distant shouts behind her. The men had made it out of the ravine.

Up ahead, the road curved around a field of corn. If she could just make it—

Intense pain exploded in the back of her rib cage as another bolt hit her from behind, knocking the wind out of her. She stumbled, twisting around to gauge the threat level.

About two hundred feet back, the hooded pursuer held up one gloved hand, palm out toward Kiana. The mage. The other three now closed in from a hundred feet away, the one she recognized from the Half Moon Inn running in tandem with a man whose crimson mohawk protruded like a saw blade from his head. The most grizzled of the three puffed just a little behind them.

Noting their proximity to each other, Kiana reached a hand toward the sky.

"Ith luziren visht."

Purple energy crackled across Kiana's eyes, which had gone completely white. A flare of bright light flashed in her outstretched hand as charcoal storm clouds gathered overhead in the blink of an eye. Lightning zigzagged through the sky, prompting deep rumbles of thunder. The druid clenched her fist, and a white-hot bolt struck the ground directly between the two closest pursuers. Both roared as electricity shot through their bodies.

Overtaking his stunned, singed comrades, the grizzled man bellowed ferociously as he sprinted toward his storm-wielding foe.

Mindful of the sharp object seconds away from impaling her, Kiana didn't see the mage preparing another spell. Fortunately, either the sudden lightning storm Kiana had summoned or his wounded allies threw the caster slightly off his mark, and his second blast, a pulse of green energy, went wide, barely tickling Kiana's hair as it zoomed by.

But it got her attention.

Maintaining her focus on the magical storm above, she looked behind her and whispered, *"Nebela samat."*

Roiling mist surrounded her, and she vanished, reappearing twenty feet up the road a moment later, still engulfed in a rapidly dissipating cloud. The second she reappeared, she clenched her fist, this time bringing lightning down on top of the mage. The scream that ensued informed Kiana that this caster was, in fact, a woman. The hit knocked her to her knees.

More leaves vanished at the crook of Kiana's elbow.

Momentarily losing visual contact when Kiana teleported, the three thugs had halted in their tracks, but only for a second. Reacquiring their target, they resumed course.

One of the two she'd hit with lightning called out in a thick, gravelly voice, "You're ours, bitch! You can't outmatch the Obsidian Web."

Kiana's energy flagged, the strain of maintaining the storm too much. A glance at her arm revealed a lone leaf beginning the initial arc of its descent. If the attackers reached her, they won.

There are too many of them, she thought. *I can't do this alone. Nelami, help me.*

The closest thug would reach her any second, the other two not long after. Turning her back on her assailants, Kiana fled as fast as her elven legs would carry her. Twenty more feet and she'd be around the bend, momentarily out of sight behind a wall of corn. Maybe she'd have enough time to hide.

"AHHH!" Kiana screamed as a sword bit deeply into the flesh of her side. The magical electricity coursing through her body abruptly disappeared as her focus wavered. The storm vanished as quickly as it had appeared.

"You will pay for the lives of our friends, druid. You will die as they did. But first, you're coming with us." This voice lacked the gravel of the first but more than made up for it with menace.

The man pulled back his sword, the blade now glistening with Kiana's blood. The injured elf reached a hand back toward him and released a spurt of flame the size of a coconut as she continued to move along the road, clutching her side with her other hand. Senses heightened by battle, he dodged the flame and kept coming.

They weren't going to stop. She had to stand and fight.

Sensing the pursuer just behind her, Kiana waited until the last second and turned, pulling the dagger strapped to her thigh free and thrusting it in front of her. The blade sank deep under the man's ribs, a look of shocked confusion crossing his face. He dropped his sword and fell to his knees. Down the road, the other thugs stopped dead in their tracks, also staring in shock.

With little time before the moment passed, Kiana yanked her dagger free and quickly appraised the situation. The mage had regained her feet but didn't seem like the most immediate threat. Kiana turned her attention to the fighters. Each wore a large metal medallion around his neck.

Harnessing what power she could, likely the last of it, Kiana pressed a hand to her chest. "*Ardentz metilia.*"

As the last leaf vanished from Kiana's arm, the medallion around one of the pursuers' necks glowed white hot, tiny silver lightning bolts sizzling across the surface, searing into his flesh. Already slightly charred from being struck by the much larger lightning bolt, the guy dropped to one knee, growling in pain.

"You fucking . . . aaaaahhh!" the other guy yelled, charging Kiana with even more ferocity.

He was less than ten feet away. And the mage could hurtle another bone-cracking spell her way any second. The woman's hood was thrown back from her coal-dark hair, and Kiana saw the feverish intensity in her icy blue eyes.

Blood continued to seep from the druid's side. Desperate, she looked within, searching for any power she had left. All druids came into the world with the ability to access minor magic from each of the druidic disciplines, even before receiving a Regent Tree, and without the need for a verbal invocation. *Water and ice, fire and light, earth and flora, lightning and thunder, wind and healing.* Kiana raised a hand and released another small shock of flame, hurling it at the oncoming thug's mohawked head. The fire glanced off his shoulder, barely slowing him.

This was it. She was done.

Crunch.

The sound of bone splitting hit Kiana's ears at the same moment a massive black bear collided with the muscled but fleshy man before her, sending both beast and prey tumbling along the road. Just beyond where they landed, the mage held one hand up, green energy crackling around her open palm.

And then the spell fizzled out.

Terror gripped the caster's face. Backing up, she started frantically muttering words Kiana couldn't hear.

The bear finished mauling its first victim, who now lay in a motionless bloody heap, and turned its attention to the mage.

Leaning into her staff for support, Kiana stretched a hand toward the mage, sending her druidic flame racing at the frenzied caster. Just before the fire made contact, an ear-shattering ringing erupted from where the caster stood, a visible shock wave of sound pulsing out from the ground.

The mage crumpled to the dirt.

Confused, Kiana stared at her palm.

How did . . .

Hit by a wave of wooziness from blood loss and what was likely a cracked rib or three, her knees buckled.

Strong hands grabbed her from behind and helped gently lower her to the dusty ground.

"Whoa, there. I've got you."

"Waterfalls," Kiana whispered, closing her eyes against the dizziness.

"What's that?"

She smiled up into familiar amber eyes. "You smell like waterfalls."

Tash smiled back at her, the air around him still vibrating with arcane power. "Haven't heard that one before, but I like it."

Warmth spread down Kiana's body. Maybe it was the blood. Maybe not. At the moment, she was too dizzy to care.

"How did you find me?"

"When you didn't show up for our rendezvous, we figured you got held up along the road and decided to come find you." Aravel finished jogging back to them, no longer in the shape of a bear. Instead of dark fur, she wore a dark-green sleeveless top with brown leather padding across the chest, a wide brown leather belt with various straps and buckles, and a brown leather skirt over leggings made from the hardy but flexible fibers of a clypernia plant, a favorite among Tribali's druids. Her flaxen hair and golden skin shone in the bright midday sun.

The man with the superheated medallion lay behind her, deep claw marks carved into his chest.

"Turns out those bracelets Tash made come in real handy. Helped us home in on your location." Aravel dropped to her knees beside her friend, hand pressed to the wound in her side. "When you said time was of the essence, I didn't think this was what you meant."

Kiana coughed out a pained laugh, her ribs screaming at her for doing so. From behind her she heard snuffling, and Snow came running to her side. She hugged him. "Surprisingly, this *isn't* what I meant."

Gold light glowed in Aravel's palm and sparkled across her irises as she whispered druidic words of healing.

"Well, in that case, I feel like we're in for one heck of a story."

CHAPTER NINE

By the time Kiana finished telling Tash and Aravel about her whirl-wind twenty-four hours, Aravel had turned the six-inch gash in Kiana's side into an angry pink line that would fade with time. They'd sought shelter from the sun under the old oak, deciding it best not to venture back into the Hollows. The Obsidian Web still wanted blood.

"So, you've been attacked by these Charcoal Web people twice in one day. Interesting start to your big adventure." Aravel sat back against the oak, legs planted in front of her for her arms to rest on. Wind rustled the pointed leaves that were just beginning to turn fiery shades of red and orange above her head.

"Obsidian. But yes." Kiana nodded her agreement. "Thank Nelami for you guys. I'd be dead if you hadn't found me when you did. Tash, that spell you used on the mage—your timing was impeccable. For a second I thought I'd acquired a crazy thunder spell." She laughed, then grimaced. "Please don't tell my father about this. Can't go letting him think he's right all the time."

Tash chuckled. "Your secret's safe with us."

"I've never killed anyone before, but when I saw that mohawked buffoon about to stab you . . ." Aravel made a small growling noise in the back of her throat. "Maybe I've been spending too much time in predatory forms, but instinct just took over."

"And here I've been giving you a hard time for shirking your spell-casting practice to play shapeshifter." Kiana shook her head. "Never again."

Aravel grinned and flicked a mud-caked leaf from her boot, which Snow ran to inspect. "So, what now?"

"Battle Tree, I think."

Tash cocked his head, eyebrows arching in surprise. "What's in Battle Tree?"

"Answers, I hope. When I was there last year with the Trinete Delegation, I met a druid who works in the library, the Mystic Lyceum. I never ended up going, but she told me about a collection they have with information on the five Orders. At the time, I was merely expanding my studies, but if the Deep Ones really have Freya's Crystal, that library might have information on what they want to do with it and how we can stop them. There's also the small matter of locating the Ice Druids."

Aravel's brow furrowed in deep consternation. "You were in Battle Tree and *didn't* go see the continent's biggest library?"

Not expecting this reaction, Kiana stuttered, "I—it—I didn't have that much extra time."

"Didn't have time for *books*?" Aravel shook her head. "Do I even know you anymore?"

No words came to Kiana's open mouth, so Tash stepped in.

"Wouldn't it be more prudent to try to stop the Deep Ones *before* they can use the Crystal?"

Kiana broke eye contact with Aravel, finally finding her voice. "We don't know what they want it for, or where they are. I don't know about you, but I'd rather enter into this armed with as much information as possible. We're not going after some brainless bog giants you could trick with a little prestidigitation. I've read the legends. Deep Ones are clever; they plan. They've been underground for centuries, long enough to become mere bedtime story villains. The fact that they're making a move now is significant. The last time they poked their ugly"—she grimaced—"*ugly* faces above ground, there was a demon war."

"Okay, so let's say we get to Battle Tree and discover what they could possibly want a druidic artifact for. Then let's say that we manage to find out where the Ice Druids have been hiding for centuries, assuming they still exist at all. You're proposing that we three"—he gestured among them—"then take on enemies legendary for their almost successful bid for dominance over the entire Realm of Eventide?"

"Ideally, no."

Tash propped an arm on his knee. "Explain, if you would."

"My hope is that by the time we encounter the Deep Ones, we'll be among a city of allies. If we do this right, we locate the Ice Druids and warn them that the Crystal has fallen into dangerous hands. *Then* we go after them."

"Why not simply tell your father?"

Kiana sighed. "Between the werewolf war up north and the pirates playing hide-and-seek in the sea, the druids are already stretched too thin." She leaned forward. "I know this sounds dangerous, and I will understand if you think I'm crazy and want to go back to Tribali, but I believe we can do this. I've dedicated my life, what little I've lived of it so far, to the study of druid history. Since I joined the Conclave, I've been the only voice speaking up for the restoration of balance. This is my chance to act upon the views I've been espousing for years."

"And if we run into the Deep Ones first?"

Kiana's face grew serious. "Then Nelami be with us."

"Very well." Tash stood, brushing dead grass from his hands and pants. "May I suggest we move on and continue our plans elsewhere? When those four Web hooligans don't return to their bosses, I'm sure others will be sent after them, and what they're going to find will no doubt place you even higher on their hit list. If it hasn't already. I'd say two battles is plenty for one day, and I imagine they won't travel far outside their borders in pursuit."

"Fair enough." Aravel rose effortlessly to her feet as Tash offered Kiana a hand up.

Strength mostly recovered but still happy for the help, Kiana clasped Tash's hand and pulled herself up. Her ribs emanated only an echo of the pain from before. And better still, her Regent Tree boasted three renewed leaves already, thanks to the brief period of rest in the bolstering embrace of nature. Yet another reason she preferred her forest home to cities.

"Regretting coming to join me yet? Some might call this more than a little reckless." Kiana shouldered her pack.

Tash reached out and straightened the circlet atop Kiana's head, which had fallen askew during the fight despite the braids holding it in place. Jade-inlaid leaves decorated the metal's vine pattern, making it a near-perfect companion to the ring she now wore on her middle finger.

"More than a little reckless. Sounds like just my game," Tash said. "I never had any intention of bowing out. I simply wanted to be the voice of reason for once."

"You're sure?"

"Indeed." He smiled. "I'll happily walk whatever path you choose right alongside you."

A faint dizziness buzzed through Kiana's head as a tingling sensation sparked throughout her entire body. This time she was sure it wasn't blood loss.

Aravel clapped, snapping her out of it. "Great. Now that we've got that cleared up, let's go kick some monster ass."

"Technically Deep Ones aren't monsters." Tash banished a patch of dirt from his knee with a snap of his fingers. "They're simply a devoutly evil race hells bent on enslaving Eventide and anyone who gets in their way with their insane psionic powers that allow them to read and control minds or bring enemies to their knees with an incapacitating psychic aura. Or so I've read."

Loathing puckered Aravel's mouth into a circle of disdain.

"So, monsters, then."

Tash squinted. "I guess so."

"Well, now that *that's* out of the way." Kiana made a grand gesture with her arms. "Shall we?"

And with that, the four companions set their sights on Battle Tree.

Two uneventful weeks slipped by as the companions traveled through the plains with little more than farmland to break up the monotonous landscape. They passed most of the time reliving favorite memories or practicing new spells. Kiana and Tash spent nights around the campfire reading while Aravel learned to shift into any new creatures they'd encountered along the road. Mostly birds and rodents, forms which Snow took great delight in chasing.

Just when the importance of their mission started to blur in their minds, Kiana and company at last came into view of the wall around Battle Tree. Delicate patterns of tessellating shapes adorned the coppery filigree.

"Thank Nelami. At last," Aravel said. "I was beginning to think there were only cows and thorn grass left on this blessed continent."

"Yes, you may have mentioned it a time or two," Tash said. He lowered his voice to just above a whisper. "Or thirty-seven."

"I'm sorry, was my boredom with our scenery bothering you, Mr. Can Cast Beautiful Lights at Will But Chooses Not to in Our Hour of Need?"

"Says the druid who can literally alter natural surroundings."

Kiana sighed. While she was used to Aravel's moods and quirks, Tash had never spent much time with her on his visits and was now being thrown into the churning seas unprepared.

"But we're here now!" she tried.

Aravel planted her fists on her hips and surveyed the scene ahead. "It really is beautiful. Not exactly the wall I'd expect from a city called 'Battle Tree,' but it's nice to look at."

Tash shook his head. "To the naked eye the wall might appear merely decorative, but something ancient and powerful infuses the metal with magical defenses that would deter the largest of armies should the city go into lockdown—an enchantment so strong that no outsiders, and very few insiders, seem able to identify its origin. I've studied it myself once or twice. The latent energy alone is incredible."

"Thank you, O Master of History."

Kiana headed off further discussion. "Shall we?"

Walking through the nearest eastern gate of the city led the party into the Merchant Ward. Much like Old Home, Battle Tree was composed of distinct districts, though instead of rings, the city spread out like a wheel, with sections taking up different-sized slices of the circle. At the very center was the Hub, where nobles such as Battle Tree's highly respected Archduke lived. The Hub also housed the Mystic Lyceum, the heart of the city.

As they passed through the gate, Kiana noted the same phenomenon she had on her last visit: a crackling hum of energy that seeped into her as she stepped through the boundary.

"What was that?" Aravel asked as she hurtled through the arched entrance, apparently having felt the same sensation.

"I'm not sure," Kiana replied. "I felt it the last time I was here too."

"That," Tash said, "is one of the great, and many, mysteries of Battle Tree."

Both women looked at him.

"Something about Battle Tree heightens magical abilities, amplifies power. Rumors abound regarding the source, but like the wall, it's one of the city's most closely guarded secrets. I'd guess a rare few know the true answer."

"Heightens abilities, you say?" Aravel looked at her hands with one arched eyebrow.

She summoned a ball of druidic fire to her palm, the same minor conjuring Kiana had used so desperately in Old Home to prevent herself from being impaled by an advancing blade.

"Ari . . ." Kiana said in a low voice tinged with warning.

Staring intently at the flame, Aravel flexed her hand, ignoring her friend. With a roar, what had started as a small orb of fire ignited into a four-foot-high spike of flame. Passersby ducked out of the way, startled. Snow crouched to the ground with a growl.

Kiana and Tash raised their hands toward Aravel's flame simultaneously.

"*Prodicsht aquai*," Kiana hissed.

A stream of water materialized overhead as if being poured from a large invisible pitcher, dousing the flame.

Tash lowered his hand, spell unspoken.

"Aw, hey. What'd you do that for?" Aravel shook out her soaked hand, lips curved in a dejected frown.

"Are you out of your mind? You don't just walk into a new city and summon a tower of fire." Kiana kept her voice to a harsh whisper. Around them, people continued to gawk.

"It was just a little spell. Not like I shot sunlight from my eyes or called a tsunami down from the heavens." Her eyes brightened. "Do you think I could do that here?"

"No," Kiana and Tash said in unison.

Aravel's face fell.

"Even if you could, I'd say a little more discretion would be wise," Tash said quietly through a disarming smile directed at those who continued to stare.

Eventually the locals lost interest in the spectacle and wandered off about their business.

Kiana put a hand gently on her friend's arm.

"There's going to come a time very soon when we're going to want to avoid drawing attention to ourselves at all costs. Maybe that's something we should start practicing now."

Aravel gave a dramatic sigh. "Fine." She moved past her companions, muttering something about people who hated fun.

Kiana and Tash exchanged a knowing look and, both shaking their heads, followed after her.

Though filled with bustling throngs just like its counterpart to the east, Battle Tree's Merchant Ward hummed with less frenetic energy than Old Home's Merchant Ring. People walked with both purpose and an ease that spoke to a more relaxed mindset, much like Tribali. Kiana had noticed this contentedness during her last visit, as well. Having spent little time here, Kiana could only hazard a guess that it might have something to do with the city's leader, Archduke Hiran. He maintained a much more reciprocal relationship with the people he served than the Archduke of Old Home, taking an active interest in day-to-day affairs to ensure continued peace and prosperity. Little had been seen of Old

Home's Archduke the last few years. He appeared to wrap himself up in his own affairs rather than keep in mind the concerns of the populace.

To be fair, Battle Tree wasn't facing an incursion of Deep Ones like Old Home. Their very presence could be enough to disrupt a city's tranquility. Who knew how long they'd been there before druids started to disappear?

"So, where can we find this new friend of yours?" Aravel asked as they passed the cart of a gnome selling brightly colored rugs.

"I imagine at the library, given that's where she works," Kiana answered. She held up a hand and politely shook her head as the rug seller called out an offer for a pretty lady.

"Does your library pass allow for guests, or will we have to wait outside?" Tash ran his slender fingers along a strip of deep-blue silk hanging from a rack.

Kiana stopped in the middle of the path, nearly causing Aravel to run into her.

"What?"

Tash stopped a few steps ahead and half turned back to her. "Your pass. Can you bring in guests?" When Kiana didn't respond, he rubbed the back of his neck. "Oh, sorry. I assumed when you said you'd met someone who told you about the library that you'd gotten a pass."

"No."

A group of six humans split in half and moved around the three elves and the fox blocking the way.

"Well, that presents a bit of a problem, doesn't it? Accessing the Hub's finer amenities, like the bank or the library, requires special permissions. You can't just waltz in uninvited." He paused. "I thought you'd been here."

"I was . . . with a delegation of ambassadors from Tribali. I presume they had the necessary documentation and didn't trouble me with the details. And the only building we visited in the Hub was the Archduke's headquarters."

"Hmmm," Tash responded.

"Who has to invite you?" Aravel asked.

Tash turned his gaze to the other druid. "Anyone who lives in, or holds a high enough position in, the Hub."

"Like the Master Apprentice of the library?" Kiana said ruefully.

Tash's mouth cocked into a crooked grin. "Precisely."

"Wonderful. Amina left out that little tidbit." Kiana sat heavily on a nearby wooden bench with a wrought iron back. "So, now what?"

"Wait." Aravel pointed an accusatory finger at Tash. "How do *you* know about these passes?"

Tash put his hands on his hips, eyes on Aravel's finger.

"My family has done business in Battle Tree for generations. We even have an account at the Bank of Ash." He met her eyes. "This isn't my first time here."

"So you could get us in." She motioned back to Kiana. "Or at least get *her* in."

"Maybe. Assuming we still have a library pass in the vault box."

Aravel mirrored Tash's stance, hands indignantly on her hips. "And you weren't going to mention this?"

"I hardly got the chance, before now, did I? We've been talking about this for all of two minutes."

Aravel scoffed. "Are you going to completely ignore the two *weeks* we spent getting here?"

"Like I said, I made an assumption." He held up an apologetic hand. "My fault."

"Look, it doesn't matter now," Kiana said by way of intervention. She turned to Tash. "Do you think you could check and see if you have a pass?"

He hesitated.

"What is it?" Kiana asked.

Another moment's hesitation, and then he said, "Nothing, nothing. Let's get to the Hub and I'll see what I can do."

"Great." Kiana eyed him quizzically.

As they made their way to the center of the city, Aravel surveyed their surroundings. Pink-blossomed shrubs separated the merchant carts along the main thoroughfare. Behind the row of vendors, lines of trees interspersed with fountains filled the space before another section of merchants. Children used the intervening space as a makeshift park, chasing each other in a game of tag while parents chatted idly on benches.

"Why do they call it Battle Tree?" she asked after they'd been walking for about fifteen minutes.

Tash frowned in thought. "I'm not sure. It hasn't come up in my reading on the city's history. Obviously a tree played a key role in a battle of some kind at some point."

"But which one?" Aravel spun in a circle as she walked. "You'd think a tree worthy of naming a city after would be a little more prominent. I don't see any especially spectacular trees about." She pointed to a particularly thick oak with limbs curling off in all directions. "But I'm definitely keeping that one in mind in case I ever learn to treewalk and need to get back here."

"Maybe the tree was destroyed in the battle?" Kiana suggested, admiring the deep-yellow leaves rustling along the big oak's branches. She, too, committed the tree to memory. If she truly were to become High Druid, Nelami would almost certainly grant her the power to treewalk.

"There it is," Tash said, pointing ahead.

"What, the tree?" Aravel's head perked up.

"No, the Hub."

"Oh my," Aravel said, voice low in wonder.

Ahead, a beautifully ornate wall, even more stunning than the one surrounding the city, encircled the Hub. Pulses of blue magic raced at intervals along the copper-and-brass filigree. Shapes formed from the negative space along the top of the wall resembled an array of ancient runes. Farther down, the patterns opened up into tree branches and arcane symbols. Massive stone buildings towered above the barrier, their smooth walls glistening in the afternoon sun. Guards stood at attention at the entrance directly in the travelers' path, their green uniforms crisp and tidy.

"Pardon me a moment," Tash said, turning to the ladies to block their way.

"What're you doing?" Aravel eyed him suspiciously.

"Just a little cleanup." He waved his hands over each of them in turn, including Snow, the grime from their travels that hadn't been washed away by their bathing in a stream that morning vanishing in the blink of an eye. "There"—Tash wiped his hands together—"much better. We're about to enter the realm of the city's elite. The guards are far more likely to let us pass unmolested if we look the part."

Snow shook himself out, his freshly fluffed fur gleaming coppery red in the sunlight. Tongue lolling, he smiled up at the noble, who responded with some scratches under the fox's chin.

"Where were you when I spilled Grandmother Owl's special ink on her prized yeti-skin rug?" Aravel inspected his handiwork. "My hands were stained indigo for days from trying to clean that up before she got home."

"Never mind you, what about the rug?" Tash resumed course for the Hub. "Can't imagine the trouble she went through to acquire such a thing."

Kiana laughed. "Grandmother Owl took care of the rug just fine. Aravel's pleas for mercy, however, went unheeded. She thought a fitting punishment for her carelessness was 'the mark of the menace,' as she called it."

Tash laughed. "Seems she had you pegged early on."

Aravel brushed an invisible speck of lint from her shoulder. "I don't know what you're talking about."

In truth, Grandmother Owl had taken pity on Aravel after three days of desperate scrubbing. Though not related by blood to either Kiana or Aravel, the old woman considered both of them family and took special interest in their druidic training as well as doting on them as adopted granddaughters. Ancient even by elven standards, the woman was the finest mentor Kiana could have hoped to have. Also the most mysterious, always favoring riddles over direct conversation.

May your steadfast tutelage help me in this quest, Grandmother, Kiana thought as they neared the gate.

Soon, the four friends stood at the entrance to the Hub. The guards made no move to stop them as they entered, but Kiana could feel their scrutinizing gazes upon them as they passed, though the guards' heads never turned an inch. As she stepped through the gate, a visceral wave of nearly intoxicating magical energy washed over her, even more powerful than the one at the city's entrance. The sensation, while fleeting, left her buzzing.

The Hub more than lived up to its name. Buildings and denizens central to the continued prosperity of Battle Tree sprawled out in all directions. Wide stone paths paved the way from structure to structure, a pleasant change from the dusty roads they'd traveled for so long.

"The Bank of Ash is just over there." Tash pointed to a stunning structure on the left made entirely of glass.

Inside the lobby stood a large, well-pruned ash tree. Leaves blazing with the deep reds and burning oranges of autumn continuously fell in a lazy drift to the floor, new leaves sprouting in their stead.

"I'll pop in and see what I can find, then come meet you at the library." He nodded toward the center of the Hub.

Kiana turned to the massive circular stone building and smiled. After being unable to visit during her previous journey here, she couldn't wait to see what literary treasures awaited inside.

Aravel's mind stubbornly stayed on other matters. "Who in Nelami's vast domain of nature and the sea builds a bank out of glass? That seems like one of the worst ideas ever, a heist waiting to happen."

Tash shook his head. "Like with most of Battle Tree, there are enchantments on that building you wouldn't believe. In fact, it's probably one of the most secure places I've ever been. If you step one foot inside without the proper authorization, guards will be on you before your second step has a chance to fall. And I would challenge you to try and break that glass, but I fear you'd actually accept, and we would have no time to evade authorities after you failed spectacularly."

Aravel snorted.

"Then I guess it's a good thing you have the proper authorization." Kiana smiled. "So, we'll see you at the library, then?"

"Indeed. I shouldn't be long." He paused and rubbed an earlobe.

"Is something wrong?"

He dropped his hand. "No, I'll catch up with you shortly." He turned and headed for the bank.

Kiana stared up at a single wall containing more books than she'd ever seen in her life. And given that reading was her favorite pastime, that was actually saying something. She'd seen more than her fair share.

"Seas of mercy . . ." she whispered. "I may never leave."

Aravel nodded silently in agreement, mouth hanging open wide enough for an apple to fit in. Tash stood just behind them, still chatting amiably with the clerk who had admitted them.

All around, as far as the eye could see, books rose floor to ceiling on towering shelves of dark wood, some freestanding with arched tops, others built into the walls. The smell of aged parchment and leather hung heavy in the air, though every spine of every book appeared immaculate, perfectly preserved in this haven of learning.

Small spheres of dancing light flitted about, darting between rows before speeding back to places unknown. Apprentices of varying ranks milled about as well, half wearing sage-green tunics bearing the symbol of a large tree in gold, the other half wearing lavender bearing the same symbol. Some had one of the little orbs of light hovering near their shoulders.

"What are they?" Aravel whispered near Kiana's ear.

"We call them finders," a male voice said.

A man wearing a tunic of both sage and lavender approached from the right, a small but friendly smile on his lips. A leather band tied back his shoulder-length blond hair, and his thoughtful green eyes shone with a wisdom beyond his thirty-something years.

"They help the apprentices locate specific books," he said. "Or people."

Kiana nodded slowly, still lost in the wonder of this place.

"I imagine it's a lot of inventory to keep up with," she said quietly as Tash came up to stand beside her.

The man smiled. "So it is." After a pause, he held out a hand in greeting. "My name is Wyatt Foxheart. I'm the Master Apprentice here at the Mystic Lyceum. I understand you're looking for Amina."

"Wha—" Kiana's head twitched to the side. "Yes. I thought Amina was the Master Apprentice." She regarded him more carefully. "And I thought the apprentices were all druids."

He straightened. "We are."

She frowned. "But you're . . . human."

A soft laugh escaped through his nose. "I am that. Our ties to Nelami are somewhat unique here in Battle Tree."

"Define 'unique.'" Aravel pinned him with a suspicious squint.

"I'm afraid that would be a dive into history I don't currently have the time for. Suffice it to say, magic is weirder here."

"So we've noticed." Kiana darted a quick glance at Aravel. "Okay, a conversation for another time. That doesn't explain what happened to Amina."

Wyatt looked at his boots for half a moment before restoring eye contact. "I'm sorry to be the one to tell you this, but Amina is dead."

"What?" Kiana blinked at him, trying to accept the information. "How? When?"

"Three days ago. She was found at her home. We're still investigating the cause of death."

Kiana placed a hand on her abdomen and sucked in a slow breath, calming her emotions. Tash wrapped an arm around her shoulders, and Snow leaned against her legs.

"You two were good friends, I take it?" Uncertainty trembled in Wyatt's words.

With a quivering breath, Kiana shook her head. "No, we'd only met once, last year. I was visiting Battle Tree from Tribali with a group of diplomats sent by my father. Amina attended one of the meetings, and we got to talking about books and all things druid. She invited me here on my next visit. She was lovely."

"Tribali? Are you Ozmand Paletine's daughter?" Wyatt asked.

The surprise on Kiana's face matched that of Wyatt's tone. Tash and Aravel both looked at Kiana, their surprise apparent as well.

"One of them, yes," she said. "Do you know my father?"

Wyatt shook his head. "Unfortunately, no. But his name is well known here at the Mystic Lyceum. I hope to have the pleasure of meeting him now that—" He paused and cleared his throat. "In my new role."

As High Druid, Ozmand would indeed make it a point to visit the new Master Apprentice in Battle Tree. Kiana wondered if he'd heard about Amina yet.

Aravel leaned into Tash, playfully bumping an elbow against his ribs. "Looks like you're not the only one with family clout here in ye olde Battle Tree."

"Indeed." His voice lilted up with a note of intrigue.

Clearly having overheard the whispers, Wyatt said to the group, "High Druid Paletine has more than earned our honor and respect, given the amount of conflict he's been tasked with overcoming in his time. His wise leadership and prowess of nature's magic are a rare combination these days." He bowed slightly to Kiana. "It would be an honor to assist you however I can."

Kiana reciprocated the bow. She also noted the barb in his comment about leadership and wondered if he felt the same way she did about the politicization of the High Druid mantle. The previous High Druid had done little more than sit on councils advising Amarra's leaders on proper crop care. At least, that was how it felt to Kiana, based on her reading and the passing comments of older druids in Corval.

"So"—Wyatt stood fully erect, placing his hands behind his back—"how *can* I help you?"

"Well, I was hoping to gather any information you have on the five Orders. Specifically the Ice Druids, to start."

Wyatt frowned. "Is there something in particular you're looking for? The history of the druids is vast. You could be here for days."

"Can't say that would be the worst thing," Aravel said, mostly to herself, eyes wandering the shelves.

Kiana hesitated. "I'm mostly interested in the last couple centuries, anything that might help us find where they ended up." Seeing suspicion flash across Wyatt's brow, she added, "As daughter of the High

Druid, I'm hoping to restore the Orders, help reforge the bonds that have been lost to time."

The Master Apprentice nodded thoughtfully. "Does this mean you intend to follow in your father's footsteps?"

Kiana hesitated, weighing her response. "If I'm worthy, yes."

Wyatt smiled. "Well, I can think of a few texts that might be a good place to start looking for clues, if there are any to be found. Perhaps you'll have better luck than others."

"Others?"

Amused, he said, "You think you're the first to seek out the lost Ice Druids?"

Kiana blushed. "No, of course not."

He opened a palm, and one of the finders flitted over to him. He cupped his hand around the orb for a few seconds and then released the light, which flew off toward a far shelf of books.

"Come. I'll take you to a table where you can read to your heart's content." Wyatt stepped back and gestured for them to follow.

He guided them to a grand mahogany staircase leading to the second floor, a trek that took several minutes due to the vastness of the library. Dark wood gleamed like polished glass beneath their feet as they climbed. Cresting the top stair, Kiana noted dozens of round oak tables in a large circular room. Seven or eight other patrons sat reading, clustered to one side. As Wyatt motioned the group to a table near the back center, Kiana gasped in surprise at seeing several books already waiting for them.

"These should be enough to get you started, I would think," Wyatt said. "Should you need anything else, just place your palm over this"—he produced a finder and placed it in the middle of the table—"and I will be with you as soon as I can."

"This is wonderful, thank you," Kiana said.

With another bow, Wyatt turned to leave.

He'd made it only a few steps when Aravel cried out, "Wait!" She cringed at the volume of her voice and glanced around to see if she'd caused offense, but none of the other patrons so much as looked up. They remained still, heads down, apparently lost in their books. Softer, she said, "Wait."

Wyatt returned to the table. "Yes?"

"Why is this city called Battle Tree?"

Wyatt's smile faded, and it took him a moment to answer. Kiana noted the shift in demeanor with puzzlement.

Finally he said, "Legend has it that long ago there was a great battle between two powerful mages, a battle which took place beneath a massive tree. As the fight waged on, the tree began to absorb their magical energy, creating a barrier around them, protecting passersby from the magical onslaught. This city was later built around that tree." He motioned to his chest. "Our tunics honor that history. Sage and lavender were the colors of the orders of those mages."

"So where's the tree?" Aravel asked.

Wyatt's eyes flicked to Kiana before settling back on Aravel. "I'm afraid that information is lost to history." He glanced behind him. "I'm terribly sorry, but I have other business that must be attended to for the moment. I'm happy to answer further questions at a later time."

And with that, he left them.

"Well, that was weird," Aravel said.

The strange interaction had sent a tingle up Kiana's arm. The sudden cold of her owl ring alerted her to something amiss.

"He's definitely hiding something," she said quietly.

"Who isn't?" Tash murmured.

He pulled out two chairs, one for each of his companions, then settled in across the table. Snow curled up on Kiana's feet, snoring within minutes.

"I'm going to have to drag you out of here, aren't I?" Tash said with a smile, flipping through the text on top of the stack, a small green leather-bound book.

Returning his teasing smile, Kiana took the next book in the stack, one with a deep-blue cover etched with druidic runes. She opened to the first page.

"Shall we?" she said.

For the next two hours, the friends devoured the books in front of them. As the minutes flew by, half a dozen more patrons joined them in the reading area, though Kiana barely gave them a second glance, being thoroughly absorbed in her own reading—none of which contained anything remotely useful about the Ice Druids aside from notes on their solstice rituals. On the verge of requesting more books, she sat up straighter when a passage caught her eye.

The Seeds of the Five Orders

The Tempest Tree locks in a beast from the
depths in the heart of a never-ending storm.
The Whisper Tree guards an ancient creature in
a ring of woods by the sea.
The Oasis Tree keeps a hidden threat in the fiery
lands that shift with the wind.
The Ember Tree guards against a battle ending.
The Shiver Tree stands strong, countering fire
with ice.

The language was old, an ancient form of Elvish Kiana struggled to translate. Thank Nelami for Grandmother Owl's insistence on linguistic studies. As she read on, Kiana's persistence paid off.

"That's it!" she cried, standing and almost knocking over her chair in her excitement, startling Snow awake. "I think I know where the Ice Druids are."

She'd barely gotten the words out when every head in the room turned and looked at her in unison. A silvery film glazed all twenty-eight eyes now locked onto her, small black veins spidering out from the irises.

"What the . . ." Aravel trailed off, disbelief more than alarm widening her eyes.

"Oh no." Fear hushed Kiana's voice to the faintest of whispers.

As if of one mind, everyone in the room stood at once and turned toward the three elves, forming a semicircle in front of them. Weapons appeared in hands all around them, poised for battle. Tash rose slowly from his chair. Angry, guttural growls rumbled from Snow beneath the table.

"You're too late," said a male human with a rapier standing near the middle of the group. His glassy eyes fixated on Kiana.

The elf narrowed her eyes at him. "I beg your pardon?"

"We have already located the Ice Druids. Your plan will not succeed. And we cannot allow you to leave this place." He spun his rapier. "Alive."

"Well," Kiana said, gripping her staff tighter, "on that we have to disagree." The tremble in her voice belied her calm facade.

Each of the Deep Ones' thralls took a step closer.

Lifting her staff several inches off the floor, Kiana whispered, "Nelami, help us," and slammed the wood back down, triggering the magical vines as her Regent Tree went violet. At the same time, she reached out her other hand and placed it over the glowing orb in the center of the table, which instantly shot out of the room.

The scene erupted into chaos.

Fourteen mind-controlled beings moved forward in a wave. That same instant, three black shards streaked into the crowd. Three opponents fell, large holes torn through their chests, edges sizzling with acidic residue. As they hit the floor, their eyes cleared of the cloudy film.

"Those don't normally pack that kind of punch," Tash said, shifting so that none of the thralls could get around behind them. "Magic is enhanced inside the library as well. Duly noted."

The remaining thralls split into two groups of four and one of three, the latter heading straight for Kiana. Just as they reached out their hands to grab her, she spun her staff and shoved it in front of her horizontally.

"*Tona vat.*" An angry gust of wind pummeled into two of them.

The spell whipped their heads back and knocked them into one of the recently vacated tables, toppling books and furniture and sending the two men sprawling. Books from nearby shelves clattered to the floor as well. The two thralls didn't get back up. The rapier-wielding man peeled off from the group approaching Tash and headed for Kiana.

"Now's your chance, Aravel," Kiana called. "And try not to burn down the library."

The warning turned out to be unnecessary. Hands held high, Aravel twisted her palms as if around an invisible ball. A glistening column of silver-and-gold moonlight enveloped three of the four thralls rushing toward her. They wailed as the dazzling energy keeled them over.

"Ha!" she cried. "Did you see the size of that Shimmer? Three down!" A short sword slashed the air a mere inch from her chest. She leaned back just in time. "Whoa!"

"Ach!" Tash gripped his arm where a dwarf with a mace had landed a glancing blow.

The injured arm straightened out from Tash's side, and a long sword of rippling amber materialized in his hand, solidifying into a gleaming bronze blade etched with black arcane runes. He swung for the dwarf's head but managed to catch him across the chest instead. The edges of the wound hissed as acid ate into the thrall's flesh. Two glazed-over eyes stared at Tash for a moment, the film slowly clearing. The dwarf collapsed to the floor.

Kiana abandoned an incantation and shouted, "Look out!" as three more thralls converged on Tash.

Attention elsewhere, the druid didn't see the man approaching her. With surprisingly strong hands, the thrall gripped one of Kiana's arms and yanked her around, placing his other arm around her neck in a chokehold.

To Kiana's left, Tash parried a blow from a half-elf wielding a long-sword, but a man with an axe approached from his other side. Unable to speak in her current predicament, Kiana took a note from Aravel and pointed a hand toward the axe man, unleashing an enhanced tower of flame that burned into his side. His clothes caught, and he fell to the floor a shrieking column of conflagrated flesh.

Aravel's fourth opponent, a human woman, thrust forward her short sword, slicing into the druid's side half a second before her form shifted into a sleek, muscled tiger. Her cry of pain transformed into a fierce growl. Razor-sharp claws from two massive paws dug into the neck of her attacker, a mortal wound.

Snow launched himself from under the table and bit into the calf of the thrall restraining Kiana. Another yelp of pain joined the cacophony, and the man's grip loosened slightly, but still not enough for Kiana to break the grapple.

Tash had managed to eliminate the threat of the half-elf and turned his attention to the woman now coming at him with a quarterstaff. He raised the hand not wielding his bronze sword.

"*Kishtal pitek*," he growled.

Acid streamed out from his palm, searing into her chest. She was dead before she hit the ground.

Kiana gasped as the man's grip tightened around her throat with renewed fervor. Stars burst across her vision.

The man stabbed his rapier down toward Snow, but Kiana shoved herself back into him, throwing him off balance enough to make him miss his mark.

"Snuh," she rasped, unable to properly form the word.

Fortunately, the fox had enough awareness to leap back to avoid being skewered by the man's second attempt.

"You've lost this fight." Tash stepped between the fox and the tiger, facing their final foe, who was using Kiana as a shield. "Let her go."

"Move, or we will kill her," the man said, his voice devoid of inflection or emotion.

Wariness narrowed Tash's eyes briefly before he motioned vaguely to the bodies scattered around the floor.

"What 'we' would that be? It's just you now. And even if you manage to stop one of us, the others will kill you where you stand."

"Such arrogance," the man said. "That's what often gets your species killed."

"*I'm* arrogant?" Tash said. "You just watched your friends get obliterated and still think you have a chance."

Movement back by the stairs caught their attention. Three more eye-glazed thralls stepped into the room.

Tash stared hard into Kiana's eyes, mouth set in a grim line. He turned to face the new threat.

"We'll say it one last time. Stand aside," the man said.

Tash swung his head around and leveled his gaze at the man, amber eyes flashing. "Never."

"Then die."

The new arrivals moved forward. Two steps in, a ten-foot-high wall of green-and-lavender magic suddenly encircled them, and Wyatt Foxheart appeared at the edge of the tables. Three other apprentices emerged from the opposite side. No sooner had the magical barrier closed around the thralls than Tash turned and rushed at the man holding Kiana, blade at the ready.

Shifting his focus to the hand holding the rapier, the man relaxed his death grip on Kiana's throat, and she seized the moment. Pushing the man's arm away from her neck with a grunt, she ducked down and spun away, turning just in time to see Tash's sword sink into the man's shoulder, the parry by the rapier enough to prevent him from being impaled through the heart. He gritted his teeth and dropped the sword, unsheathing a dagger from his belt and aiming it at Tash's side.

Kiana plunged a hand overhead and summoned a column of light, anxiety rising as she realized she was a moment too late. The dagger bit into Tash's flesh.

"*Sanye dolim.*" The incantation flew from her mouth in an echoey hush.

Strands of purple magic weaved through the wound in Tash's side, knitting it back together. The final thrall crumpled to the floor in a cloud of golden smoke, taking his dagger with him. Kiana rushed to Tash.

"Are you okay?"

He gave her a reassuring smile. "Absolutely. Thank you."

Blood still seeped from his arm and side.

Kiana placed her hands on the wounds. "*Sanye dolim.*"

As more healing energy coursed through Tash, Wyatt stepped farther into the room, the magic wall vanishing to reveal three desiccated bodies. Kiana had never seen such a spell from a druid but didn't have time to dwell on it before several more apprentices came running up the stairs.

"What is the meaning of this?" Wyatt asked, face a mask of barely controlled anger.

Something about the fight didn't sit right with Kiana. "To be honest"—she looked around at the host of bodies now covering the library floor—"I'm not entirely sure." She shook her head.

There was another one.

She counted the bodies of the original attackers. Thirteen.

One got away. How?

"Is there a place we can talk?" She looked briefly at the other apprentices before looking back at Wyatt. "Privately?"

The Master Apprentice took in the damage around him for a moment. Something hot still simmered beneath the surface. He offered a curt, "Sure."

Kiana turned to their table to grab the book she'd been reading just before the fight. It was gone.

"What . . ."

She ducked under the table, searching.

"What's wrong?" Tash stood behind her.

"The book, the one I had before. It's not here."

The group scanned the area, to no avail, before turning and following Wyatt, puzzled.

Books covered every square inch of the walls in the Master Apprentice's office. He motioned to the two chairs sitting in front of his desk. Kiana and Aravel sat, Snow between them, while Tash leaned against one wall of books.

"First, I am so sorry about . . . all of that." Kiana swallowed hard, throat parched.

Wyatt lowered his eyes and then looked back at the distraught druid.

"Some of Battle Tree's finest citizens met their ends today." The Master Apprentice leaned back into his chair. "It's not going to be an easy message to deliver, particularly to Archduke Hiran, but I have connections that can help ease the blow."

"There was no other choice. Their minds, they—"

"I know, I saw," Wyatt cut in. "The loss is regrettable but"—he sighed wearily—"necessary. But what led a group of Deep Thralls to my library? And how did they get in?"

Gathering herself, Kiana said, "I recently learned that the Deep Ones have resurfaced and come into possession of a relic known as Freya's Crystal."

Wyatt's head tilted up, but his face remained neutral.

"You've heard of it," Kiana stated.

"Yes."

"Well, until two weeks ago, I thought it merely a legend. But now I believe the Crystal actually houses one of the Seeds of the Druid Orders. Specifically, the Shiver Seed."

Wyatt remained silent.

"But . . . you already knew that." Kiana leaned back in her chair, chagrined.

"I'm familiar with the legend, as well as the Druid Orders. I, too, pieced that particular puzzle together. The Shiver Seed was placed inside the Crystal for safekeeping. A disguise, of sorts."

"So you had the information I wanted all along."

"On the contrary. You said you wanted to know the location of the Ice Druids. That I don't know. No one does."

Kiana eyed him skeptically. "Okay. So how is it I've never heard of the Seeds until now? My father is High Druid, for Nelami's sake."

"The Seeds have been around for millennia, created by each of the Druid Orders to protect against dangerous entities. Each Seed corresponds with a tree that acts as a magical barrier to keep these entities trapped, unable to escape into the world. As the Orders began to scatter and isolate, many druids dying off, knowledge of the Seeds fell into legend. Only a select few still know of their existence. I know merely because I have read every book on druid history in this library. And I assure you, the references are few."

"What entities?" Tash asked.

Darkness flashed across Wyatt's eyes. "The Five Terrors." He moved his gaze back to Kiana. "If the Deep Ones have the Seed and know where the Shiver Tree is located, more than just our world is in very grave danger. And you, Lady Kiana, may be the druid we've been waiting for to renew our hope for the future."

CHAPTER TEN

A ridiculous sense of inadequacy intertwined with reawakened fear settled across Kiana's shoulders. She shifted in her seat, gaze darting to her companions, who appeared equally overwhelmed. Deep lines creased Tash's brow as he stared intently at Wyatt.

Ever the first to speak, Aravel broke the silence. "The Five whats?"

"Terrors." Wyatt's eyes didn't leave Kiana's. "Over the last few millennia, Amarra has faced five potentially world-ending threats, creatures of tremendous power bent on destruction and death." Wyatt leaned forward, hands steepled in front of him on his desk. "They became known as the Terrors. When the first arose, magic users of all kinds started working toward a solution to capture and contain the threat."

"Why not just band together to kill them?" Aravel said.

Wyatt held up a finger to silence her. She frowned slightly but held her tongue.

"Dark magic powers these creatures. If killed, the Terrors are reborn stronger, more dangerous, than they were before, so the casters had to come up with something that would imprison them instead." He picked up a finder from his desk, idly turning it over in his hands. "It was the druids who came up with a solution. Over time, each of the Orders took on one of the Terrors, producing a Seed that, when planted, grew and powered a Tree that would keep the Terror locked away as long as the Tree stood. Whenever the magic of the Seeds began to wane, the High Druid performed the ritual to renew them, ensuring the Terrors stayed trapped."

Kiana's brow furrowed. "I don't understand how none of us have heard of these Terrors before. If they're that big a threat, how does the whole world not know?"

"The enormity of the threat they pose is the very reason their existence has been wiped from record." Wyatt set the finder back on his desk. "Once the druids trapped them, they planted the Trees in locations that were unlikely to be found. If someone were to damage the Trees significantly enough, even before the Seeds deteriorated, the Terrors would be released."

Kiana rubbed her hands down the arms of her chair thoughtfully. "When was the last time the Seeds were renewed?"

"If the legend is correct, and the water jinn tried to steal the Shiver Seed centuries ago, then not for a long, long time."

"And how long does the power of the Seeds last?" Tash asked.

Some indecipherable emotion passed over Wyatt's face. "I imagine time is running short, which is why your timing is impeccable." He nodded toward Kiana. "If what I've heard is true, you may be destined to reestablish the mantle of High Druid as a position of true leadership and power, to reunite the Orders. As a result, your fate may be inextricably linked to that of the Seeds."

And what exactly have you heard? she wanted to ask. Instead, she pressed back into her chair and blew out a breath of disquiet. "We've got to get that Seed. All the more reason to get to the Ice Druids as fast as we can."

Surprise dawned on Wyatt's face. "You found them?"

Kiana nodded. "The book I was reading just before the thralls attacked. The one that's missing. I found a clue, as well as some sort of riddle about the Terrors. I think I know where they ended up."

Aravel looked at each of her companions in turn. "Okay, I'll ask. What in the Three Hells are these Terrors, exactly?"

Wyatt shook his head. "I don't know for sure, other than beings of great power. Monsters, devils maybe. Most of the information has been lost, buried beneath the sands of time. All that remains are vague references, riddles, like the one Kiana found. Sometimes secrets must be kept even from trusted allies."

Kiana flashed him a look.

"Do we think it's safe to presume the Deep Ones mean to unleash whatever Terror resides beneath the Ice Druid's Tree?" Tash moved to stand between his companions' chairs.

"Or control it," Wyatt said. "Whatever beast lies beneath the Shiver Tree could aid them in their war against the Shadow Wraiths."

"Shadow Wraiths? *More* monsters?" Aravel groaned.

"The Shadow Wraiths and Deep Ones have been at war since time immemorial, if you believe the legends," Tash said. "There was even a time the Deep Ones were thought to have been all but eradicated. Somehow they always come back."

"You know your Eventide lore." Wyatt crossed his arms and regarded Tash with something akin to admiration.

Tash smirked. "'More knowledge, more power' may as well be the Ilirian family motto."

"Not the worst I've heard."

"Well"—Kiana pushed back from Wyatt's desk and rose—"we need to get moving." She looked at the Master Apprentice, who also stood. "Any chance you have a teleportation circle handy?" she asked wryly.

Wyatt grunted in amusement. "The odds of finding one that happens to align with your journey, wherever it may lead, are slim. The chances of access even slimmer."

Kiana nodded. "Just thought I'd check." She knew all too well that most teleportation circles had been destroyed in a war well before her time. Only a few remained on the entire continent, and those that did required special permissions to access.

Wyatt smiled, though it barely reached his eyes. "Well, it seems I have some investigating to do to discover how more than a dozen Deep

Thralls made it past the guards and into the library." He tugged down his tunic. "I wish you well on your journey."

Tash and Aravel made their way out of the office, but Wyatt placed a gentle hand on Kiana's arm, holding her back.

In a low voice, he said, "I hope that, if all goes well on your quest, you will return to Battle Tree. We have much more to discuss."

Kiana frowned but nodded.

"And I'm sorry about Amina."

A shiver of realization quivered up Kiana's spine. "It was the Deep Ones, wasn't it? They were trying to get the location of the Ice Druids out of her, or access to the library, at the very least. It's why they stole the book I found." *And that must also be why they were kidnapping druids from Old Home. Information on the Shiver Tree.*

"Given the circumstances, I'm inclined to believe that's the case. The state of her body was consistent with a psionic attack." His voice didn't break, but Kiana sensed a deep sadness hovering beneath his words. "And given the level of mind control we just witnessed, and the number of thralls, more than one creature is here in Battle Tree. You need to be careful."

Noticing Aravel's head pop back in the door, Wyatt released Kiana's arm.

"Safe travels."

"This is somehow way worse than we imagined." Tash stood with his hands on his hips just outside Battle Tree's city limits. "We have no way of knowing how close the Deep Ones are to their goal. If they mean to unleash this Terror, whatever it is, Amarra will need more help than the three of us."

Snow yipped.

"Sorry. Four."

A ghost of a thought scratched at the back of Kiana's mind, but unable to fully grasp onto it, she pushed it away.

"All we can do is get to the Shiver Tree as fast as we can and pray we're not too late."

Tash nodded. "Anything in the riddle you found offer a hint as to what the Deep Ones are after? The Terror?"

Kiana summoned the passage to her mind. "The Shiver Tree stands strong, countering fire with ice."

"Fire, huh?" Tash scanned the sky, likely rummaging through the veritable tome of trivia stored in his brain. "That would make sense, given their enemy."

"Whose enemy?"

"The Deep Ones'. If they're still at war with the Shadow Wraiths, a beast of fire would serve them well. The stories I've read portrayed a weakness to fire."

Kiana thought back over what she'd read, the rest of the riddles. The elusive thought solidified in her brain, and she whirled back toward Battle Tree.

"Nelami's mercy," she rasped.

"What? What's the matter?" Tash came up beside her, alert.

"Battle Tree," she said quietly.

Tash cocked his head. "Yes?"

She kept her eyes locked on the city. "The fourth entry, 'The Ember Tree guards against a battle ending.'" She turned to Tash. "Battle Tree is guarding one of the Terrors. It fits with the story Wyatt told us."

Aravel stood and joined them. "But Wyatt said the tree was lost."

Kiana gave a single curt nod. "And sometimes you keep secrets even from trusted allies."

"So, what, the two mages are locked away somewhere in Battle Tree? I thought he said the Terrors were monsters, demons even." Aravel's face scrunched up in puzzlement.

Kiana shook her head and sighed. "I don't know, but it's a problem for another day. Right now, we have to get to the Ice Druids and stop the Deep Ones from releasing whatever is imprisoned there. Or wielding it."

"I know I was just feigning the voice of reason earlier," Tash said, "but don't you think it's time we called for reinforcements? This new information changes things."

Again something drifted around the edges of Kiana's mind, a nagging feeling.

"No, not yet."

"Why not?"

Scratch, scratch, scratch.

"Because that would mean revealing the Ice Druids' location, and I'm not prepared to do that yet."

Tash folded his arms across his chest, his expression curious. "But the Deep Ones already know where they are, so what does it matter?"

"Maybe they do; maybe they don't. Why did they steal the book with the riddles? Why did they wait to attack us until I said I knew where the Ice Druids were? Why were the thralls still here at all? They could just be trying to buy themselves time, get us out of the way to ensure a clearer path. If we send a message to Tribali, they could intercept it. As we've just discovered, they could have people anywhere under their control. You said yourself that the Hub is not an easy place to infiltrate."

Tash dropped his head and heaved a heavy sigh. "All right. We go it alone for now." He secured his pack across his chest. "Where to?"

Kiana winced. Tash looked at her incredulously.

"You're not going to tell *us*?"

"No." It almost came out a question.

"You're joking, right?" Aravel said, matching Tash's expression of pure incredulity.

"I'm sorry, I don't want to risk the information falling into the wrong hands." Kiana rubbed her thumbs vigorously against her fingers. "I promise I'll tell you as soon as I think it's necessary. For now, I'm asking you to trust me. If they catch you, they'll kill you for the information. I can't live with that."

"But—" Aravel started to protest, but Tash held up a hand.

"It's okay." He walked up to Kiana and placed his hands on her shoulders. "We've followed you this far. We're not going to stop now."

"Thank you." Gratitude ebbed the worry from her face.

Tash smiled crookedly and gave her a wink.

Weary from the fight but eager to be on their way, the trio took the road leading southwest out of Battle Tree, Kiana guiding their way. The southern edge of Watchman's Forest would be their home for the next couple of days before they hit the miles upon miles of plains and low hills leading up to and through Harrian. Knowing Aravel's current distaste for such bland terrain, Kiana kept this tidbit to herself for the time being. No sense starting up the ribbing early.

The brief rest outside the city allowed Kiana time to replenish her druidic reserves by two leaves—the only ones she'd lost that day—but the prospect of further encounters with unfriendly beings kept her on constant alert. Nearly three hours into their trek, a tingling began around her left index finger followed by a now-familiar coolness, a warning from her owl ring. Sounds of movement in the trees to the northeast caught her ear. She froze, prompting her friends to do the same. Footsteps crunched over twigs and fallen leaves.

"Someone's coming," she whispered, listening harder.

Crunch, snap, crunch, crunch, crack.

"It's a group." She turned to her friends and pressed her palms together in front of her chest, swiping her right hand away and making a short, quick cutting motion. "*Nelim marvige.*" The incantation settled on all four of them, whispers of purple magic. Kiana pointed to a collection of boulders to their left. "Quick, over there."

Aided by Kiana's spell and an elf's natural furtiveness, the party hurried to the rocks, their footsteps light as air.

They didn't have to wait long. Peering through gaps in the boulders, they watched six humans march past, eyes glazed, weapons in hand. Each silvery eye searched the forest for its quarry. One of the thralls snapped his head toward the boulders. Kiana stopped breathing. She held deathly still, terrified of even blinking. Her hands held fast to Snow.

The thralls came to a sudden halt. They stood motionless long enough for Kiana to regret holding her breath before one by one peeling off and marching northwest.

Only after they were out of sight did Kiana release a shuddering exhale.

"Well, that was close." Aravel collapsed against a boulder.

"Indeed it was." Kiana ran her fingers through Snow's fur. "Let's hope that's the last we see of them."

Vast stretches of plains and meadows eventually gave way to the dry, dusty landscape along the southern rim of Harrian, across the river from the Akkra desert. Nearly two more weeks of hard travel and little sleep made for a few raw nerves among the party, exacerbated by the fact that the Deep Ones—or, at least, their thralls—had been relentlessly pursuing and attacking them since they left Battle Tree, though fewer each time. No matter how much distance they put between themselves and any form of civilization, still the companions were hunted. The tedium and exhaustion made keeping their spirits up impossible.

Late morning lapsed into early afternoon on their twelfth day out of Battle Tree as the Midlane River came into view. Snow sensed its presence even before keen elven ears detected the sound of the gently flowing waters. Barking out three short yips, the fox sprinted forward. Before he got his paws to the sandy banks, an eagle dove into the river thirty yards from shore.

Aravel popped up out of the water, flipping her sopping hair back over her head, her scouting form dropped.

"Yes! I haven't missed flowing water so much in all my life!" She eased onto her back and lazily propelled herself toward shore. Snow splashed toward her.

The other two elves cast wary glances toward the tree line to the west, a normally welcome sight that now merely aroused fear of what could be hiding among the foliage. Three and a half peaceful days had passed since the last attack, the longest gap between confrontations yet. Kiana knew they were on borrowed time.

"I'll keep watch. Go enjoy the water." Tash pulled the canteen from his pack as he spoke.

Deep muscle aches and profound weariness prevented Kiana from making her usual polite protests. She simply nodded and moved toward the riverbank, eager for a moment's rest.

"Ki, hop in! The water feels fantastic." Aravel flung a handful of water into the air for emphasis, letting it rain upon her face.

Kiana reached to unlace her leather armor but hesitated. Behind her, Tash sat on a large stump, eyes scoping the area for anywhere an enemy could hide. His face showed no signs of the worry consuming Kiana. Only intense concentration furrowed his brow.

Fur heavy with water, Snow trudged up the bank and nudged his nose into Kiana's palm, letting out a wet snort.

"Hey, take it easy." Kiana withdrew her hand from her fox's snout with a chuckle. "I'm coming."

Shedding her corset, bracers, and cloak, Kiana stepped into the water, its chill easing up her legs, causing goose bumps to sprout up on her flesh.

"By the tides, that's cold," she muttered, taking a few more steps out into the river.

"Isn't it glorious?" Aravel shouted, floating about fifty feet away. "How have we gone this far between rivers?"

Kiana turned her face to the sun and closed her eyes, reveling in the dual sensations: the icy prickles rippling along her calves and the soothing warmth spreading across her cheeks.

"I know. It feels like ages since—"

Kiana stopped short, the sound of indistinct shouting pulling her from her moment of bliss. She turned back toward Tash.

From the tree line, a cloaked figure, hood tossed back to reveal shaggy brown hair framing an olive-toned face, raced toward them, one palm held out. To the figure's left, Tash rose and angled to intercept.

Now facing the intruder, Kiana could make out his words.

"Get out of the water!" he shouted. "Hurry, now, get out!"

As he got closer, Kiana could see he carried a longbow with a copper quiver slung over his back. She opened her mouth to speak but snapped it back shut when Snow went wild beside her, frantic barks piercing the air, paws dancing on the shore. His eyes stayed on Aravel.

Looking back toward her friend, Kiana felt the hair on her neck stand on end. Ripples had erupted near the center of the river and hurried toward Aravel, who now stood in the water thirty feet from shore, eyes wide in apparent confusion.

"No," Kiana whispered, followed by the much louder, "Aravel, get out of the water!"

Catching Kiana's gaze, Aravel flicked a look over her shoulder.

"By the tiiiiiiides!" she screamed, clumsily running through the thigh-deep water.

Realizing the ripples—and their source—were rapidly gaining on her, Aravel swung her arms up over her head and jumped, her elven form giving way to an eagle once more as she rocketed into the sky in one graceful movement.

With her friend safe, Kiana turned to put some distance between herself and whatever horror now raced toward her. Tash had intercepted the hunter, and they both watched her from fifty yards away. The druid managed only a few steps in their direction before she saw Tash's eyes go wide. He started forward. The hunter raised his bow. In a flash, he nocked an arrow.

Whatever had their attention, Kiana didn't want to waste time looking back.

"Nebel—"

Something strong and slimy cinched around her middle, cutting her incantation short and knocking the air from her lungs. Two arrows impacted the thing that held her with audible thuds.

A sharp pain exploded in her side. She let out a strangled cry.

Two bolts of amber magic streaked by the druid's head. The sizzle of damaged flesh crackled in the air. Half a moment later, the sound of violent splashing rose up from the water, and Kiana again felt a sharp stab in her side. The more she struggled, the worse the pain.

Tears mingled with the river water wetting her face, and the slimy thing suddenly jolted her into the air—ten feet, fifteen. At last, she could see her attacker. The sight stole whatever breath remained in her lungs.

Below her, a massive octopus thrashed about in the water, each of its eight tentacles at least twenty feet long. Dozens of bony spikes protruded from its mottled purplish flesh.

Thud thud.

Four arrows now pierced the tentacle slowly crushing the life out of Kiana's body.

Moments from losing consciousness, Kiana spotted an eagle alight three feet away. In an instant, Aravel resumed her elven form, careful to avoid the arrows and magic slamming into the flesh around her. She hurled a ball of fire into the appendage holding Kiana.

The octopus let go.

One of the creature's bone spikes ripped out from Kiana's side as the tentacle retreated, prompting a rasping cry of pain. She'd plummet to her death unless she could refocus her magic.

"Lenith qua plum."

Aravel's words floated on the wind. The spell wrapped Kiana in a cocoon of air until she gently wafted downward, light as an autumn leaf cushioned by the breeze. Another barrage of attacks whizzed past her.

An inhuman shriek pierced the air. The monster flung three tentacles high and lashed out with them. One struck Kiana eight feet from the ground, swatting her like a bug from the air. The force of the blow broke Aravel's enchantment, turning Kiana into a living projectile. She slammed into the earth.

Bones cracked. Skin tore. Kiana heard another shriek, momentarily believing it to be her own scream of agony. But no sound would leave her mouth save for a few hopeless grunts. Her lungs labored for air, gaining little.

"Kiana!"

Tash's shout sounded miles away. Time slowed down, and a white haze crept into the corners of her vision. Fuzz filled her ears, her brain. Something jostled her head, and pain lanced all the way from her neck to her toes. Above her, she could make out the faint outline of Tash's face. He spoke to her, his voice muted, like he was under water. Or maybe she was underwater. She tried to smile at him, but even that small effort cost her. She coughed up warm liquid. The taste of copper bit her tongue.

A warm palm on her face. Pressure in her side. The refreshing scent of waterfalls.

These were the last sensations before blackness took her.

CHAPTER ELEVEN

"She's lucky to be alive."

"I can't thank you enough for all you've done. We had no idea."

"I did nothing. Thank Madame Lesant."

Voices floated at the edge of Kiana's consciousness. Though she understood the words, the heavy fog clouding her mind prevented her from grasping any meaning. Who was Madame Lesant? Who was lucky to be alive? Why were these voices chattering away in her bedroom while she was trying to sleep?

An attempt to roll onto her side brought it all screaming back. The octopus. Unbearable pain. Somehow she had survived. Barely, based on the level of pain and brokenness she remembered.

She moaned.

"Tash! I think she's waking!"

Aravel's voice, much closer than the others she'd heard, brought Kiana back to herself.

One eye slowly, carefully blinked open. Three faces stared down at her, two familiar, one not. She opened her other eye. A wiggle at her feet brought her attention to Snow, who whined softly into the blanket over her legs.

They appeared to be in a large tent. Crystals of all colors and sizes hung from the fabric ceiling, a few reflecting the sliver of light coming in from somewhere to Kiana's left. Potion vials filled rickety collapsible shelves at the foot of the cot on which Kiana lay. The air smelled herbaceous and fresh, like a summer garden ready for harvest.

"Thank the gods, we've been so worried." Tash crouched beside Kiana's cot and tenderly grasped one of her hands with both of his, forehead lined with concern.

"What happened? The last thing I remember is being knocked out of the air by that . . . beast."

Aravel shifted where she sat on the bed beside her friend.

"When we got to you and saw the severity of your injuries, I knew it was beyond my skill to heal. Reyan, here"—she nodded toward the face Kiana did not know—"told us of a powerful healer here in his village. We brought you to her immediately. That was hours ago. For a while there, we weren't sure even she could save you." She hesitated. "If we'd been even a few minutes later, we would have been looking for a temple instead of a healer."

The words sank in slowly.

We're still weeks away from the Ice Druids, and I've already almost died.

Kiana tried to keep the shock off her face, but Aravel knew her too well.

The elf cleared her throat dramatically, eyes brightening. "But here you are! Awake and as beautiful as ever." She scowled. "Unfortunately, I can't say the same about all of your things."

"What do you mean?" Kiana frowned.

From the table beside them, Aravel picked up the crushed, splintered remnants of Kiana's trinket box, the now-former home of some of her most sentimental possessions.

"You landed on your pack somehow. The box was destroyed, and some of your clothes have a few too many holes now, but everything in the box came out okay." She scooped the box's former contents off the table and handed them to Kiana, who cupped her hands to accept the items. The metal jasmine flower landed on top. She'd forgotten about it entirely. She pressed it to her circlet, magically affixing the blossom to the metal. A perfect fit.

In her other hand, the brass button caught the light from a gleaming crystal. With a silent prayer to Nelami, Kiana looked at Tash. He was gazing at the button, a shadow of a smile on his lips.

"May I have my pouch?" Kiana said, trying to ignore the flames of embarrassment tickling her cheeks.

Tash bent down and shuffled some things around on the floor, coming back up with a brown leather pouch. He held it open for Kiana to deposit the earring, staff shard, tooth, and button inside.

"Thank you." She moved to sit up, expecting every bone and muscle in her body to object. Only her ribs twinged. "Huh."

"What is it?" Tash shifted on the cot to offer her the support of his arm. "Still in pain?"

Baffled, Kiana shook her head and used Tash's arm to pull herself upright the rest of the way. "Hardly any at all. My ribs are a little sore, but it's almost like it never happened. This healer of yours must be powerful indeed. If I'd tried to heal wounds as severe as you say, it would have taken days to reach this point. Maybe longer." She looked to the stranger standing behind Tash, meeting his piercing green eyes, nearly the emerald color of her own. Slightly duller, they had an almost haunted look in their depths. Wisps of umber hair hung about the man's dirt-stained face, the rest pulled back behind his head. He looked to be in his late twenties, early thirties at most. "You must be the man who tried to warn us." She bowed her head briefly. "Thank you."

Reyan tilted his head in acknowledgment. "Sorry I didn't get to you sooner. I was out hunting when I heard your voices. Everyone in these parts knows better than to go into the river, so until I heard splashing, I didn't know there was trouble. Made my way to you fast as I could."

"So, this . . . creature . . . it attacks anyone who goes into the river?"

Reyan nodded soberly.

"Why? Where'd it come from?"

The hunter shrugged. "The first time it appeared was about six months ago. My brother Eris and I were out hunting when the screaming started. By the time we got to the river, the bastard had already killed two fishermen." Reyan turned his head away, eyes downcast. "Eris died trying to save the third."

Hot tears pricked at the corners of Kiana's eyes, heart shattering at the thought of losing a sibling.

"I'm so sorry."

Tash squeezed her hand.

"It's been tormenting your villagers for six months and no one has gone out to kill it?" Aravel's disbelief scrunched her face into a scowl.

Reyan's tone hardened. "Believe me, we've tried. The damn thing is clever, though. Seems to be able to tell the difference between innocent fishermen and trained hunters who are there to kill it. Only shows its face to the unsuspecting. You show up with axes and bows? Won't hear a peep from it."

"Those spikes—" Kiana felt a phantom pain in her side at the words. "I've never seen anything like that on a giant octopus before." She bit her bottom lip and frowned. "To be fair, I've only ever encountered one other, and it was in the ocean. But I haven't heard of such a thing before either. Not to mention the fact that, even for a giant octopus, it was enormous."

Disdain curled Reyan's lip. "It's an aberration, a mutant. Some gods-awful experiment or the result of a curse, maybe."

"Who would do that?"

"Well, now, what's this?" a strange, brittle voice said from the direction of the shaft of light.

Aravel's question went unanswered.

Peering past her companions, Kiana caught sight of an incredibly old woman standing in the opening to the tent. She wore a long mauve dress and matching slippers, and her white hair fell past her shoulders in two long braids, each fastened with what looked like strips of extra material from her dress. Deep wrinkles creviced her face. Two yellowish eyes peeked out from under heavy lids. Her hands appeared to have more spots than unblemished skin. All of her features appeared too old, as though she might wither into dust at any moment.

"Our patient is awake, is she?" the old crone asked, obviously rhetorically. "You had this lot pretty worried." She waved one ancient-looking hand in the general direction of the group.

"You must be Madame Lesant." Kiana pressed her palms together at her chest and bowed her head. "I understand I'm greatly indebted to you." Kiana raised her head and dropped her arms, looping one with Tash's in the process.

The old woman looked at her curiously.

"Perhaps." She waved a hand dismissively and approached the cot. "First things first: How do you feel?"

"Miraculously, like I didn't just get crushed to within inches of my life by a massive, malevolent octopus."

"Inches is being a bit generous, my dear. Wouldn't you say?"

Kiana's throat tightened with the horror of her near death.

"So I've been told, yes." She felt Aravel's fist tighten where it sat against her thigh.

"Good thing that son of a lich skulked back to its cave after, uh"— she looked at Kiana and grimaced—"you know. Otherwise I would've lit that thing up like a bonfire on Midsummer's Eve."

"It didn't realize you had so much company, I reckon." Reyan perched on a stool. "Wasn't looking for a fight, just a quick meal."

"Whoa," Aravel said, standing and turning on Reyan. "A little decorum wouldn't go amiss. That meal was almost my best friend."

Reyan shrugged one shoulder. "Just telling it like it is."

"Well, this party already has someone to do that, thank you very much." Aravel smoothed the fabric of her shirt. "Anyway, after seeing what that thing did to you—you know, just your everyday mutant octopus—I admit I have a little more reluctance when it comes to the possibility of encountering that Terror." Immediately upon finishing the sentence, Aravel's eyes went wide.

The old woman's head snapped in her direction.

"I mean, you know, that terror that I have of . . . of . . . werewolves." She cringed slightly. "The things we're hunting."

From behind her, Reyan said, "You're hunting werewolves?" He crossed his arms slowly. His expression revealed some combination of curiosity and disbelief.

"No, of course not." Aravel chuckled. "Werewolves. Psh." Her eyes landed on Kiana and Tash, who both stared at her pointedly. Laughter aborted, she swiveled her head back to Reyan. "I mean . . . yes. Werewolves." She nodded firmly, mustering all the conviction she could.

"Stick to the truth, my dear. You're a dreadful liar." Madame Lesant moved to a box in the corner and began rummaging through its contents. "Besides, werewolves are more of a Northland problem. Only get one down here once in a blue moon." She shuffled more things about in the box. "So, you're going after one of the Terrors, eh? Dreadful business, that. Wouldn't want to be in your shoes."

"You know about the Terrors?" A hint of trepidation mingled with the surprise in Kiana's voice.

The crone chuckled. "When you've lived as long as I have, dear one, you learn about a great many things. Some make you see the world as an endless marvel, while others, well, they make you dread the next sunrise. Aha!" She pulled a pendant from the box. From the end hung a circular black stone studded with hundreds of shimmering specks, like the night sky on a chain. A small hole through the center housed the loop of the gold chain.

Kiana eyed the pendant warily.

"Anyway"—Madame Lesant's eyes narrowed and focused intently on the druid's—"I've certainly heard whispers of the Terrors in my time, tales of faceless beasts that want to destroy the world, now locked away by the druids. I hope that you find safe passage. You're headed west?"

Kiana hesitated. "Yes."

"To Mooreland?"

"For the time being."

"So, not your final destination, then."

Kiana cleared her throat. "My apologies, but I'd rather not say."

The crone tilted her head curiously to one side. "I assure you, dear, that no one can eavesdrop on my tent. My business is my own, and while you're in here, your words are protected as well."

Kiana held firm. "Nevertheless, I'd rather keep the information to myself for the time being. The Deep Ones have a way of getting information from people."

Reyan stiffened on his seat. "Deep Ones? What do they want with you?"

Kiana sucked her lips between her teeth, torn by indecision.

"They want the Terror too," Madame Lesant said for her, voice a low rasp.

"I—" Kiana clamped her mouth shut. "Seas of mercy," she whispered, her mind racing back through all of the encounters they'd had with the thralls so far, half a dozen attacks. "I was right."

Tash studied her. "How do you mean?"

"They've only been trying to kill you and Aravel. They were trying to take me alive." Scenes of battle flipped through her head, one after the other. "They never come at me with deadly force."

The implication hit Tash as well. "They really don't know where to go. They've been tracking you so you'll lead them to the Shiver Tree. Just like you suspected in Battle Tree."

"Wait, seriously?" Aravel looked between her two friends. "We've been playing into their hands all along?"

Kiana nodded.

"I suspect that's why they've been so relentless in their attacks," she said. "They're trying to drive us forward faster, keep us off balance. If they kill you two, so be it. Maybe they get lucky and get me alive, so they can take me back to their masters, who will then suck the information out of my head. Either way, they get what they want."

"So what do we do?" Aravel clenched and unclenched her fists, her way of tamping down anxiety. It was what she'd been doing the first time Kiana laid eyes on her. The motion summoned an intense wave of affection for her friend.

"We have to find a way to lose them," Tash said.

"But how do we do that? We don't even know how they're tracking us."

Setting one end of his bow on the ground, Reyan said, "I may be able to help you with that."

Madame Lesant twirled the pendant. The starry specks caught the light, reflecting it back brighter than before. "As can I."

CHAPTER TWELVE

Terror swells inside her as she struggles to move her legs. Her arms hold their position, bent at her sides, poised for flight. Even her head stays frozen in place, eyes wide with the fear that now burns through some intoxicant clouding her mind.

He is speaking again, taunting her. His words sear into her brain, battling her own thoughts for attention.

Nelami, help me. *Her silent plea resonates through her mind, an entreating whisper from another self.*

Something pulls her backward, an invisible force dragging her through the sand. Cool water laps against the backs of her legs, and icy prickles radiate out from her chest.

Please! *Her prayer becomes more urgent as a strange rippling sensation washes through her body.*

He stands before her now, eyes cold and mocking, like his words. This time as he speaks, he holds up his hand, and she watches in horror as that which she's been chosen to protect flies into the hands of her enemy. The chain breaks free from her neck with a tiny metallic snap.

"Why?" she suddenly cries, her voice strangled and broken, foreign to her own ears.

He takes a step closer.

"To survive," he snarls.

The young druid channels every ounce of will she still possesses into moving her limbs, but her body is no longer her own. With a gasp, she locks eyes with her tormentor. A malevolent smile creeps across his face. Suddenly, the world swells, then collapses, and everything goes dark.

Kiana woke drenched in sweat, gasping for breath, the memory of her dream still vivid in her mind. Her fingers fumbled at her neck, half expecting to feel where the chain had been ripped from it. But the young druid in the dream hadn't been her.

Soran.

The name appeared in her mind like it had always been there, though she was certain she'd never heard it.

Beside her on another cot, Aravel stirred.

As silently as possible, Kiana slipped out of bed, shushing Snow when he chuffed in protest, and out the front flap of the old woman's tent. The crone had offered to let them spend the night with her before setting off on their way the following morning.

Stepping out into the night, Kiana relished the cool air brushing her cheeks, a lover's caress, refreshing after her all-too-real dream. She stopped between Tash and Reyan, who sat on stools on either side of the tent. They'd taken first watch in case the Deep Ones made a move during the night. They were overdue.

"Everything okay?" Tash asked, looking up.

"Yes, fine," she replied, still sounding slightly out of breath to her own ears. "I came to relieve you."

"It's only been a few hours," Reyan drawled sleepily.

"And considering I spent a fair portion of the day unconscious, I'd say that's plenty for me tonight."

The men exchanged a glance.

"I'll stay up with her. You go get some rest." Tash adjusted his position on the stool.

Kiana cocked her head to one side, amused. "What, you don't trust me?"

The noble let out a surprised bark of laughter. "Couldn't be further from the truth. I'd simply prefer to have two pairs of eyes looking out for trouble after the day's events."

With a nod, Reyan headed away from the tent, presumably toward his own home. Once he was gone, Tash studied Kiana's face.

"Are you sure you're okay? You look flushed."

"I'm fine, I promise." That sinister smile flashed into her mind again. She winced. "I had a dream. It was . . . unsettling. And it felt so real, more like a vision than a dream."

"Oh?" Tash shifted to face her but kept his head on a swivel.

"Yes. It was like I'd witnessed the moment the water jinn attacked the Ice Druid for the Shiver Seed. Stole the Crystal right off her neck."

Tash's eyes ceased their roaming and fell upon Kiana in surprise. "That must have been upsetting."

"It was strange. It was like it was happening to me, but I was aware that it wasn't me in the dream." She scrunched up her nose. "If that makes sense."

"It does. I've often had dreams in which I'm someone else."

"You have?"

He pressed his lips together, maybe regretting his words. Before he had a chance to respond, a rustling sound caught their attention.

Holding up a stilling hand, Kiana whispered, "It's coming from the east."

"Stay here. I'll go check it out," Tash whispered back.

The moment he stood to investigate, a doe bolted into the village and abruptly stopped thirty yards away. She glanced behind her, waiting for the two fawns they could now see trailing her. The family of three stopped to drink from a water barrel the villagers' horses shared before wandering toward the west side of the town and out of sight.

Kiana let out a sigh of relief.

"I'm tired of jumping at every little noise."

"Well, if Reyan is as good as he says he is at eluding pursuers, we may be able to rest a little easier in a few days."

"Then let's hope he's not all talk. If we can't shake the Deep Ones, I don't see how we can keep going, leading them right to the Ice Druids like a bunch of chumps."

Tash nodded thoughtfully and resumed his steady scan of the village.

The rest of the night passed without incident. Aravel got up to relieve Tash so he could get a few hours of rest, and the women spent the remainder of their time enjoying the cool stillness and the heavy scent of night-blooming jasmine, which grew in abundance all around the village.

The sun rose a brilliant orange, streaking the sky with deep pinks and purples. Tash poked his head out of the tent to ensure all was well and then set about building a fire over which to cook breakfast. Reyan joined them shortly after, a pig carcass slung over his shoulder. The smell of cooking meat finally rousted Snow, who had been lying on his back on Kiana's cot, legs akimbo, snoring softly while everyone else began their day.

The two druids sat near the fire but tried to avoid eye contact with the wild pig roasting on a spit above a pot of boiling potatoes and peas.

"Caught this fella yesterday," Reyan said, gesturing to the pig, "so he's nice and fresh."

Kiana offered a polite smile, ignoring the pang of sorrow in her stomach. "I'm sure he is, but I'll stick to the potatoes." She tossed several sprigs of rosemary she'd plucked from the village herb garden into the pot. These she followed up with a sprinkling of Tribali sea salt Aravel had brought along.

"You don't eat meat?" Reyan's mouth held a frown of confusion bordering on scorn.

Both women shook their heads. Snow, meanwhile, stood next to the fire, drooling.

"Once you've had a conversation with a pig, it's sort of hard to see them as a meal again," Aravel said as she magically mended some of the holes in Kiana's clothes from the day before. She'd all but perfected the art of growing and manipulating natural fibers.

"You've had a conversation with a pig?" Reyan's confusion turned to skepticism.

Aravel looked up from her task.

"Uh, yeah." Her eyebrows pulled together. "Well, you know, not a philosophical discussion about the meaning of life or anything, but he told me where I could find some nice Corvalian truffles, and . . ." She trailed off, noting Reyan's dubious expression. She pressed her fists into her hips, elbows out. "Didn't you say you were a ranger, a guardian of the forest? Don't you have an affinity for nature like we druids do? Without the delightful magic, of course."

Reyan snorted. "I may not have magic, but . . ." He pulled a pouch from his boot and dug two fingers into the contents. He brought out a pinch of orange powder and sprinkled it over the roasting carcass. The sizzling intensified, and the skin immediately began to brown. Reyan smiled. "I can't produce fire or water at will, but this Dust of Decadence will cut the cooking time of any meat to minutes. Likewise for baking bread, curdling cheese . . . whatever you need. Quite the time saver when you have a hungry village to feed. As for consorting with animals, we rangers tend to stick to those who are . . . brighter. Like him." He nodded to Snow and tossed him a few already cooked scraps.

Aravel rose slowly from her log, eyes blazing. Her words came out slowly and perfectly enunciated.

"Excuse me, *sir*! I'll have you know that pigs are *very* bright creatures. Those truffles were among the best I've ever tasted." She lifted her chin in the air, looking down her nose at their new friend.

Reyan held his hands up in mock surrender.

"Apologies. Had I known, I never would have killed this little guy." He dug a knife into the fully cooked pig, slicing a piece of the juicy meat and depositing it on his plate.

"Really?" Aravel said, head lowering.

The ranger's smirk knocked the hope off Aravel's face.

"Harrumph," she grumbled, sitting heavily back down on the log and snatching up Kiana's clypernia pants. Eyes squinting, she focused intently on the spell she used to weave the fibers back together.

The pants burst into flames.

"Salt and sky!" Aravel shouted, dropping the pants in the dirt and leaping up.

Fortunately, Tash arrived with a pitcher of water just in time, promptly dousing the flames.

"Maybe we should calm down a little before we use any more magic, eh?" he said soothingly, holding the pitcher out to Kiana.

"*Prodicsht aquai*," she whispered, flicking her wrist upward.

Water refilled the pitcher.

Aravel's eyes bored into Tash's. She sat back down and whipped the pants off the ground, spraying dirt over Kiana's feet.

Reaching tentatively toward her pants, Kiana said, "Do you want me to—"

"I've got it!" Aravel snapped, tugging the fabric out of her friend's grasp. She cleared her throat. "Sorry," she said meekly. "But I'm fine. Thank you." And she set back about her task, this time with no incendiary mishaps.

Several children from the village scurried over to their campfire and held out plates, which Reyan heaped with meat and potatoes. The kids chattered excitedly the entire time. Kiana's gaze moved past them. Several adults watched them warily but kept at a distance.

"We don't seem to have made a great first impression here," Kiana said.

Reyan followed her gaze over his shoulder. He observed the people for a moment before he turned back to his roast.

"Don't mind them. They're just edgy because of the octopus and . . . everything. They'll come around when they're hungry enough. Meat has been in short supply lately." He watched the children scamper away with their generous breakfasts, Snow following behind them to make sure they didn't drop anything. "Having that damned aberration lurking in the local watering hole has scared away most of the wildlife. I've spent weeks on the hunt, and still Estlin hasn't seen pig in more than a month." His gaze stayed fixed on the children, filled with a deep and consuming sadness Kiana knew all too well. Still, she kept her sighting of the three deer the night before to herself.

"Pity," Aravel muttered, irises flashing with gold as she tended to the scorch marks on the clypernia fabric.

Keeping one wary eye on her pants, Kiana stirred the potatoes, Tash settling on the log across from her.

"You spend weeks at a time alone in the forest hunting?"

Reyan eyed the druid. "Sure, sometimes. I used to go with my brother from time to time, before he . . ." The ranger coughed. "But mostly I like the solitude."

"Sounds lonely," Aravel said, half to herself as she concentrated.

Reyan shrugged this off. "I'm a bit of a lone wolf."

Kiana watched the ranger for a moment in silence. There was an obvious strength about him, a quiet confidence, and at the same time a deep and penetrating gloom.

"Well, once we've completed our quest, we'll be happy to come back and help you get rid of that . . . thing," she said. "You know, assuming we survive."

Aravel straightened and shot Kiana a look of surprise.

"We will?"

Trepidation fluttered behind Kiana's rib cage.

"Yeah." She swallowed hard. Memories of spiked tentacles and abject horror rose to the surface of her mind. She pushed the thoughts away. "Of course." She nudged Aravel's foot and nodded toward where the children feasted on their meat. "These people are suffering. And isn't that what we're out here for? Going on adventures, saving the world one quest at a time?"

"Um, first of all"—Aravel held up a single index finger—"it was one *enchanted grove* at a time, and something tells me this octopus isn't going to doff its proverbial hat and skedaddle just because we conjure some rain and wind and threaten it with angry, semisentient vines." As the final hole mended, she held Kiana's pants up to the light and examined them. "I mean, unless you think giant mutated octopuses—" She paused and muttered, "Octopi?—have some hitherto-undiscovered fear of fast-moving air." Satisfied, she proffered the pants to Kiana. "Do you?"

With a withering yet somehow still loving look at her friend, Kiana took her pants, exchanging them for a bowl of potatoes, which Aravel accepted gratefully.

"No, I don't. But you're the one who was so eager to come with me, to see the world in all its terror and glory. I realize we've faced a bit more danger than maybe we anticipated at first." Aravel scoffed, but Kiana continued as if she hadn't heard. "But the mission is still the same: find our path, bring back the Orders, and do whatever good we can along the way. Besides, I'd think our"—she looked quickly toward Reyan, then away—"other adventure would be more concerning than the future threat of an octopus."

Kiana's eyes involuntarily found Tash's. Tremors seized her stomach at the look on his face, a blend of admiration, affection, and something buried just a little deeper, harder to pinpoint. Sadness, maybe. With a small smile, he nodded and returned his gaze to his food.

Does he think of her when he sees me? Of my failure?

Kiana gritted her teeth and swiftly dispelled the tormenting questions. Instead, she called to mind Ravaini's words, the reassuring ones. The ones that meant her own mind was the problem.

Stop projecting, she told herself.

This exchange of glances between druid and sorcerer, however brief, did not go unnoticed. When Kiana turned back to Aravel, her friend was eyeing her curiously. In a most un-Aravel fashion, she let the matter drop without a word.

"You're right. If we can help, we have a duty to do so." Aravel turned to Reyan, who had been watching this whole conversation with interest. Straightening her posture and raising her head in an exaggerated show of dignity, she said, "Mr. Ranger, should we not perish in our quest to rid the world of the Deep Ones plague and all it entails, we would be most pleased to return here and roust thine foul beast from your ancestral waters." She bowed her head and offered a respectful curtsy.

Clearly unsure of what to make of this proclamation, Reyan looked back and forth between Tash and Kiana before rolling his head in an awkward, confused nod.

"Thank you. We'd obviously appreciate any help we can get. Though, as I've said, the thing doesn't reveal itself when people show up to kill it."

Aravel placed a hand on Reyan's shoulder and, voice grave, said, "My good man, Kiana is right. If we survive the task we are about to undertake, that oversized water blob better cross its very, very, *very* large tentacles and hope it can find a cave somewhere we can't get to it."

After the mishap with the pants, Reyan glanced warily at Aravel's hand where it rested on his shoulder.

"Right. I'm sure a giant octopus will seem a far easier quarry after facing down a Terror, which"—he pointed at each of them—"still hasn't been fully explained to me, by the way."

"With any luck, you'll never need to know." Tash set aside his empty plate. "Once you've helped us elude the Deep Ones, I imagine you'll be eager to return home."

Reyan pursed his lips and offered a vague nod.

"Speaking of"—Kiana stood and brushed her hands together—"we should head out soon. I'd love to make up some distance after losing most of the day yesterday."

"Agreed. I'll see about restocking our rations." Tash stood and began collecting dishes. Snow appeared by his side in an instant, checking the ground for fallen morsels.

Kiana stepped toward the tent. "I'll—"

"Sounds perfect!" Aravel put a stopping hand on Kiana's arm and draped her other arm over her friend's shoulder. She smiled at Tash. "We'll meet back here in, say, ten minutes?"

The elf gave her a look of suspicion but merely nodded and returned to the tent.

"Can I talk to you?"

It was Kiana's turn to be suspicious.

"I suppose," she said, drawing out the last syllable.

"Great. Let's go pick some herbs to take with us."

Outside of earshot from the tent, a small path wound into the forest. Along the edges of the trail grew patches of moonwort, blue thyme, and glaceria root.

The druids had just stepped into the shadow of a large evergreen tree to gather some thyme when Aravel blurted, "So, are we going to talk about this Tash thing?"

Startled, Kiana's eyes widened. "I'm sorry?"

Aravel stepped directly into her friend's eyeline. "You're probably the most perceptive person I know, but when it comes to seeing hopeless, all-consuming love staring you in the face, you're as blind as a Sola-crucian dwarf bat." She held out a hand, index finger up. "Which are actually blind, by the way."

Kiana's mouth went dry, and heat prickled her cheeks.

"I—I, uh . . ." She shook her head vigorously. "What? No."

"I've seen the looks, the way he finds excuses to touch your hand or your cheek. And you should have seen him after that octopus—" She stopped, pressing her lips together. "Point is, Tash is in love with you. All the flirting and romantic gestures were cute at first, but now it's just painful. If you don't feel the same—which I doubt, by the way, if the color of your face right now is any indication—then for Nelami's sake, put the man out of his misery. Hells, put *me* out of *my* misery. If I have to watch him bite his tongue because you've secured him at arm's length one more time, I'm going to hang myself with your stupid, flammable pants." Finally done with her tirade, Aravel crossed her arms and blew out a quick breath.

Tears crested the rims of Kiana's eyes and gently spilled onto her cheeks.

"Oh, honey." Aravel unfolded her arms and went to Kiana, pulling her into a hug. "I'm sorry. You know I would never hang myself." She stroked Kiana's hair soothingly. "My end will almost certainly be in a firestorm of glory." She bobbed her head. "Maybe a hailstorm."

Through her constricted throat, Kiana snorted out a laugh.

"Well, that's a relief because I was mostly worried about my pants," she said in a voice choked with tears.

Aravel snorted in return. Pushing back slightly, she wiped a tear from Kiana's cheek.

"Really, though. What is it?"

Taking a moment to gather herself, Kiana dried her face and took a long, deep breath.

"I've loved Tash since the day I met him." She cleared her throat. "But—"

"So help me, Kiana Paletine, if you say one word about him blaming you for—"

Kiana held up a hand, cutting her off.

"*But* I cannot imagine a worse time to bring it up. For Nelami's sake, we're traveling across the continent to take on an enemy who may very well smite us in a single breath."

"So, then, what *better* time to tell the man you love how you feel? You may not get another chance!"

Exasperation forced a small groan out of Kiana. Aravel narrowed her eyes.

"There's something else. Something you're not saying."

Kiana chewed the corner of her lip.

"Ha! That, you do that"—she pointed animatedly at Kiana's mouth—"when there's something you want to say. Or don't want to say."

Eyes squeezed shut, Kiana mumbled, "I don't know how to talk to him."

Aravel's pointing hand dropped to her side. "Huh?"

Opening her eyes, Kiana said a little louder, "I don't know how to talk to him."

Confusion contorted Aravel's face. "False. You talk to him every day. I've seen you, for weeks now. You're actually quite proficient at it."

"That's not what I mean," Kiana said, hands fidgeting. "Talking to him about our journey or home or magic is easy. It's nice." She grimaced. "It's the other stuff."

Momentarily struck dumb, Aravel only stared at her, mouth slightly agape.

Kiana clarified, "The romantic stuff. Anytime the conversation might steer that direction, I get panicky and . . . awkward. Even if I wanted to broach the subject, test the waters, I can't get the words to come out."

Something dawned on Aravel. A squeal of laughter escaped her.

"Tides be, you're *right*. Like the other day, when he pulled the brambles out of your hair, and I thought you might finally kiss him, and you dropped your pouch on his foot and then headbutted him in the chin when you looked back up from what you'd done. Or when he gave you a black lily and you said something that sounded like, 'Horkay, imblesh agorku.' Or when—"

"Okay! Yes, you obviously see what I mean." Bright-red splotches colored Kiana's cheeks.

"Sweet Nelami's mercy, who would have thought the stately, collected Kiana Paletine would have trouble talking to boys?" At a look from Kiana, she amended, "Men."

"It's not all men, just Tash. It's like his presence melts my brain." She sighed. "Among other things."

Aravel still stared at her in bewilderment. "Huh. I . . . huh." She laughed.

"Well, now that you've gotten your amusement from it, perhaps you can understand why I haven't simply thrown myself into his arms. And that's to say nothing of the fact that his fiancée did die because I—"

"Kiana Paletine!" Aravel took a step forward, face stern.

Three sharp yips interrupted them as Snow came bounding into the forest.

Kiana took advantage of the save. "Well, this has been fun, but we should get back to the others. They're probably waiting for us."

Kiana stepped back toward the path, leaving Aravel a few steps behind, a look of remonstration still on her face.

"Oh, wait!" Kiana stopped dead and turned. "We haven't picked any herbs."

"So?"

"You don't think they'll find it odd that we came out to pick herbs and returned empty handed?"

"You think they'll actually notice?" Aravel scoffed. "I have plenty of herbs in my pack. They'll never know the difference."

As they strolled back into the village, they saw Tash and Reyan waiting for them by the now-extinguished campfire, bags packed and ready to go.

"Find what you were looking for?" Tash asked, handing Kiana her pack and staff.

Aravel patted a pouch hanging from her belt. "Yup. Nice, yummy herbs ready for blending."

"The moonwort is extra potent this time of year. Great with tubers. Find any?" Reyan asked, securing his bow across his back.

"What're you, the High Inquisitor?" Aravel snapped.

Perplexed silence settled on them for a moment.

"Are you always this excitable?" Reyan asked, eyes wary.

"No, Mr. Ranger, I am not. But it's been a stressful couple of days. Or weeks." After a deep breath, she concluded, "Apologies for my outburst . . . ssss."

"You know my last name's not actually Ranger, right?"

"Oh?"

"It's Thein. Reyan Thein."

"Well, Mr. Thein, it's a pleasure to formally make your acquaintance. I'm Aravel Zavir, this is the lovely Kiana Paletine, and that there is the esteemed Tash Ilirian." She gestured to each of her companions in turn, then clapped her hands together. "Everyone acquainted?"

Snow yipped at her feet.

"Ah, sincerest apologies. And this is Snow."

The fox wagged his tail happily, tongue lolling.

"*Now* we're all acquainted. Let's get to evading."

Dense mist spread a mile in all directions as the travelers left Estlin, conjured by Kiana and Aravel as an added precaution against their dogged pursuers. Only their five-member party could pass through the fog unimpeded by the visual impairment. The people of Estlin had agreed, albeit reluctantly, to the inconvenience of having their village shrouded in obscurity for a day.

True to his word, Reyan led the group expertly through the terrain, his stealth nearly on par with that of Ravaini, whom Kiana had seen slip unnoticed past their father on more occasions than she could count, practicing to be the spy—and other things—she had now become. The protective pendant Madame Lesant had provided kept any of the companions from being located even by magical means. How the old healer had known they'd need the pendant before they did was a mystery she wasn't telling.

Traveling alongside a river came as a blessed relief. Though cautious when nearing the banks, the party kept the water if not within view, at least within earshot. Even just the sound of running water soothed their fraying nerves. Dense tree growth finally replaced the sparse woods they'd traveled through thus far as they approached the border of Mooreland, putting Akkra's arid sands and Harrian's barren plains behind them.

Despite all their precautionary measures, conversation all but ceased their first day of travel. Even Snow remained subdued. All ears strained for even the tiniest sound that might mean the Deep Ones persisted on their trail. Day one passed with no such evidence, and the collective sigh of relief as they made camp that evening was the loudest noise any of them had made in hours. When Kiana settled next to the fire for her nightly meditation before bed, the snapping of a twig beneath her mat startled her as though it had been the clash of swords in battle. Her cry of surprise nearly made Tash drop his book into the licking flames.

Day two passed much the same as the first, though tongues loosened little by little as the morning wore on. By dusk, friendly banter and even spurts of laughter resumed.

"We should reach the crossing to Mooreland by midmorning tomorrow," Reyan said, dropping his pack on a stump, his indication they were stopping for the night. "And the river should be safe here for anyone who wants to freshen up."

"Egads, yes please," Aravel said, stretching her arms over her head.

"Yes, and you can all feel free to wash your own damn clothes this time," Tash said, waving a finger around at each of them. "I'm tired of being the designated laundress."

"Launderer."

"What?" Tash looked at Aravel.

"A laundress is a woman. You are our designated *launderer*."

Tash scowled at her.

"What? I'm perfectly happy to wash my own clothes. That little trick of yours"—she waggled her fingers in an imitation of his spell—"is just so darn handy."

"She's not wrong," Kiana said, enjoying the look of exasperation that flickered across Tash's face before being replaced by a wry smile.

Aravel laughed gleefully and then placed a reassuring hand on Tash's arm. In a faux-serious voice she said, "Fear not, good sir. We will bathe our own garments this night." She looked at Kiana. "Ladies first?"

"Actually"—Tash stepped forward—"I was hoping I might have a moment alone with Kiana. Perhaps she and I can clean up first while you and Reyan set up camp?" He inclined his head to Kiana. "If you don't mind, of course."

What could only be described as a rampaging horde of butterflies made Kiana clutch her pack closer to her abdomen.

"Of course not," she said with her best reassuring smile. "Why would I?"

Don't panic.

"Wait!" Aravel said, striding between them. Apprehension pulled her features into a comical mask of alarm.

"Is there a problem?" Tash asked.

"Yes!"

No, Kiana thought, willing Aravel to get the message.

Tash glanced at Kiana, who ever so slightly shook her head, and spread his hands out before him, palms up. "What is it?"

"I . . . uh." Aravel looked around, clearly desperate for any explanation of her interjection that might make the tiniest bit of sense. "I . . . need, um . . . the herb pouch!" she finished triumphantly.

Tash looked to where the pouch hung from Aravel's belt.

"That herb pouch?" He nodded to the sack.

Aravel followed his gaze.

"Aha! Yep! Here it is. Heh heh." She put her hands on her hips. "Thought Kiana had it last."

Beside Tash, Kiana squeezed her eyes shut, grimacing.

Tash was still staring at Aravel. "Well, now that you . . . still have it, any further objections?"

Aravel pursed her lips and shook her head.

"Grand!" Tash motioned for Kiana to lead the way.

"Stay here," Kiana whispered to Snow. His wagging tail slumped.

Leaving their gear with their companions, the two elves made their way cautiously to the water, ears alert for any sign of company in the surrounding woods. They walked in silence for the three minutes it took to get to the river's edge. Only thinking about the blooming cycle of a snow lily kept Kiana from opening her mouth and unleashing whatever unstoppable nervous prattle lurked there.

Once they reached the water, Tash bent to remove his boots.

"Any more unsettling dreams the last couple of nights?" he asked.

The abrupt break in the silence pulled Kiana back into the moment.

"Oh, uh . . ." She frowned. "No, nothing." She paused, removing her cloak. "Though I have been waking up thinking about snow a lot."

Tash removed his coat, belt, and vest. "Well, he is a big part of your life."

Kiana furrowed her brow. "What?" Realizing what she'd said, she quickly added, "Oh! No, not Snow." She mimed pointy ears. "Snow, the wintry precipitation."

"Ah." Tash laughed. "That is stranger." Shirt and pants still on, he held out a hand. "Shall we?"

Wearing just her green travel dress, which needed to be washed anyway, Kiana took his hand without a second thought. A familiar tingle of energy passed between their skin, along with a familiar longing. They moved to the water.

"Ahhh, yes." Tash relaxed into the river, letting the water come up to his chin. "Feels great."

Kiana mumbled in agreement, eyes scanning the surface for signs of a disturbance. The only ripples were their own. She dug her toes into the sandy river bottom.

"Still nervous in the water?"

Kiana chuckled. "Just a little." She dipped her head back, letting the water soak into her long, wavy hair. "Strange, isn't it? Being brought up in Tribali, the ocean was my safe place, my comfort. The water was practically my second home. But here, this river . . ." She trailed off as the octopus's ugly, mottled head floated into her mind's eye.

Tash let her words hang in the twilight air for a minute.

"I have a confession to make," he said at last.

Nelami's mercy, Kiana thought as her muscles tensed.

Feigning nonchalance, she said, "Oh?" Inside, everything screamed.

"I haven't been completely honest with you."

Caught slightly off guard, Kiana managed to maintain her calm facade. She turned to him and saw his eyes focused intently on her face. "How's that?"

A sigh laden with weariness and resignation poured from Tash. He let his eyes drop, but only for a moment. Without another word, he stood to his full height. Water cascaded off him. The river now at his waist, he pulled his shirt off over his head.

Kiana inhaled sharply.

Black and bronze scales dotted the flesh on either side of his abdominal muscles. He turned, and Kiana could see more scales around his shoulder blades and down his back ribs. It wasn't until this moment Kiana realized she'd never seen him with his shirt off before. Though focused on absorbing the meaning of what she was seeing, she took a moment to appreciate the finely sculpted musculature of the man who was laying himself bare to her.

"Draconic ancestry," she muttered, forcing her eyes not to linger too long.

Tash nodded once and turned back around.

"I don't understand," Kiana said, head swaying in astonishment. "Why would you wait until now to tell me this?"

"Because my family is very private about their past. Our lineage is . . ." He searched for the word. ". . . complicated. Secrecy has been drilled into me since I was a child." Bitterness hung heavy in his voice. He averted his eyes. "There are details about the Ilirian ancestry that some of my relatives would kill to keep concealed."

Kiana frowned. "Having dragon blood in your lineage is nothing to be ashamed of. In fact, I know some who would keel over with jealousy if they knew. It's so rare. And a dual lineage, bronze *and* black dragon—I've never seen anything like this before."

"Aside from myself, nor have I."

Kiana looked at him. "The rest of your family isn't this way?"

Tash shook his head. "I'm the only sorcerer in my generation, which isn't unusual given how rare they—*we*—are. My father was the first after three generations of evocation mages. He's"—he cleared his throat—"not like me."

"I'm still not clear on why draconic lineage would be seen as anything but enviable."

Tash gave a half smile. "Enviable, perhaps, if the dragon falls on the high end of the morality spectrum, a Dragon of Order. You may not be aware, but black dragons are incredibly rare to find in draconic lineages. Almost nonexistent. The same goes for red dragons. Both are among the worst Scions of Discord. The few mages throughout history known to have red or black dragon in their blood have been some of the most heinous criminals or vicious tyrants Amarra has seen." His mouth flattened into a thin line. "This is a secret my family has kept for centuries. If word got out, the repercussions in Highmane would be, shall we say, unacceptable to my father. His place on the Council would be forfeit. All those aristocrats he so loves advising would shun him in an instant."

"But you're telling me."

Tash's face softened for the first time since his confession began.

"Yes," he breathed.

Kiana stood and moved to him. She reached out a hand, stopping short of touching him.

"May I?"

He nodded almost imperceptibly, his eyes warm but cautious.

Running her right hand over the scales on his left side, she marveled at their solidity, like built-in armor. She could see now where the thrall's dagger had pierced his side, just missing the protective layer that covered his most vital organs. She thought back to that fight and the sizzle of Tash's arcane sword as it sliced through their enemies.

"I suppose this would explain your tendency toward acid magic." She ran her fingers over the bronze scales. "But black dragons, don't they breathe—"

"Death," Tash finished for her quietly.

He wasn't wrong. Black dragons could exhale clouds of necrotic energy that desiccated their victims. Thank the gods black dragons were so rare. If Tash was the rarest of mages with the rarest of bloodlines, who knew how powerful he could become. Or what the cost would be.

Kiana furrowed her brow, fingers playing lightly over bronze before moving to black. Where the bronze had a warmth to them, the black were cold as steel.

"Bronze dragons are Scions of Benevolence, Dragons of Order. Surely that negates some of the stigma you'd face from the black dragon lineage."

Tash breathed a laugh and lowered his eyes.

Moving on. She let her fingers fall away from his side, reluctantly.

"Are there more scales?" As soon as the question left her mouth, Kiana willed the words to come back, realizing what few places remained to be revealed. She hazarded a glance at his face.

To her immense relief, he smiled kindly, a hint of playfulness dancing around his eyes.

"Just a few."

She nodded and focused intensely on not saying anything else embarrassing.

"I didn't want to have this hanging between us," Tash whispered into her hair. "Secrets can be toxic."

Kiana sought his eyes.

"Thank you for sharing this with me."

They stood like that for a time, frozen in a moment neither wanted to interrupt nor knew how to move forward from.

Unsure of what to say, Kiana switched tacks.

"Well, as long as we're confessing things, there's something I should tell you as well."

"Is that so?" Tash said, his casual demeanor reemerging as the conversation shifted. The moment lost, he tugged his shirt back over his head. "And here I thought my family had the monopoly on secrets."

"It's not a secret . . . per se." Ignoring the roiling unease shooting outward from her navel, she met Tash's gaze. "For someone who was raised by a diplomat to *be* a diplomat, I've never been great at expressing myself around, well, certain others. I find navigating emotional waters infinitely more difficult than sailing a physical ship through even the stormiest of seas." She paused, opened her mouth, closed it. Try as she might, no more words came.

Once again, Tash came to her rescue.

"It's okay. You don't owe me an explanation. You don't owe me anything."

The kindness in his words gave her a second wind.

"There's just so much happening right now, but—"

"It's okay," Tash repeated softly.

Kiana shook her head. "It's not. I need you to know . . ." *How much I care about you.* The words failed her, but she poured the emotion behind them into her eyes and fixed them on Tash, her face pleading with him to understand.

To her great surprise, he nodded.

"I do."

"How?" she rasped, her throat constricting as an overwhelming wave of emotion washed over her. She wanted so badly to cast off her fear and guilt and pull him to her, never let him go.

It was as if he were reading her mind. Rather than answer her question, he pulled her into a hug. He didn't let go until her breathing leveled out and the muscles in her back relaxed. Even then, his embrace lingered.

When they did finally part, Tash laid his hands on her shoulders and cocked his head to the side.

"This may come as a shock, but I'm actually pretty good at reading people. Comes with the territory, I suppose. All those hours at court navigating the murky waters of greed and manipulation." He let his hands fall away. "I assume your 'herb-gathering mission' with Aravel, masterfully disguised though it was, was her long-awaited best friend intervention, and given her reaction to our coming here together tonight, the conversation didn't go in my favor." A lopsided grin accompanied his chuckle.

"First of all"—Kiana pressed the tip of her index finger into his chest—"decoding Aravel's less-than-clandestine activities hardly qualifies you as an expert at reading people."

Tash laughed. "Okay, I'll give you that. And second?"

Her finger lingered for a moment before moving to tuck a piece of sodden hair behind her ear.

"I wouldn't exactly say the conversation didn't go in your favor."

Arcane magic buzzed in the air as Tash passed a hand over Kiana's head. He clutched a lock of her now-dry hair between two fingers and gave it a light tug.

"Happy to hear it. Perhaps we can talk more about it when the fate of the world is in a less precarious balance?"

"Gladly." She smiled, feeling another weight lift from her.

The hoot of an owl drew their attention. High in a tree several yards from the riverbank, a small owl watched them. As they turned to face it, the bird left its perch and soared farther into the trees.

"You must be joking," Kiana said indignantly. "Was that Aravel?" She'd seen her friend shift enough that the markings appeared uncannily familiar.

An uncharacteristic disquiet came over Tash.

"You don't think she heard . . ."

Sensing his unease, Kiana placed a hand on his arm.

"It probably wasn't even her." She glanced at the trees. "But just to be sure, maybe we should get back to camp." She started moving toward shore.

"Kiana." Tash grasped her hand to stop her.

She turned back to him.

"What I told you, about my family . . . about me . . ."

"Your secret's safe with me."

Still he hesitated. "I appreciate that. And while I don't want secrets to come between us, I also need you to understand that there are other things about my family that I'm not at liberty to discuss."

Kiana nodded, her face tight with concern.

"For better or worse, we are the stewards of secrets, and I already catch enough criticism from them for perceived disloyalty to the family due to 'misaligned priorities.'"

"I understand."

He squeezed her hand. "Thank you."

Back at camp, Aravel sat on a stump, stoking the fire. Snow lay at her side, ears turned toward the new arrivals, though his eyes remained on the pot Reyan was filling with what must be their dinner. Still poking at coals, Aravel scanned her friends' appearance.

"Welcome back." She raised a querying eyebrow at Kiana. "Feel better?"

"Much, thank you," Kiana replied airily. Casting a brief look over her shoulder at Tash, she added, "Have you two been here the whole time?"

"We gathered some firewood and a few tasty-looking mushrooms. Other than that, yeah. Just setting up camp and making dinner." She frowned. "Why?"

Kiana let out the puff of breath she'd been holding. "No reason."

"All right." Aravel rose and handed Kiana the stick. "Your turn to poke the fire. My turn to tend to my lady needs."

Everyone froze.

"Whoa, okay, not how I meant that to come out. I didn't mean"— she looked at Kiana and Tash, hand waving between them—"not that I . . ." She hung her head. "Forget it. Come on, Snow."

The fox tore his eyes away from the pot, now sitting atop the fire, for only a second.

"Dinner won't be ready for a while. Come on."

Reluctantly, the fox followed Aravel. Before they reached the edge of camp, Reyan called out.

"Hang on, can I get some of those herbs you picked in Estlin? Maybe some blue thyme for the mushrooms?"

Aravel's face flushed. She fingered the herb pouch hanging accusingly from her belt. An owl landed in the branches above her head, his peaceful hoots filling her silence.

Finally, she said haughtily, "No, you may not."

And with that, she left the camp, leaving a confused Reyan crouched by the fire.

CHAPTER THIRTEEN

The crossing to Mooreland took place at the narrowest point of the Mid-lane River. Two hundred yards separated the banks, and a ferry docked on either side. Two dwarves—brothers, by the looks of them—helmed the ferries, and each sported a greataxe strapped to his back. Approaching the dock with her companions, Kiana noted that the pair seemed to take immense pleasure in shouting insults back and forth whenever they passed one another around the midway point.

"Go faster, ya orc-brained phlegm wart. Me daughter could pull 'arder than you."

"Heh heh, so I hear from the tavern boy, ya ignorant weasel face."

"Shut yer ugly yap 'ole, Digger!"

"What's 'e matter, Graves? You got an eye on the boy yerself?"

"Eat dung buds, ya stupid arse!"

And on it went.

When the one called Digger reached the near bank, two half-elf clerics disembarked looking more than a little annoyed. A familiar symbol adorned their shields.

"Must be headed home to the Temple of Alsäm," Reyan posited as they passed. "Not known for their sense of humor around there."

"Speaking of heading home, I imagine this is where we part

ways." Tash stuck out a hand to the ranger. "Thanks for all your help."

"Actually"—he ignored the hand—"if it's all the same to you, I have some business in Garrison and would be happy to accompany you a little further." With a glance at the druids, he added, "Unless you're not headed that way."

"We are." Kiana cast wary eyes around but saw no one except the dwarf awaiting them on the ferry. "And we'd be happy to have you join us awhile longer."

"'Ey, you lot!" Digger called. "Yous plannin' on crossin' today or what?"

Bustling toward the dock, Kiana pulled out her coin purse. She appraised its meager contents.

"Guess I underestimated travel costs a bit. Restocking rations in Battle Tree ate up most of what I had left." She jangled the few remaining coins. "We might need to find a source of income soon if we're going to make it to—" She caught herself. "Uh, where we're going."

"I've got this one." Tash gave her elbow a squeeze and produced a handful of coins from his coat pocket. "How much for the group of us?" he asked the ferryman.

"One silver." The dwarf's eyes landed on Snow and narrowed. A muscle twitched in his neck, where a dragon tattoo wound its way up to his face, the creature poised as if ready to let loose flames upon the dwarf's nose. "Three silver."

Looking as though he might protest, Tash seemed to think better of it and acquiesced.

Once on board, gear settled around them, the companions watched Digger slam his wrists together, summoning a glistening magical rope that anchored to the far dock. He began to pull them toward the opposite shore with his extremely muscly, extremely tattooed arms. Aravel waved her hand through the shimmering rope but met only air.

"So, what business do you have in Garrison?" Kiana asked.

Sharpening his dagger with a whetstone, Reyan answered without looking up. "Left some raw materials with a blacksmith there. He's making us some armor and weapons we hope might help us drive out the octopus."

"What kind of weapons?"

"What raw materials?"

Tash and Kiana asked their questions in unison.

Perhaps deciding which question to answer first, Reyan hesitated. He looked to Kiana.

"Some metal ore—"

"Get off the river, ya rotting sack of sheep butts!" Digger suddenly shouted.

"Eat trouser wind!" came the reply. Graves made a rude gesture with his left arm, which boasted even more tattoos than his heavily inked brother's.

After a fleeting pause, Reyan continued, "—mined in the Harrian mountains. We bought it off a trader several months ago." To Tash he said, "I've commissioned harpoons, javelins, and crossbows, mostly. Things we can use at a distance. Most of the villagers lack innate magic."

Tash raised his eyebrows. "With armor on top of all those weapons, how do you plan to get everything back to—"

"Yer ma's a whore!"

"She's yer ma too, dipshit!"

"—back to Estlin?" he finished loudly.

Reyan dropped his hands, still holding dagger and stone, between his bent knees. "I reckon I'll buy a cart."

"And horses?"

The ranger gave Kiana a look of mild exasperation.

"You all certainly ask a lot of questions."

Both elves shrugged.

"I tend to take an interest in the people I travel with," Kiana said. "Not trying to pry."

"Your face looks like the south end of an ice buffalo!" Aravel shouted after Graves, who'd almost reached the other side of the river.

Digger rounded on her.

"Don't no one talk to my brother that way," he snarled.

"But you just . . . I heard . . ." she stammered.

"Oh no," Kiana mumbled.

She and Tash stood as one and raised supplicating hands toward the dwarf.

"She meant no offense," Kiana said. "Sometimes she just gets carried away in the moment."

"Yeah, I thought it was a show of respect or something. How you relate to each other."

"Respect?" Digger balked. "For that boil-faced buffoon?" He scoffed.

A strangled word tried to leave Aravel's mouth. She stamped a foot and tossed one hand out to the side demonstratively.

Tash masked his chortle with a cough while Kiana put an arm around her friend.

"Let it go, Ari."

"But—"

"I know."

"We're here." Digger released the magical rope and it vanished, eliciting a soft glow from the cuffs he wore around each wrist. "Make sure you don't leave nothin' behind. 'Specially that furry little menace." He pointed a stubby, hostile finger at Snow.

The fox tilted his head, still sitting quietly and minding his own business.

"I'm sorry, has my fox done something to annoy you?" Kiana bent to gather her pack and to stroke the fuzzy red ears.

"Not yet, but I seen them foxes tear up my neighbor's chickens somethin' awful. Terrible sight." He glared at Snow. "Don't you be gettin' no ideas."

"I assure you, all chickens are safe around this fox."

Digger looked unconvinced.

"Come, friends, let us leave this fair gentleman to his task. We have business of our own to attend to." Tash slung on his pack and motioned to shore.

The party happily disembarked.

This side of the river appeared strikingly lusher than the Harrian side. More species of trees sprouted up all around, and a smattering of blue and purple wildflowers adorned the ground on either side of a wide country road that disappeared into the distance.

Kiana turned to ask Tash a question and ran squarely into Aravel.

"What in the great sea are those?" Aravel said dreamily, wide eyed.

Up ahead, two pine lemurs wrestled in the dirt. About the size of human toddlers, they had impossibly fuzzy chestnut-colored fur with white rings running down their long tails. Two rounded ears nearly the size of Kiana's fist sat atop their heads. Their white faces featured large, round, expressive eyes. They fought wildly over a pine cone.

"You haven't seen a lemur before?" Reyan asked.

"Not one that looks like that." Her voice came out in a hush. "Tribali only has cave lemurs. They're cute but totally black, so their features are hard to make out. Not like these. Those eyes . . ."

Kiana leaned toward her, eyebrows knitting together. "Are you about to cry?"

"No," Aravel squeaked, clearly fighting back tears.

"Go make a new friend," Tash suggested, nudging her with his arm.

"I wouldn't recommend that," Reyan countered. "As you can see, pine lemurs are quite territorial about their food, and those tails have one of the strongest grips I've ever seen. You could choke a giant with that thing. Like iron, they are."

"But they're *so cute*," Aravel whimpered.

Beside her, Snow whined.

"You're cute too," she reassured him before giving her attention back to the lemurs.

One finally wrested the pine cone from the other and launched himself from the ground into the nearest white fir—a forty-foot jump. Undeterred, the other followed after. Both disappeared into the trees.

"I think I'm going to like it here," Aravel said.

Kiana smiled. "Let's go find out."

Picking up the rest of their things, they headed west down the dirt road. Years of consistent cart travel had produced deep ruts along the lane. Reyan took the lead while the others walked three abreast several paces behind, Snow trotting along between them, hopping over the grooves in his own little game.

"This road will actually take us all the way to Garrison, though it narrows some where the swampland gets particularly boggy," Reyan said over his shoulder.

"Right, swamps. Thank the gods we've mastered those air-pocket spells," Aravel whispered to Kiana.

The other druid nodded and squinted ahead. She could already smell faint traces of decaying plant matter and peat.

"You come this way a lot?" Aravel asked, louder.

"This is my fourth time," Reyan said. His head remained in constant motion, eyes scanning their surroundings.

"So, no."

"Never had much need. My father took me to Garrison once when I was a boy to get my first bow. When that broke a few years back, I returned for an upgrade." He wiggled the bow he now carried in his hand. "Garrison has some of the most renowned armorers and blacksmiths in Amarra. As you might have gathered from the name, it was once just a human military base. They've become a self-sufficient city, attracted dwarven smiths and gnomish merchants, but their central trades are still the same."

"My father has had some trade dealings with Garrison." Kiana placed one cupped palm over the other. "*Delecht beshas.*" When she lifted her hand, eight figs lay in her palm. She proffered them to each of her companions as she continued, "During the last demon war, Tribali supplied Crucian metal to what was then the military base to craft more effective weapons. We've tried to keep a relationship going ever since."

"How are you able to conjure different fruits every time?" Aravel plucked up another fig. "Mine always come out as sort of bland, extra-large blueberries."

"I guess I'm just that good." Kiana winked.

"What's Crucian metal?" Reyan tossed the stem of his fig aside.

"Metal crafted from the ore found around the coast of Tribali and Solacru. Its inherent properties are particularly effective against fiends like demons and devils."

"How have I never heard of this?"

Aravel reached for a third fig, but Kiana dropped the last three into the box Tash had given her the bracelet in. Aravel scowled.

"Two is plenty," Kiana chided. "As you well know." The basket she'd secretly left behind in Estlin would be enough to keep them all full for at least a week. As Aravel reluctantly withdrew her hand, Kiana said, "Crucian metal is actually quite rare, even more so now that pirates have spent decades raiding our shores, stealing what we do have and slaughtering our people." Rage bubbled up anew as she spoke. "It's sacred to Tribalians, so we don't part with it lightly."

From her position behind him, Kiana saw Reyan merely nod. Tash hugged her to him with one arm, resting his cheek briefly atop her head. Even this minor show of affection triggered a deep pang of longing. They walked lost in their own thoughts for a bit, until, to their right, two massive stone feet came into view atop a hard patch of earth.

"What's with those things?" Aravel asked. "That's the third set of ruins I've seen since we set out on this road. All feet."

"Yeah, you'll see them every hundred yards or so, alternating sides," Reyan said. "Sometimes other body parts are still there. Not sure what they signify, or what they used to look like, but they're everywhere, along every road in Mooreland. Thousands of 'em."

"Strange." Kiana leaned over to get a closer look at the feet. The stone itself was ancient, easily centuries old. "Must be quite a story there." She scrolled through the annals of her memory but came up empty on Mooreland history. Another topic to add to future studies.

"I actually think I read something about this recently." Tash crouched beside the ruins.

"Of course you did." Aravel rolled her eyes. "Between you and Kiana, half of Amarra's literary offerings have been consumed. Have you spent a single night not staring into the pages of a book? How did you even pack so many?"

"I only packed one."

"So you're a prolific but slow reader?"

Tash stood. "I only need one. It's enchanted to contain up to thirty volumes of my choosing."

Kiana popped to her feet. "Seriously?"

He grinned. "I can create another for you when all this is over, if you like."

"What about the feet?" Reyan interrupted.

Kiana swallowed her glee.

"Huh? Oh." Tash knelt again. "I only recall a brief reference, but I think they were some type of memorial."

The sound of heavy clanking pulled their attention from the sculpted feet. Up the road, a cart with a canvas covering, wheels caked in mud, rattled toward them. Two gnomes lounged on the driver's bench, one strumming a lute while the other coaxed a lively tune from a flute.

"Oy, 'ello there!" the one with the lute shouted in a high, melodic voice. "Lovely day, innit?"

The gnome's blue eyes sparkled with unbridled delight, and Kiana found herself smiling at the infectiousness of the emotion. The thought suddenly struck her that it had been some time since she'd found joy in little things, like a sunny afternoon. Or a book that could hold thirty volumes.

But as the cart drew closer, a twinge of unease swept over Kiana. The horses trotted at a normal, steady pace, but something in their eyes tickled the back of Kiana's neck, raising her hair just a little.

Fear.

Slightly widened eyes revealed dilated pupils that darted from side to side. The equine mouths champed harshly against their bits. The behavior stood in stark contrast to the languid manner of the cart's passengers. The gnomes seemed utterly unperturbed, both lost in the rapture of their musical harmony.

Kiana reached out to the horses with her mind, seeking connection. A scream javelined into her brain. With a gasp, she took an involuntary step backward, palm snapping to her forehead to ward off the intrusive sound.

Tash turned to her, concern creasing his brow.

"What's the matter?"

The cart passed and Kiana severed the connection, hand still pressed against her pulsing head. She took a moment to catch her breath.

"I'm not sure."

As they marched on throughout the day, eventually seeking a nice camp for the night, Kiana couldn't shake the disquiet creeping through her. Something had frightened those horses. Whatever it was could still be out there.

You're flinching at ghosts. Her sister's voice echoed through her mind, the phrase emerging from a sea of childhood memories. Ravaini used it every time Kiana overthought a situation or let her anxiety ruin a perfectly good time.

Everything's fine, she thought, holding on to the memory, to the specter of her sister.

An owl screeched in the distance.

Night fell on their first day in Mooreland. The terrain had shifted to be more swamp than anything else, so they stuck close to the road to camp in order to find dry land for their bedrolls. Aravel crafted a hammock to sleep in, and Tash teased her about wanting to be closer to the lemurs. She didn't deny it. In truth, Aravel always preferred to be among the branches. Rather than gifting her a cottage like Kiana's when they turned twenty, Ozmand had a special tree house built for her. The trend caught on, and Corval now had a miniature city sprawling through the trees.

Now deep into autumn, the sun's weakening rays could not contend with the deep shadows the party found themselves traveling through. A new, bitter cold grew with the dark, pressing up from the ground and wrapping around them like a shroud. Kiana's cloak kept her comfortable, as promised, and she thanked Ravaini daily for such a precious, opportune gift. The others huddled closer and closer to the flames licking out from the campfire.

"Why are you sleeping over here?" Kiana asked Aravel, who was lounging in her hammock, cloak pulled tight. "It's freezing." She nodded toward the fire. "I'm taking first watch with Tash, so there's plenty of room. We can stick close, share heat."

Aravel smirked. "I'll bet you can."

No flush hit Kiana's cheeks, no anxious fluttering in her stomach. She just smiled serenely.

"Wow, you've really come a long way since your 'imblesh agorku' days." Aravel nudged her friend with her elbow. "I'm proud of you."

"Gee, thanks."

Something caught Kiana's ear—an eerie sound floating on the breeze. Someone was crying. Softly at first, then louder, until the sound crescendoed to the unmistakable wail of a child.

"What in the hells . . ." Aravel whispered.

Tash and Reyan had joined them, ears turned to the noise.

"I'll check it out," Reyan said quietly.

Kiana grabbed his arm. "No. I think we should all go together." Unease gnawed through her gut. The horses' demeanor, the shriek of fear, nagged at her. "We shouldn't split up in the middle of an unfamiliar swamp at midnight."

Kiana worked to control the anxious spiral of her thoughts as they walked. What was a child doing in this swamp in the middle of the night? Was the source of the sound the reason for the intense fear she'd sensed in the horses? Could the noise be just a trick of the wind?

Calm down. It could just be the wind. She repeated these thoughts in her head, over and over.

But the closer they got, the more certain she became that it was not the wind. Up ahead, through an opening in the trees, they could see the remnants of a fire and what looked to be a camp in disarray. Scattered coals from the campfire formed a haphazard oval around half-burned logs. Two bedrolls lay rolled out near the far edge of the debris. A leather satchel sat abandoned against the base of a tree, contents spilling out. Left index finger burning beneath her ring, the Owl's Wisdom sharpening her focus, Kiana also noted marks in the dirt twenty feet to the left of where she had entered the camp. Someone had been dragged.

The wailing intensified.

"Hello?" Kiana called softly. "Anyone—"

Shooting pain lanced through her head, cutting her off. She doubled over, hands pressed flat against her temples, eyes shut tight. The agony threatened to rip her skull in two, boil her eyes in their sockets. She'd never felt anything like it. Any second might be her last, a swift death on the heels of unbearable torment.

And then it was over, the pain swept away in an instant. She stood up into eternal dusk.

A jagged landscape of hazy blues and grays replaced the swamp. Barren, lifeless snags now stood in place of the trees dripping with decaying vegetation. Fog rolled along the ground, swirling to the rhythm of a nonexistent wind.

"*Where is it?*" said a voice that came from nowhere, everywhere. The raspy whisper grated against Kiana's mind.

"Where is what?" The druid's gaze darted around for the source of the other voice. Had her own lips even moved? She wasn't sure.

Up ahead, from the misty darkness, emerged a figure cloaked in black, hood pulled low. Black smoke twisted around the feet, spiraled up and around the arms.

Kiana felt herself moving forward, unable to stop. She sent silent commands to her muscles, urging them to resist, and felt more stabbing pain in her head. A knife between the eyes.

"Aaaahhh!" She gritted her teeth but kept shuffling forward.

"*Kiana!*"

Tash. His voice sounded distant, barely discernible, as though he existed on the opposite end of whatever this hellscape was. Maybe in another world altogether. She tried to call back, couldn't.

The cloaked figure hovered only a few yards ahead now.

"*Where is it?*"

The voice grew louder but still lacked direction. Did the figure speak? Was someone else here?

The hood fell back.

Two shadowy eyes stared at Kiana from an otherwise featureless face.

Veins of pulsing black ran along the top of the head, down the cheeks, along the throat. The whirling smoke whipped into a frenzy.

Fear dug its icy fingers into the back of Kiana's neck. She willed her feet to stop, pressed her heels into the ground. Her movement slowed, slightly.

"Where is the Shiver Tree!"

The abrupt shrillness of the voice sent chills across Kiana's chest and down her arms. There was no mouth to speak. Every word fell like a psychic assault.

In the distance, that world from before the pain, Kiana heard Tash's faint voice. *"Don't let it touch her!"*

Does he mean me? The pressure in Kiana's head intensified, scrambling her thoughts. She shook her head, jostling the pendant around her neck.

"Ssso that'sss how you've kept out of our sssight," said the oddly sibilant voice.

The monster stretched out a hand, magic arcing out from his palm and connecting with the pendant. Intense heat flared at Kiana's chest. She screamed.

Something flickered to the Deep One's left. A shape formed from the mist, familiar, friendly. The ghostly outline of Aravel lunged at the Deep One, ethereal scimitar raised, a faint blue aura surrounding it. As the weapon slashed downward, a scream pierced Kiana's brain. A hideous sound, like a butcher's cleaver hacking through muscle and bone.

The Deep One vanished in a swirl of red smoke, taking with him the dusky, fog-laden hell. Kiana came to in a new nightmare.

She stood back in the swamp with her dagger drawn, wrist pressing against the resisting force of Tash's left arm. She had him pinned against a tree. She gasped and dropped the dagger.

"I'm so sorry," she panted. "What did I do?"

Pushing himself from the trunk of the bog oak, Tash rubbed a hand down Kiana's arm. He pointed to something on the ground behind her. She turned to find a man dead on the ground, a longsword beside him. Two arrows pierced his chest. Something about his face looked familiar.

Farther back, another man lay dead, acid still sizzling at the edges of his wounds.

"You didn't do anything. Not by choice," Tash said. "This time, the thralls didn't come alone." He looked at Aravel, who stood twenty feet away, between two trees. She still held her scimitar. Black goo dripped from the blade, vanishing into smoke before it hit the ground. Kiana read panic or bewilderment in the wideness of her eyes.

"Forgive my language, but what the fornicating hells just happened?" She held her scimitar at arm's length to avoid any splatter.

Tash looked at Kiana. "A Deep One was here, in the disturbingly pallid flesh. He seemed to be controlling you."

Kiana shuddered. "I didn't know what was happening. He had me in some kind of hallucination, asking me where the Shiver Tree was." She looked at Tash. "I could hear your voice, though. You said not to let him touch me."

Tash nodded and bent down to the thrall's corpse. He pointed at a black smudge on the man's temple. "I noticed similar marks on other thralls we've fought. Didn't piece together for me until now." He stood. "I think a Deep One has to make physical contact in order to fully take over someone's mind, hit that point of no return. He only got you from a distance."

Like Ravaini's friend in Old Home, Kiana thought. "Makes sense," she said.

"Oren wasn't so lucky," Reyan added somberly. He pointed to the first body. "He's from Estlin. He knew I had business in Garrison. Maybe the Deep One enthralled him as a guide since we threw them off our trail. Whatever the case, looks like they found this camp and forged another thrall to greet us." He indicated the second corpse.

"I'm so sorry, Reyan," Kiana said.

The ranger lifted his head and squinted into the trees. Kiana didn't press.

"How did you get rid of the Deep One?" she asked.

"The creep had some sort of magic-dampening field around him," Aravel said, joining them around the body. "So I pulled out my trusty old friend." She held up the scimitar, now almost clean. The blade's orange tint gleamed in the moonlight. "Seems he didn't like the feel of Crucian metal in his shoulder. Teleported right on out of here."

"They can teleport?"

"So it would seem," Tash answered grimly.

Kiana sighed. "Fantastic."

The last of the Deep One's blood fell from the blade with an audible hiss. Aravel's head and shoulders jerked in a shiver.

"Well, good. At least it's not getting creepier."

"Let's hope it was just the two of them," Kiana said, still shaking off the effects of the illusion, not sure she could trust her eyes. Or her hands. She made sure to secure her dagger against her thigh, then tried to still the trembling in her fingers as she felt for the chain around her neck. She tugged the pendant out from beneath her dress. A jagged, diagonal crack bisected the midnight stone.

"How the hells did that happen?" Aravel said.

Kiana closed her eyes. "The Deep One. He knew the agate was concealing our location."

"Are you all right?" Tash said gently from beside her.

Kiana wobbled her head, neither a yes nor a no.

"I can still feel him in my head. Just traces, inklings, but there nonetheless."

Tash squinted into the darkened swamp. "We'll keep an extra-sharp watch tonight, pick up the pace tomorrow. Maybe we can get ahead of them somehow."

Kiana nodded her muddled head. She needed sleep. Maybe a good night's rest could clear her mind.

CHAPTER FOURTEEN

A ship glides along the water, white sails billowing in the summer wind. Beneath the clear blue sky, crewmen stand at their posts, going about their daily tasks. Ten people move about the top deck. Why have they come here? What do they want?

Invisible among the waves, she floats closer, appraising. Portholes line the starboard side, several open. That's her way in. Under the guise of a swell in the sea, she rises to the level of an opening and enters. She moves through the compartment. Voices drift, muted, down the passageway. She passes one closed door after another before coming to the source of the sounds.

"The time is drawing closer. This will eliminate the need to manipulate the ore ourselves."

Through the gap beneath the door, she sees the one who speaks. An elf, pale and haughty. His black hair falls down his back. A piece of dark leather, pierced by a carved wooden stick, holds one section of his hair back. A strange symbol adorns the leather. Foreign. His finger taps a piece of parchment on the table.

"Father, I understand time is of the essence, but grave robbing? If they find out, it could lead to a different war entirely."

This voice is of a younger male, the speaker blocked from view. She sees only an arm resting on the table.

"They're far too preoccupied with the pirates to look closely at our affairs. I'm certain they'll attribute our theft to them as well."

Fury begins to swell in her core. For the first time in ages, she feels the call of her people. Though centuries have separated her from her druidic brethren, their fight remains hers.

"But—"

"Do not question me!" the older man booms. "I will not have Highmane fall because you are weak and scared."

She gathers herself, a brewing tempest. Renewed clarity burns through her mind. This will not stand. The storm inside her builds quickly. She races down the passage, strength and fury growing. Shouts echo somewhere behind her, but she pays them no heed.

As she bursts through the hull, wood splintering around her with the force of her explosive exit, only one word reaches her ears, reverberating around her.

"Tash!"

She vanishes into the mist.

Crying out with the ghost of a sob, Kiana woke. Beside her, Tash remained unmoving, still at rest. Even through the perfect warmth of her cloak, Kiana felt a deep, penetrating cold settle into her bones. Her hands trembled. Again the name Soran flitted through her mind.

The sound of her startling awake drew Reyan's stare from where he perched on a stump at the edge of camp on sentry duty. Through Kiana's sleepy haze and unshed tears, his eyes glowed in the early-morning light. He gave her a querying look, which she waved away, and he went back to scanning the trees.

Kiana had relived the day of the explosion countless times over the last year, always guessing at the unknowns. To see it from this alternate perspective filled her with renewed anguish. Was it real?

If this was, in fact, a vision and not a mere dream summoned by the anxieties of Kiana's subconscious, the people on that ship had been killed by Soran's anger. And that wasn't even the most alarming revelation.

The elves of Highmane were involved in the theft of the Crucian metal.

Had that been Tash in her dream, talking to his father? Or was it his older brother, Tem? She'd recognized Kellen immediately, though her dream self did not know him. Kiana had seen him minutes later that day, fighting through the debris to get to shore. The leather he wore in his hair bore the Ilirian family crest.

Tash couldn't possibly know, Kiana thought. *He would never go along with it.*

Their conversation from the week before came back to her in flashes.

Secrecy has been drilled into me.

The most heinous criminals or vicious tyrants Amarra has seen . . .

He'd been hiding something that night. Even as he opened up to share his secret, a part of him had stayed closed off. Now the possibilities buzzed in Kiana's brain like a swarm of angry bees.

She couldn't take this right now. Not after the Deep One.

The Deep One.

Kiana could still sense the faintest tingle of his presence in her mind, like a dream she couldn't quite remember. Was he the one responsible for these visions of Soran, first her assault and now her existence as the wild jinn? Had he invaded her mind before, triggered them somehow? She pressed her palms to her head in frustration, then turned to Tash. Seeing his face as he slept, she tried to imagine him being complicit in desecrating the graves of her people, stealing from them. She couldn't do it. The Tash she knew would never be party to such a violation. But Tem? He'd seemed so kind too. None of it made sense.

Tash stirred. Before he could wake, Kiana rose and went to Reyan, stepping over a sleeping Snow and Aravel, who had given up on her hammock after all. The fox had moved to her sometime during the night, sharing his warmth along the length of her torso. His head popped up as Kiana passed.

"Everything all right?" Reyan asked quietly as Kiana approached. Snow enjoyed a deep stretch and then joined her.

"Yes. Just a bad dream. How much further to Garrison?"

"Should arrive by midafternoon, I reckon." He finished sharpening an arrow tip and blew on it.

Kiana nodded. "I'll find some breakfast."

"No fruit today?"

Too on edge to think about food, the group had been living on Kiana's druidic conjurings. Since one piece of whatever fruit she produced—lately figs or huckleberries—contained enough nutrients to replace an entire meal, no one had bothered gathering any other sustenance.

"I think we should change things up a little. I won't be long."

As she and Snow passed Tash, he stretched, now fully awake. "Where're you headed?"

She couldn't meet his eyes.

"Just going to find something for us to eat that isn't enchanted fruit. I'll be back soon."

"You want some company?"

"No."

The word came out terser than she would have liked. He gave a curious tilt of his head. Since she couldn't bring herself to look at his face, she could only imagine which expression touched his beautiful features. Confusion? Did he frown, hurt? She'd worry about it later.

"I mean, I'm taking Snow. And I really won't be gone long. Maybe you could build up the fire."

She stepped around him, Snow at her side. They'd only made it a couple of yards beyond camp when she heard the fire roar to life.

She walked with no idea where they were going or what she was looking for. She wanted to clear her head. Food would be a lucky bonus.

A quarter mile from camp, they came to a mossy lake deep in the swamp. Struggling to catch her breath, more from emotional stress than from hiking aimlessly through the mucky bogs, Kiana descended a small slope, Snow ahead of her, and dropped onto a peaty rock. Her reflection distorted with the movement of the water.

My relatives would kill to keep concealed . . .

My relatives would kill . . .

Kill.

"Stop it!" she yelled at the lake, jumping up. Snow crouched, ears back.

Her heart beat fast and hard against her ribs. Breath came in shallow gasps. She felt sharp pain as her fingers squeezed into her palm, nails burrowing. Several minutes passed before she sank back onto the rock. Snow trotted over and rested his chin on her leg.

She slipped a hand into her leather pouch, fingering the brass button within. Doubt crept into the edges of her thoughts. Maybe this was all too much for her. She'd left home with purpose, partly to find herself, but instead she'd found danger and deceit around every corner. They'd been lucky so far, but that only lasted so long. Luck wouldn't stop the Deep Ones. Perhaps she wouldn't either.

"Must have been some dream."

Kiana whirled around at the sound of the voice. Tash stood at the top of the slope, hands in his pockets. The druid tensed.

"How did you find me?"

He raised his left arm, the one with his bracelet. She instinctively fiddled with her own.

"You seemed upset. Reyan mentioned you'd had a bad dream, so I thought I'd come check to make sure you were okay." He took a couple of steps closer.

"What business does your father have in Solacru?" Kiana blurted before she could stop herself.

Tash halted, uncertainty narrowing his eyes.

"What?"

With a deep breath, Kiana continued shakily. "The day your ship sank. You said your father was going to negotiate a trade deal on Solacru." She balled her hands into fists. "What was the deal?"

When his answer didn't come immediately, fear began to blend with the anger working its way to the pit of her stomach.

"What was it?" she pleaded, voice cracking.

The outburst caught him by surprise. He lifted his hands, placating.

"Kiana, what is this about? I don't know what the trade deal was for. And we never made it there anyway." He took another couple of cautious steps forward, as though he were approaching a dangerous animal. "I refused a position in my father's business endeavors, so I wasn't privy to details. Another source of my father's disappointment in me. Orchelle and her father were going, so I tagged along for some time with her."

The mention of Tash's fiancée doused a bit of Kiana's anger. She'd heard the part about his refusal to join Kellen's dealings before, the first time he confessed to the animosity growing like a brambled wall between father and son. This time, curiosity got the better of her.

"Why?"

"Why what?" Frustration, maybe anger, seeped into his tone, sharpened it.

"Why did you refuse a position in your father's business endeavors?"

Now his anger flared hotter, though Kiana didn't know at what. Or whom.

"Are you going to tell me what this is about?" He kept his voice remarkably level. Perhaps his anger was not with her after all.

The vision swam in her head. All of the emotions, both hers and Soran's, hit her anew. For a moment, she thought she might be sick. She wavered on her feet.

"Kiana," Tash said, coming the rest of the way to her.

She didn't resist him as he gripped her arms, holding her steady.

"Please tell me what's going on," he said, the entreaty in his voice cutting through her anger.

"I saw him," she answered almost inaudibly.

"Saw who?"

She cleared her throat. Keeping her voice as even as she could, she said, "Your father, in another vision. The day your ship sank. At least, I think it was a vision." *No, certain.* "He was in his quarters talking to someone." The arm on the table flashed into her mind's eye. Details came slowly into focus. Smooth skin, slender fingers. An obsidian ring.

She looked down to where Tash held her. He wore a bronze ring on his right hand. The counterpart to the other, the one she saw on Tem's hand the night they came to Corval with Laera.

"Your brother," she said, grief flooding through her at having to say the words. "They were talking about robbing Tribali's graves for Crucian metal."

"They *what?*" The vehemence in Tash's voice sent birds scattering from trees. His eyes flashed angrily, and Kiana could actually feel magical energy radiate off him.

She pressed on, reminding herself his anger was not with her. At least not yet. "Your brother didn't like the idea, but your father said he wouldn't let Highmane fall because of Tem's weakness." *How does Crucian metal help Highmane?* She was too busy watching Tash's reaction to give it much thought.

For a moment Tash didn't speak, processing the information. Then realization dawned.

"And you thought I knew?" Those five little words spilled over with so many emotions. Surprise. Indignation. Hurt. He let go of her arms and stepped back.

Guilt washed over her at his pained expression. She clutched her chest, fingers slipping around her amethyst pendant in a hopeless bid for the comfort it usually provided.

"No, of course not!" Her insides twisted into knots, tumbling into each other, tightening. "I thought if you knew about the deal, you could prove the dream wrong, tell me it was rum or lasha wood you were there for. I'd never believe you capable of such a thing." *I love you.* She begged him to sense those three words, couldn't bring herself to say them out loud. Not in this state.

He regarded her silently for a moment. The impassivity of his face cleaved her heart. Did he believe her? Finally, his face softened and he moved to the water, eyes downcast.

"To answer your earlier question, I've chosen not to be a part of my father's business dealings because I don't always approve of the second parties involved." He sighed. "The other night, you said my family turned out fine in spite of the black dragon in our lineage." He faced her again. "I'm not convinced that's entirely true." His features darkened. "If what you saw is real, and not just some dream, then I'm certain it's not."

"You've suspected your father of other offenses?"

The hardening of his face told Kiana he was done with this line of questioning.

"If my father is in fact involved in the theft of Crucian metal, I will do whatever I can to ensure he is brought to justice. You have my word. But I'm not going to stand here and air my family's every transgression."

"Of course. I'm so sorry. I didn't mean to pry."

His anger deflated slightly. Heaving a weary sigh, he reached out to her. She pressed into him, desperate to wipe away the tension, meld herself to him.

"If anyone should be sorry, it's me. How could I miss this happening right under my nose?" He hugged her tightly, and she could still sense the peculiar tingle of sorcerous magic emanating from him.

In her mind, Kiana saw a black glove dripping with blood, a crow mask in a dark alley.

"Sometimes it's hard to acknowledge the dark sides of the ones we love."

After a moment of silence, Tash said, "Did you see it happen?"

Kiana broke the embrace to look in his face. "Did I see what happen?"

"The explosion. Do you know what caused it?"

She felt herself as the water jinn again, the rage swirling through her. Wood splintering around her.

"It was the water jinn, the one who used to be an Ice Druid. Her name is Soran."

"How do you know that?"

Kiana shrugged. "Part of the vision. When I woke up, I just . . . knew."

His expression clouded. "So you were right. She was the figure you saw that day."

She nodded, but it quickly turned to a shake. "If these are actually visions, and I'm increasingly certain they are, yes. I just don't know where they're coming from. What if the Deep One is still affecting my mind somehow?"

"Can you still feel him?"

"Yes," she whispered. "But something about these dreams, these visions, it feels right. Like I'm seeing the truth. There just . . . there has to be more to it." She hated herself for the next words that left her mouth. "Is there something else you're not telling me? About that day?"

The question had the predicted effect. Indignation turned Tash's body rigid, his expression something Kiana wished never to see again.

"There are lots of things I'm not telling you, Kiana. I've already said so. But I don't see how any of them relate to either the Deep Ones or the Shiver Tree." He peered out at the lake through narrowed eyes. "It's bad enough having a family who questions my allegiance, my devotion." His voice lowered. "After everything we've been through, I didn't think I'd have to face the same from you." He pulled a cloth pouch from his coat pocket. "We should go. I saw some tree nuts on the way through that we can take back for breakfast."

He brushed past her and she watched him go, her stunned rebuttal resting on frozen lips.

A few hours later, the bone-weary travelers caught sight of the city of Garrison atop its legendary plateau. All that could be seen of the city itself from the party's position down below was a large stone wall erected around the perimeter, which ran up to within thirty or forty yards of the plateau's edge. The steep cliffs surrounding the city on all sides would be nearly impossible for enemies to scale without the benefit of flying mounts or loads of extra gear. The strategic positioning was flawless.

"Kiana and I won't have a problem, but how are you ground-bounds going to get up there?" Aravel said, breaking the uncharacteristic silence she had maintained since breakfast. Though she'd cast curious glances between Kiana and Tash all morning, likely speculating about the fresh tension, she'd kept her thoughts to herself. Now she stood with her fists on her hips, staring up at the perimeter wall.

"They've rigged up a pulley system, one on either side of the plateau, that carries people to the top." Reyan tucked his bow across his back. "I recommend we all take the southern lift. They have a tendency to shoot things out of the sky when they fly too close to the city unannounced."

"Friendly folks," Aravel muttered.

"Smart folks," Reyan corrected. "When you live in a city with a rep-utation for being impenetrable, you keep it that way."

"Then let's go meet them!" Aravel set off, leading the party toward the plateau.

Two burly humans stood guard on either side of the lift, both clutch-ing glaives. Inside the lift, another human held a crossbow. All three men watched Kiana and crew carefully as they neared.

"Something we can help you with?" the one with the crossbow asked once they stood within speaking distance.

"I've some business with Brek," Reyan said. "I'm here to pick up my order." He pulled a token from a pouch on his belt and held it up.

The man nodded and inclined his head to the others.

"And you lot?"

"They're with me," Reyan declared, his tone not inviting discussion.

"Very well."

The man opened the small wooden gate and let them onto the lift. Five people and a fox didn't even fill the spacious compartment halfway.

"Is this how you spend your day?" Aravel asked the man. "You just wait down here in case someone needs a ride to the city?"

The man glared at her.

"Not that it's any of your business, but it just so happens we're ex-pecting some folks any minute. Normally I'm topside on guard duty."

"I didn't mean to imply operating this contraption isn't a noble pursuit. I just can't imagine there's a pressing need for such a devoted position every day."

"Normally. Lately, you'd be surprised."

The lift reached the top of the plateau. Everyone, save for the oper-ator, got out. The moment the others disembarked, the man began his journey back down without so much as a goodbye.

"Like I said, friendly folks." Aravel cocked an eyebrow at Reyan.

Half a dozen more guards stared down at them from a catwalk atop the perimeter wall. Most held glaives like the two below, but a couple sported longbows, arrows nocked.

"State your business," one of the guards called down.

"We're customers of Brek, here to pick up an order," Reyan hollered back, token in an outstretched hand. The symbol on it flashed blue.

"You and half the continent," the man retorted bitterly.

The companions traded puzzled glances. A few seconds later, the massive wooden gate creaked and started to open, its mechanism clinking and clanking under the strain of the weight.

The inside of the city very much resembled the outside. Stone walls, though shorter than the one the group had just entered through, ran throughout the city in an almost mazelike fashion. Squat stone buildings peppered the scant open areas. Soldiers patrolled the passageways in either pairs or orderly lines of four.

"If I didn't know better, I'd think these people were actively at war," Kiana said as eight more soldiers marched by.

At the city center they found a huge citadel, no doubt housing a smaller version of what they'd just walked through. Around the edges of the square, various shops and carts sold an assortment of food and wares. The distinctive clang of metal on metal drew them to a shop with an anvil and hammer carved in the stone above the door. Immediately to the left of the blacksmith's forge was a potion shop. Row upon row of jars and vials of all colors filled the shelves, some freestanding, others covering every inch of wall space. The plaque above the door read "Potions of Mercy."

"Feel free to look around. I'm not sure how long I'll be." Reyan disappeared into the forge.

"I think we should see what they have," Aravel said, peering in through one of the potion shop windows.

"Worth a look, I suppose," Kiana conceded tentatively. The lightness of her coin purse weighed proportionately heavily on her mind.

As if reading her thoughts, Tash said, "You two go ahead. I'm going to go see about replenishing our financial resources. Maybe there's an adventurers' guild in town we can get a quick job from."

Without waiting for a response, he headed to the opposite side of the square.

"What is going on with you two? You've been acting weird since breakfast. And that's coming from me." Aravel pressed a hand to her chest.

"Nothing, we're fine."

"You're something, but it's not fine. Tash has barely looked at you since you got back from gathering nuts."

Putting on her best conciliatory smile, Kiana looked at her friend.

"Like I said, it's nothing. Let's go."

She squeezed into the shop, taking care not to bump into any of the precarious shelves standing about the place. Snow lay down outside, wagging tail a safe distance from myriad breakable objects.

Inside, a medley of odors hung in the air. The acrid smell of vinegar stood out strongly against the somewhat less noticeable aromas of clove, juniper, and rainwater. Farther into the space, something peaty—fresh moss, maybe—tickled the nose.

"Good day, folks. Something I can help you find?"

A gnome with purple pigtails emerged from the back of the shop. A pair of round, black-rimmed spectacles perched on her nose, specks of blue liquid dotting the lenses. Keeping her eyes on her patrons, she plucked the glasses from her face and wiped them absentmindedly on a stained rag hanging from her green canvas smock.

"Just browsing, I think," Kiana said, looking around. "Though I'm curious. What's a Potion of Mercy?"

The gnome made a sweeping gesture with her hand.

"All the potions you see in this shop." She smiled impishly. "I'm Mercy."

"Ah, got it," Kiana said. She tapped a finger to her temple.

"Hey, look." Aravel held up a jar. "Balm of Fire Defense. Might come in handy if I have to fix your pants again."

Mercy gave them a quizzical look.

"Long story," Aravel mumbled, setting the ointment back down.

"How much do your wares typically go for?"

Mercy finished cleaning her glasses and plopped them back on her face. She shrugged.

"Depends. Potions run the gamut as far as strength and rarity. Cost runs anywhere from twenty gold to seventy-five thousand."

"Seventy-five thousand?" Aravel cried. "What potion costs seventy-five thousand gold?" She whipped her head toward Kiana. "That could feed the entire city of Corval for, what, a year? Maybe two?"

With a mischievous grin, Mercy beckoned them to the counter and hopped up on a stool that allowed her to see over the top. From underneath she pulled an intricately carved wooden box. She took a key from a string around her neck and inserted it into the lock. Inside, a vial filled with a roiling white-and-violet liquid lay nestled in a bed of plush gray velvet. Constant flashes of miniature silver lightning bolts illuminated the contents. Like all of the other vessels Kiana had seen about the place, it bore a stopper carved with an ornate *M*.

"The Tempest Potion. One of my finest achievements, and very rare indeed because it's so tricky to brew. Makes you strong as the Tempest Lord it's named for and allows you to harness the power of lightning and thunder without being harmed by either. Plus, anyone who touches you will get, well, a wee bit of a shock. You can also summon the winds and use them to fly. The effects last for an *entire day*." Her voice had become almost reverent, pride shining from her eyes like a parent watching her child perform the First Rite.

Both druids stood mesmerized by the swirling potion, awed by its power. Mercy snapped the box shut.

"But I can't imagine what two nice-looking elves like yourselves would need such a potion for." She replaced the box under the counter. "So, what are you here for?"

"Mostly passing time while our friend attends to some other business, though perhaps some healing potions wouldn't go amiss."

"Those I have! A variety of potencies. What suits your needs?" Her eyes drifted briefly to Kiana's Regent Tree. "Something supplemental would suffice, I take it?"

Let's hope so, Kiana thought. She willed away an unwanted memory of the Deep One's sinister face.

"Sure. How much are they?"

"Thirty gold apiece."

"I'm sorry?" Kiana squeaked. "Your lowest-potency healing potions are thirty gold?"

Mercy pursed her lips. "Not just mine. That's about the universal rate. As someone who uses magic to heal, I assumed you'd appreciate the value."

"Yes, of course. I apologize if that sounded rude. I've just never had the occasion to purchase a healing potion before. The number caught me off guard." She picked up an intriguing vial, the viscous contents churning like liquid steel laced with a subtle iridescent gleam. "How much is this?"

"The Potion of Divine Armor? Twenty-five hundred gold."

With an inward groan, Kiana set the potion back in its slot.

"So that's a no on the healing potions then?"

Kiana apologized to the gnome and turned to Aravel. "Let's hope Tash finds us some work."

"Isn't this city populated entirely by soldiers?" Aravel asked. "How does anyone afford these?"

"Locals tend to stick to simple healing potions and basic buffs—my bread and butter, you might say—but Garrison has a reputation that brings visitors from all over in search of the finest weapons and armor. You may have noticed I'm opportunely situated directly next to Brek's forge. Many of those seeking superior battle gear also have a need for potions. Just last week I sold three invisibility potions and two of those divine armor brews." Her eyes fell to the cracked pendant around Kiana's neck. "Your charm is broken," she said, brow furrowed. She leaned in. "Is that an Agate of Night's Veil?"

Kiana held it out for her to see.

"Took something pretty vicious to crack this."

The druid offered her a wan smile. *If only you knew.*

The gnome gave both druids an appraising glance.

"Tell you what." She reached under the counter and pulled out a second intricately carved box. Luscious green silk lined the interior, and a wooden ring sat atop the shiny folds. "I have this ring that I've been meaning to enchant in my spare time, expanding my business, if you will. But as you can see"—she waved around the shop—"I don't actually have spare time." She picked up the ring and held it toward Kiana. The wood was a gorgeous, richly hued rosewood. "If you infuse a little of your magic into this—I can show you how—I'll fix that there pendant for you."

Kiana twitched her head, stunned. "You can do that? You *would* do that?"

Mercy folded her arms across the counter, ring still pinched between two fingers. "Like I said, I'm trying to expand my business, and having an actual druid magnify this Ring of Thorns would save me loads of time. Don't get many of your kind around here." Nodding to the broken pendant, she added, "But I am, of course, quite proficient at creating and tinkering with enchanted objects." She winked, as all magically inclined gnomes were known for their skills at both tinkering and enchantment—even gnomish druids, the only nature mages known to have any proficiency with the arcane arts.

With a mere glance at Aravel, Kiana undid the clasp around her neck and passed the agate over to the beaming merchant. She took the ring in return.

"Let's go to the back for a few, shall we?"

Thanking Mercy profusely for her assistance a short time later, the two druids excused themselves and left the shop with one final, wistful glance back at the tantalizing inventory. Kiana rubbed the good-as-new pendant between her fingers.

Back outside, the druids scanned the area for any sign of their other companions. A woman hocking steaming loaves of bread across the square bent to pick up a dropped coin. As she did, she exposed a section of stone wall bearing an assortment of charcoal smudges. Kiana's eyes sharpened. Someone had scrawled "Be Vigilant" in haphazard script.

"What . . ." She probed her memory, trying to summon the phrase.

Old Home. She'd seen the words in Old Home.

Odd.

At that moment, she spotted Reyan strolling toward them from the citadel, not the blacksmith's. He was empty handed.

"Where's your cart?" Aravel asked.

"Turns out, Brek has been flooded with orders for weapons and armor from Byce. Apparently there's some big brouhaha down there. My order won't be ready for another few weeks."

"I'm sorry." Kiana squinted toward the forge. A tall figure, neck to toe in gleaming plate armor, pushed his way in, shoulder-length blond hair wafting behind him in the breeze. "Are there any other blacksmiths here?"

"Yes, but none with the skills of a Brek. They're practically legendary masters of their craft."

"*A* Brek?" Aravel said. "I thought the man's name was Brek."

"Sort of." Reyan spun the top off his canteen and took a long pull before continuing. "Technically it's a title, only given to the greatest blacksmith masters. They have their own names, but everyone just calls them all Brek. They seem to prefer it."

"And you can afford that level of craftsmanship?" Aravel folded her arms.

"Me?" He snorted. "No. This is for the entire village, remember? Took some saving and a few extra merchant expeditions, but we scraped together what we needed."

Before Kiana could ask how much, a large group of half-elves in battle-worn armor entered the square and marched toward the blacksmith. There were probably twenty in all.

"Looks like the customers from Byce are here." Kiana watched as one by one the first five soldiers entered the forge. The rest moved toward the citadel. Except the five at the back.

As Kiana returned her attention to Reyan, something niggled at her, owl ring flaring in warning. Movement caught her eye, and she grabbed Reyan and pulled him back just as one of the half-elves drew a sword and swiped at the ranger.

"Hey!" Aravel yelled.

All five soldiers looked at her, eyes glazed—except for one.

"How . . ."

The two shortest of the thralls lunged at Aravel with glaives. One reached for her back, fingers grasping at the hilt of her scimitar. She ducked out of the way and rolled, standing up in the form of a jaguar, teeth bared, fierce feline face radiating menace.

"So much for outpacing them," Reyan shouted, unsheathing his dagger and slashing at the nearest thrall, who slashed back, connecting with Reyan's forearm.

The door to the forge burst open, and the tall armored man stepped through. The symbol of Xendal, God of Light and Holy Fire, was etched onto his breastplate. Distracted by this new arrival, Kiana didn't get fully out of the way of the glaive coming toward her. The blade gouged her left arm as she threw it up in a defensive motion, drawing a thick line of blood. Snow growled furiously. The glaive came around again, a straight shot toward Kiana's heart. She knocked the attack aside with her staff, barely dodging away from a potentially fatal skewering.

"What is going on here?" the holy warrior demanded.

Two of the eye-glazed thralls looked his direction, and recognition flitted across the paladin's features. He raised a newly polished longsword.

Kiana took advantage of the diversion and leaped aside, tucking and rolling out of range. When she stood back up, the paladin was already cutting down one thrall and rotating to hit another.

"What do you think you're doing?" One of the soldiers who had gone toward the citadel was running back toward the forge, the others in tow.

"These men have been taken by the Deep Ones," the paladin shouted back, not stopping his swift assault. He grabbed one of the thralls in a chokehold and spun him to face the soldiers. "The men you knew are already gone."

Taking note of the silvery eyes, the soldier sputtered in confusion.

"But . . . how?"

Reyan stabbed one of the thralls through the heart with his dagger.

The fight was over almost before it began. Aravel still stood ready to pounce, waiting for a spot to open up in the fray, but the paladin had made quick work of the enemies. He pulled his sword from the chest of the one soldier whose eyes had been clear.

The men from Byce gathered around their slain comrades.

"I don't understand," one said. "How did this happen? The Deep Ones . . . they've been gone for centuries. How do you know it was them?"

"Where have you come from?" the paladin asked, ignoring the man's confusion.

"Byce," the soldier answered. "We arrived via the territory's only teleportation circle a day's walk from here, in the city of Arkem. But these men, they joined us just outside the city." He pointed to the body most recently impaled by the paladin's sword. "This one had a written order from our commander in Byce to accompany us, and his eyes were fine. He was the only one we saw up close. They followed in the lift separately."

"Take me to where you encountered them," the paladin said. "Now. And if there are any more abominations within this city, let us cleanse it."

He pulled a cloth from his pack and wiped the blood from his sword before sheathing it. Then he stepped over the bodies he'd just piled up in the street. When he got closer to Kiana, he stopped.

"You are injured," he said.

Kiana looked down to see blood dripping from her fingers. She dabbed at the wound.

"I'm fine, really. Thank you for your assistance."

"You are sure?" he said. "I can help."

With a smile, Kiana declined.

"Very well. Go with Xendal. If—" He stopped short, sharp gaze drawn to something behind Kiana.

She turned to see what had caught his attention. Thirty feet back, almost hidden among the onlooking crowd, stood a figure swathed in black. Smoke seeped from the sleeves of the cloak. From under the hood, cast in shadow, two solid black eyes peered.

"Sweet gods," Kiana exclaimed in a near whisper. "Not again."

Beside her, the paladin drew his sword.

"By Xendal's light, I will cleanse thee!" he shouted. His blade ignited in divine flame, metal glowing white hot.

Screams met this proclamation as onlookers scattered, leaving the Deep One standing alone. It threw its arms wide.

A deafening noise that was part hiss, part screech suddenly reverberated through Kiana's brain. She winced at the psychic attack and ducked into a defensive stance. Behind her, the sound of weapons being drawn mingled with grunts of pain. A number of the people closest to the Deep One collapsed.

The paladin charged. When he was within a few feet of his target, he swung. His sword hit air. The instant before the attack, the Deep One gripped a glowing pendant about his neck. There was a flash of green, a plume of red smoke, and the being vanished.

"That's impossible," Reyan said from Kiana's right, voice indignant.

Fear had paralyzed the druid's throat. She threw the ranger a questioning glance.

"Teleportation is impossible in Garrison. Part of their defensive measures."

"Apparently not anymore," Aravel said, standing up out of her feline form.

The trio watched the paladin bark orders at the soldiers from Byce. He led them off at a run, presumably to hunt down the Deep One and any remaining thralls.

"Should we go with them, search the city?" Aravel said.

Kiana watched the sure movements of the paladin, radiant fire practically blazing from his eyes.

"I think they can handle it on their own." She tried to hide the fear still trembling through her voice. Her head throbbed. "Maybe we sit this one out." She pointed to Reyan's arm. "You okay? Looked like a bad cut."

Reyan lifted his arm and inspected it. His sleeve was torn, but there was no wound.

"Lucky. He just missed me." He adjusted the fabric. "The guy handled his blade like a rookie. Must have been a new recruit."

Kiana frowned. "Guess so."

She thought of the glaive coming at her heart. He'd gone for the kill shot. Kiana paled.

They know.

"What's the matter?" Aravel asked.

Kiana swallowed roughly. Casting her gaze around, she asked, "Uh, we have a problem. Has anyone seen Tash?"

The companions shook their heads. Kiana sighed. She placed a hand on her arm and whispered a healing spell that knocked one purple leaf to her elbow before it vanished. The wound sealed just enough to stop bleeding.

"Well, I could certainly use a drink while we wait for him. Who's with me?"

A tavern called the Rope Ladder stood several doors down from the potion shop. They settled in and ordered meads all around. Kiana positioned herself where she'd have a clear view of the window and kept an eye out for Tash—as well as any more enemies that might have made it into the city and past the holy man of Xendal.

Aravel accepted a mug from the bartender gratefully, followed by Kiana. Both druids savored long sips of the honeyed brew, Kiana willing it to steady her nerves. This day was not off to a great start. She glanced out the window. Still no Tash.

"I just wish we could go one whole week without seeing hide nor tendril of those horrid, horrid creatures and their stupid puppets." Aravel cradled her mug.

Reyan grunted.

"Agreed." Kiana perched her elbows on the bar and rested her forehead on her fists. Her bracelet dangled an inch from her face.

"Oh, for Nelami's sake," she chided herself. She focused on the bracelet and immediately felt Tash's presence. He was close. She looked out the window and, sure enough, saw him saunter into view, apparently unharmed. Relief flooded through her.

She watched Tash consult his own bracelet, and a minute later the bell above the tavern door clanged brightly as he entered and made his way to them.

"Tash," Kiana said. "Thank the gods."

Thunk.

A heavy leather pouch landed on the bar beside her.

"That should get us by for a while longer."

Momentarily confused, Kiana eyed the bag and noted gold coins gleaming all the way up to the brim.

"Where did you get that?"

Tash barked out a laugh rimmed with bitterness.

"What's the matter, still don't trust me? Please, do let me know what else I can do to prove my fealty."

Turning on her stool, Kiana lifted her face to him, ready to bite back this time. Beside her, Aravel tensed, ready to defend her friend but unsure of the situation. Her eyes flicked back and forth between them. Kiana pushed up off the bar and stood. Tash's expression went from irritation to concern faster than she could blink.

"What happened?" He took her arm gingerly in his hands and inspected the deep wound running almost the full length of her wrist to her elbow, skirting the tattoo on her forearm. Blood still smeared across her arm and shirt. "Who did this?"

"The Deep Ones have found us. Again," Aravel said, relaxing slightly but still wary. "Where were you?"

"What? How'd they get in?" He produced a small vial filled with red liquid from a pocket near his hip. "I found a bank, figured that'd be faster, and easier, than trying to scrounge up an adventuring job."

"And did you *rob* it?" Reyan hefted the bag, eyes widening as if inspecting a foreign creature.

Tash frowned at Reyan and proffered the healing potion to Kiana.

"Don't you know who Tash's family is?" Aravel asked the ranger.

He looked at her blankly. "No."

She paused, apparently having expected a different answer. "Oh. Well, they're super rich, so . . ." She gestured to the bag of gold with both hands and made a popping sound with her lips. "That's nothing."

"Not nothing," Tash said, though his eyes still examined Kiana.

Reyan gawked at the pouch a few seconds more before setting it back on the bar.

"It's okay. I can heal it more later," Kiana said, declining the healing potion and jabbing a thumb toward her mead. "I was more interested in getting one of those at the time."

"What can I get you, sir?" the bartender asked.

With barely a glance at the man, Tash said, "Whatever they're having is fine."

The bartender gave a shallow bow and grabbed another mug from a shelf.

Tash wrapped Kiana in a hug, which she melted into gratefully.

"I'm so sorry I wasn't there." All trace of Tash's resentment after their spat had disappeared, at least for the moment. Something that felt like remorse filled the void. "How many were there? What happened?"

Kiana did her best to recount the events, still marveling at the paladin's impressive fighting prowess. Tash, clearly shaken, exhaled slowly.

"If they know we're here, we should move on as soon as possible. There might be more of them in the city."

"Not if that paladin had anything to say about it." Aravel smiled behind her mead. Almost to herself, she added, "I wonder if he always talks like that. 'I will smite thee, villain!'" She chortled.

Kiana ignored Aravel and spoke softly. "That's not the only reason we need to be moving quickly."

"Oh?" Tash leaned into the bar.

"One of the thralls tried to kill me."

Aravel squinted. "Uh, yeah, Ki. That's kind of what they do."

"No," Kiana said, infusing her next words with the weight of heavy significance. "They tried to kill *me*."

Tash straightened. "You think they found the Ice Druids."

Kiana set her mug on the bar top. "They must have finally figured out the clues in the book they took from Battle Tree." Kiana's face fell. "They were likely tracking us as a backup plan in case they couldn't solve it on their own. And now, they don't need us anymore. We really need to pick up the pace."

"How many have been killed and how many more have to die before this is over?" Reyan said from beside them, mostly into his mug.

"I'm sorry we dragged you into this," Tash said. "Bet you're looking forward to getting home."

Reyan downed the rest of his mead and slammed the mug on the counter. The bartender arched an eyebrow in warning.

"I want to stay."

"What?" Kiana asked.

"With you all. I want to keep going with you and see this thing through."

"What about Estlin?"

"For now it makes little difference if I'm there or not. I can send word back to them with the updated timeline from Brek. If I'm not back by the time the gear is ready, someone else can get it." He looked from face to face. "Whatever you're up against, you clearly need additional strength. I can't really explain it, but I've been restless of late. Seeking purpose. Maybe this is it. Please, let me help you."

"You understand what you're walking into?" Kiana said. "And that I can't tell you anything more than I already have until I deem the time is right?"

"I do."

An intensity beyond anything Kiana had seen in Reyan so far gave him a slight flush. The look of a hunter. He held her gaze steadily, and she nodded.

"Great, welcome to the team!" Aravel raised her mug. "Now we have to figure out how to lose them again, especially with kid gloves off. They may not need us anymore, but I doubt that means we're off the hook." She tipped the remaining mead into her mouth.

"It's a shame we lost that veiling charm," Tash said.

Kiana quirked her head at him. "Oh, about that." She held up the mended pendant, a grin brightening her face.

"You fixed it?" he said, surprised, and maybe more than a little impressed.

"I wish I could take the credit, but no. We swapped favors with an enchantress down the way. She mended the pendant, and, if she's as good as I think she is, she made it extra resilient. If we can lose the Deep Ones here, we might be okay. For a while, at least."

"You mentioned heading north, so I still think we should head for Eastdale," Reyan said. He pulled out a map, tapping his finger on a dot northwest of them. "It's a refugee haven, of sorts, as well as a trading post. A protected city. Might be a nice respite from the Deep Ones just in case they still track us somehow." He looked at Kiana. "Would this take us off course?"

The druid shook her head, smiling.

"Okay, great. So what's the plan for losing them this time?" Aravel said.

Kiana looked out the window. Crows scavenged crumbs and scraps by a baker's cart. She fingered the pouch of gold.

"I think I have an idea."

CHAPTER FIFTEEN

Two winter finches perched on the perimeter wall above Garrison's southern entrance. They preened themselves in the autumn sun, unheeded by the soldiers on patrol. Below them, Tash, Reyan, and Snow boarded the lift to leave the city. Once the three passengers reached the base of the plateau, the finches stretched their wings and soared off to the northwest.

On the ground, sorcerer, ranger, and fox hiked due west. Dense woods loomed half a mile ahead and covered most of the land between Garrison and Arkem. The trio trekked toward them at a steady clip. To their right, the two small birds vanished on the horizon.

Four hours later, Kiana and Aravel sat around a fire cooking up a pot of vala beans and brewing tea. Savory smells from their collection of herbs mingled with the spice of the tea and wafted through the muggy, bug-dense air.

"Do you really think this is going to work?" Aravel poked a stick into the boiling beans.

"I don't see how it couldn't. Even if they somehow saw us leave, who's going to track two tiny finches miles through the swamp? And unless they have All Sight, which I don't believe they do, they're certainly not going to see the others. If the pendant works, we should be okay."

"Speaking of, where are they?"

Setting aside her tea, Kiana tuned in to her bracelet. The mental tug was strong. "Not far. They should be here any minute."

Snow bounded through the trees fifteen minutes later. Excitement sent his entire backside into a frenzy of wiggles. Tash followed, with Reyan bringing up the rear. Both looked utterly exhausted.

"How'd it go?" Kiana asked, rising to greet them.

"I think we're clear. Once we were out of sight in the woods, we took the invisibility potions and spent the next hour moving at the fastest pace we could maintain before the effect faded." Tash eased himself down onto a log. "And I don't think we left any trace behind for them to follow, should they try."

Reyan joined Tash on the log and peered into the pot. "Smells good."

"Vala beans!" Aravel cheered. "Forgot we brought them. One of my favorite things from home. Just as good as any meat." She dipped a spoon into the beans and brought it to her nose, inhaling the aromatic steam deeply. "Mmm, yeah."

Reyan shot her a look. He pulled out a stick of jerky and gnawed off a bite.

"Anyway, we did what we could. Only time will tell for sure. And if they do know the location of the Ice Druids now, they may not waste the effort in tracking us anymore." Tash took the bowl of beans Kiana handed him. "Thank you."

"I don't know how they're traveling—I assume through the Shadow Core still—but I figure we can cut up through the swamps and pass into Southland by the southwest edge of Storm Lake. Even with the heavy bogs, it should be faster than trying to go around."

Aravel's head popped up. "Ha! I was wondering if they might be somewhere in Southland. Lots of cold mountains up that way to trap a fire monster in."

Kiana gave a nod of affirmation, her burden of secrecy lightening just a little. "Since the Deep Ones seem to know anyway, I suppose there's no harm in telling you now that we're alone. I believe they've made their home in one of the mountains just to the northwest of High Crag." She scrunched up her lips. "I'm just not sure exactly which one yet."

"How do you know?" Reyan asked.

Feeling rather proud of herself, Kiana allowed a rare smirk of satisfaction to cross her lips. She reached into her bag and pulled out her well-worn copy of the *Nature of Druids* book.

"It was actually this that helped me make the connection. The book I was reading in Battle Tree was written by one of the old High Druids from the time before the Orders dissolved. She had just finished some sort of ritual at the new, secret home of the Ice Druids. She was the only one outside the Order who knew where they'd gone." Kiana opened the book and started flipping through pages. "At one point, she mentions 'the warmth of the desert haven.' At first, I thought it was a location, especially translating over from such an old form of Elvish, until I remembered . . ." She plopped the book in front of her and pointed to the top corner of a page. A blossom with a blue-and-white center and brilliant orange petals was painted there. "The desert haven is a flower that grows along the northern border of Southland, but only high in the mountains. High Crag and the mountains northwest of it are the only places it could be, and High Crag itself is too populated for the Ice Druids to have lived there undetected for so long."

Tash blew out a breath. "Okay, up toward High Crag it is." He paused and gave her a crooked smile. "Nice work putting that together."

Kiana beamed. "Doesn't hurt that I've read this book a couple dozen times."

"High Crag," Aravel repeated. "High Crag . . ." She rolled the name around in her mouth as if tasting its veracity. "I wonder what the odds are of us running into a powerful druid between here and there. We could sure use a treewalking spell right about now." She looked forlornly at her arm, her Regent Tree's scant leaves clustered around the middle-most branch. "I wonder if I'll ever have that kind of power."

Beside her, Reyan shoveled beans into his mouth.

"What do you think?" Aravel nodded at his bowl.

Swallowing, Reyan dipped his head from side to side. "Not bad."

Aravel waited for some kind of elaboration, eyebrows raised expectantly.

"Certainly no match for meat, though."

The druid gave him the side-eye and went back to her own food.

Kiana contemplated their situation, fingers worrying the pendant at her chest. "I'll send a message to my father via blitz falcon tonight with our situation and timeline. That will give him a chance to start gathering troops. The bird should reach Tribali in a couple days. Nelami knows we'll need all the help we can get once we find the Shiver Tree."

"Don't suppose you feel like telling me about this Terror now?" Reyan looked around the group pointedly. "I've traveled with you this far, faced just as many dangers since we left Estlin. You still going to keep me in the dark on what exactly we're up against?"

Kiana paused a moment. "That's the thing. We're not sure what it is."

"What?"

With a sigh, Kiana gave him the information they'd learned from Wyatt Foxheart in Battle Tree. When she finished, Reyan began shaking his head.

"Is there a problem?" Aravel said.

The ranger let out a laugh, a sound they definitely weren't used to hearing. A hint of mirth lifted the sound.

"You're all insane," he said at last.

"You mean because we four are taking on an army of Deep Ones and maybe an ancient evil beast so dangerous it took the combined power of all the Druid Orders to capture it?" Aravel's casual tone clashed mightily with the absurdity of her words.

"Well, yes."

"We're calling for reinforcements." Kiana looked at each of them resolutely. "They'll come."

"Hopefully before you're staring down the chasm of impending doom." Reyan's lip curled in a half smile.

"You asked to come," Tash reminded him. "No one's making you stay."

Reyan held up his hands. "I'm not complaining. I'm still prepared to see this through." He lowered his hands. "I just thought I should let you know how crazy it sounds."

"Trust me, we're aware," Kiana said dolefully.

No one said anything else for a minute, perhaps afraid to give voice to the million what-ifs floating around their heads. They'd cross those bridges if they came to them.

"As long as we're confessing things, there's something else you should know." Kiana waited for all eyes to settle on her. "I've been having visions. They started in Estlin. Only two so far, but I think somehow Soran, the Ice Druid, is showing me what happened to her. And to the Shiver Seed."

Aravel looked at each of them, then back to Kiana. "What now?"

"At first, I thought the Deep Ones might somehow be responsible, but that doesn't feel right."

"Nelami, maybe?" Tash ventured.

"It's possible, but these feel too, I don't know . . . *chaotic*. The first vision was barely a snippet, more feelings, really. I'm not getting proper context. Why would Nelami do that? And why would she reveal your father's complicity in the theft of Crucian metal through Soran's eyes?"

Aravel started to come up off her mat. "I'm sorry, *what*?"

Kiana spent the next couple of minutes relaying what she'd learned from the visions so far, from Kellen and Tem's betrayal and Soran causing their ship's explosion to the water jinn stealing the Shiver Seed.

"Okay, if it is Soran communicating with you . . . *how*?" Aravel probed.

Kiana pulled in her lips, having no answer.

"Something to sleep on," Tash said. "And if you don't mind, I think I'll pass on first watch tonight." He arched to stretch the muscles in his back. "Slogging through swamplands at a near run for that long really took it out of me."

"Don't worry about it. I'll take first watch." Aravel waved her hand toward the group. "You three get some rest."

"I can stay up with you," Kiana offered.

"No, really. I got it. No blubber-faced mind thief or his shiny-eyed puppets are going to sneak up on me tonight." The druid's eyes flared purple and gold.

"No, I don't think they will."

After sending off the blitz falcon with a lengthy message to her father, followed by an hour of meditation devoted to the study of magic, Kiana tucked herself snugly between Tash and Snow. For a time she stared into the fire, unable to quiet her mind. Eventually, she squeezed her eyes shut and focused on the sound of feathers rustling on the wind, the smell of earth and honeysuckle and musk. In her mind's eye, jade streaks of magical energy formed intricate patterns, ever changing. A pleasant sensation caressed her forearm, like the tickle of seagrass, and her eyes shot open. She looked down grinning, watching as four new leaves unfurled along a branch of her Regent Tree. These weren't recovered from magic spent—her tree was growing. All of the real-world casting experience she'd been getting was paying off.

"I'm sorry about earlier," Tash whispered into her hair, breaking into her thoughts and diverting her admiring stare.

Kiana rolled over so they were face to face, provoking a disgruntled whine from Snow. "About what?"

"I shouldn't have gotten so upset." He grunted a breath through his nose. "I'm so used to facing accusations of disloyalty from my father that I suppose I see lack of trust everywhere I turn."

"You had a right to be upset. I shouldn't have questioned you. You have to know that I trust you completely. I just . . ." She shook her head, thinking it might dislodge the rest of the sentence from her brain. "I think I'm more rattled by these visions than I'd care to admit."

Tash ran a finger across her hairline and down her jaw. A shiver of pleasure followed the line he traced. "You're reliving someone else's traumatic experiences. Anyone would be rattled by that."

"I suppose." She bit the inside of her lip. "I wish I knew where these dreams, *visions*, were coming from."

"Give it time. I'm sure the pieces will fall into place."

Oh, how I hope that's true.

With Tash's reassurances floating in her mind, at last Kiana found the peace to sleep. The night stretched on in tranquil silence around her.

Mountains sheathed in gowns of snow grace the landscape as far as the eye can see. She sits atop an icy ridge, booted feet dangling over the vast chasm of mist and shadow below.

"The Tree will be safer here, away from prying eyes. I know it's not easy to leave the only home you've known."

The voice that speaks is weathered, escaping a throat that has surely seen many years. Kiana's head—no, Soran's head—does not turn from the view. A feeling of insignificance overwhelms her as she takes in the ancient, towering peaks.

"I'm fine, really. There is plenty to like about this new place. And Northland is not the same home I was born to. The time was right to leave." *She hesitates to speak the question that brought her out here, but she must know.* "Why have I been chosen to attend the renewal in Tribali?"

Rustling breaks the stillness behind her. The mystery woman moving closer.

"You've shown great promise. The elders agree you will make a fine High Druid one day. The replanting of the Mother Tree is a beloved ritual. Being chosen as our representative is a great honor."

Soran nods. Trepidation tingles along her spine, pulses a heavy beat behind her eyes.

"I've never been out on my own before."

"You will be far from alone. The festival will be filled with druids from all the Orders."

"Then why will I be the only one of our Order to join?"

Silence, then more rustling. A hand rests on her shoulder.

"There's much work yet to be done here to establish this place as our new home, to ensure the Shiver Tree is safe. Maintaining the stasis spell during replanting was no small feat, and we need time to confirm everything is as it should be. But we have every faith that you will do us proud."

At last Soran turns to look at the source of the craggy voice. A gnome in the winter years of her life looks upon the younger woman with kind blue eyes. Her deeply lined face tells the story of many adventures past. Snowy white hair falls down her back in a thick braid.

Kira. Her name is Kira.
"May Freya be with you, dear one."

"Ahem."

Kiana's eyes snapped open.

"Sorry, love," Aravel said, her face inches from Kiana's. "Hate to wake you—you looked so peaceful—but the menfolk think it best we be getting on our way."

Rubbing the crusty remnants of sleep from her eyes, Kiana stretched the nighttime kinks from her back.

"What time is it?"

"Late enough in the morning that breakfast is no longer reheated vala beans. It's more like"—she cast a grimace over her shoulder at a pot sitting above a pile of ashes—"sad, gloopy vala beans."

"What?" Kiana shot up from her bedroll. "Why did you let me sleep past breakfast?"

"Like I said, you looked so peaceful." Aravel drummed her fingers on her thighs, lips pressed together. "And I thought maybe you were having another one of your visions, figured it was best we let you get some more rest."

Kiana dropped her gaze to the ground, the memory of the vision still fresh. "You figured right."

"Oh? Anything useful?"

"I saw her home, Ari. Soran's home."

"What? That's great! Now we don't have to wander aimlessly through a vast and frigid mountain range."

Kiana scrunched her mouth to one side.

Aravel's excitement fell away. "You still don't know which mountain."

"Sorry."

The other druid sighed. "Maybe next time." She handed over a steaming mug. "Drink this; then we'll head out."

Kiana obeyed, slurping down the strong, citrus-scented tea. Notes of hibiscus and orange filled her nostrils, reminding her of home. She wondered how her father was doing, what he would say if he knew the things she'd been through on this quest. What she still planned to do. And Ravaini. What trouble had she found these last weeks? A sudden, deep ache filled her chest. This latest dream, Soran apprehensive about leaving her home to fulfill a greater purpose, unlocked a sense of kinship with the other druid Kiana had heretofore not experienced. She, too, had been reluctant to leave everything she knew. May her own fate be kinder than Soran's had turned out to be.

"You're up," Tash said, pulling Kiana out of her reverie. He stood at the outer edge of camp, Snow at his side. "How do you feel?"

What a complicated question, Kiana thought. "Great," she said instead. "I think I needed that little extra rest."

"Seemed so." He approached with something resting on his palm. "I figured I'd spare you having to eat that culinary travesty"—he nodded at the cold, congealed beans—"and got you a muffin instead."

"A muffin?" both druids said in unison.

"Where in the great realms did you find a *muffin?*" Aravel's eyebrows furrowed. "In a *swamp.*"

"There was a charming little bakery near the bank in Garrison. I saw this in their window display and knew I had to get it." He turned back to Kiana. "Candied lemon. Your favorite, if I'm not mistaken."

Another wave of homesickness washed over Kiana as she took the muffin from his hand.

"No, you're not mistaken at all." She inhaled the sweet scent of sugar and citrus. "Thank you."

"A-*hem.*" Aravel held her hands out from her sides, palms up. "You just bought the one muffin?"

Smiling, Tash reached into a side pocket of his pack and produced a second muffin wrapped in thin cloth.

"You know I couldn't forget you," he said.

"Cinnamon!" Aravel cried, apparently ignoring the slight stress put on the word "couldn't." She snatched the muffin eagerly from his hand. "You're not so bad, after all."

"What's the holdup?" Reyan called from behind them.

"Sorry, coming," Aravel called back, eyes glued lovingly to her muffin.

"Wait." Kiana straightened her back, purple energy dancing across her eyes. "*Nes mergi atur.*"

Visible only to Kiana, purple lines of magic rippled around each of the companions' feet as pockets of air created a razor-thin layer beneath them. She stepped onto a mucky puddle. The spell formed a translucent disk beneath her boot, keeping her firmly on the surface rather than sinking into the goopy mess.

"Okay, now we can go."

Aravel walked up front with Reyan, regaling the ranger with lists of her favorite pastries from back home as they went. When she ran out of pastries, she moved on to soups, and then fruits and vegetables. He was a good sport about it, though he did cast the occasional look of entreaty over his shoulder to Kiana, who merely offered a wink and a smile.

Tash buttoned his coat against the cold as they ventured into a deeply shadowed bog. Tendrils of moss hung from branches like threadbare, decaying shawls. Tash parted a curtain of yellow green for Kiana to pass through.

"You had another vision." A statement, not a question.

"Yes," Kiana said. "Different from the others, though." She dodged around the withered limbs of a long-dead tree.

"How?"

"I saw Soran before she left for the festival in Tribali, at her home. She was a gnome before the curse turned her, like most of the Ice Druids. And she was talking to someone about the replanting of the Mother Tree."

"What's that?"

Kiana shook her head, eyes on the jumble of roots and vines in their path. "I'm not sure. What they called the Monarch Tree maybe?"

"Well, let's hope you dream some solid answers soon."

Eventually, after two more days of onerous trudging, nights crowded around the campfire, and no more revelatory dreams, the marshy landscape gave way to rockier ground, the damp air growing crisper, cleaner.

Storm Lake now lay unseen but foreboding a day's walk to the north-east. Black, craggy mountains jutted up from the earth before them like rotted, broken teeth taunting them in a crooked smile. Smaller hills rose on either side of the travelers, lining a wide swath of shale-coated ground like stolid stone sentinels. Puffy white clouds dotted a stretch of pale-blue sky, the weather still tenable. To the northeast, blue gave way to silvery gray, and the clouds grew angry and black, moving swiftly with the force of unseen winds.

"Oof. Up and over, then?" Aravel frowned at the steep, jagged bar-rier on the other side of the river, now ten miles ahead.

"Don't really have a choice," Kiana said. "To get to the pass we'd have to skirt Storm Lake"—she tilted her head toward the swirling clouds—"and from what I surmise, that's far more dangerous than scal-ing some mountains."

"Why would you think that?" Reyan bent down and picked up a hunk of shale. He smacked it against another, bigger hunk and watched it break apart. He tossed what remained in his hand away.

"I read about it in a book."

Reyan leaned sideways and looked at the druid. "Another book?"

Kiana crossed her arms over her chest, oddly defensive. "Yes, an-other book. *A History of the Sky Druids.*"

"Sounds like a page-turner. What exactly did it know about the lake?"

"The Sky Druids are the masters of thunder and lightning. They were naturally drawn to Storm Lake as a settlement, especially given their reclusive nature, so I imagine they know quite a lot. The book says that the storm above the lake never ceases, that its waters are treacher-ous and virtually impassable, and that its shores are perilous to those who travel too near."

"Not untrue, but not wholly accurate either," Tash said.

"In what way?" Despite the fact that Tash had proved knowledgeable in so many areas, Kiana had a hard time believing he could know more about the lake than a book about the people who lived there.

"The lake does indeed roil beneath a never-ending storm, and passage across is treacherous, but the shore—at least some of it—can be accessed without too much trouble. The pass into Southland is frequented by traders."

A distant crack of thunder shuddered through the air, punctuating Tash's statement.

"You're probably thinking of the eastern shore, near Stormfront," Reyan said to Kiana. "Those borders are fiercely guarded. I doubt too many travelers venture through there without stirring up trouble."

"Why would the book indicate the lake was dangerous from all sides?" Kiana queried.

"You said it yourself. If the Sky Druids are hermits, they probably didn't want visitors." Tash shrugged.

"In that case, we head for the pass. According to the map you showed us, it should pop us out less than a day's walk from Eastdale."

With everyone in agreement, Kiana set off behind Aravel as they renewed their course to the river. She tied her hair into a braid, tucking the loose strands up front into her circlet. After two more steps, the world flashed white. Kiana felt the ground give way beneath her, there one minute, gone the next. She reached out to stop her fall, but her hands touched nothing. Everything vanished.

Garlands of jasmine and moonflowers drape across the square. Fire crackles in the night air, its light sending shadows across the stone platform erected beside a young elm. Music plays on the breeze. Everywhere people dance and twirl, laugh and cheer. The warm air smells of pine and the sea.

A faint chill hides in the breeze, though Soran barely notices, used to the cold. Around her neck hangs an ever-present chill in the form of a crystal so white it seems to glow. She strokes the pendant protectively, focused on the precious thing within.

"The rum is good, no?"

Soran spins around at the sound of the voice. At her side stands a young water jinn, about her age, his skin a barely translucent blue, hair a constantly moving wave of cobalt curls. She looks down at her own hand, which is holding a small glass of dark, aromatic liquid. A faint buzzing moves through her head.

"Yes, quite." She feels her lips stretch in a smile.

The jinn holds out a hand.

"I'm Mer."

Shale underfoot. Four hands gripping arms. Cold air on the face.

"Kiana!"

Reality crashed back into focus. Tash and Aravel each had hold of one of Kiana's arms. Reyan stood behind them, keen eyes alternately searching for danger and falling with concern upon the dazed druid. Snow paced frantically back and forth behind him.

"What the . . ." Kiana came fully back to herself. "That was new."

"What was new?" Aravel's voice came out an octave too high. "What in the salty seas just happened? I thought a Deep One had you again."

Tash's intense gaze read her like a book.

"A vision?"

Kiana nodded. "Apparently they don't just happen at night anymore."

"Anything useful?"

Kiana's slight frown was answer enough.

"If you're good, we should keep moving," Reyan said.

The druid nodded.

Picking carefully across the uneven terrain, the party remained tense, alert. Whether concentrating on keeping their footing or wary of another dream lapse, Kiana wasn't sure. For her part, the druid pondered the visions.

Why were they out of chronological order?

Was the Mother Tree really the Monarch Tree?

Why did the water jinn, and the Deep Ones, want the Shiver Seed?

Were any of them going to make it out of this alive?

She had no answers.

Bitter cold wind from the northeast slapped at their faces for the next few hours. Kiana pulled her fur-lined hood farther down her head and sent yet another silent thank-you to her sister as the magical cloak seeped warmth back into her cheeks. The bottom edges of Tash's long coat flapped wildly in the persistent gusts, and Aravel fought relentlessly with her own cloak, her irritation visibly growing every time the hood was snatched off her head.

"Tides of terror, this wind is ridiculous!" She let out a growl of fury as her hood whipped back from her hair for what must have felt like the thousandth time.

"With these hills on either side of us, conditions are perfect for creating a giant wind tunnel," Reyan shouted over the turbulent howl.

"Then thank the seas we're almost to the river."

Another twenty minutes of walking, and they reached the edge of the shale valley, the hills dropping behind them to reveal a rocky riverbank. The wind still blew from the northeast, buffeting them from one side, but the intensity of the gales lessened drastically without the hills surrounding them. They all rubbed hands over their chapped faces with relief.

Against the typical laws of nature this close to the lake, the river raced past them with uncontained fury, as though it were a caged bull freed from a pen and intent on crushing anything in its path. Whatever force controlled the storm seemed to be hurling the water out toward the sea with intentional ferocity. Though this area was only a little wider than their crossing to Mooreland, the journey would be much, much more perilous.

"Um, are we sure we want to cross here?" Aravel bent closer to the speeding current and was rewarded with a blast of spray to the face as water collided with rock. She hopped back and glared at the river. "Maybe we try further south?"

"There's no telling how far down the current stays strong. Could be all the way to Cinder Island." Reyan's face darkened. "And we don't want to cross there."

"Cinder Island?" Kiana said, voice quiet. "You mean—"

"Home of the fire giants, yes," Reyan finished for her. "What's left of them, anyway. I think I'd rather take my chances here."

"Well, I know how I'm getting across, but how do *you* propose to cross two hundred yards of angry river in one piece?" Aravel flung the question at both men.

Neither answered, but Kiana moved closer to the water, a smile tugging at the corner of her mouth as she gazed to the far bank.

"I have another idea."

"Oh?" Tash stepped to her side.

"Well, the same idea as before, actually." Kiana eyed Tash up and down. "Slightly modified."

"Intriguing. Do tell."

Kiana turned to face the whole group.

"Aravel, you and I shift into giant eagles. The form should be big enough to carry these two across." She gestured to Tash and Reyan. "That way we don't even have to touch the water."

Snow yipped at her feet.

"Yeah, what about Snow?" Aravel said on behalf of the distraught fox. "We'll likely each be able to carry only one passenger, and he wouldn't be able to hold on should something happen."

Kiana wiggled her fingers and felt the magic building in her chest. Her eyes flashed purple as the leaves on her arm animated and darkened. Her lips curled in an elated smile.

"It's fine. He's going to be a giant eagle too."

"Ummm." Aravel jutted her hip to one side. "Pardon?"

Kneeling in front of her furry companion, Kiana rubbed her hands along the sides of his face and down his back in soothing motions.

"You've got this. Just stay with us and you'll be fine."

The druid stood and held her palms up in front of her, focused on the newest leaves of her Regent Tree. As she curved her hands around each other and pushed her palms out, one in front of the other, she whispered, "*Fasalia figue suen.*"

Purple energy danced across her eyes. In front of her, red fur sloughed away, replaced by reddish-gold feathers. The pointed snout curved into a sharp yellow beak. Front paws elongated out to the side and became wings, while hind paws stretched into fierce talons. The fluffy tail short-ened and narrowed into a tuft of feathers. The whole transformation took only five seconds.

Four violet leaves vanished into the druidic ether. The fox turned eagle hopped up and down.

Pleased with the result, Kiana stepped back. The others looked on with a mix of surprise and awe.

"When did you learn to do that?" Aravel said quietly, mouth hang-ing slightly agape.

"It's one of the spells I've been meditating on at night," Kiana said. "Thought it might come in handy when I finally grew my power enough to use it." She rolled a shoulder and held out her arm. "Guess I'm there."

Aravel gasped and held her own arm up to Kiana's. Even after Ki-ana's loss of four leaves, she still had four more than Aravel. Simply having enough leaves didn't always mean a spell would be within a dru-id's reach, though. More powerful spells took time to learn. Kiana had felt the morphing spell unlock within her the previous night.

"Guess I have some catching up to do." Aravel summoned a spark of electricity to her wiggling fingers.

Reyan approached Snow and, gauging his new size, nodded in ap-proval.

"I think this just might work."

"Let's find out," Tash said, a mischievous grin giving his face a rogu-ish quality that sent desire flooding through Kiana. She grinned back.

Both druids stood next to Snow and extended their arms down their sides, fingers stretching toward the ground. In unison, their forms shifted to match the eagle between them. Kiana's eagle form shook her dark-brown feathers, spreading her wings wide. Aravel's giant golden eagle let out a high-pitched scream that was quickly whipped away by the wind.

"All right. Time to go." Tash approached Kiana's flank. He swung himself onto her back in a motion so smooth he seemed weightless.

Things didn't go quite as effortlessly for Reyan. Unaccustomed to mounts, the ranger first grabbed a fistful of feathers and tried to mimic Tash's graceful jump. His usual dexterity failed him in that moment, and his knee caught Eagle Aravel in the side, forcing an annoyed whistle from her and ending in Reyan lying supine on the rocky ground. He propped himself up on his elbows and examined the situation. Then, hopping onto his feet, he jogged twenty feet away, turned, and sprinted toward the large bird. With a flying leap, he landed perfectly on her back, though his momentum knocked another irritated grunt from her.

"You good?" Tash asked once Reyan appeared settled.

Reyan lifted two fingers in the air, a signal in the affirmative.

All three eagles took flight at once, launching themselves up and over the rushing waters.

WHOOSH.

The air current that hit them when they made it over the river felt like a battering ram. Kiana and Snow were knocked sideways and slammed into Aravel, causing both passengers to nearly lose their grip. Tash clung to Kiana's feathers with all his might, ducking behind her head to lessen the effect of the squall trying to shove him off her back. Reyan now hung precariously from Aravel's wing, both of them fighting to regain an upright position. Snow tumbled haphazardly through the air for a few seconds before managing to right himself.

The wind would not relent. Every time the companions started to make progress across the river, a gust blew them off course. Kiana felt Tash's grip start to fail just before his thighs pressed against her with renewed force, as if he were focusing all the strength he had into his legs. She turned her head and caught a glimpse of him raising a hand shimmering in an amber glow toward the tempest.

"*Veters espoktro*," he growled.

Slowly but surely, almost reluctantly, the force of the wind shifted. As soon as the air yielded, the eagles shot toward the opposite shore. Tash's body began to shake when they were just over halfway there, the effort of keeping the impossibly powerful wind at bay a fight he would lose before long. This wind seemed to have a will of its own.

Fifty more yards. Kiana felt Tash's legs begin to slip again. Funneling all her focus into speed, she kept her eyes glued to the rocky bank ahead, praying to Nelami to keep them safe just a little longer. Tash clenched his legs tighter, stopping himself from further backward movement just as Kiana heard a cry from her left. She whipped her head to the side and watched in horror as Aravel and Reyan were tossed by a rogue air pocket. The ranger lost his hold.

No! Kiana screamed in her mind, watching helplessly as Reyan fell toward the murderous waters below while Aravel fought to maintain altitude.

Ten feet above the river's surface, a streak of reddish gold snatched the falling ranger from the air.

Snow! You glorious, wonderful creature! Relief quenched the fiery terror that sizzled in Kiana's chest.

Distracted by the nick-of-time rescue, Kiana felt Tash's pull too late. They'd reached the other bank, and Kiana was headed straight for a snag, its dried-out, lifeless branches ready to impale her feathered body. And Tash's.

Letting out an earsplitting screech, she veered left, colliding with Aravel yet again. A tumbling mass of flesh and feathers crashed to the ground.

CHAPTER SIXTEEN

"That could have gone better," Aravel groaned from where she lay atop Kiana's legs. She glared up at the dead tree. "I will make you *firewood*!"

"Mmm," Kiana moaned.

"Everyone okay, though?" Tash fought to untangle himself from the two druids. Once propped on his elbow, he scanned everyone for injuries.

"I suppose that depends on your definition of 'okay.'" Aravel rolled onto her side. Blood carved a crimson path down her left cheek.

"At least we're on the right side of the river now." Panic jolted Kiana's head off the ground. "We did make it to the other side, right?" Her eyes darted around to take in their surroundings.

"Hey, you're all alive!" Reyan jogged up to the others, completely unscathed. Thanks to Snow. "That was wild."

Snow, a fox once more, whined his agreement from behind the ranger, fur ruffled and dotted with leaves and twigs. He seemed otherwise unharmed, though he'd clearly sustained some kind of injury to revert back to his vulpine form so soon. Only the imminent threat of unconsciousness should end the spell early.

"Here." Reyan clasped Aravel's arm, hauling her to her feet, where she wobbled uncertainly. The ranger steadied her with a hand firmly gripping her elbow. He used his sleeve to wipe at the blood trickling from a minor laceration just below her eye.

Beside them, Tash helped Kiana stand, clearing the dirt from her clothes, hands, and face with a flick of his wrist and a glint of amber magic.

"Thanks." She caught his arm as he moved to brush debris from his right shoulder. "You're hurt."

A foot-long tear in his shirt revealed a cut that ran across his abdomen, exposing a band of bronze and black above where torn flesh seeped blood into white silk.

Tash glanced at the wound indifferently, though he pulled his coat closed and rebuttoned it where it had come loose. "I think it's safe to say we all took a bit of a beating there. No need to waste magic on a trivial scratch." He gave her a reassuring smile. She relented, knowing his elven blood alone would handle the cut before too long.

Balance regained, Aravel stared at the foaming current, jaw jutted slightly forward. The scratch on her face was now barely a memory. Apparently she didn't feel the same about superficial wounds.

"What is it with rivers around here? Every time we get near one, something tries to kill us."

All at once, the current slowed, its pace now that of a normal river winding its lazy way to the open sea miles away. The crashing of rapids against rock ceased. No more frothy spray sprinkled the air. The party gaped.

"Maybe—"

A roar so loud that the ground vibrated beneath their feet cut off the rest of Reyan's response. Everyone froze, the sudden, inexplicable change in current forgotten.

"What—" Kiana bit off her question as a boulder smashed into the ground behind them with a thundering crash. Snow screamed in warning, ears flattened against his head.

Tash wrapped his arms around Kiana and whirled them out of the way as the enormous hunk of rock rolled toward them with unexpected velocity. Aravel and Reyan dove in opposite directions out of the boulder's path.

"What now?" Kiana screamed. Confusion and frustration burned through her.

Can we not have a moment's peace?

Another roar split the air. Kiana tracked the sound to its source.

"By the tides," she breathed, eyes wide.

Tash cursed beside her.

"RUN!" Kiana bellowed, feet already moving over the stony, unforgiving ground, Tash on her heels.

Aravel and Reyan had barely regained their feet when Snow shot by them in a blur of orangey red and white. They took one look back the direction he'd come from and quickly fell in behind him.

"Mother of pearl!" Aravel shouted.

Farther down the bank, two towering humanoid forms lumbered toward them, clubs larger than Tash held aloft in grimy, giant fists. Dull expressions slackened their faces as they stomped toward the travelers. Noses like lumpy potatoes sat beneath eyes shadowed under prominent brow ridges, and the mouths housed teeth that, though decayed and stained with gods knew what, could easily rip flesh from bone. One was bald, with angry scars running down each side of his scalp; the other sported a bushy mess of brown hair matted beyond the help of any comb.

Every couple of steps the giants let loose unintelligible howls and swiped at more boulders, sending the hefty projectiles hurtling ahead with questionable precision but terrifying force.

"I thought the giants lived further south!" Aravel cried, missing a step as the impact of a boulder juddered the ground beneath her.

"Fire giants, yes," Reyan said, catching her arm for balance as he came up alongside her. "Those are bog giants. They roam freely throughout this mountain range. They've expanded their territory from Mooreland."

"And you didn't think that was an important piece of information?" Aravel screeched.

The ranger dodged flying debris from another impact, then proceeded to nearly trip over a thorny vine that snaked out from between the rocks. "Shit," he cursed, exasperated. To Aravel he said, "Hadn't come up yet."

Battling both uneven and unfamiliar terrain, the party was losing ground. All except Snow, who bounded swiftly a good fifty feet ahead of them now. Behind them, the giants loomed higher by the second.

"Aravel, *Motea Libreth*!" Kiana shouted. At the same time, she clasped Tash's hand in hers. "*Mothiri librenti et miri.*" Aravel followed suit with Reyan, murmuring the same incantation just seconds behind the other druid.

As the magic took hold, their feet suddenly became unencumbered by the sliding rocks, grasping brambles, and haphazard rises and falls of the river's shore. They moved on air, finally gaining some distance between themselves and their pursuers. The giants roared in outrage as their prey slipped steadily from their grasp.

"You're a genius!" Aravel panted as a furious bellow echoed off the mountains, followed by a meaty thwack.

Chancing a backward glance, Kiana watched as one giant stumbled, righted himself, and then took a swing at the other. The huge fist connected with the fleshy collarbone, knocking the second giant back a few steps.

Kiana set her sights back on the path ahead. Several more yards and they were sheltered in the shadowy embrace of a thick stand of evergreen trees. They wasted no time losing themselves among the full branches of heavily scented needles. No thundering steps followed in their wake.

"I think they lost interest," Kiana said, breathless, peering carefully back through the trees. "Too busy with each other, now."

Tash shook crumbled bits of boulder dust from his coat. "Thank the gods they're dumber than a sack of yew wands." The sound of a heavy impact rumbled through the trees, then more shouting. "Let's hope they don't have more family nearby."

Aravel sprawled out on the ground, arms and legs flung out from her sides, eyes glued to a spot somewhere near the top of an ancient white fir.

"So much for tricking them with a little prestidigitation." She threw Kiana and Tash a significant look before rolling her head back to center. "This day is the worst."

"I don't know, I wasn't overly fond of the day a giant octopus tried to turn my bones into powder."

Aravel let her head fall to one side. "Fair."

Shivers ran along Kiana's arms, though not from cold. So many fights, trials, and close encounters set her nerves on the ragged edge. And plenty more still lay ahead.

Aravel sat up suddenly, propped on her left elbow. "What's that?"

The other three travelers moved to see where her finger pointed through the foliage.

Hanging from a gnarled fir limb twenty feet off the ground was a large net. Bloated legs dangled between the mesh.

"A snare," Reyan said. "Probably the bog giants'. They prefer their meat on the riper side." His voice was flat, a hunter assessing the work of another, but his face took on the stony mien of disgust. "We should cut the poor bastard down. Bury him before the giants can come back for him." He cast his gaze around the other trees. "Keep an eye out for more traps."

They stood beneath the gently swaying body, appraising the situation.

"That smell is . . ." Aravel suppressed a gag. "Not good." She pressed a fist over her mouth and nose.

The hand that hung through a gap in the ropes was marred by a scar in the shape of a broken sword, the top third of the blade bent at an acute angle.

"The mark of the thief," Tash murmured. "This man has been tagged by the clergy as a criminal."

Kiana clenched her fists. Visions of pirate raids in Tribali tried to sneak into her mind, unbidden. "Let him hang there." She started to turn away.

"I agree he's not worth the trouble," Tash said, "but if he is, in fact, a thief, perhaps he has something of value we can put to good use."

Kiana turned back to him, amused. "You want to rob the thief?"

"His corpse, yes." Tash shrugged a shoulder. "He certainly doesn't need his material possessions anymore."

Kiana looked up to the limb from which the net hung. The trunk of the tree was bare up to that point, no other branches to climb. The pines and firs surrounding it were the same.

"How do you propose we get to him?"

Reyan's fingers danced on his bow.

"I can try to shoot him down."

Aravel pushed past the ranger and stood at the base of the tree.

"Keep it in your quiver, Mr. Thein. I've got this."

Taking a step back, the druid tucked down and launched herself at the grand fir. Midway through her jump, her form shifted, and a pine lemur hit the bark and scurried up with incredible speed.

"How long do you think she's been waiting to do that?" Tash whispered to Kiana.

"Since the moment she laid eyes on those lemurs, I'm sure."

Aravel had spent far more time over the years developing her shape-shifting abilities than Kiana, while Kiana's spell casting outpaced Aravel's. Where Aravel could see a small- or medium-sized animal one time and assume its form, Kiana had to acquaint herself somewhat better with them. She'd made an effort to increase her repertoire of bird and feline forms, sometimes taking special trips with the sole purpose of finding new cats. Aravel's collection of critters ran the gamut.

Lemur Aravel made it to the net, hooked her tail around the limb, and swung down so she was more or less eye level with the dead thief. She then began rummaging through the corpse's pockets, tiny arms dexterously thrusting in and out of the gaps in the rope. When it came time to search lower pockets and the man's pack, which he still held in the crook of his rotting arm, she dropped onto the net, curled her tail around a loop about a third of the way down, and continued her investigation.

The results were a mixed bag.

First she dropped a lock-picking set bound in black leather, followed promptly by two daggers. Tash and Kiana let out simultaneous cries of "Hey!" as the blades hit the ground near their feet. Tash scooped them up. Next came a pair of steel pliers, which Reyan grabbed and fiddled with while they waited for more items to fall.

With all eyes on the adorable primate, Snow traipsed up to Kiana's side and dropped a plump muskrat on her boot, a trail of pink blood leaking down the brown leather. He tilted his head back and snorted a happy chuff.

"Ugh, Snow," Kiana chided, sliding her foot away from the dead rodent. "You know you can keep those things to yourself."

The fox pushed his prize closer again with his nose. He looked up and whined.

Kiana shook her head. "I don't want it."

Dejected, Snow lay down and put his chin forlornly on his paws.

Kiana sighed. "I know you're just trying to contribute." She bent down and picked the muskrat up by the tail. "Thank you." She tossed it to him, and he lurched to his feet, snatching the rodent from the air and trotting off to gobble it down in peace. At least he'd offered.

Kiana looked at her boot and grimaced.

Tash chuckled and waved away the gore in a flicker of amber.

"That truly might be the most useful trick I've ever seen," the druid said as a heavy leather pouch and a ring of keys hit the dirt.

Above them, Aravel had cut an opening in the net with a third dagger and now struggled with something in the thief's pack. Sitting against the ropes, tail still secured, she tugged hard with her little lemur hands, her nimble feet holding fast to the bottom of the bag. Finally, an iron lockbox popped out. Aravel inspected it for a moment before dropping it through the hole she'd made. Before the box even finished its descent, she emitted a high-pitched squeal of delight—or maybe surprise or alarm, hard to tell with a lemur—and scrabbled about in the pack for a moment before producing a vial. An empty vial, from the look of it.

Lemur Aravel held the vial over her head like a trophy, chattering wildly.

"She seems awfully excited about an empty vial," Kiana murmured.

"It's not empty." Tash smiled, eyeing Aravel as she collected a few more items in one furry arm and leaped back onto the trunk of the tree. The trip back to the ground was somewhat less graceful than the ascent, thanks to the loot practically spilling from her grasp.

Reyan had caught the lockbox before it could hit the ground, saving anything breakable inside from potentially shattering, and now sat with his back to the tree, going through the lock-picking set. Snow, done with his afternoon snack, settled down beside him to watch.

Back on the ground, Aravel deposited her finds at Kiana's and Tash's feet. In a blink, she reverted to her elven form. She still held the vial.

"Look!" She held the empty-looking vial up to Kiana's face. A few specks of what might have been dust floated lazily within the tube.

"Yes, I see it," Kiana said, suddenly noticing a detail she hadn't seen from far away. An ornate *M* on the vial's stopper. Recognition dawned, and Kiana smiled. "Another invisibility potion."

"How great is that?" Aravel took back the potion and admired the imperceptible contents. "And we didn't have to pay another nine million gold for it, or whatever those ridiculous prices were. I still can't believe we used up almost all of Tash's gold on those invisibility potions for that plan of yours."

Kiana bent and picked up the third dagger that Aravel had dropped with the other items—a small mirror, a silver pendant, a full wineskin, and another leather pouch—and turned it over slowly in her hand.

"If he had this, why didn't he cut himself free?"

Aravel stopped ogling the potion and furrowed her brow.

"The thief? I highly doubt he was thinking too clearly when he got caught in that net."

Kiana and Tash both looked at her.

"What do you mean?" the sorcerer asked.

"Oh, he was poisoned, for sure. Probably stumbled into the trap half-dead already and couldn't summon the strength or presence of mind to free himself."

"How do you know he was poisoned?" Kiana asked, suddenly wary of the blade in her hand.

"Well, aside from the fact that he was covered in his own vomit"— she turned to Tash—"could've used your fancy fingers for that one, by the way," then continued, "his eyes and tongue were both swollen and purple, and his veins had a distinct dusky hue."

Kiana relaxed. "He ate moonshade berries."

Aravel tucked the invisibility potion in her belt and hefted the two leather pouches she'd scavenged. "Yep. Some people just don't appreciate basic survival skills."

Three consecutive grunts of frustration came from the ranger doing battle with the iron box. Tash walked over and stood above him, arms crossed over his chest. A look of amused curiosity quirked his lips into a half smile.

"You've never done this before, have you?" the sorcerer said, more of a confirmation than a question.

"What makes you say that?" Reyan asked blithely, jiggling a long piece of metal in the lock, to no avail.

"Lucky guess."

Reyan's jiggling became more desperate. Tash took a couple of steps back from him. Almost imperceptibly, he rotated his fingers in a movement that mimicked opening a door. As he did, Kiana heard the barest hint of a whisper.

"Otchkryst."

The lock popped open.

For a second, Reyan just looked at the box. He dropped the lock picks.

"Couldn't have done that any sooner, eh?" he said without looking back at Tash.

Caught, the sorcerer scowled. Reyan spared him a glance.

"I have very good peripheral vision. And hearing." He lifted the lid.

Inside, amid a bed of smaller gemstones and platinum coins, three enormous diamonds glittered in the diffused light filtering through the trees. Upon seeing them, Aravel's eyes practically matched their size. The two leather pouches dropped from her hands, forgotten.

"Holy Lady of the Wilds, who did this man rob? The Tors?"

"I imagine Amarra's long-dead royal family would have had better security than to allow a lone rogue to break into their vault." Kiana picked up the dropped pouches. Peeking inside, she found one to be full of ball bearings—useless—and the other contained an assortment of gold and silver coins. She shook her head in wonder. "Why in the wild realms was a man this rich wandering around in the middle of nowhere? And eating moonshade berries?"

"Maybe he wasn't alone, and this was just his cut of the loot." Aravel reached into the box and plucked one of the diamonds from its opulent crib. "Or maybe he robbed someone, some *bank*, near the pass, and this was the quickest escape route to avoid capture." She tossed the sparkling stone from hand to hand. "Whatever the case, now *we're* going to be this rich and wandering in the middle of nowhere."

"You don't think we should try to restore these items to their rightful owners?"

Aravel stared at her. Tash remained unmoving, arms crossed, a look of mild amusement tugging at his features. Reyan paid them no heed and instead began sorting through the gems and platinum while Snow dozed beside him.

"I mean, what if someone is looking for it?"

Tash stepped forward. "And so your plan is to, what—place an advert about a small lost fortune? I'm sure no one would step up to claim that." A teasing smile played on his lips as he reached for her. "I appreciate your desire to do the right thing, always, but these gems could have come from anywhere. Imagine the good uses they could go toward in our hands."

Embarrassment heated Kiana's cheeks. Her sheltered naivete suddenly felt like a millstone strapped to her back as she fought to swim across the ocean of real life, drowning her in useless guilt and misplaced optimism. After all the years she'd spent studying balance, morality, and diplomacy, all the years she'd watched her father persevere under the stress of leadership, she finally understood how little was black and white. Wisdom lay in shades of gray. Somehow it took robbing the corpse of a thief to come to terms with that.

Out of the gloom of her thoughts, a feathered mask appeared. The crow offered but a moment's silent testament before vanishing back into the void.

"You're right," she said, shaking her head. "Of course, you're right. I don't know what I was thinking." She ran a hand over her hair self-consciously, fiddling with her circlet.

"You were thinking of the poor fool who was duped by our decomposing friend up there." Tash's gentle voice soothed Kiana's shame like aloe over a burn. "I hope you never lose that selfless desire to help others, but it's okay to take care of yourself first, sometimes."

The cooling effect of Tash's words spread. Too quickly. Icy streams poured through Kiana's body. When she breathed, she could almost see the mist of her exhales. Tash's face distorted, blurred. And then the world fell out from beneath her.

Bodies twirl and sway through the night. Spirits are high. Tomorrow, the Mother Tree will be replanted in Tribali, the Seeds renewed. But tonight, they dance. And drink. Solacrucian rum hums a happy tune through Soran's brain. She and Mer have jigged, waltzed, and quickstepped their way through the last few hours, feeding off the energy of the crowd, off the light in each other's eyes.

Freya's Crystal pulses waves of cold across Soran's chest. She pays it no mind; the heat of the rum and Mer's touch and the bodies all around burn through any chill she might encounter. In fact, if anything, she's too warm.

"Do you want to get out of here for a bit? Catch our breath, cool down?" Mer says this softly in Soran's ear. A mind reader, perhaps.

In response, Soran nods, smile lopsided with spirits and giddiness.

He takes her along a wooded path to the shore, their hands clasped tightly as they race through the trees. The alcohol has begun to throb gently behind Soran's eyes. If not for Mer's secure grasp, she surely would have stumbled by now. The world seems to be tilting ever so slightly on its axis.

Their feet hit the sand. Soran slips off her sandals and digs her toes into the cool, soft granules, watching as her feet sink lower. She giggles but doesn't know why. When she looks up, Mer is staring at her. Not the friendly, warm gaze from before. His eyes are hard, shimmering orbs of ice and malice.

As if she's waking from a dream, Soran's head snaps to the side. Four hooded figures lurk in the shadows, chanting softly.

"What's going on?" Soran asks, her voice a small croak.

Mer only smiles, a cruel quirk of the lips.

"Here she is," he suddenly yells, "bearer of Freya's Crystal!"

Instantly sobered, Soran clutches at the Seed around her neck. She moves to flee, but her body has stopped obeying her commands. She's frozen in place. Terror swells inside her as she struggles to move her legs, her arms, anything. All effects of the rum have vanished from her mind. She watches in a haze of confusion, fear, and anger as Mer steps toward her. The other four figures move with him, their chanting growing louder.

"The time of our suffering is at an end. We will no longer sit quietly by while our world fights for existence. While you and your people do nothing to help us."

Nelami, help me, *Soran pleads, her mouth paralyzed, words unspoken.*

The chanting has reached a crescendo. The hoods fall back, revealing four more water jinn.

An invisible force begins pulling Soran backward, dragging her through the sand. Cool water laps against the backs of her legs. Icy prickles radiate out from her chest. She's reached the sea.

Please! *Her prayer becomes more urgent as a strange rippling sensation washes through her body.*

Mer stands before her now, eyes cold and mocking, like his words. This time as he speaks, he holds up his hand, and she watches in horror as the Shiver Seed flies from her neck into his translucent grasp.

The rippling sensation continues, and she starts to regain a little movement. She looks down to see where her legs meet the sea and gasps. Where once her body was, only water remains. She is *the sea.*

"Why?" she suddenly cries, her voice strangled and broken, foreign to her own ears. The words barely make it out.

Mer takes a step closer.

"To survive," he snarls. "We have Freya's Crystal, and you are forever banished to the sea, cursed to roam the island's coast as a forsaken jinn. Can't have you giving us away, now can we?"

"Why not just kill me?" Soran croaks. She tries again to protest, to beg, fight, and curse. Further words refuse to form, her voice stolen like the rest of her.

With a smirk, Mer holds the Crystal up to his face. "I'm afraid I must leave you now and get back to the festival." He clenches his fist, and ice engulfs it. He grins. "Your precious tribe told us the Seed couldn't help us. We'll just see about that."

He turns and walks away. The other jinn step forward. As one, they turn sideways, swing their arms in a circle, then push their palms out toward Soran. The resulting wave of magical energy sends her flying backward, away from the Seed, away from her family, away from the life she was only beginning to step into. The weight of her loss, of her failure, crushes her. She closes her eyes and lets the water take her.

With a sharp, desperate inhale, Kiana came back to herself. Tash had one arm around her waist, one hand cupping her cheek. His forehead almost touched hers.

"You're okay," he said softly.

Tears prickled at the corners of Kiana's eyes. She raked more air into her heaving lungs and wrapped her arms around Tash, letting her cheek rest against his chest.

"Why is this happening?" she whispered.

His arms enveloped her, held her up against the sudden desire to cave in on herself.

"I don't know, but I'm here. We're all here."

"She was so scared." Kiana felt the fear flow through her again, not her own, but as real as if she'd been there. She pushed back from Tash, one hand still gripping his coat. "It was the same as the first vision I had, but . . . more. The water jinn wanted the Shiver Seed to save their world somehow, so they took it from Soran and cursed her so she couldn't reveal what they'd done. They blamed the druids for not helping them."

"Well, the Deep Ones found out anyway," Aravel said. She offered Kiana some water.

As Kiana drank, Tash said, "When you say they wanted the Seed to save their world . . . how does that work, exactly?"

"He didn't go into detail." Kiana swirled the water bottle, thinking back.

Aravel snapped her fingers. "That's it!"

Kiana stopped swirling. "What's what?"

The other druid pointed to the bottle. "Maelstrom!"

"What?" Kiana held the bottle away from her. Tash and Reyan both shifted away slightly.

Eyes alight with excitement, Aravel threw her hands in the air.

"I know something about Water Realm history that Kiana doesn't?"

Clenching her jaw against her exasperation, Kiana managed to say, "And I can't wait to learn it."

"Likewise," Tash added.

Aravel dropped her arms. "Right, sorry." She cleared her throat. "Ages ago, around the time Soran must have lived, the water jinn faced tyrannical subjugation by a power-hungry despot who went by the name Maelstrom. Subtle, right? Anyway, his all-consuming desire to rule the Water Realm nearly destroyed the whole plane. I don't remember all the details, but at the time, beings from here in the Primary Realm rarely interfered in Elemental Realm matters. The water jinn were almost wiped out as a result." She turned to Kiana. "That must be what they were talking about."

It fit. The timing was right, and all the details seemed to match up with what Mer had said in the vision. But . . .

"How would the Shiver Seed help them, though?" Reyan voiced the question that was rolling around in Kiana's mind.

"That's a good question. If Wyatt is correct, the Seeds were created to trap the Terrors, not some rogue jinn."

"The imprisonment spell might not necessarily be specific to the Terrors. Or maybe the Seeds have other powers we don't know about," Tash said. He rubbed a thumb over Kiana's hand that still clutched his coat. "Yet."

Aravel gagged.

Kiana flinched. "What?"

"I'm sorry, it's not you. I was trying to hold it in." She swallowed another retch. "That salted body, lords of hells. Can we go somewhere else?"

"I second that." Reyan stood, tucking the pilfered items he'd retrieved into his pack.

"Right, we should move out of the giants' hunting ground anyway.

We've lingered too long." Kiana whistled to her dozing fox, and they set off deeper into the pines.

Half an hour later, they halted. Kiana's heart sank.

Trees as far as the eye could see twisted in blackened snarls, every needle dead upon the forest floor. Sap ran black down the corrupted bark.

"Another blight." Aravel approached the nearest afflicted tree. One hand stroked the trunk. She looked at Kiana. "Do you think we could . . ."

"Yes, of course." She looked at their companions. "Give us a minute. Well, perhaps twenty of them."

The druids stood at the edge of the blight, fingers intertwined, eyes closed. Together they beseeched their goddess.

"Blessed Nelami, Lady of the Wilds, our hearts seek communion with thee. We call on your grace for aged and for child, the power of nature and sea."

They repeated the hymn once more before their words shifted, a druidic cleansing ritual pouring out of them, lines of magic spreading from their feet toward the decaying thicket. They kept at it, fervor growing with every streak of purple and gold, until all at once they stopped. They opened their eyes.

A layer of green glowed beneath the brown, crunchy needles littering the ground. Gradually, the light seeped into the base of the trees, zigzagging up through the pattern of the bark.

"It's working." Aravel clasped her hands beneath her chin.

"It will take some time, but hopefully that's enough of a start." Kiana nudged her elbow. "Look at that, your first blight abroad. Just like you wanted."

"Do you think this will give my Regent Tree a nudge?"

"Undoubtedly."

"Hmm. Which branch? Jade or Spirit?"

"I imagine you'll find out soon."

Aravel rubbed her hands together. "I do love surprises."

"Here," Reyan said, suddenly at Aravel's side holding up a gorgeous purple sapphire.

The druid nearly jumped out of her skin.

"Aaahh!" she screamed. "Where did you *come* from?" She planted a hand against her chest. "I think my jaguar form just lost one of its lives."

"Sorry," the ranger said. He looked down at his feet. "These hunting boots are charmed to be virtually soundless." He held the gemstone back out, a little more awkwardly this time. "I found one that's the same color as your eyes, if you want it."

Aravel blinked. "That's so . . . nice." Confused delight lifted the word. She took the stone. "Thank you."

Kiana smiled at the exchange, but the sight of the gem forced her mind back to Freya's Crystal, the Shiver Seed, and their earlier conversation. They were still missing something. Perhaps Soran would have more answers for her soon. The thought both intrigued and nauseated her.

CHAPTER SEVENTEEN

Lightning danced a staccato, chaotic rhythm in the eastern sky where bluish-purple clouds roiled. Every half minute or so, deep, echoing booms of thunder reverberated through the hills, a beat faintly out of time with the constant motion above. The air felt electric. This close to Storm Lake, the force of the raging tempest was palpable, a physical presence warning away curious passersby.

The travelers stood atop a hill less than a mile from the churning shore of the lake. Even with the advantage of height and proximity, they could not see the water, which lay shrouded in heavy mist.

"It's beautiful," Aravel mused. "You know, other than the menacing-darkness-of-doom aspect."

"This storm has been raging for centuries," Tash said. "Most people don't even remember a time when the lake wasn't here. This used to be a lush valley."

A familiar foreboding hollowed out Kiana's gut and sent goose bumps down her arms. The library in Battle Tree came screaming back to her.

The Tempest Tree locks in a beast from the depths in the heart of a never-ending storm.

So she'd found Terror number three. It had to be. How she had not made that connection earlier—instantly, really—baffled her. The lake had been, and perhaps still was, the home of the Sky Druids, after all. She attributed her delayed realization to the stress of nearly being killed on multiple occasions over the last couple of months. For a minute, she simply watched the hypnotizing waltz of vapor and electricity, imagining a great, unknowable beast doing the same from below the surface of the lake. Was it sleeping, or did it face an eternity of imprisonment fully aware of its circumstance? Did it matter?

"You do know an awful lot about the history of Amarra." Aravel lifted an eyebrow. "Maybe I should pick up a few books next time the opportunity presents itself."

Tash smirked. "There's at least one thing you can thank my father for." He pointed toward a gap in the mountains ahead. "We should keep moving. The pass is just on the other side of this hill."

Kiana's friends began their descent, Tash pausing when he realized she hadn't followed. She remained transfixed by the unseen lake.

"Is something wrong?"

"The lake," she said. "It's guarding another Terror."

Aravel groaned. "You mean we're going to have to come back here?" She pointed to the electric clouds. "*There?* Are you sure?"

"'The Tempest Tree locks in a beast from the depths in the heart of a never-ending storm.' Where else could it mean?"

"Maybe we visit that one last. The Sky Druids don't like company anyway, right?"

"Right."

Casting one final look at the lake, Kiana huffed out a breath of resolve, lips set in a firm line.

I'll be seeing you soon, she thought. *Whatever you are.*

Descending the hill took far less time than ascending, and by late afternoon the travelers found themselves standing at a well-worn path between the mountains. Memories of a thousand journeys, of millions of rainy days and blazing afternoon suns, were etched into the sheer, rocky cliffs on either side.

"Heldur's Pass." Reyan's voice had a wistfulness to it Kiana hadn't heard before. Not that she had a lot to go off. He didn't talk much.

"Any horrible beasts we should know about before we go in there?" Aravel asked wryly, the shock of the encounter two days ago still too fresh for all of them.

Reyan's eyebrows and shoulders joined forces for a noncommittal shrug. His mouth inverted the movement with a fleeting frown.

"Could be."

Fists clenched, Aravel took two steps closer to the passage and leaned forward.

"If there are any giants in there, just look out!"

Tash nodded his head thoughtfully.

"That's done it. I'm sure we're all clear now."

Choosing to ignore his sarcasm, Aravel gave a curt nod.

"Darn right."

"Do you think we can make Eastdale by nightfall?" Doubt strangled the note of hope in Kiana's question. She looked at Reyan.

For a moment the ranger didn't answer, eyeing the passage before them. He turned abruptly to Kiana.

"It would go much faster if we flew."

Kiana wiggled her fingers, amethyst flecks sparking in her eyes.

"I think that can be arranged."

Three giant eagles soon shadowed the entrance to the pass. Mounting went far more smoothly the second time around, though Aravel still insisted Reyan ride on Snow's back, seeing as how they "had such a connection last time." She decided she'd fly a little ahead of everyone and make sure no surprises waited in the nooks and crannies of the mountainside. To everyone's great relief, the biggest surprise they got was a herd of mountain goats staring them down from their precarious perches among the crags and outcroppings.

Reyan hadn't hunted in more than a week, out of respect for the druids' distaste for consuming animal flesh, not to mention a lack of appetizing options, but Kiana could see one of his hands caressing his bow as they passed the herd. He'd been a little more on edge lately, keeping a little more distance each night around the fire. She made a mental note to suggest he forage some meat for himself, Tash, and

Snow when they landed. Maybe that would sate the hunter's urge for a while.

The farther they traveled from Storm Lake, the bluer the sky and the colder the air. The chill was still autumnal rather than the breath-seizing cold of winter, but even Kiana's resilient beast form felt the drop in temperature as the miles sped by. Luckily, flying cut their travel time significantly. About an hour into the pass, when the shapeshifting spell on Snow was waning, Kiana sent up a piercing shriek and touched down on the hard-packed dirt. The others did the same. Just ahead, the landscape opened up into Southland. Eastdale waited for them just around the edge of the northern mountain.

Snow yipped and shook out his fur as the eagle form gave way. Dozens of red hairs danced away on the breeze.

"Guess we walk from here." Reyan pointed north. "Should only be a few hours to the edge of Eastdale."

"It'll be nice to sleep in a proper bed again, in a proper room," Aravel said. "As much as I love spending time in nature, the nights are becoming a little too frigid for my coastal blood to handle." She spent some of her nights as a bear, Kiana now realized, for added insulation against the cold.

The familiar specter of guilt reared its head, needling Kiana's gut. She'd grown so used to her cloak's comfort that she had started to forget the others didn't have the same temperature control. Such a simple thing had become an invaluable part of her.

"There haven't exactly been a great many options for accommodations," Tash said. He glanced at Kiana with a soft smile. "Merely an unfortunate side effect of the path we've chosen."

Of late, Kiana felt like he'd begun reading her mind, sensing her self-deprecating thoughts and brushing them away before they could take root in her mind. This new, unexpected level of connection with him startled her.

"He's right," she agreed, "but once we hit Eastdale, there should be towns along the rest of our journey we can seek shelter in, until the last day or so, at least. And given our recent influx of coin"—she hefted her brimming purse for emphasis—"we may even be looking forward to a few nights of luxury."

The thought brightened Aravel's eyes.

"Can you remember the last time you had a nice soak in a tub? Or a tray of still-steaming biscuits and perfectly ripe fruit set before you like you're one of the Tors themselves?" She let her mind wander through the daydream, eyes unfocused on the path ahead.

"You can order all the fruit and biscuits you like once we hit Eastdale." Kiana smiled.

The city of Eastdale lay nestled against one of the larger mountains in the Oxidian Range. Size-wise somewhere between Battle Tree and Estlin, the town sprawled out in a collection of low buildings and dusty streets, with larger homesteads rimming the outer northwest edge. The scant information she'd heard led Kiana to believe the city had grown from a small fishing village into the largely self-sufficient home of expert weavers, stonemasons, and other artisans. With political chaos on almost all sides, Eastdale also served as a neutral haven for travelers seeking respite from whatever wars were being fought at home.

The five companions stood at the southern edge of the city, watching the lights flicker against the darkening sky. The shape of the full moon began to form above them. As if attracted by a magnetic force, Kiana's head swung to face north-northwest. Mist clouded her vision, and she could see Soran's boots dangling above the black chasm between mountains. The ones mere days away. They were close now. So very close.

Are we ready? Kiana thought. *Am I?* They'd faced down enemies along the way, but she'd never knowingly walked into a battle.

She thought of home, of Ravaini and her father, of the Tide Hunters who'd given their lives to stop the pirate raids on Tribali's shores. She thought of her mother, her face now a waning image time threatened to snatch away forever. And she thought of Soran, ripped from her life and cursed to spend eternity lost and alone.

Kiana's fingers tightened around her staff. She was ready.

"Are you okay?"

Tash's tender voice broke her from her thoughts. His hand touched her lower back just above the hip, spreading warmth into her skin despite the cold.

"I am," she said, and meant it. "Let's go find a place to stay for the night, get some food that doesn't include the words 'berries' or 'beans.'"

"Gods, yes," Aravel mumbled. "Who would have thought I'd ever get tired of those?"

An archway over the road into the south end of town carried a sign that read, "Welcome to Sanctuary." The party halted abruptly in the middle of the road.

"Um, did we come to the wrong place?" Aravel said.

"No, this is the town," Reyan said. "They must have changed the name."

The rhythmic clip-clop of horse hooves clattered behind them, and they turned to find a man driving a cart practically bursting at the seams with bulging sacks of gods knew what. At least, Kiana *thought* he was driving the cart. As he drew closer, she realized with no small amount of astonishment that he was, in fact, dead asleep. The brim of his battered bucket hat fell just below his eyes. He sat leaned back against the seat, arms folded across his chest, reins tucked into his belt.

"Excuse me, sir!" she called when he was within a few yards.

The man woke with a snort and nearly toppled off the bench seat.

"Wha—what's that?" He pushed back the brim of his hat and glared at the elf standing primly at the side of the road, her companions just behind her. "Who are you? What do you think you're doing, scaring an old man like that?" The burr in his speech rolled his *r*'s gently.

Sensing the disturbance, the two horses pulling the cart slowed. The driver snatched the reins from his belt and called them to a halt.

"My apologies. I did not mean to frighten you." Kiana inched forward. "I was hoping you might answer a question for us."

The man said nothing, just continued glaring, wild gray eyebrows furrowed.

Kiana cleared her throat. "We've been traveling for many days to reach the city of Eastdale and were told this is where it would be." She gestured to the archway. "Have we been misinformed?"

For a moment Kiana thought he might not answer. Finally, his glare relaxed, and he spoke.

"No, you've not been misinformed. We've just changed our name, is all. Seemed more fitting given the amount of refugees we've taken in these last few months." He looked over the group, assessing. "You up from Byce?"

Kiana glanced back at her friends.

"No, we're not."

"Is that where the refugees are coming from?" Tash asked.

"The odd one, now, sure. But most come down from Northland. The war seems to be reaching a bloody climax up there. Again. Folks just want to live in peace."

"And what's happening in Byce?" Kiana couldn't help but think of the downtrodden soldiers that had arrived in Garrison. Something down there was driving the need for weapons. Trouble seemed to be coming from all directions these days.

The old man's face closed off a bit, letting the question hang unanswered in the chilled air. He pulled his lips into his teeth and gave them another appraising look.

"Don't rightly know. All's I can say is the folks that come up from Byce have seen some things that set their minds on edge. Don't like to talk about it. We don't pry."

Kiana nodded. "Fair enough."

By this point, Snow had come up beside Kiana and was sniffing at the cart's front wheel. The man's eyes tracked him.

"That's a pretty little fox you got there."

Something in the man's stare made Kiana's stomach fall toward her knees, and she suddenly had no desire to find out what filled the sacks he carried. She stepped to block Snow from view.

"Thank you." Though her voice remained polite, the hardened set of her face made her point clear. *Back off.*

The glint in the old driver's eyes died. A wan smile crossed his face.

"Don't you worry. No one here'd ever go after a pet." He waved his hand dismissively. "But you should know, given our cold winters here in the shadow of the mountain, one of our core trades is . . ." He trailed off but nodded toward Snow.

Kiana sensed Reyan shift behind her. She bit back the wave of nausea threatening to toss her empty stomach.

"Thank you for the warning, Mister . . ."

The old man grunted. "Higgles."

"Mr. Higgles. And for the information." She dipped her head. "We've kept you long enough. Have a wonderful evening."

Clearly uncomfortable, Mr. Higgles ducked his head and flicked the reins. "And you as well," he mumbled.

They watched Mr. Higgles and his cart of mysterious goods disappear beneath the arch before they followed. Most of the buildings on the south end of town appeared to be taverns and inns. Rows of windows revealed fires blazing in stone hearths, tables set with food and drink, patrons laughing and dancing and otherwise throwing off the cares of the day.

One establishment in particular caught their eye. Set back slightly from the road, with a long stone walkway leading to a cerulean door with a gold knocker, the white building stood two stories tall, with two white columns on a wide front porch. Candles flickered in the windows, which were lined with gauzy cream curtains. The sound of a lute wafted from within. An arched gate stood open at the head of the stone path. The sign hanging from the top of the arch featured a fox silhouette filled in with an array of colors. It read, "The Painted Fox."

"Seems like a solid choice to me." Aravel gave Snow a good scratching under the chin. "Can't go wrong with a fox."

Snow leaned into the pets, chuffing with pleasure.

Aravel rose, and the three elves stepped forward down the path, fox out front. Reyan held back.

"If you don't mind, I'll catch up to you later."

Four heads turned back to him. He fiddled with his bow.

"Of course," Kiana said. "Take whatever time you need. We'll get a room for you."

The ranger dipped his head and headed off into the dusky streets.

"What was that all about?" Aravel asked.

"I think we've deprived him of his milieu a little too long," Tash said.

"What are you talking about? We've been camping and tromping through forests and swamps for weeks. Isn't that what rangers are all about? He even told us he practically lives in the woods."

"I more meant the thrill of the hunt," Tash clarified.

"You mean he misses killing things?" Aravel's voice held a bit of heat.

"Not everyone—"

"No use speculating," Kiana interrupted. "He'll tell us if he wants to." She turned back to the inn and nodded. "Ready for some proper meals?"

After allowing Tash to magic away the worst of their travel grime, the trio made for the warmth of their first indoor repast in days. A little bell jingled merrily as they stepped through the door as blue as a summer sky.

Just inside, a tall woman in a flowing white dress stood behind a wooden dais in a curved alcove, the sleeves open along the outsides of her arms and tied atop her shoulders. The rich mahogany hue of her skin contrasted beautifully with the billowing fabric of the dress. Her dark hair tumbled in silky waves down her back.

"Good evening," she said, her voice low and placid, a soothing, lyrical sound. "My name is Maryn. How may I help you this evening?"

Kiana felt herself smile, lulled by the welcoming tone. "We were hoping to get a few rooms for the night."

Soft lighting from the wall sconces and candles on the windowsills filled the room. The dining area sat to the left behind a thick velvet curtain, the same cerulean shade as the door. Kiana could hear muted chatter and laughter through the fabric. Directly behind Maryn, two staircases split off, one to the left, one to the right. The steps were built from a dark, shiny wood, while the banisters and railing up top were painted white.

"This place is beautiful," Kiana said.

"Thank you." Maryn flipped open a guest book in front of her. "I've been lucky these past few years, and business is booming. I just completed my expansion in the spring." She pulled a quill from an ink pot on top of the dais. "Three rooms, you said?"

"Four, if possible," Kiana said.

Maryn shook her head slightly. The movement jostled her hair away from her ears, and Kiana noted the not-quite-elven shape. "I'm afraid I've only three rooms available tonight." She eyed the party. "Does the fox need his own room?"

Aravel snorted. "He does rather fancy himself a prince some days."

Kiana smiled. "Actually, we have another companion joining us in a little while."

"I don't mind sharing a room with Reyan," Tash said. "If this foyer is any indication, I'm sure the floors are plenty comfortable in the rooms." He flashed a charming smile at Maryn. She reciprocated with a polite one of her own.

"Your room will have a chaise longue that should be adequate for a second guest."

Tash grinned. "See? Perfect."

"Psh, don't be silly," Aravel said. "Kiana and I can share a room. Certainly won't be the first time."

"I'm sure that's true, but this is supposed to be your lavish night of luxury. Don't you each want your own room to luxuriate in?"

"Reyan could be gone for hours. I'm sure one of us can partake of his room's luxuries while he's out."

Tash looked at Kiana, who shrugged. He threw up his hands in surrender.

"Fine, fine. I'm only trying to be accommodating."

"And we appreciate it." Kiana tucked her arm around his waist in a half hug. She looked at Maryn. "We'll take the three rooms."

"Very well."

Once they'd worked out the details, they retreated into their rooms, which were simply but beautifully appointed. As promised, each room had a velvet chaise in addition to a large, downy bed. Aravel promptly threw herself onto the mossy-green covers and let out a groan of pleasure as she sank into the feathery nest of comfort.

"Can't beat this," she murmured.

Kiana poked her head into the modest room at the back right.

"Oh, I think I can." She pointed at something out of Aravel's sightline.

Reluctantly, Aravel pulled herself from the bed and joined Kiana in the doorway. Pure, unadulterated joy washed over her face.

"A tub!"

Kiana laughed and kissed her friend on the cheek. "I'll leave you to it."

As she closed the door behind her and moved farther into their shared room, she heard a muffled, "I *love* water!"

Gathering a few of her things and Reyan's room key, Kiana walked over to Snow, who'd taken up residence on the forest-green chaise within seconds of entering the room. She kissed him on the top of the head.

"Be back in a little bit."

He deigned to offer a small chuff but did not open his eyes.

Kiana slipped out of the room and almost immediately ran into Tash.

"Oh! So sorry." She laughed. "Didn't expect to find you out here." She stepped back from him with a twinge of confusion.

He'd changed clothes, looking dapper in black pants, a crisp white shirt, and a wine-colored vest. He also looked and smelled delightfully clean. His hair sat perfectly mussed atop his head, as always.

"Have you washed already, then?" she asked. She'd only been in her room for five minutes, tops.

"I have," he said with his trademark crooked grin. "Thought I'd pop down to the bar and have a drink before we meet for dinner. Would you like to join me?"

Kiana looked down at herself and the clothes she'd worn for two days straight.

"I was actually going to grab a bath in Reyan's room before heading down, since Aravel is using ours and may never come out."

"Oh, well, feel free to use mine if you like. That way if Reyan comes back before you finish, you can avoid any . . . awkwardness."

"I wouldn't want to impose," Kiana said softly. Somehow a flirtatious smile found its way onto her face without her permission.

"No imposition at all," Tash said, matching her tone. "In fact,

I insist." He opened his door and waved her in grandly. "I'll save you a seat at the bar." He bent and gave her a kiss on the cheek, then wandered off down the hall.

Kiana stood rooted to the spot for a moment, sudden desire running hot through her blood. She let the beating of her heart calm down before she stepped into Tash's room and closed the door behind her.

When Kiana found Tash at the bar, he was deep in conversation with a silver-haired human sporting a well-trimmed beard and mustache. Just as she sidled up to one of the stools, both of them reared back their heads, laughing heartily but not loudly enough to disturb the pleasant ambience.

"Sounds like I've been missing out on the party," Kiana said, then thanked the bartender as he promptly set a glass of water in front of her.

"Kiana!" Tash cheered, clearly enjoying himself. "So glad you've joined us." He paused a moment, subtly taking her in.

She'd changed into her nicest dress, a silvery-blue gown that made her pale skin luminous, and her dark tresses tumbled loosely in relaxed waves. The Agate of Night's Veil hung between her breasts, sparkling brightly, somehow reflecting more than the low candlelight about the room.

Collecting himself, Tash motioned to the man beside him. "I'd like you to meet Mavric Aldeers, a noble bard who hails all the way from Dulin!" He turned to his new companion. "Mr. Aldeers, may I present the lovely Kiana."

"Pleasure." Kiana offered her hand.

The handsome entertainer stood from his stool and clasped her fingers, bending deeply at the waist.

"Oh no, it very much seems the pleasure is to be all mine, my lady."

Tash laughed and slapped the man on the back. Kiana gave him an indulgent half smile.

"So, Dulin?" she said, taking a sip of her water. "I thought that was dwarven country with all the mines down there."

"Right you are, my lady. Right you are." Mavric picked up his glass of amber spirits and tossed it all back. "Ah. You see, when I was a lad, I was traveling with my father, a trader from the western edge of Harrian, when he met a beautiful woman named Elsbeth, a hill dwarf from Dulin." His words slurred ever so slightly, and Kiana wondered how long he'd been here at the bar. He plowed on. "She so charmed him that he gave up his wandering lifestyle and settled down with her. I spent the next eight years there, till the travel bug bit me again and I set out to have my own adventures. But I go back every couple years and spend time with siblings, the nieces and nephews, writing all my tales down as bedtime stories for the children. I'll always consider Dulin my home, now." He gestured to the bartender for another drink. "What about you? Tash, here, has been a bit cagey on the details, but it sounds like you're out having a grand adventure of your own. If you ever need someone to jot it down"—he winked—"you just let me know." He noticed the water glass in Kiana's hand. "And please, let me buy you a real drink."

Before Kiana could respond, the bartender set a glass of honey-colored liquid beside her.

"Hope you don't mind," Tash said. "I took the liberty of ordering you a local mead, but I'm more than happy to drink it if you'd like something else."

Kiana picked up the drink and took a sip, savoring the sweet flavor, a hint of elderberry rolling over her tongue.

"It's perfect, thank you." She looked back at Mavric and raised her glass. "Thanks, anyway. And yes, I suppose we are having a bit of a grand adventure." She smiled at Tash. "Just passing through East—er, Sanctuary before making our way west to Crestlake."

Tash's head flinched toward her, and she leaned against his side, keeping her smile on Mavric. The Deep Ones may have already discovered where the Ice Druids ended up, but that didn't mean Kiana planned to broadcast their location to the whole continent after they'd taken such care to hide from the world.

The man gave them both a curious look.

"Crestlake, eh?" He swirled his fresh drink on the bar top.

His tone and manner indicated he'd caught the lie, but Kiana fixed her smile in place and didn't look away. She couldn't even deceive a drunk man.

"What amazing wonders draw you there?"

Kiana hesitated. Crestlake was the first name of a city in Southland she thought of that was west of where they now were. She racked her brain trying to recall any details, things to do, people who lived there.

"We thought we'd have a look around their Splendored Caves. From what I hear, the sheer volume of gemstones that make up the walls is astounding."

Thank the gods for Tash.

The Highmane noble peered into his glass nonchalantly and swirled its contents. The lie sounded so natural. Maybe she could learn a thing or two from him.

Still unconvinced thanks to Kiana's initial blundering, Mavric let the subject drop anyway.

"Well, sounds like a lovely adventure. Did I tell you about the time—" He raised his glass toward Tash and sloshed whiskey over the side. "Whoopsie."

Without a second thought, Tash flicked away the spill with a tiny burst of magic. Mavric's eyes brightened.

"Ah! I thought I sensed a fellow user of the arcane arts." Mavric eyed Tash as if appraising a fine jewel. "You're too chipper to be griffin blood, and you have too much sense about you to be fey blood." He gave a playful wink. "So, phoenix, then?"

Tash clinked his glass against Mavric's. "Right you are."

"Ha!" The mage slapped his hand against the counter. "Thought so! Haven't come across one of your kind in ages." Kiana averted her face to avoid betraying Tash's lie, but Mavric's eyes locked onto something over Tash's shoulder. "Oh my," he murmured.

Both Kiana and Tash turned to follow his gaze. The blue velvet curtain swayed, having just admitted a radiant Aravel. Never one for too many fineries, she'd opted to wear her favorite deep-blue skirt with a high slit up the right side and a matching halter top that hugged her slender frame. A gold belt joined the two together. After enjoying her first bath in weeks, her face positively beamed. Atypically, her long blond hair lacked any adornment and fell naturally straight down her bare shoulders and past the middle of her back.

Spotting her friends across the room, she waved and headed their direction.

"Friend of yours?" Mavric asked, straightening the cuffs of his pale-green shirt, which was embellished with gold trim.

"Indeed she is," Tash said as Aravel squeezed in next to Kiana with a hug.

"By the maritime gods, that was the best thing to happen to me all week." The druid placed a hand on her hip. "No exceptions." She held a finger up at Tash. "Not even the lemur thing." She plunked a silver coin down on the bar. "A glass of your finest wine, good sir!"

The bartender gracefully snapped up the coin and moved off to fetch her drink.

"I don't believe we've had the pleasure of meeting," Mavric said, reaching out a relaxed hand, palm up. "Mavric Aldeers, at your service."

Aravel flashed Kiana a "who's this" look.

"Forgive me." Kiana held out an introductory hand. "Mr. Aldeers, this is Aravel. Aravel, Mavric Aldeers."

"So he said." Aravel placed her hand in his skeptically.

He pressed his forehead to the back of her hand lightly before looking back up.

"A true pleasure."

"Ladies and gentlemen," said a familiar voice.

Kiana looked to a low stage in the corner of the room nearest the window. Maryn stood regally, front and center, arms up in the pose of one about to make an announcement. Behind her, the full moon glowed like the watchful eye of a nocturnal god.

"I thank you all for joining us this fine evening. For those who have just arrived, welcome to the Painted Fox." She dipped her torso in a shallow bow. "Some of you may know our next performer, who has come again to grace us with songs of distant lands." She made a grand sweeping motion as she said, "I humbly present Mavric Aldeers!"

"Ah, such tragic timing," Mavric said to Aravel. He gave his shirt a tug and stood. "Perhaps we can speak again when I have finished."

"Perhaps."

Mavric bowed deeply and made his way to the stage. The instant his feet ascended the platform, full performer mode took over, every gesture exaggerated, faux humility pouring out of him like wax from a melting candle. The buzz from his whiskey seemed to evaporate as he soaked in the enthusiastic applause from the crowd for a minute before bringing it to a hush.

As he began his first song, Aravel turned to her friends.

"Let's order something to eat. I'm famished."

They each enjoyed a decadent meal, blissfully unconcerned with the tab they had started. The wine flowed, the food kept coming, and Mavric sang song after song of vanquished dragons, smote hydras, and dazzling damsels in distress. By the time the friends lounged, sated, in their chairs, half the patrons had cleared out of the dining room, but Mavric kept on.

"I think, perhaps, it's time to call it a night," Kiana said, happier than she'd been in ages. For just one night, she refused to think about what the Deep Ones might be up to, where they might be. Whether she and her friends were already too late.

"I think the lady is right," Tash agreed with a smile. "I'll settle the tab."

On their way back upstairs, they left Reyan's key with Maryn, who assured them she'd get it to him when he arrived.

"I hope he's okay," Aravel said as they climbed the steps.

"I'm sure he's fine." Kiana meant to reassure herself as much as Aravel.

At Tash's door, the two druids bid him good night.

"Rest well, ladies." He slipped into his room.

In the druids' absence, Snow had moved to the bed and lay on his back, mouth agape, snoring. He barely stirred when they entered.

"Would you rather share the bed with a fox, or have the chaise to yourself?" Kiana asked.

"Either is fine by me."

"Why don't you take the bed. Feel free to kick him off if he's in your way."

Tossing off her clothes and tugging a simple slip over her head, Aravel snuggled in beside Snow. She leaned into the mass of pillows and seconds later entered the beckoning world of dreams.

Kiana moved to the balcony doors and pulled the brass button from her pouch, which she'd set on the table there. She rolled the thing between her fingers in a familiar, comfortable motion as she pondered the visions she'd endured so far, the snippets of Soran's short and tragic life. Fear, loneliness, anger. Such awful emotions to keep as constant companions. No wonder time had worn away at her sanity.

Kiana looked at herself in the glass of the balcony doors. For a brief moment, she saw Soran's face—what she intuitively knew it looked like—overlap with the reflection of her own, a trick of the mind. How long would she let her own fear, her guilt, keep her from taking the risk she'd so long avoided?

Dropping the button on the table, Kiana left the room.

The look on Tash's face was one of utter surprise when he opened the door to her knock. His vest was gone, shirt partially unbuttoned, boots stashed neatly beneath the table. The perfect sweep of his not-quite-tousled hair remained untouched.

"May I come in?"

"Of course." He stepped to the side, allowing his surprise to be replaced by tempered delight. He closed the door behind her and ran a hand quickly through his hair. The locks fell right back into place. "Is everything all right?"

Kiana took in the details of the room with a quick sweep of the eye. Where her room was greens and dark wood, sunny yellows and brilliant whites made up the space here. She spun to face Tash.

"I wanted to thank you."

He cocked his head to the side, confusion knitting his brow. "For what?" A small laugh stuttered his words.

"For always being there." She sighed. "I know it might sound silly, but you always seem to know just the right thing to say to save me from myself."

He took a couple of steps toward her, so they were almost touching, and he lowered his voice to just above a whisper.

"Kiana, you hardly need saving by me. Or anyone else, for that matter."

She smiled and resisted the urge to lower her eyes. Instead, she held his warm gaze intently. "I've been letting fear get in my way." She hesitated. "Fear of what you think when you look at me."

Confusion returned to his face. "And what, pray tell, would that be?"

"For the longest time, I thought every time you looked at me you remembered what happened the day we met. That maybe you blamed me, somehow. I know I did."

Confusion morphed to concern. "Why in the world would I blame you? None of it was your fault." His voice was gentle, almost anguished. "You have to know that."

"Sure, a part of me knows. But Tash, you lost your fiancée." She regarded the floor, gathered herself, looked back up. "That's a pain that's hard to get past. I would never dream of interfering with your grieving period."

Tash took a step back. "My—" His face relaxed, something falling into place for him. "I thought you knew." He sighed. "What happened to Orchelle was tragic. Yes, I grieved her passing. But Kiana, our betrothal was arranged by our fathers. A marriage of opportunity. That trip to Solacru was only the second time we'd ever met. I only went because I wanted to know at least a few details about the woman I was to marry before we found ourselves sharing a life."

Sometimes the truth was hard. Other times, it could set you free. "So . . ."

Tash stepped back into her space. "So I never truly loved her. My heart has been free all along."

A lightness settled over her. "And all this time I've been hiding behind a lie I've told myself so I didn't have to face my feelings."

He tilted his head. "And what feelings are those?" He brushed her hair behind her ear.

The last of her defenses evaporated. Finally, the words fell, quiet in their utter sincerity. "I love you."

The look on his face was everything she'd hoped for and more: joy, relief, pleasure. Love. He finished closing the distance between them. When his lips met hers, the endless ache of longing she'd carried these last months finally lifted away. His hand on her face, in her hair, undid her completely.

Tonight, Kiana Paletine chose happiness. Fear and loneliness could haunt some other poor souls.

CHAPTER EIGHTEEN

Smoke rises into the night sky, ash from the burning trees dusting the sand and sea. Screams echo in the dark. Fear, anger, and suffering blur into a single sound of loss and pain, a keening that is almost too much to bear. Each new cry, every clang of metal on metal, sends a fresh spike of anguish through Soran's soul.

She can't stop them. And it's not the first time she's tried.

As soon as she caught sight of the black flag flapping in the wind, the ship of bones and death sailing in from its hellish berth, the terror took hold. No matter how much she wishes to intervene, to blow the ship and its fleet to the end of the world, she can never get near. Not to the pirates. The curse won't let her.

So she watches, punishing herself for her weakness, her inability to break the curse's hold. She watches as the pirates pillage the land and kill the innocent. She watches the people of Tribali stand and fight to protect their shores. An endless cycle of bloodshed.

Names float on the wind, the ones who have been lost. The mourning will be great.

I'm so sorry.

She sends the words into the void, a feeble penance to those she cannot save. Though tears will not come, the lost and lonely druid feels rent in two.

Moonlight bathed the balcony in silvery light. The cold attacked Kiana like a living thing, clawing at her cheeks, nipping at her fingers and toes. The thin silk of her robe did nothing to deter the assault.

I don't remember coming out here, she thought dazedly. She put a hand to her face. It came away wet. Again. She tucked her hands into her armpits and filled her lungs with a long, deep breath.

She heard a muted curse from inside followed by, "Kiana?"

Tash appeared on the balcony beside her, a thick woolen blanket in his hands. He threw it over her shoulders and hugged her to him, rubbing vigorously up and down her arms.

"What are you doing out here? It's freezing." He pulled his own robe tighter around himself. The bronze scales adorning his calves peeked out beneath the hem.

"I guess Soran brought me out here," she said distractedly. "I think she likes the cold."

Tash noticed her tearstained face and gently wiped away the dampness with the sleeve of his robe. He kissed her forehead.

"You say that like she's in control of these visions."

Kiana quirked her head at him. "I think she might be." She shivered violently.

"Come on, let's go back inside." Tash led her back into the room and shut the balcony doors against the chill. He pulled her into a warm hug. "Do you want to talk about it?"

Kiana leaned into him. Her mind went back to the day she had the first vision. The fight with the octopus, Madame Lesant's tent. Her broken trinket box. Another memory, further back, tumbled into her mind. With a gasp, she reached up and untangled the metal jasmine blossom from her hair, detaching it from her circlet and stepping back from Tash.

"What is it?" he asked.

Kiana closed her fist around the flower and shut her eyes.

A young elf sits on the shore as the sun sets on the horizon. She looks beautiful with a bloom of white jasmine adorning her auburn hair. Soran has seen her before, watched her play in the surf, swim in the waves. Soran saw her the day she sent the Highmane elves to the undersea, her rage an unstoppable tempest that splintered their ship like kindling. The elven girl tried to save them, not knowing what they were. But she would.

Tonight, she looks sad, lost. Soran knows she can't get too close, but she senses something in her. Something about her feels quintessentially good.

She's the one, *Soran thinks.* I know it.

On the seafloor, she finds the bit of Crucian metal, jetsam from one of hundreds of ships that have sunk or sailed here. Being a druid made of water has its perks, though they are few indeed, and Soran soon shapes the metal into a flower to match the elf's chosen adornment.

If you are who I think you are, you will be able to take this part of me, to understand it.

She clutches the metal in her watery grip and focuses every last bit of druidic power she has into it, imbuing it with her memories, haphazard and scattered though they are. The years, the centuries, have shattered her mind. She tries to find order in the chaos. She hopes she succeeds.

Kiana opened her eyes with an odd feeling of relief. Still distraught by the memories she'd been living, at least now she knew for sure where they came from, why they plagued her. A sense of wonder puckered her mouth into a curious O.

"I've never seen Crucian metal used this way." She turned the blossom over in her hands. "Soran sent this to me. She was watching me the night you came down from Highmane with Tem and Laera. She imbued the metal with her memories, a piece of her soul." She stroked the petals.

Tash held her in his eyes and waited.

"I think that's why I kept thinking about Old Home, and why her story came to mind so readily when Ravaini mentioned Freya's Crystal. Soran knew it was close and was trying to tell me what happened, guide me to it before the Deep Ones could find the Shiver Tree. But her memories are jumbled, confused. Her mind is . . . broken, somehow." She squeezed the flower against her palm. "She blames herself for the pirates. Something about the curse won't let her interfere with them, give aid to Tribali when they attack. She couldn't stop . . ." Her voice hitched.

Tash cupped his hands over hers. "Your mother?"

Kiana looked out the window. "It wasn't Soran's fault," she whispered.

"And it wasn't yours. Or your father's, or Ravaini's. The pirates are a scourge, a bloodthirsty plague on Amarra, and the fault lies with them alone."

"I know. And they will rue the day they set foot on Tribali's shores. Ravaini will see to that. I will see to that. When this quest is finished."

Tash smiled. "Soran knew what she was doing when she chose you."

Kiana tucked the blossom back into her hair. "And I don't intend to let her down."

When morning came, Kiana lay with her back flush against the curve of Tash's torso, his arm draped over her waist. Despite the events of the night, she'd managed to get a full night's rest and felt lighter than she had in months. Maybe ever.

"Do you think Reyan made it back okay last night?" she whispered.

Tash snorted. "I'll pretend it doesn't hurt a little bit that your first thought is of another man this morning."

Kiana rolled over to face him. He smiled and pushed her hair from her face.

"I'm sure he made it back just fine."

Kiana made no response.

"Would you like me to go make sure?" he asked, already shifting toward the edge of the bed.

"You wouldn't mind, would you?"

"Not at all. I can see to breakfast while I'm out."

"Oh, that's okay. We should be moving along soon. We can grab something on our way out." Kiana scooted out of bed. "I should be getting back to Aravel now, anyway."

Tash finished pulling on his pants and moved to Kiana.

"It's a shame we can't stay another night. Who knows when we'll have a bed this comfortable again?"

Kiana slid her arms around his slim, bare waist. Her fingers traveled up until they found the bronze scales below his shoulder blades and soaked up some of their warmth.

"I'm—"

Three modest raps on the door interrupted her thought.

Quickly, Kiana slipped back into her dress from the night before as Tash went to the door, tugging on a shirt and fastening it just enough to cover the scales on his torso. The man who stood outside the door looked like he hadn't slept a wink, his hair and clothes disheveled and dirty.

"Reyan!" Kiana exclaimed, moving closer to the door. "What happened?"

The ranger registered no surprise at finding Kiana in Tash's room in an evening gown just after sunrise. At least not outwardly.

"Nothing. Got in late, tried to catch a few winks, didn't have time to clean up."

"Where were you?" Tash asked.

With no hesitation, Reyan simply said, "Out."

Tash leaned on his arm against the door. "Yes, we gathered that much."

Face impassive, Reyan said, "Rather not talk about it, if it's all the same to you." Something in his eyes warned away further questions.

The diplomat in Kiana told her not to press, while the protector in her screamed for answers. She settled for a compromise.

"You've asked us to trust you, so we hope that you feel you can do the same with us. If you change your mind, we're here." She looked from one man to the other. "Why don't you go clean up and we'll meet back here in half an hour, get ready to head out."

Silently, Reyan returned to his room a few doors down.

"I'll let Aravel know to join us here." Kiana padded across the hall to her own room.

The door opened before she touched the knob. Aravel stood dressed in her leather armor and usual traveling clothes, hair pulled back in a cluster of braids. She caught sight of Tash, shirt still mostly open, propped on one arm across the hall. Surprised delight immediately lifted her face into a grin. She crossed her arms and leaned against the doorframe, Snow peeking out from behind her legs.

"Looks like Reyan's not the only one who missed out on some sleep last night." She jerked her head toward the end of the hall. "Heard him come in just an hour ago."

Kiana darted her eyes back to Tash, who calmly acknowledged Aravel with a sideways tilt of the head.

"Ladies," he said. "See you shortly." He slid back into his room and closed the door.

When Kiana turned back to Aravel, her friend's eyes opened as big as the previous night's full moon, the grin still trembling on her lips, threatening to split her face in half. Kiana stepped past her, and Aravel swiveled to follow.

"I have so many questions," she said. "How . . . when . . . what—"

"Soran is, in fact, responsible for my visions."

The declaration stopped Aravel short. Her smile faded.

"Wait, what?"

Kiana grabbed her pack, pulled out a fresh set of clothes, and considered her leather padding and bracers. She glanced at Aravel.

"Why are you wearing your armor?"

The second complete shift in conversation apparently gave Aravel mental whiplash, and she shook her head as if warding off a gnat.

"I, what"—she faltered—"we're quite possibly still being hunted by

Deep Ones. Who knows what the day will bring?" She flung out her arms. "What about Soran?"

Kiana frowned. Extra precautions couldn't hurt. She pulled out the rest of her gear. As she dressed, she filled Aravel in on her latest visions.

"So you think the visions didn't start earlier because you had the flower in a box?"

Kiana considered the logic. "The night I found the flower, I had it on me when I slept, so initial attunement likely started then. That's why I woke up thinking about Old Home. Not because Ravaini lives there, but because Soran knew the Shiver Seed was there and was trying to prompt me to go to it. That's partly why I felt the need to leave as quickly as I did. Then once I joined the flower with my circlet, the magic fully activated, and the visions started." Strapping her dagger to her thigh, Kiana paused with her finger on the hilt. The familiar weight of the Crucian blade brought on a sudden, intense longing to have her sister there with her. She sent a quick prayer to Nelami for Ravaini's safety. Gods knew what she'd gotten herself into since Kiana had last seen her. Maybe when all this was over, they could join forces.

"I did wonder about that. You're usually such a planner. I thought your haste was because, you know." She held out her left forearm. "No more Regent Trees for those new initiates."

"That was certainly the other part of it."

Kiana finished pulling on her boots and turned. Aravel quirked an eyebrow.

"What?"

"Oh, you know. Just wondering if there's anything else you want to tell me. Maybe about last night."

Though she had no intention of discussing details about her night with Tash, Kiana couldn't keep the smile from her face. She took a moment to relive the thrill of his touch, the feel of his body pressed to hers. With effort, she pulled herself from the memory.

"Sorry, no time for such things. We have a Tree to find."

"Okay, we travel at speed for as long as we can hold the pace." Kiana selected a biscuit from the platter Tash had obtained while they'd waited for Reyan to be ready. Ever the thoughtful gentleman, he'd ensured it was heaped with warm biscuits, muffins, and fresh fruit. Aravel nearly fainted with joy.

Reyan raked a hand through his still-damp hair. The bath had done him good, but he still bore dark circles under his eyes that spoke of a sleepless night.

"I suggest flight for as long as we can sustain it," he said, stifling a yawn.

Words of agreement spread around the room.

"All right, if there's nothing else, let's be on our way. Who knows how far the Deep Ones have gotten by now."

Kiana picked up her pack from where it sat by her feet and rose from the chaise lounge. She took only a moment to commit the details of the room to memory, hoping to return one day with Tash, before following her friends out the door.

Pine trees lined the cobblestone road out of town, each one individually decorated for a festival Kiana didn't recognize. Glass ornaments of all colors hung from the lowest branches, while braided strands of different-colored twine wrapped around those closer to the top.

"Pity we can't stay for whatever *this* is." Aravel craned her neck to admire the rainbow theme of the nearest tree. "I can smell the buns being baked from here."

Kiana smiled. "Maybe we can come visit next year. Did you see the library down the way? Bigger than Corval's by half. Wouldn't mind spending a day or two in there."

Aravel's eyes lit up, mouth open to respond, but before she could speak, a loud creaking sound erupted behind them. A scream followed. Spinning toward the source of the commotion, the party watched a humanoid figure lurch out from a fresh opening in a large pine tree bordering the road and collapse at a woman's feet. The magical door closed seconds later.

The companions sprinted toward the figure, now prone on the ground. A small group began to gather around them.

"Where am I?" the fallen man croaked through his ruined throat. Blood ran from his ears. Dirt encrusted his white robes, face, and hands. Over his left breast, a gold embroidered symbol caught Kiana's eye: the trunk of a tree with roots spreading in a half circle below, with six shards above.

"Sweet seas," she whispered. "He's an Ice Druid."

The man, an elderly half-elf, reached toward Kiana, then immediately withdrew his hand and clutched both sides of his head, his face contorted in a grimace of immense pain. More blood leaked out of his ears and the corner of one eye, and he let out a horrible moan.

Slowly, he reached back out. "You've been touched." He pointed to the jasmine blossom. "The magic, it drew me here. You have to help us." He coughed and moaned again, hands firmly pressed against his graying temples. "The Deep Ones—" A scream of pure agony interrupted his words. He caught his breath and continued, "They've found us."

CHAPTER NINETEEN

"They've found the Tree." The Ice Druid squeezed his eyes shut against whatever torment ravaged him. "And they have the Seed."

Murmurs rippled through the crowd.

"What's he talking about?"

"Who is he?"

"What tree? What seed?"

"Somebody get Mayor Lachden!"

Panic shot through Kiana like a bolt of lightning, electrifying her nerves in the worst possible way.

We took too long.

Snow's frantic yips seized her attention. She whipped a scrap of parchment out of her pack and hastily scrawled five words: *It's happening. Please come now.*

Surely her father had received her message from the blitz falcon by now. She prayed he had troops to spare. She fixed the note to Snow's collar and held the fox's face tenderly in her hands.

"Get this note to my father as fast as you can. Go, now!"

The fox yipped once and vanished in the blink of an eye.

Kiana turned back to the writhing Ice Druid.

"How did they find you? How many are they?" Questions continued to bubble up in her mind. She tried to focus on the most pressing. "How can we get to the Shiver Tree in time?"

The Ice Druid's eyebrows arched in as much surprise as his agonized face allowed. He extended a feeble hand once more, and Kiana grasped it in hers. His skin felt ice cold and parchment thin.

"I can't hold it off much longer. The spell—I can't defy them anymore." His head rolled back toward Kiana, and she noted the faintest hint of a black smudge on his temple. "Please go. Help them. Tell them I tried." His voice came out a bare whisper. With a shout that contained all the fury and all the pain now coursing through him, he lifted his arms toward the pine tree, his movements labored. Upon his left forearm, a blackened Regent Tree flailed as though assaulted by a hurricane. Hundreds of leaves blazed an angry red as he growled, "*Aperata ent arberia Monj.*"

Silver energy zigzagged up the tree, and a magical doorway reopened under a high arch.

"Go. Hurry." They were the last words the Ice Druid spoke. His eyes closed, breath slowed. The red glow of the Regent leaves dimmed to flickering embers.

Tears flooded Kiana's vision, but Tash grasped her arm, fingers firm.

"We have to move. Now. Before the spell drops."

Amid a chorus of alarmed shouts, the four companions maneuvered around the body and strode through the tree into an unknown future. The magical gate sealed behind them.

The world they stepped into was one of nightmares. Emerging from a massive Korvisian cedar on a wide, icy plateau hundreds of yards across, the companions paused to take in their new surroundings. Bodies lay strewn about everywhere, some Ice Druids, others a horrifying shape that looked like a pale brain on eight black, spidery legs. Way up ahead, the ice narrowed and dropped off in a sheer cliff. The tops of nearby mountains surrounded them. The tree they had come through somehow grew straight from the ice. The nearest mountain loomed behind them, abutting the plateau.

Absolute, baffling silence enveloped them.

"This isn't High Crag," Aravel said quietly.

Kiana shook her head. "Just west of it, I think." She focused inward, tethering herself to the space and opening a channel of magic that she then sent outward: a homing beacon for those who knew how to use it. She prayed Snow had delivered the message to her father in time. He would find her.

She stepped forward. The plateau flashed white.

They pass through a ten-foot gate of ice and metal, the sound of chimes tinkling through the air as the barrier magically seals behind them. A tunnel opens up ahead, leading into the glacier, deep-blue ice surrounding them.

"She's still at rest. The replanting was successful," Kira says, motioning Soran into the passage.

"Do you think the Deep Ones will come for her again?" Soran's footsteps echo dully off the frozen walls.

Kira takes a deep breath. "We're well hidden here, our location not in any records. I don't see how they'd find us now."

They round a corner and follow the slope that winds into the heart of the glacier.

"Besides," Kira continues, "once we have the new Mother Staff, our defenses will be greatly enhanced."

The burden of expectation reasserts itself atop Soran's shoulders.

"But as High Druid, Ilestra will have the staff, in Murano."

"For now, yes." Kira stops and turns to Soran. "But Ilestra's time will end. Before long, the staff will pass to you."

Soran accepts her words with a nod. They continue around another curve. Before them the interior of the glacier opens up into a vast, spherical cavern. From here, Soran can see a massive root ball encasing an immense orb made entirely of ice. A soft blue glow emanates from the shell. Before the women can move farther, a shout from above stops them.

"Oy! Kira, Soran. It's time. Come now."

Kira sighs. "Later, then."

As they turn to leave, Soran traces a finger along the wall, gathering the cold. The feel of home.

Kiana's own world fell back into view slowly.

"I think Soran just showed me where we need to go. The Ice Druid colony is built into the glacier below us. There's a tunnel that leads inside. The Shiver Tree is there." A sensation of cold damp drew her attention to her hand. A touch of melting frost dotted one fingertip. "Our connection is definitely getting stronger."

"Great." Aravel turned 360 degrees as she crept forward. "Remind me again what exactly the book said about this Terror?"

Kiana had gone over the words so many times that they flew from her mouth almost by rote.

"The Shiver Tree stands strong, countering fire with ice."

"Right. Fire. So, what are we thinking? Demon lord? Demented devil?"

"The Deep Ones favor fire as well," Kiana said. "Maybe the Terror is the lord of their race?"

"Queen," Tash said, head in constant motion as he assessed their position.

"What?"

"If I'm not mistaken, Deep Ones spawn from a queen." He shook his head. "Whatever the case, let's hope we don't have to find out."

Aravel bent down to examine one of the brain-creature corpses.

"What in the name of the great wide deeps are these things?" She shifted to get a better look at where its face might be. "No eyes, ears, or mouth that I can see. Just . . . gross, gooey tissue."

A tingling sensation crawled up Kiana's arm from her owl ring, and she snapped her head to the left. Something moved at the edge of the precipice, a scratching sound stealing closer.

"Something's coming," she whispered.

Heeding her warning, the group readied itself. Everyone dropped their unneeded gear at their feet. Kiana unclasped her cloak and let it fall, sacrificing warmth and comfort for greater freedom of movement.

Tash whirled his arms, muttering, "*Keldes bronyec.*" Magic light engulfed him and left him shimmering in a metallic aura that gradually faded but provided a layer of enchanted armor.

Reyan had an arrow out of the quiver and nocked in under a second.

From the scabbard on her back, Aravel drew her scimitar, spinning the hickory hilt around a few times before tucking her hand securely against the simple gold guard. Though she usually favored shapeshifting in battle scenarios and had plenty of spells at hand, she'd grown fonder of the blade since its success against the Deep One in Mooreland. No one could ever accuse her of being a typical druid.

An eerie calm settled over Kiana as she focused her magic, a spell ready on her lips. Vines engulfed the wood of her staff and secured it to her hand. The last couple of months had been building up to this. Whatever happened, they'd made it.

Four of the nightmare brains appeared over the southeast edge of the cliff, their pointy legs scrabbling over the ice, thin black veins pulsing beneath their gelatinous skin. The resemblance to the flesh of the Deep Ones did not go unnoticed. Before the fourth brain had even finished cresting the overhang, an arrow slammed into the lead creature. A screech pierced Kiana's mind, nothing audible but rather a mental dagger of sound. Out of the side of her eye, she noticed her companions jerk their heads in response.

"They're telepaths!" Kiana yelled. "Guard your minds!" She hurried ahead and held her position, focus fixed on a point midway between the creatures and her friends. "Come and get it," she muttered.

Tash and Aravel ran forward, paths diverging to flank, Tash's arcane sword materializing in his hand as he moved.

"Mother of seas!" Aravel grunted, momentarily losing her footing on the slippery surface. She righted herself and continued forward.

Two more spider brains emerged over the precipice, all six now charging ahead. Another arrow struck the one in front and it fell, but not before sending another stabbing scream into their minds. A third arrow barely missed the rearmost brain as the creature slipped on the edge.

As Tash and Aravel came almost within melee range of the creatures, four of the five brains moved within Kiana's focal point. The spell flew from her mouth the same instant.

"*Pehrec terra.*"

The words were no sooner off her lips than the ground erupted in a mass of thorny vines in a thirty-foot radius around the tiny monstrosities. Every creature within the circle wailed in telepathic rage. The two frontmost aberrations limped from the trap and into the range of the waiting Tash and Aravel. In what looked like almost choreographed unison, the two warriors sliced into the brains with their respective blades. The already injured foes went down hard, wisps of smoke curling out of their fallen bodies.

"They're weak. Save your bigger spells for the Deep Ones," Tash called out.

As if illustrating Tash's point, the two brains still caught in the center of the spike pit perished before they could exit the trap, their bodies torn and seeping black goo and smoke as they dragged themselves through the barbed points. Skirting the treacherous ground, the final brain creature launched itself toward Aravel at a full gallop. Two well-placed arrows knocked it to the ice, where it slid to a stop at the druid's feet.

"Okay, that wasn't so bad," Aravel said, shoving the impaled brain away with her boot. "Great job, team."

"I'm sure there are plenty more where those came from, so stay sharp," Tash said, striding to Aravel's side. He handed her a vial of bright-red liquid.

"A healing potion? You know I'm a druid . . ."

Tash smiled and nodded to her sparse Regent Tree. "Just in case. Your magic isn't infinite." He moved back to where Kiana and Reyan stood and handed them red vials as well. "I did a little more shopping while we were in Garrison. Figured these would come in handy about now."

"When did you have time to do that?" Kiana accepted the potion and tucked it in her belt. "Oh, right. While we were facing down a Deep One and his thralls."

Tash threw her a look that was part sheepish, part defensive. "After I visited the bank, on the far side of the city, before I found you at the pub." He pulled out two more vials. The translucent purple contents of each sparkled in the light. "Potions of Mental Resilience. They should help protect against the effects of the Deep Ones' powers." He wiggled the vials in his fingers. "But I only have two."

Kiana held up her owl ring. "This should help protect me."

"I have defenses as well," Tash said, handing one potion to Reyan.

Aravel joined the group and accepted the second. "And let's not forget we have that invisibility potion. Could also come in handy here." She handed Reyan two arrows she'd retrieved.

A trembling sensation started vibrating up from the soles of Kiana's feet. She shook out her hands and watched her staff reabsorb the magical vines as the energy within it faded. "We should keep moving before all the adrenaline from that fight wears off," she said. "My body is literally vibrating with it."

Aravel stared at her feet.

"I don't think that's adrenaline. I feel it too."

The tremors grew stronger, bits of ice on the ground now visibly quaking.

"Well, that can't be good," Kiana said.

A terrible, cacophonous crash exploded behind them.

A monster of fire and ice burst out of the ground. Ten legs supported its twenty-foot-long, armored body, and its insectoid head housed a gaping maw of sharp, menacing teeth. Fiery spikes ridged the creature's sides, while the rest of the bluish body looked chiseled from the deepest of ice. The tail ended in a curved point like that of a scorpion. The tip blazed hotter than a blacksmith's forge.

"Holy mother of tides," Aravel whispered.

"Shit, move!" Tash yelled as the monster charged.

Following Kiana, who sprinted right, the sorcerer resummoned his arcane sword. Just as the creature came within range, mouth open wide, Tash turned and swung his blade, slashing at the side of its face. The thing hissed in pain, and freezing vapor poured from the gash, engulfing Tash's arm.

"Ahh!" he yelled, grabbing at his sleeve, which was freezing solid around his arm.

The distraction gave the creature an opening to swing its head back for another go, jagged jaws snapping at Tash. With maybe an inch to spare, the sorcerer rolled out of the way. An arrow plinked off the monster's hardened shell, followed almost instantly by another.

"Argh!" Reyan yelled as his second attack proved equally as ineffective as the first. He spat a few expletives into the wind and snagged another arrow from his quiver.

The misfired arrows caught the creature's attention. It whirled around to face the ranger and a battle-ready Aravel.

"Keep your distance!" Tash shouted, summoning a wave of heat to thaw his sleeve.

"Not a problem," Reyan muttered, nocking another arrow.

"Not a problem at all," Aravel agreed. She swept her right hand back over her left shoulder, torso rotating for added torque. As she did, a long vine of thorns materialized in her hand in a surge of golden light. She twisted her body back to the front, lashing out with the string of barbs, which extended until it struck home against the ice monster's cheek. More vapor gushed out, but not far enough to reach the druid.

Kiana watched all this happening while preparing her own assault. Making sure Tash was clear, she reached up to the heavens, eyes going white.

"*Ith luziren visht.*" Purple energy crackled across the druid's eyes in time with a silver lightning bolt that arced down from the sky.

The electricity cracked into the creature's body with a sizzle that made the beast rear back in pain seconds after Aravel's thorns struck its face.

Tash took advantage of the exposed neck and let loose a stream of acid, further enraging their opponent as not vapor but liquid fire oozed from the wound. Apparently unsure of who posed the greatest threat, the monster focused on the first thing it saw when its head came back down.

Aravel.

The beast charged with a hiss of fury. Its jaws snapped shut on flesh, eliciting a howl of pain. But not from the druid.

Aravel lay shocked on the ground, where Reyan had just body-checked her. The ranger now writhed in the closed maw of the huge monstrosity. He struggled against the force of the jaws, trying to pry them open as teeth sank farther into him.

"No!" Aravel screamed, rolling onto her feet and drawing her scimitar in one fluid motion.

"Wait!" Tash yelled, but too late.

In a fit of fury, Aravel stabbed her blade into the creature's neck. The weapon dug in, but a gush of molten fire immediately repaid the druid for her efforts, blasting her face. She cried out and fell away, hitting the ice hard, blade still lodged in the monster's swaying neck.

Kiana's protective instincts raged as she watched her friends take damage she could do nothing to stop, and she clenched her fist, searing more magical lightning into her target, guarding Reyan from the spell's harmful effects with a shielding aura. The singed wound from the first lightning strike split and widened as sparks skittered along the creature's exoskeleton.

Tash grabbed Aravel and pulled her to a safe distance.

"*Vulshben raguet,*" he snarled, backing away, hand snapping forward to complete the spell. Five glowing darts of amber energy shot ahead and collided with the vulnerable space between two of the creature's body sections.

The fight in Reyan waned. Blood poured from wounds in his back and side as the monster attempted to swallow him whole. In a desperate show of strength, Reyan slipped a dagger from his boot and slammed it into the roof of his captor's mouth, hanging on with everything he had. His life truly did depend on it.

Mad with violent rage and pain, the creature lurched to the side and swung the rear of its body in a wild arc, whipping its tail sideways into Kiana. Fire seared into the druid's back and side at the same time that the deepest cold she'd ever felt shocked her system into submission. The force of the blow sent her sprawling across the ice. Air rushed out of her lungs, leaving her gasping for breath. Her lightning spell wavered. Gritting her teeth, she just managed to maintain her connection. A flurry of amethyst sparks flashed in her eyes.

Aravel recovered her feet and summoned a beam of ethereal, scorching light down onto the creature's back, syncing with a final bolt of lightning from Kiana. The two spells intertwined in a brilliant flash. The damage proved enough to force the creature to release Reyan, the ranger rolling from its mouth amid a puddle of bile and flame.

Kiana watched, aghast, as the biting jaws lunged forward in an attempt to recover their escaped meal, but Tash was too quick.

"*Razbethna!*"

His voice boomed across the plateau, and a thunderous ringing resonated out from a shock wave that knocked the creature prone. Liquid fire and shards of ice surged out from the thing with tremendous velocity, striking them all. As the echo from the attack dissipated, the creature remained still. So did Reyan.

"No no no no no," Aravel cried, rushing toward him. Her burned, bleeding face grimaced in pain that went deeper than her physical injuries. She pressed her hands against the two deepest wounds she could find, her fingers instantly coated in blood.

"*Sanye dolim,*" she said in the otherworldly voice that marked druidic healing spells.

The ranger's chest rose in a deep intake of breath, and his eyes fluttered open. Pain clouded his features.

"Stay still," Aravel instructed. She produced the healing potion Tash had given her only a minute or two earlier. With zero hesitation, she popped the stopper and tipped the contents into Reyan's mouth.

Burns and gashes across his face and arms began knitting back together. The rattle in his chest quieted, his breathing returning to normal. Still battered and far from tip-top shape, the ranger rolled onto his side and propped himself on one elbow.

"Thanks," he rasped.

Careful not to put pressure on still-open wounds, Aravel pulled him to her tightly.

"I can't believe you did that," she said shakily, voice cracking with tears.

Suffering a string of burns across her left arm from where she had shielded herself from flying fire, and a cut on her cheek where ice had met flesh, Kiana dragged her aching body off the ground and moved to join Tash. His hand instinctively went to her back. She winced when his palm touched the burning patch of cold left from contact with the creature's body.

"*Sanye dolim*," the druid whispered, watching amethyst magic weave around the burns on Aravel's face, healing them. Her friend didn't even notice. She held on to Reyan like a life preserver in a storm.

"You're hurt," Tash said, obviously noticing her grimace at his touch.

"We're all hurt," Kiana sighed. "I'm okay. For now." She inspected the lifeless body of the creature that had nearly eaten Reyan. At a volume meant for only Tash, she muttered, "I have a feeling things will only get much, much worse from here."

"We can hold here, wait for help to come. Your father could be on his way as we speak." Tash nodded toward their two companions. "Taking this much damage early on puts us in an even more precarious position."

Kiana watched Aravel help Reyan to his feet. The ranger masked his pain well, but not well enough.

"Maybe you should stay here, rest up a bit," Kiana suggested.

Realizing she was talking to him, Reyan demurred.

"I'm fine. The longer we wait, the more we risk the Deep Ones getting what they came for."

"Reyan, you almost died. Stay here. We'll scope out the threat. You can catch up to us in a bit."

He shook his head more firmly.

"No. I'm coming with you." His eyes hardened. "Trust me, I'm good."

Kiana moved slowly toward him, watching his eyes. Where she thought she'd find fear, apprehension, she found only resolve. She extended a hand to him. He clasped her arm with a strong, sure grip. Fingers tightening, she channeled more healing energy into this steadfast companion, Regent Tree shimmering amethyst.

"If you're sure."

"You said something about the colony being built into the glacier?" Aravel stomped a foot against the ice.

"Yes, we need to find a way down."

Here.

The word tickled Kiana's ear, barely more than a whisper of the breeze.

"Did you hear that?"

Tash scanned the open space around them. "Hear what?"

We are here.

Kiana turned west. Mist obscured her view. When it passed, her eyeline was much lower. She guessed about a gnome's height. Near the far edge of the plateau, off to one side, she knew there would be a subtle dip. She pointed.

"There's a staircase. Leads down and around the glacier."

Tash joined her, peering forward, the distance too great even for elven eyes to make out such a detail. "Should I ask how you know that?"

"I don't. Soran does."

CHAPTER TWENTY

Kiana's vision returned to normal as they hustled back to the tree they'd come through to deposit any gear that would slow them down. They held on to weapons, potions, and a few tools and shed the rest. The shock of the cold made Kiana hesitate over leaving her cloak, but she wanted as much freedom as possible.

After pouring one last flurry of healing into Reyan, they began their descent.

Narrow stairs led off the plateau and down to what Kiana now knew would be towering columns of druidic dwellings carved into the ice, reaching up to meet the glacier's outcropping. Images of one of the homes flashed through her mind: a multicolored braided rug, two wool chairs, lines of dried fruit along the walls. The images vanished when Kiana's foot slipped and Tash had to tuck his arms beneath hers to keep her upright.

"Do all Ice Druids wear special shoes or something? These stairs are deadly. Ah!"

Kiana heard Aravel slip behind her and turned. "I could use magic to get us down safely, but I don't know if that's the wisest course of action given what we likely face ahead."

"Whoa!" Aravel took one more step and landed on her backside with a thud. "Okay, this *will not* do." Brushing herself off, she crouched on the offending stair. Thick fur with black spots erupted over her body. When the transformation was complete, the snow leopard shook her head. She brushed by her companions with barely any room to spare and trotted downward with ease.

"Remind me why we didn't have you two fly us down, again?" Tash steadied himself against the glacier.

"I can only shapeshift a couple times a day, and I don't know if I'm going to need that for later, I haven't grown that part of my abilities like Aravel."

They eased around a curve leading to the front of the glacier. Kiana's breath caught.

The glacier they were descending jutted out over a sheltered valley of gardens below, which sloped up to the ice columns filled with druidic dwellings. Filtered blue light bathed everything beneath the glacial outcropping as the sun worked to penetrate the thick layers of ice. Plants grew all around, adapted to this strange light by taking on faded hues of blue and purple, others the most brilliant white nature could achieve. The farther out from the shadow of the ledge, the more variety of color, until a veritable rainbow of fruit trees and flowers adorned the landscape. On this day, however, carnage stained the would-be paradise.

At the base of the stairs, the party could already see a gruesome field of death. Far more bodies than they'd encountered above gathered in bloody heaps among the columns, many friendly, many foe, from spider brains to ice golems and trolls.

So much death. How long had the battle been waging?

"Looks like the Deep Ones brought more backup," Kiana said. "Who knows how many creatures they have under their sway by now."

Let my father find us quickly. She sent the urgent plea to the feet of Nelami.

Commotion caught her eye as she came upon Aravel, who had stopped on the stairs. She let out a low growl.

Down below, five gnomes sprinted into the colony, lost to sight moments later among the massive columns. Giving chase were three ice trolls.

"We have to help them." Kiana pointed. "Ari, go!"

The snow leopard raced down the stairs. Kiana threw a hand at everyone else's feet.

"Mothiri librenti et miri."

She chose not to watch the leaf vanish from her arm. The companions rushed down the stairs.

Sounds of battle ricocheted through the colony. Spells bellowed in the druidic tongue, attacks striking yielding flesh.

Dodging through the maze of columns and bodies, Kiana and her friends came upon the source about fifty yards to the northeast. The Ice Druids they'd seen fleeing stood tattered and panting, one resting on one knee over a sizzling and very dead troll. The other two trolls were nowhere to be seen.

At Kiana's approach, the four druids still standing whirled her direction, hands and lips ready with spells.

Kiana held up her hands in a gesture of peace.

"We mean you no harm. We're here to help."

Confusion sent their eyes darting between each other before settling back on the newcomers. The oldest-looking gnome, a boy of maybe eighteen, stepped forward.

"I am Kezrac. How did you find us?"

"I'm Kiana, of Tribali. One of your elders"—she faltered a moment, realizing she hadn't gotten his name—"a half-elf, he came through a tree in Sanctuary saying the Deep Ones had found you. He asked for help and sent us back the way he came."

"Sanctuary? Geshrem was supposed to go to Stormfront." Emotion filled the young druid's voice, choking his next words. "But he's alive? Geshrem? Have others come?"

Kiana suddenly felt as though she had never come down from the precipice, and now someone was poised to shove her over the edge. Tash came up beside her, and she sensed his desire to save her, to take the horrible task of relaying the devastating news from her shoulders. She placed a gentle hand on his arm and signaled him off.

"I'm so sorry." She kept as much of the tremor from her words as she could. "He asked us to tell you that he tried. He was strong until the end. He made it long enough to open the tree and get us to you." Kiana blinked back the tears rimming her eyes. "But I'm afraid it's just us."

Their faces crumpled at the news but quickly recovered. They'd already seen untold desolation this day.

"We five had just returned from training when we came upon this"—Kezrac gestured around him—"calamity. There were monsters everywhere. Geshrem stumbled out of the gate, near death. We were hoping he'd make it to the Council in Stormfront so that they could dispatch reinforcements to help us. Only a few of us remain." He motioned to a fallen Ice Druid. The gnome leaned against a dead golem, face slack but eyes open. "And those of us who do may yet perish."

"What happened to him?" Tash asked.

A scowl pulled the gnome's brows together, and he kicked a dead brain creature.

"These beasts—they link you to the hive mind of the Deep Ones and overwhelm your mind, drive you mad. Our friend, he may heal in time, but for now he is left with the mental capacity of a snow beet." Collecting himself, Kezrac continued, "The Deep Ones attacked swiftly, with a great many beasts at their command." He gestured to the corpses at their feet. "I'm not sure how much longer we can fend them off."

"Where are the Deep Ones now?" Kiana said.

The boy's face sagged beneath the weight of his response. "The two I've seen have already made it to the tunnels."

"Just two?" Tash asked.

"More may have come since the attack began, but I cannot be certain."

A look of part confusion, part relief passed between Kiana and Tash.

"We have to stop them. They cannot be allowed to access the Shiver Tree." This came from a second gnome, a girl of perhaps sixteen. A winter stoat perched atop her shoulder, beady eyes narrowed at the strangers.

"Shaerna's right," Kezrac affirmed.

"Don't worry, that's why we're here—to stop them, retake the Shiver Seed, and restore the trees." Kiana turned to Tash. "We need to get to the tunnels."

Kezrac and Shaerna shook their heads in unison, faces stern.

"The gate is locked," Shaerna said. "That's why we're out here. Only an elder can open it . . ." Her gaze fell to Kiana's arm. "You have the mark."

Kiana glanced at her Regent Tree. Only then did she note through a torn sleeve that this gnome had only a seed upon her forearm. She assumed the others would be the same—initiates.

"Our Tree has not granted a mark in some time. We've been unable to maturate."

"Your Tree?" The realization hit Kiana almost immediately. "The Shiver Tree. It's how you get your Regent Trees."

Shaerna frowned. "Of course it is."

The Trees must be connected. The Monarch Tree has to be the Mother Tree then, right? With the failure of the Monarch Tree, none of the druid Trees are working.

"So this will get us through the gate?" She indicated her mark.

"Yes."

"Then we mustn't waste more time." The question that had been nagging her finally broke free. "What do the Deep Ones want?"

Kezrac cocked his head, confused. "Lystrix."

He said this as though it were the most obvious thing in the universe. Kiana's mind found no entry for the name in her memory.

A snarling growl interrupted any clarification she might have received. All eyes looked up to where an ice troll rushed past a nearby column. His tusks gleamed with drool and blood in the muted blue light. Another was close behind.

Kiana readied her staff.

"No!" Kezrac shouted. "Get to the Shiver Tree! Make sure it's safe. We'll take care of this. Go." The expression on his face brooked no argument.

Shaerna was already releasing a spiked orb of druidic ice, hurtling it toward the first troll.

"Go!" Kezrac shouted one last time before turning his attention to the fight. He placed one hand on his chest and muttered a spell under his breath. Dim blue light—much too dim—spread out from his fingertips.

Kiana raced back the way they'd come, friends in tow, trying hard not to think about the fate she was leaving these young druids to.

Halfway back to the stairs, she slowed. Her vision blurred again, and she turned her head, seeking something through the haze. She pointed west through the columns of homes, where the valley ended and the glacier began.

There loomed a high gate covered in druidic runes.

"The tunnels are through there," Kiana said.

A light, warm breeze blew a strand of hair across her face, carrying a floral scent. She held out a hand against the wind, flooded with a feeling of nostalgia she should not have. Her eyes fell on the slope spreading out below them. Vibrant orange petals glowed in the morning sun, the flowers' blue-and-white centers glittering with what looked like tiny ice crystals.

"Desert haven." She smiled. "The flower that led us here."

"Led *you* here," Aravel corrected, stretching out of her leopard form. "Thank Nelami for your obsession with that book."

"Come on, the gate." Tash sprinted west.

The iron gate stretched twenty feet up and across to guard the vast entrance to the tunnels through the heart of the glacier. Inside was total darkness. The hum of tremendous magical power vibrated through Kiana in a startling shock wave.

"Whatever enchantment is locking that gate is strong." She felt a whisper of cold brush across her arm. Her Regent Tree responded, a silver glow outlining the mark as the cool sensation intensified.

The gate started to open.

"It's working."

Tash started for the gap.

Stop!

The command registered at the same time Kiana saw two white eyes awaken in the gloom.

"Hold!" Kiana cried.

They all froze just as two black, leathery hands bigger than Kiana's torso slammed into the gate, gripping the bars. Grimy white fur ran along tree-trunk-sized arms leading toward a chest padded with the same tough skin as the hands. A roar bellowed from an apelike mouth where two tusks jutted up from the lower jaw. Fearsome eyes glared out from beneath a prominent brow. They were clouded over, the Deep Ones' mental barbs already piercing the creature's untamed mind.

"They have a *yeti*?" Aravel shouted.

"Fall back!" Kiana called, already turning to run. Even free of a Deep One's control, a yeti was exceedingly dangerous. Under the sway of such evil, who knew what violence one could achieve?

After only a few yards, Kiana felt the cold on her arm fade. The gate clanged shut behind them, a snarling yeti still trapped on the other side. Still, she ran until they'd reached the stairs.

"Okay, so the gate's no good to us. Now what?"

A chuffing sound punctuated Aravel's question and sent a spike of alarm through Kiana.

Snow?

She spun around, heart racing at the thought of her furry friend being dragged into this hell.

A fox did sit some ten yards down the slope of the valley, piercing blue eyes calmly observing the companions. This fox was pure white and twice as fluffy as Snow would ever be.

"Hello there," Kiana crooned.

The hoarfox let out another chuff, body twitching with the sound.

"Do you know how we can get through there?" Kiana inched forward, careful not to frighten this new friend.

I do.

The voice startled Kiana back a step. The fox yipped.

This is Nix. Let her be your guide.

Kiana crouched. "Soran?"

Yes. I am here.

"How?"

You carry a piece of my soul. I felt the connection to my home the moment you stepped through the great cedar. But you must hurry. The Deep Ones have already reached the Tree, and I can feel the pull of the curse, dragging me back. I do not know how long I can resist. Follow Nix.

With that, Nix launched herself forward, climbing the stairs.

"What just happened?" Aravel's gaze followed the fox, who stopped fifteen feet up and looked back, waiting.

"The Deep Ones have already found the Shiver Tree. Soran is going to show us another way in. Follow the fox."

"That's Soran?"

"Sort of. I'll explain later. We have to move." Kiana started upward.

Reyan caught her arm. "Whoa whoa whoa, you mean we have to climb back up those stairs?" The incredulity in his voice would have been comical if the fate of an entire people didn't hang in the balance.

"You'll be fine. The spell on your boots should last a few minutes longer, at least."

"Nevertheless . . ." Aravel stretched her arms toward the ground. White, black, and gray fur sprouted from her arms, up her shoulders, and down her back. Within seconds, the thick winter coat transformed her entire body. She bounded up the stairs, everyone else racing behind.

CHAPTER TWENTY-ONE

Kiana did her best not to look at the giant ice monster melting into the plateau. Liquid fire still pooled around the body, sending up a curtain of steam.

"Is that going to be a problem?" Tash asked.

"I certainly hope not. Not much we can do about it at the moment." Kiana watched Reyan studiously avoid looking at the creature that had almost killed him as they hurried to catch up with Nix and Aravel, dodging around the corpses littering the ground.

Just before reaching the hole where the giant scorpion monster had broken through the ice, Nix halted. She whined, dancing around the opening.

"Through there?" Kiana peered into the hole.

This will lead you to the Ice Druid tunnels. The Shiver Tree is at the heart of the glacier. I fear I cannot help you beyond this point. Please hurry. Save them.

"What about you?"

The fox blinked at Kiana, ears twitching. She bolted off into the white expanse.

"We'll find you," Kiana whispered.

The monster's burrow swallowed the companions in icy silence.

About thirty feet down, the burrow crossed another passageway, this one far smoother and wider than that of the beast.

The tunnels were quiet. Too quiet. Kiana listened hard, straining her ears for sounds of battle, of resistance or chaos. Nothing.

"Which way?" Tash said, voice low.

"Soran didn't say. She just said the heart of the glacier." She turned northeast. "I'd guess that direction. But maybe . . ." Tentatively, she touched her circlet, finger caressing the jasmine blossom.

A figure floats above the sand, hand outstretched, long cloak billowing out around booted feet. Five water jinn turn to face this intruder. Almost instantly they assume offensive postures, ready for battle.

Something about the floating figure is wrong. What Soran thought to be a black cape now splits, moves like a living thing. Tendrils of smoke.

The Deep Ones are here, Soran thinks.

The jinn do not attack. Instead, they double over in pain, hands clutching at their heads. Two remain this way. The other three, including Mer, right themselves. Mer reaches out to the sea, pulling water toward himself, shaping it into a spear. He hurls the weapon at the Deep One, hardening it to ice as it flies. The psionic adversary dodges the projectile and launches an orb of fire back at Mer. The spell explodes in the water jinn's face, his reaction too slow to stop it. He cries out.

The other two jinn send twin disks of pinwheeling water at the Deep One, the edges razor sharp. At least one hits, sending the creature flying back through the air.

Soran's vision wanders, movement at sea catching her attention. Three ships float out toward the horizon. A pit of dread settles in her watery stomach. By the time she turns back to the shore, five jinn lie on the ground, unmoving. How long did she look away? Time feels different now, each second both a flash and an eternity.

The Deep One holds something in his hand. A chain. The Shiver Seed, encased in snowy crystal, sways in the breeze.

They have It. *Soran's mind races, panicking.* Please, Nelami, don't let them find her.

The pull of the tide is too strong to resist. Exhaustion falls on Soran like a crashing wave. She allows herself to be drawn out to sea, eyes struggling against the weight of sleep and tears that won't fall. At last, she sleeps.

Kiana let her hand fall.

"Mm. Not exactly what I was hoping for."

"Didn't get directions to the super-secret hidden monster?" Tash said, cracking a brief smile.

Kiana shot him a look. "No, but Soran's memories are still in there, still jumbled. And I did learn that the jinn never got what they wanted from the Shiver Seed. A Deep One was there in Tribali, ready to take it as soon as the jinn had it in their possession."

"Whatever this Terror is, the Deep Ones want it badly." Tash pointed down the northeast-facing passage with his sword. "Should we see where it leads?"

Kiana turned to the snow leopard and the ranger, both of whom possessed better directional instincts than she did. She could track, certainly, but these tunnels were oddly clean.

"Thoughts?"

Aravel uttered a cross between a mew and a growl and took off down the tunnel.

"I guess that settles it," Tash said.

They dashed after the big cat.

Kiana whispered, "Do you think she actually heard something, or—"

"Shh!" Reyan turned with a finger to his lips, stopping abruptly midstride.

Aravel had stopped too, sniffing the air.

"There's something down that way." Reyan pointed down a tunnel that jutted off to the left.

The tunnels were dim in the blue filtered light, but keen elven eyes easily pierced the gloom. Reyan, too, seemed to be managing okay in the subterranean environment.

"Looks like it dead-ends about sixty feet ahead," Tash said after a moment. "But there is something down there. Looks like . . ."

"Rubbish," Kiana finished for him. "It looks like piles of detritus." She shook her head. "Let's go."

After another couple of minutes of travel, the main tunnel branched off into three passageways. Kiana pointed left.

"That one takes us closer to the heart of the glacier. I think that's the way."

They'd made it no more than ten yards into the leftmost passage when the bodies started appearing. Unlike the other corpses they'd encountered so far, these were far along in the decomposing process, mere piles of gleaming bones.

"How long have these bodies been down here?" Kiana bent down to inspect the nearest skeleton. Each bone bore distinct grooves. Kiana swallowed a lump rising up her throat. "Sweet seas." She shot to her feet to escape the sight.

"What is it?" Tash hunched over to get a better look. "Acid?"

"No, not acid. And they didn't decompose. Those grooves . . . they've been picked clean. Something ate them."

A low growl rumbled in Leopard Aravel's throat.

"Agreed," Kiana said. "Let's keep moving. Keep your eyes open."

Taking deliberate steps so as not to tread on the bones of the dead, the party continued down the tunnel at a relatively steady pace, Tash heading up the pack. What started as a body or two every ten to fifteen feet eventually became clusters of three or four, about half of which clearly weren't humanoid. Enemies had fallen in nearly equal numbers, almost all of them reduced to skeletons. But not the spider brains. They were left whole.

"At least the druids put up a fight," Kiana said, hoping to evade the crushing wave of sadness poised over her head at the sight of so many brethren lost. She began muttering a prayer to Nelami. Then something ahead chilled her blood.

A leather-clad body slumped in the passage, the head smooth with black veins crisscrossing in a chaotic web. A Deep One, also left whole. Kiana's heart rate ticked up a few beats.

"They got one," she whispered. "Maybe they stopped the other too."

"We can only hope." Tash bent to inspect the corpse of the enemy they'd feared for weeks.

"Help."

The voice came as Aravel and Reyan hunched over the Deep One, trying to glean anything they could about how to fight it most efficiently.

"Did you hear that?" Kiana whispered.

Tash nodded. He stood and took a few slow steps, head cocked to one side, listening.

"Please, help."

Something about the voice troubled Kiana. She could hear it, but she couldn't pinpoint any distinguishing features of the voice. Was it high? Was it raspy? Male? Female? And where was it coming from? It was as though she forgot the sound as soon as it faded.

"What's going on?" Reyan called softly from behind Tash.

"Someone's crying for help," Kiana said, still trying to make sense of the voice.

"I don't hear anything," the ranger said after a pause.

The tunnel's width allowed them to travel two or three abreast, so Kiana moved to Tash's side and walked in tandem with him farther down the opening. Five steps, six steps, slow and steady. Soon, a gruesome sight emerged from the gloom.

"Blazing hells." Tash's muted curse carried back to Reyan's attentive ears.

"Is that smell what I think it is?" he asked.

Up ahead, maybe sixty feet, a mound of bodies blocked half the tunnel. These were not skeletons but freshly deceased Ice Druids, trolls, and other unidentifiable creatures.

"If you think it's a mountain of dead bodies, then yes," Tash said.

Kiana pressed a hand over her mouth to stop herself from gasping. Or gagging.

"Help!"

Urgency punctuated the cry, and Kiana and Tash both rushed forward. They halted at the mass of corpses, eyes frantically searching for any that might still be alive. Their search abruptly ceased when two tentacles sprang out from the grisly heap and grappled them both about the waist. The elves cried out in surprise and pain as the barbed appendages tightened around them.

Panic edged into Kiana's breathing, flashbacks from the Midlane River smacking her like a fist. Instead of giving in to the fear, she grasped the leathery tentacle with her free hand.

"Infurian vulneri."

Gashes opened up along the rough flesh as concentrated lightning spread out from Kiana's fingers in flickers of arcing magic. The tentacle released and retracted as whatever beast it belonged to snarled. In response to the loss of one quarry, the other tentacle smashed Tash into the hard wall of the tunnel.

"Ungh," he gasped as the air rushed from his lungs. With both arms pinned at his sides, his sword hung useless from his hand. Feet pounded down the corridor behind them as Reyan and Aravel joined the fray.

A fleshy face with clouded, glowing eyes popped up from the pile of dead bodies.

"I don't have a shot!" Reyan yelled.

His shout was drowned out by a growl as Aravel tore into the tentacle holding Tash with knifelike fangs.

The creature attached to the tentacles rose up from its hidey-hole with a shriek. Thick, leathery skin covered the four-legged body, its long snout ending in a screaming mouth filled with dozens of pointy teeth—the same type that lined the four tentacles protruding from its sides. Perfect for tearing flesh off bones.

The head hovered at the end of a long, oscillating neck, seeking its next target. The obvious choice was the snow leopard chomping down on its flailing appendage. The bite connected, and the creature got a mouthful of fur.

Tash took advantage of the distraction and broke the grapple. Sword arm free, he swung the blade at the eyes, blinding one. The ensuing scream echoed off the walls, making Kiana wince as she drove her staff into the top of the thing's head. A second later, two arrows sank into one of the corpses between Kiana and the creature. She shot a frown at Reyan, who muttered under his breath as he nocked a third arrow.

Aravel pounced, wrapping her paws around the snout and biting deep into the area just behind the jaws. Two tentacles reacted by trying for another grapple. Tash hacked into one with his sword; Reyan nicked the other with a shot that finally hit something. Kiana pulled her dagger and slammed the blade up under the creature's jaw. No need to waste more magic on this heap of teeth. With a final exhale, the thing slumped to the ground.

Aravel stretched and shifted back into her normal form. "Anyone else getting really tired of telepathic monsters?" She eyed the arrows sticking out of a dead troll, then turned her gaze on Reyan, eyebrow arched. "Nice shooting, ranger."

Bottling his frustration, Reyan tucked an arrow back into his quiver. "Seems my late night has put me at a bit of a disadvantage."

"Well, I hope whatever you were doing was worth it."

The ranger said nothing.

Sensing the pending awkwardness, Kiana cleared her throat.

"Well, it looks like we found what picked those bodies clean back there."

"And what left behind the pile of garbage." Tash leaned against the wall, left arm bleeding at his side. "It's a quisculor."

Aravel frowned. "That doesn't sound like a real thing."

"They're a type of scavenger. Some places use them to clean out sewers or"—he waved around them with his good arm—"tunnels. Not usually violent, though."

"It was enthralled. I saw the eyes." Kiana resheathed her dagger and pulled out a healing potion. She handed it to Tash.

"I'm fine. Save it."

"Please? I have healing magic. You don't."

"Save yours." He pulled out a potion of his own and consumed it in a single gulp, the worst of the damage to his arm mending before he'd even stowed the empty vial. "Shall we?"

Once past the disturbingly large pile of bodies, they continued unobstructed. No more bodies littered the passage. The group stayed alert for anything else out of the ordinary.

Something tickled the edges of Kiana's perception, and she raised a halting hand. The sound of low moaning drifted through the still air of the underground maze. The timbre suggested female.

"There's someone up there." Kiana picked up the pace. "This way. Come on!"

They dashed ahead, alert but not stealthy. The tunnel curved sharply to the left, and the party suddenly faced a large window overlooking a wide, deep cavern. In the middle of that cavern, growing through a hole in a round stone platform, a tree rimed with frost dominated the view. White ice crystals sparkled fiercely, even in the faint light. Beneath the platform, the tree's massive root ball floated just above the floor of the cavern, the tangle's diameter at least three times that of the tree's crown. Inside the root ball, a sphere of blue-lit ice pulsed with veins of red.

"It's the Shiver Tree," Kiana said, voice hushed with awe.

"You have to stop them," said a pained voice to Kiana's right.

A small figure lay on the floor near the window. Her head rested at an awkward angle against a toppled podium.

"They've already been in there for too long," the gnome said with a grimace. "They can't be allowed to have her!" She moaned and wiped a bloody tear from her cheek.

Kiana's head whipped to the side, and she spotted him through the window almost instantly. Three extra-wide catwalks jutted out from various tunnel entrances into the cavern. On the one farthest across the vast space, feet hovering six inches off the ground, was a Deep One.

CHAPTER TWENTY-TWO

"How do we get down there? Can we go through the window?"

Kiana kept her eyes on the chamber, afraid to look away. She watched the Deep One's movements, small hand gestures indicative of an elaborate and intricate spell. Black, undulating tendrils of smoke coiled around the black robe, which was embroidered with green symbols foreign to Kiana. Hanging from his neck was a snow-white crystal.

No one else appeared to be in the vast space. Sensing movement from the gnome, Kiana finally tore her gaze away and looked to see the girl pointing to an opening off to the left side of the room.

"Through there. It will take you straight to them. The window is impenetrable." She was struggling for breath now, each inhale a laborious task that took her closer to death's door.

Kiana bent down, healing spell at the ready.

"No!" the girl cried, eyes sparking back to life for but an instant. "Save your spells. Stop them. One is already injured."

"Wait, more than one made it in?" Aravel asked.

"Two, yes."

Aravel sighed. "The dead one in the tunnel makes three. Knew there had to be more than the two the kid saw."

Kiana reached out to the gnome again. "If I don't heal you, you'll die."

The girl's face blazed with obstinance. "Then I'll go safely with Nelami." Grief thickened her voice. "Like the rest of my people."

When Kiana hesitated, the gnome grasped her wrist.

"Whatever happens, they mustn't gain control of Lystrix."

"What is Lystrix?"

A flicker of confusion passed over the gnome's face.

"You've come but do not know?"

Kiana ticked her head to the side in the slightest gesture of negation.

The Ice Druid frowned. "She is a Terror."

Despite the girl's weakening voice, the words carried a heavy weight, and Kiana sensed the next words to leave her lips would crush them all.

"She is a tyrant queen . . ."

Just say it, Kiana thought.

". . . and the fiercest of all the ancient red dragons."

There it is.

The panic Kiana expected did not come. Instead, her limbs grew leaden with the dread of failure. The repercussions would be mighty indeed.

"The magic of the Tree keeps her trapped within the ice of the root ball. She must not go free, nor be allowed to fall under the sway of the Deep Ones. They wish to use her in their war against the Shadow Wraiths, a war they are losing. Again. It's why only a few Deep Ones have come. The others are locked in battle with a race that means to eradicate them once and for all. Lystrix could turn the tide of the war. The power they would wield with such a beast under their influence would be tremendous. She could command any other chaotic dragon she chose, including those currently allied to the Shadow Wraiths. The Deep One army would be nearly unstoppable."

As if to punctuate the gnome's point, a loud creak echoed out from the chamber below. The girl's head tilted back in an effort to see through the window.

"The Shiver Tree is weakening. You must go. But—"

Another creak groaned mournfully from the glistening trunk, stopping the druid short.

"Don't have to tell me twice," Aravel said. She turned on her heel and raced off down the passage.

"Ari!" Kiana took off after her, but not before pressing a healing potion into the gnome's grasp.

"Be careful!" the girl cried feebly as the men joined the pursuit. More words followed, but Kiana's focus was elsewhere as she raced after her friends. They caught up with Aravel at a fork in the tunnels.

"Which way?" Aravel's hands rested on her hips, head swiveling from one opening to the other.

Attempting to orient herself to their location, Kiana pointed left.

"I think that will take us straight to the Deep One. The one I could see, anyway. Anyone looking to get up close and personal should head that way, but those of us looking for range should go right, keep our distance."

Aravel reached into her pouch and pulled out the potion of invisibility.

"Hey, Tash."

The noble looked at her over the top of Kiana's head.

"How do you feel about a little surprise attack?" Aravel jiggled the vial. "The rest of us head that way and distract him from afar"—she jerked her head toward the right tunnel—"and you go in and stab the shady blighter." She nodded left.

The corner of the sorcerer's mouth curled up in a smirk.

"I'll give it a go." He accepted the potion, then locked eyes with Kiana, awaiting her signal. Beside him, Aravel tipped the Potion of Mental Resilience into her own mouth.

Kiana felt the pressure steadily grow in her chest. There were so many things she wanted to say to her friends: words of encouragement, expressions of gratitude, possible goodbyes. She knew none of it could be said. There wasn't any time.

Instead, she said, "Let's do this."

They ran.

The brains rushed in like a gelatinous tide.

Only ten yards into the tunnel, a dozen brain creatures emerged from the darkness. Kiana conjured shards of ice to turn her staff into a mace-like bludgeoning tool to help keep the clamoring wave at bay.

"Maybe one of us should go back and help Tash," Kiana said, clubbing yet another brain. "There are probably just as many or more of these things in the other tunnel, and he's on his own."

Aravel pulled back her scimitar, awash in gooey brain matter.

"On it!" she yelled.

Without a moment's pause, she spun and raced back down the way they'd come.

"Ari!" Kiana called after her. No response came, just the fading echo of impossibly light footsteps. Kiana rolled her eyes. "I swear that girl's impulsiveness is going to get us into serious trouble one of these days."

Reyan pulled his dagger from the last brain, whipping the shadowy gore that coated it onto the tunnel wall with a flick. He looked back at Kiana.

"At least she keeps us on our toes," he said, slightly out of breath. The circles under his eyes had deepened, giving the appearance of two black eyes.

"Are you going to be okay?" Kiana thought back to the two arrows that had missed their target and sunk into the bodies right next to her. She couldn't chance Reyan hitting Tash or Aravel with a rogue arrow.

The ranger gave her a wry smile. "I'm not going to kill our friends, if that's what you're worried about." He rolled his shoulders back and stretched his neck from side to side. "I'm fine."

Another brain scurried up the tunnel, and Kiana quickly threw out a hand, hurling a small ball of druidic flame. The fire slowed the creature but did not kill it. Reyan kicked the brain as hard as he could, bouncing it against the wall. It moved no more.

"Blessed tides, how many more of those things are there going to be?"

"Let's go find out," Reyan said, setting off at a brisk jog.

The answer was zero. At last, Kiana and Reyan saw brighter light up ahead, dancing beams of blue with intermittent flashes of red.

"Okay, when we come out, we come out swinging, all right?" Kiana said, tightening her grip on her staff, magical energy vibrating through her. Every sense, every instinct, was heightened with the grim reality of imminent battle. "And keep an eye out for that second one."

"You got it." Reyan nocked an arrow and held his bow out in front of him, angled slightly down. "Ladies first."

Kiana burst out onto the catwalk, which extended only fifteen feet, a quarter of the distance to the Tree. Nearly straight ahead, more than a hundred feet away, the Deep One hovered in the same spot Kiana had seen him from above. His deliberate, practiced movements continued. Freya's Crystal—and the Shiver Seed within it—flared around his neck.

"*Fulmurien!*" the druid yelled, hand outstretched, the spell echoing around the chamber.

A bolt of radiant light shot from her hand and smashed into the Deep One's shoulder. His body lit up with a faint glow as the magic seared into him. A furious hissing noise filled Kiana's mind.

"*Insssignificant wretch! How dare you challenge usss?*" said a familiarly raspy, extrasensory voice.

The last word still reverberated in Kiana's mind when one, then two arrows flew by her on their way to the other catwalk. The Deep One spun out of the way of both shots and lifted a gloved hand. A javelin of fire wreathed in writhing smoke launched back at them. Or rather, at Kiana.

Not wanting to fall off the six-foot-wide outcropping, Kiana hesitated too long and caught part of the blast on her left side, smoke exploding up in front of her and partially obscuring her view. She gritted her teeth against the scorching pain and started to cast another spell. Before she got the chance, a bear dove through the opening behind the Deep One and collided with the monster, dragging him to the ground with her teeth.

Fighting against the grip of the bear's jaws, the Deep One held out a hand, and Kiana watched as a flood of red, crackling electricity poured over Aravel's beast form. She let out a roar, which soon turned to a scream as the bear faded back into an elf, the amount of inflicted damage too great to maintain the shift. The next instant, the Deep One reared back his head and a tortured shriek exploded in Kiana's mind. Tash suddenly appeared beside the creature, invisibility broken, sword stuck up to its hilt in the thing's side.

The sorcerer made to twist the blade, but the Deep One launched himself backward, off the catwalk, and stopped halfway to the Shiver Tree, levitating over the massive root ball.

Seizing the opportunity this presented, Kiana and Reyan both let loose their next attacks, Reyan managing to lodge one arrow in the Deep One's leg. Kiana summoned a Shimmer, the radiant energy like ghostly moonlight searing into his slick, pearly flesh. The hits redirected his fury back to his original attackers. Another bolt of fire raced toward Kiana.

She dodged left, avoiding the blast, but confusion delayed the casting of her next spell as she watched the wound she'd inflicted on the Deep One start to knit back together.

"What the . . ." she murmured. "He's healing!"

A flicker of movement drew her attention, and Kiana threw her gaze to the Shiver Tree's platform. A barely conscious half-elf Ice Druid slumped against the massive trunk. Beside him, a gnome lay unmoving, face down. Unconscious or dead, Kiana didn't know. The half-elf dropped his hands back into his lap, obviously having completed his healing spell. Silver film glazed his eyes.

"No," Kiana whispered. She focused her next spell at the base of the Tree. "*Vinai assseqi.*"

Thin branches sprouted from the trunk of the Shiver Tree and wrapped around the enthralled Ice Druid.

"No more healing spells from you," she muttered.

The distraction cost her. She looked up as a stream of acid from Tash singed only the very edge of the Deep One's cloak, and Aravel went wide with a spurt of flame. The enemy's attention remained on Kiana, its taut, mouthless face a blank mask.

"*You will not ssstop usss, young druid,*" the thing hissed in her mind, the gravelly voice still oddly sibilant given its telepathic nature. "*But you will die trying. Jussst like your friends.*"

All at once, an intense pressure bloomed in Kiana's head, like someone was trying to squeeze her brain out through her eyes. Far more intense than what she'd felt in Garrison, but not as bad as the swamp.

You're not going to get back in here, Kiana thought. She rallied against the psionic intrusion, every ounce of her willpower pouring into creating a mental block to keep the creature at bay. The owl ring around her finger burned icy hot, bolstering her resilience.

Beside her, Reyan doubled over, hands pressed to his temples, screaming.

Gods, no, Kiana thought desperately. "Fight it!" she cried.

"Aaaahhh!" he yelled. Then, just as suddenly as he'd hunched in pain, he straightened and went quiet. He turned his eyes to Kiana and drew his dagger.

Not this again.

"Reyan . . ." She backed up two steps.

"*It is weak*," the Deep One taunted. "*Now you mussst kill your friend before it kills you.*" A high-pitched cackle echoed through Kiana's mind.

Sparing a glance behind her to gauge her distance from the edge, Kiana caught sight of Tash and Aravel fending off an ice troll that must have come at them from the tunnel. Still no sign of the second Deep One. She returned her attention to the ranger now intent on killing her.

Apparently satisfied that his aggressors were well occupied, the Deep One floated back toward the icy prison containing the Terror, resuming his invocation.

"Reyan, don't do this. You have to fight it." Kiana held out a hand, spell ready, begging Nelami she wouldn't have to use it. "I've been there; I know how hard it is. But I need you to be strong here. Please. Come back to me."

He lunged.

Kiana parried with her staff and swung around behind him. With a better view of the root ball, her eyes grew wide as the red veins surrounding the orb nearly doubled in number.

"Tash, stop him!"

The ice troll now lay dead at her friends' feet. They'd already homed in on the Deep One. Tash threw his arms wide, and though Kiana could see his lips move, the space between them snatched his words.

A thunderous crack rippled out from where the Deep One hovered. And then Reyan's blade slashed into Kiana's arm.

"Argh!" she growled through clenched teeth. *Stay focused!*

She spun away and slammed her staff into the ranger's gut. It felt like the wood had banged into a stone wall.

"Stop attacking me!" she yelled.

Reyan stumbled and shook his head. He looked at Kiana and shook his head again.

He's trying to fight it.

The Deep One screamed at a frequency that felt like a vicious spear of mental sound being rammed into her brain. Then he flew toward Tash like a bat out of the unholy Abyss. Smoky tendrils lashed out, one slipping around the sorcerer's throat, others gripping him about the shoulders. Aravel hurled a ball of flame at the creature's hairless head.

"Let him go, smoky!" she yelled.

Kiana started to intervene when Reyan tried to stab her again.

"Enough!" she growled, barely evading the dagger.

She grabbed her friend's wrist as he stabbed again. This close, she had no leverage with her staff.

"Sorry about this," she whispered, dropping her staff and reaching for her thigh. The staff had barely touched the ground when she jammed her dagger into the meat below Reyan's collarbone, near his shoulder. "Seriously, fight it!"

The second the Crucian metal entered the ranger's flesh, his slackened face took on new life. He stumbled back, lowering his weapon, eyes bulging as he recovered from the mental intrusion. Then something odd happened, and Kiana was sure she was hallucinating. The ranger's eyes changed, the green irises illuminating with an eerie luster.

He locked his slit pupils on her and slowly pulled the dagger from his chest. Nothing happened. No blood poured from the wound. In fact, the wound vanished altogether.

"I'm sorry," he said, voice hoarse.

And that was when something happened that was stranger still. Reyan's features shifted, some sharpening, some elongating, until the creature In front of Kiana was no longer the six-foot ranger she'd been traveling with. Standing over seven feet tall, a grayish-brown werewolf towered above her in all his terrifying glory.

"Umm . . ." Kiana took an unconscious half step back. All other words failed her.

Sidestepping the druid, Reyan the werewolf dashed and hurled himself off the catwalk, directly at the Deep One, Kiana's dagger still in hand. The jump was impressive. Unfortunately, he never made it to his target. From the cavern floor sailed a mass of black cloth and thrashing smoke. The second Deep One threw himself into the werewolf's path, blocking access to his companion. The two creatures collided with a solid thud and tumbled out of sight.

Crazy, wild thoughts descended on Kiana like a plague of biting insects. She had no time to sort them out just yet. The monster still had Tash by the throat, and Aravel came at him with her scimitar. He dodged, but his grip on Tash loosened ever so slightly. He suddenly seemed preoccupied with avoiding Aravel's blade.

Crucian metal, Kiana thought. *It disrupts them somehow.*

Picking up her staff, Kiana readied to launch an attack but heard a snap to her right. Three narrow cracks spiderwebbed up the trunk of the Shiver Tree.

"Uh-oh."

Abandoning her plan, Kiana mentally measured the distance from her outcropping to the Tree. She hesitated. It was going to be close. With a running leap, she launched herself over the chasm. At the edge of her jump, she whispered a spell and vanished in a cloud of mist, reappearing a little more than half the distance closer.

Please let me make it, she prayed.

A glance at her arm told her she probably had only one more in her.

"*Nebela samat.*" The magical vapor engulfed her once more. She emerged just shy of the stone platform.

Gravity wove its invisible coils around her and began to drag her toward the bottom of the cavern. Stretching her arm as far as it would go, the druid felt her fingertips connect with the ledge as she fell. With a grunt of effort, she held fast to the edge, her shoulder jarring with the sudden stop. Rough ground tore into her hand.

Another shriek pierced her mind. She couldn't chance a look behind her, instead focusing her attention on heaving herself up onto the platform. Once standing, Kiana took note of the Ice Druid she'd secured to the tree. His weak struggles against her snare demonstrated just how injured he was. He wouldn't last long, and she paid him no more heed. No amount of healing could save him now. The woman beside him, another Ice Druid, still breathed. Kiana whispered a word of healing to stabilize her as she ran ahead.

Quickly covering the distance to the Shiver Tree, she placed her hands on the glacial bark, taking only the briefest moment to revel in the fact that she was here, actually touching the objective that had for so long seemed like an impossible dream. A sudden pain struck her, but it was not her own. She realized with a jolt of shock that she could feel the Tree, its weakening state. Steady streams of water dripped from the crystalline branches. Wetness coated her hands where they rested on the trunk. They didn't have long.

"*Sanye dolim*." The healing incantation escaped in a puff of frosty vapor. Immediately the cracks marring the Tree's trunk started to fuse back together.

"Kiana, look out!"

Tash's voice whirled her around in time to see a bolt of flame soaring toward her. If she moved, it would hit the Tree. If she stayed . . . Well. There was only one thing for it.

She tapped back into the natural magic coursing through her and raised her arms in front of her face. Rimed branches like those of the Shiver Tree wove together around her hands and forearms, crafting a makeshift shield. The fire hit her full force, shattering the protective branches and knocking her back into the trunk.

"Oof!" She kept her feet but felt the impact in every cell of her body. Her Regent Tree deepened to near black, and only one leaf remained.

The Deep One sped toward her, expressionless black eyes somehow blazing with hatred.

"*You will ruin everything!*" he screamed into her mind.

"Good!" Kiana shouted back.

He was close now, maybe fifteen yards away. Kiana rapidly ran through a mental list of spells she could still cast that might help in her current predicament. Ice crystals had just started to form on her fingertips when, out of nowhere, an ethereal dragon manifested in front of her, shimmering, translucent bronze scales catching some otherworldly light like thousands of ghostly gemstones.

"Holy mother of tides," Kiana gasped.

So that was Tash's mental armor—his draconic ancestry. He could summon the spirit of an ancient dragon, infusing himself with the mental and physical resilience of his protector. Across the gap, the sorcerer rested on one knee, broken and bleeding. Still, his eyes blazed with amber light. If she squinted, Kiana could just make out the spread of spectral wings behind him.

Now confronted by a gargantuan dragon spirit that blocked his path to Kiana, the Deep One seemed at a loss for what to do. The dragon relieved him of his indecision, unleashing a wave of force and acid that knocked the Deep One back onto the catwalk, sizzling and prone at Tash and Aravel's feet. Having lost his healer, the fiend now showed tremendous signs of wear. Smoke oozed from his wounds, and a thick, gooey black substance had begun to coat the pale skin of his face.

"You . . ." the Deep One hissed. "*We will dessstroy you for thisss.*"

Kiana was only half listening. The sound of falling water turned her focus back to the Shiver Tree. The once-luminous branches were fading, melting into nothing.

Suddenly remembering the dying druid in the observation room, Kiana frantically sought her unfinished and unheeded warning.

Be careful . . .

She touched her hand against the slick, wet trunk.

"Oh gods."

She spun back to Aravel, who already had her hand out over the prone form of their enemy.

"Time for you to go, tar face."

"Aravel, wait!"

But it was too late. The druid released her fiery attack, striking dead center on the thing's chest, ending him.

Don't use fire.

For a moment, nothing happened. The Deep One was dead, and Tash and Aravel draped arms wearily over each other's shoulders in a congratulatory hug. Tash released the dragon spirit back to its realm. The red, pulsing veins engulfing the orb ceased their throbbing and disappeared. Kiana should have felt ecstatic. So why did it feel like all the air had escaped the room?

The tremble started gently, barely noticeable at first. As the tremors grew, head-sized chunks of the stone around Kiana crumbled and fell away to the cavern floor. Below, the light from the orb blazed brighter.

The druid peered over the edge. Something moved within the frozen prison. Then, behind her, a deafening crack splintered the air, reverberating off the walls in a thunderous echo. Kiana ducked and turned. Her heart sank.

It was over.

The trunk of the Shiver Tree was split in two.

CHAPTER TWENTY-THREE

Kiana backed away from the Tree. If she didn't move now, she'd be just another piece of debris. Spreading her arms, she shifted into a giant eagle and carefully gripped the still-unconscious Ice Druid in her talons. Powerful wings beat down against the air, rocketing her toward her waiting friends. She promptly dropped the bird form, letting the druid fall less than a foot to the catwalk's surface. Aravel caught Kiana as her momentum threatened to send her crashing into the wall. Tash remained on one knee and felt for the Ice Druid's pulse. He looked ready to collapse himself.

"What in the kraken-infested deeps is going on?" Fear and confusion sharpened the timbre of Aravel's words. "And where the salty hells is Reyan?"

Kiana ignored Aravel's questions, eyes glued to the swelling orb. The light was almost blinding now. With a final heave, the root ball splintered. The concussive boom that ensued thumped against Kiana's chest, beat at her temples. The three companions ducked, covering their heads to guard against the frozen shrapnel flying in all directions. Then, deathly silence. The sound of Kiana's pounding heartbeat gradually filled her ears.

Debris settled around them. They coughed against the thick fog of frost and root particles as a new, hellish scent tinged the air. Sulfurous steam rose from somewhere in front of them, breaking the silence. Kiana peered toward where the Shiver Tree once stood. Somehow, the stone platform remained. There, from out of the haze, two eyes glowed.

"Well, that was quite a ride," said a sultry voice.

Stepping into view, a lithe female figure shook out a long mane of black hair. She wore a full-length red dress with slits up the sides of both muscular legs. She was barefoot.

"Uh, okay. Wasn't expecting that," Aravel whispered.

"And who may I thank for restoring my freedom, taken from me so long ago by these ignorant peasants?" The woman gestured casually above her, then cast her gaze from one companion to the next, dark eyes lingering slightly longer on Tash, who slowly, painfully rose to his feet.

"Who are you?" Kiana asked, confused. She'd studied dragons before. Red dragons couldn't shapeshift. At least, in theory.

A bewitching smile lit up the woman's face.

"I am Lystrix."

The answer was both expected and startling. Red dragons were not known for magical abilities. They tended to rely on brute force to crush their enemies. But then, when speaking of one this ancient and power-ful, Kiana supposed all bets were off. She worked to keep the fear and surprise off her face, not wanting to expose any potential weakness. Not that it would matter in the slightest if it came to a fight.

Unaware of Kiana's mental and emotional tempest, Lystrix stretched out her arms, tilting her head back to look skyward. "And now that I am free once more, I shall rebuild my empire." She leveled her smol-dering gaze on the three friends. "You. You seem like capable warriors, perhaps worthy of a place in my ranks." She held out a beckoning hand. "Join me." Her eyes widened, a peculiar madness about them. The pupils flared red.

The three elves shared a moment of bewildered silence.

"Um, sorry, that's going to have to be a no," Kiana said at last.

Lystrix smirked. "Fools, all of you." Her voice was casual, unperturbed.

On the ground, the Ice Druid stirred. The movement drew Lys-trix's stare.

"Ah, one of my beneficent captors. I should very much like to peel every inch of skin from her body." The rapid flash of violent hatred in her eyes lent troubling weight to the sentiment. "And I'll do it slowly. I'll start by ripping off one limb for every *millennium* you had me trapped in this prison." She ground out the word "millennium" like it hurt her to speak it.

Kiana took several deliberate steps forward, stopping directly in front of the waking druid. Tash shifted behind her. She imagined he was regretting his decision to dismiss the dragon spirit so quickly right about now.

The sudden burst of piercing laughter from Lystrix made Kiana flinch. It was perhaps the last reaction she'd expected. Amusement spent, the dragon-woman focused red eyes back on the group. A mirthless smile curled her lips in a mockery of joy.

"It matters not." She took one step closer and leaned forward. "One day soon, *you all will burn*." The threat in those last four words rang clear. She spit them out with a deranged vehemence, voice rasping against her throat and coming out pure acid.

Kiana braced for the coming attack. What chance they stood against an ancient red dragon, especially in their current exhausted state, she didn't care to speculate on. But she'd fight till the last. So, she knew, would her friends.

It happened quickly. Hunching her shoulders, arms held wide, the woman Lystrix slipped away. In her stead, impossibly huge leathery wings spread out from a colossal body coated in red, gleaming scales. Plumes of smoke poured from a long, horned snout beneath eyes dancing with fire. The scent of sulfur intensified. The beast stood tall on her hind feet, each clawed toe a deadly weapon in its own right. This ancient beast was bigger than Kiana could have imagined.

The druid stood rooted to the spot, petrified. She gripped her staff tighter.

The dragon let out a terrifying roar. No, not a roar. A laugh. Rearing back her head, Lystrix unleashed a torrent of fire from her mouth straight at the cavern ceiling. The heat in this enclosed space was immense. Sweat beaded at Kiana's hairline, and she longed for the cooling effect of her cloak. Everything around them shuddered. Bits of ice fell from above, crashing to the already debris-strewn floor.

After an eternal thirty seconds, the fire ceased, but the shuddering did not. A hole more than big enough to admit a dragon marred the ceiling above, daylight pouring in. Without so much as a glance at the elves, Lystrix pushed free of the platform, which crumbled beneath the force of her takeoff, and shot through the opening, out of sight. The wind from her sudden flight knocked the companions back, and they barely stayed standing.

More ice plummeted from above. The hole had destabilized the glacier, and the entire outcropping was now collapsing under the strain of the damage.

"We have to get out of here!" Kiana bent down to the Ice Druid, who now seemed to be mostly awake, looking bewildered. Deep lines denoting her advanced age etched worry across her mouth and fore-head. "Can you walk?"

"I . . ." Her eyes bulged, and she screamed.

Kiana followed her line of sight. Werewolf Reyan was climbing the wall behind them, ragged clothes stained with blood. Burn marks singed the fur along his side.

"What the fiendish blazes is that?" Aravel cried. "A werewolf?" She raised a hand toward Reyan.

Kiana grabbed her wrist. "Wait!" She still didn't quite believe her own next words, even as she spoke them. "It's Reyan."

"I beg your pardon?"

To prove the point, Reyan hopped onto the platform and reverted back to his human form. Somehow, he looked less exhausted than he had prior to falling off a ledge in the arms of a Deep One, despite his wounds. He extended his hand. In it, he held Kiana's dagger, handle angled toward the druid. She took it.

"Thank you."

Meanwhile, Aravel stood speechless, for perhaps the first time in her life.

"I'll explain everything, I promise," Reyan said. "But Kiana's right. We need to leave, now." Without asking permission, he crouched down and lifted the wounded, petite gnome into his arms. "Let's go." He turned toward the mouth of the tunnel and ran.

Tash reached for Kiana's hand, slipping something into it.

"I believe you've been looking for this."

Kiana looked down to find the Shiver Seed sparkling up at her from the white shell of Freya's Crystal. As it gleamed against her palm, Kiana felt the lifting of a spiritual burden, replaced by a wash of happiness that was only partly her own. Soran's relief crossed the chasm of time and space, filling Kiana with a tentative peace.

She faced Tash with gratitude on her lips, but on finally getting a good, up-close look at him, she instead rapidly uttered a healing spell, the biggest she could muster, sending her final leaf whirling into nothing. She wrapped the chain bearing Freya's Crystal around her wrist.

"Come on!" Aravel yelled. She threw one of Tash's arms over her shoulder, supporting him. Kiana did the same on the other side, and the three rushed out of the chamber after Reyan.

The tunnel was a heaving cacophony of cracks, groans, and the thud of ice chunks tumbling to the ground. As the glacier continued to break up, Kiana and Aravel used what minor magic they could to manipulate the terrain, easing the way through the collapsing tunnel and removing obstacles from their path. Kiana prayed they'd make it through before a total cave-in. Though Tash had consumed their final healing potion and seemed steadier on his feet, Kiana kept a supporting arm at the ready as they ran, letting Aravel dash ahead to keep an eye on Reyan's progress. Or just on Reyan.

When they reached the observation room, the world tilted.

"Get down!" Kiana dropped to the floor with Tash, Aravel beside them. Reyan hunkered down at the back of the room, sheltering the Ice Druid's body with his own. The dying druid they'd encountered here earlier was nowhere to be seen.

Ice shards rained down as a shattering splintered the air. Everything beside them fell away as the southwest half of the glacier collapsed.

The sun glared blindingly off the wintry land all around them, the contrast in lighting a shock to the system. It took their eyes a moment to adjust.

"Everyone okay?" Kiana coughed moisture from her lungs.

"Nope." Aravel pushed herself to her knees. "But for the sake of getting the hells out of here, yes."

"Who are you people?" The Ice Druid scooted away from Reyan, her leg leaving a streak of blood on the ground.

"I'm Kiana Paletine, and these—"

A hunk of ice crashed to the floor between them.

"Can we talk about this from safer ground?" Aravel brushed shards of glacier from her sleeve.

"We'll have to climb." Tash pointed at the cliff of ice now towering over them. He glanced at the druids. "Unless you two . . ."

Aravel shook her head. "I'm tapped, sorry. Need a better-than-average nap before I try to shift again."

"Then climb it is."

The going was not easy, especially in their battered state, but eventually they reached the top of the glacier. When they did, a collective gasp sent a vaporous cloud of unspoken grief into the late-morning air.

Through the valley and beyond, as far as the eye could see to the east, a sixty-foot-wide swath of charred earth scorched the landscape, a trail of devastation marking Lystrix's exit. Every tree, every shrub, every blade of grass, reduced to ash. The dragon was nowhere to be seen.

"What have I done?" Aravel whimpered.

CHAPTER TWENTY-FOUR

Kiana spun to face her friend. "What do you mean, what have *you* done? We're all a part of this."

"It was the fire, though, wasn't it?" Tears filled Aravel's eyes. She pressed a hand to her stomach. "If I hadn't killed him with fire, Lystrix would still be contained."

"That's likely true."

Kiana rounded on the Ice Druid. She was on one knee, tying a strip of her tunic around the wound on her thigh.

"Excuse me?" Kiana said, voice heated in defense of her friend. She wouldn't let Aravel bear the weight of responsibility for this calamity. "Who do you think you are?"

"I believe I asked who you are first." Her steady gaze burned with insistence. "Our Order has been sequestered here for centuries, hiding, and on the day the Deep Ones find us, you happen upon us as well? Explain yourselves."

Suddenly very weary, Kiana bowed her head. "I am Kiana Paletine of Tribali. My friends and I learned of the Deep Ones' possession of the Shiver Seed and came to stop them from gaining control of the Terror. We pieced together your location through clues found in ancient druidic texts."

"There was to be no record," the druid said quietly.

"There wasn't, really," Aravel said. "She just knows a lot about flowers."

The elderly druid cocked her head. "What?"

"Never mind."

"What is your name, *matresca*?"

Tash's use of the druidic title of respect earned a surprised smile from Kiana. And from their new acquaintance.

"I am Oohry."

Tash dipped his head as he offered his name, followed by Aravel's. Reyan stood back from the others, quiet but observing.

"So you're telling me that you four came here to save us? To stop the Deep Ones and their army of beasts? Alone?"

Suddenly Kiana was back in Old Home, sitting across from Ravaini in a dark, musty tavern.

"I'll do it. I'll take on the Deep Ones and save the Ice Druids."

"You and what army?" imaginary Ravaini asked.

"I can do this."

Her sister pursed her lips. *"I believe in you, Kiwi. But what happens if you fail?"*

A Terror is unleashed on the world.

But I can do this.

Laughter, uncontrollable bouts of giggles, bubbled up and out of Kiana like a fountainhead after the spring melt. She bent over, suddenly gasping for air as the laughter threatened to turn to racking sobs. Tash placed a soothing hand on her back.

Regaining control, she said, "Yes, that is precisely what we did. Though we didn't mean to come alone." Her thoughts drifted to her father, where he might be. Was he close? Did it matter now?

Oohry studied her. "You said you were from Tribali. Does the Mother Tree fail? Our Tree, before . . ." She cast a devastated glance at the destruction below. "The Shiver Tree had weakened to the point that it would no longer grant our initiates their marks. We were on the verge of abandoning our sequestration and sending out a delegation when . . . *this* happened."

Kiana tilted her head. "The Mother Tree . . . you mean the Monarch Tree, right?"

"Is that what you call it now? I suppose High Druid Ilestra finally got her way."

"Whoa, the Mother Tree is the Monarch Tree? *Our* Monarch Tree?" Aravel turned to Kiana. "It's been in Tribali all along?"

Oohry smiled sadly. "Forgive me, I forgot that you would not know."

"Why wouldn't we know?" Kiana stepped forward. "Why have you been in hiding for so long? What happened to the Orders?" She stopped herself before more questions could slip out.

The Ice Druid gazed at the ruined valley. "The night the Shiver Seed was stolen from the Ice Druids, the Festival of Renewal was attacked. Dozens were slaughtered, including our representative, Soran."

Kiana flinched but did not interrupt. Not yet.

"A powerful dark sorceress, Miliana Barethorn, beset the celebration with a host of demons at her command. They meant to steal all the Seeds, to stop the replanting of the Mother Tree and to free the Terrors."

"Why?" Aravel's eyes went wide.

"Because she helped create them."

"Gods," Kiana whispered.

"Fortunately, the druids were able to drive her away and kill her horde, with the aid of your people's Tide Hunters. When Soran didn't return, the Ice Druids assumed it was Miliana who had taken the Shiver Seed. Knowing what she meant to do, the Orders agreed to disperse, to ensure the Trees were hidden and beyond her reach. The Ice Tribe had recently relocated here, to Monjelé, and no one other than High Druid Ilestra yet knew of the new home. They vowed to keep it that way. They secured these borders and agreed no one would come in and no one would leave until the High Druid arrived with news that Miliana had been dealt with. Word never came."

"So you've all been isolated here ever since?"

Oohry nodded. "For generations. It's all any of us have ever known." She quirked her mouth. "Almost."

"What does that mean?" Kiana asked.

"There was one time, well before I was born, that a delegation attempted to reestablish contact with the other Orders."

"What happened?" Tash asked.

"We don't know. They never returned. Three months after their departure, the Ice Druids here in Monjelé received a magical scroll from the Warrior Council in Stormfront. They said they agreed to aid us in our time of need should it arise. We assume the delegates made some kind of pact with them. When the Deep Ones attacked, we sent an elder to fetch them, to see if the pact still stood."

"Geshrem," Kiana whispered.

Oohry raised an eyebrow. "You know him?"

"He's the reason we made it here when we did. He came to Sanctuary instead of Stormfront."

Oohry paled. "What? How?"

Kiana pulled the jasmine blossom from her hair. "Because of this."

The gnome stared at the flower, confused.

Kiana sighed. "Soran wasn't killed by Miliana Barethorn. She was cursed by the water jinn. She still lives."

Oohry started. "That's impossible."

"She sent me this blossom, infused a piece of her soul into it to guide me to the Shiver Seed. To you."

The gnome looked to be processing this information. Then she threw a hand over her mouth, gasping.

"Nelami, have mercy! The Shiver Seed! We have to find it. That Eventide fiend had it on him when he breached the cavern."

Carefully, Kiana unwrapped the chain from her wrist.

"You mean this?"

"You found it," Oohry exclaimed in a hush. She held out her hand. "May I?"

"Why not? It's yours, anyway."

"No, it is not."

The Ice Druid didn't elaborate. Instead, she reached for the Crystal. Blue light shone from within, and the crystal casing shattered. A small white Seed flew from Kiana's palm and began a close, rapid orbit around the head of her staff, as if attracted by magnetic force.

"Ah, yes," Oohry said. "I thought that might be the case. The Shiver Seed belongs to the Shiver Tree, but until such time as the Tree can be planted anew, stewardship passes to the druid deemed worthy for the task." She extended an index finger toward Kiana. "And you, my dear, have been chosen."

Kiana stared, stunned, a tear snaking down her cheek. "Just like that?"

"Just like that."

"But I don't deserve that honor. Not anymore." She felt Tash's hand on her right shoulder, a reassuring squeeze. Beside her, Aravel hooked her left arm with her own.

"I think your friends would disagree," Oohry said. "You said you came here to stop the Deep Ones from gaining control of the Terror Lystrix. That you have done."

"But at what cost?"

Oohry studied her for a moment. "The escape of Lystrix is indeed a heavy misfortune. But had she fallen under the control of the Deep Ones, had they completed their enchantment, that cost could have been even higher. You stopped that from happening, at least."

Kiana gave a weak nod of agreement but remained silent, unable to look away from the smoldering scar of wreckage etched into the land.

"What would the water jinn have wanted with it?"

Oohry turned to Aravel, brow furrowed, framing her answer.

"If I recall my history correctly, the water jinn believed that the Shiver Seed would give them the power to defeat their enemies. While the Seed does grant its bearer some powers, one Seed alone is not powerful enough for such a task. And the stasis magic infused in the Seeds only works when all five are together. The druids tried to explain this to the jinn, but they believed it a lie, a way for the druids to avoid helping them."

"And were they?" Kiana asked.

"To an extent, perhaps. But read any historical text involving interrealm relations. Druids have always tried not to interfere in the affairs of other realms."

Kiana mulled this over for a moment. "Regardless, the water jinn's curse upon Soran is an atrocity. We have to help her."

Pain deepened the lines across the gnome's forehead. "I will assist in any way I can. Once my people's home is rebuilt."

Kiana nodded. "We'll have to find the source of the curse. If she's still alive, still tethered to the sea, there has to be some kind of artifact maintaining the magic that binds her. No known curse has the power to grant immortality."

A thought floated past on a breeze of memory. Kiana felt Soran's dread at the sight of the pirate ships, her inability to approach them. She closed her eyes and breathed a sigh through her nose.

It has to be them.

"You said something about the Shiver Seed granting powers," Tash said. Kiana welcomed the change in topic.

Oohry smiled. "Yes. This Seed will stay with you until you have gathered all five and are able to replant the Mother—Monarch—Tree. With each new Seed, your powers, and those of your staff, will change and grow." She indicated the weapon. "Try it."

Kiana inspected her staff. Floating Seed aside, nothing seemed different. She inhaled deeply and channeled druidic magic into the wood.

Instead of the vines that normally encased it, frost rimed the staff, thickening into the purest of ice. Cold burst along her arm, and Kiana watched as the Regent Tree sprouted more than a dozen new leaves along a single branch. The circular mark in the center of the tree glowed, and as it dimmed, the symbol of a shard appeared at the far edge. Instinctively, Kiana knew what magic the Seed held.

"This is amazing," she whispered.

"Yes, and it will only get better." Oohry held up a finger. "But I warn you, if the Seed has chosen its new bearer, time runs short to renew all the Seeds. The Trees have already begun to fail. Please, you must locate each one as quickly as possible. If they are not renewed before the Mother Tree dims, the Terrors will be free."

"Before it dims?" Kiana said.

"The lights that dance among its boughs. They signal that the magic is still in place. If they die out, all is lost." Her head snapped toward the horizon. "It seems we have yet more visitors this day."

Kiana followed Oohry's gaze. The sight that met her sent her heart leaping into her throat, and she choked back more tears.

Down the valley, a line of warriors, at least fifty strong, approached from the southeast. Even from this distance, Kiana recognized the man marching at the head of their formation, his silver hair blowing in the wintry wind.

"Father!" she cried.

CHAPTER TWENTY-FIVE

Ozmand Paletine saw his daughter running toward him from the ruined glacier when she was still a long way off. Relief flooded his face. The tense set of his jaw relaxed, and the hardened gaze that had been soaking in the destruction before them, trying to make sense of what they were seeing, softened with paternal love.

"Kiana!" He broke away from his warriors and ran to her.

When they collided, she threw her arms around his neck, and he lifted her from the ground, squeezing her tighter than he'd ever squeezed before. She squeezed right back, not wanting to let go, still convincing herself he was even real. They stayed this way for some time.

"My Kiana," he said, stroking her hair. "When I got your message, I feared we'd be too late. I could only get us within an hour's march of your beacon by treewalk." He eyed the remains of the druid colony. "But here you are, alive." He rubbed an affectionate thumb down her cheek, a line of magic trailing the digit and healing the wounds on her face. "What happened here? Did the Deep Ones do this?"

Words lodged in her throat, and she worked to get them out.

"No, the Deep Ones are gone. We managed to stop them from getting control of the Terror—a red dragon—but she . . ." A suffocating surge of grief blocked the rest of the sentence. She shook her head. "Please don't be angry. I should have asked for your help sooner."

Compassion drew Ozmand's features down in concern. "Oh, dear one, I'm not angry. And you made the right decision to leave Tribali."

She looked up, confused. "What do you mean?"

Ozmand took a steadying breath. "After you left, Deep Ones started popping up anywhere that had a high concentration of druids, including Corval. They kidnapped and tortured nearly two dozen, obviously looking for information. We trekked all over the eastern regions trying to stop them for weeks, until they suddenly vanished. If you had sent word of your mission, they may have found the Ice Druids even sooner."

Kiana felt sick with both loss and relief. She squeezed her father's hands tight.

The remainder of the party joined them, having taken their time climbing down from the remnants of the glacier. Reyan kept a little distance from the others. He'd redonned his cloak, but tattered bits of cloth still showed beneath. Ozmand took in their appearance with some alarm. He stepped back and raised his arms as if to encompass the group in a hug.

"Sanas omnisten."

Healing energy cascaded through all of the wounded travelers. Tash took his first full breath since the Deep One had nearly choked the life out of him, the eager inhale audible. Kiana slipped an arm around his waist and pulled him toward her. He complied readily. He placed her cloak around her shoulders and hugged her to him with one arm. Kiana gaped.

"Where did you find this?" She fingered the lining of her cloak. "I was certain it was lost to the mountain of destruction."

The sorcerer wiggled his fingers. "Recovery spell. Found theirs, as well." He pointed to the other two companions. "Figured I'd risk the Chaos for a little warmth."

Kiana smiled. Though sorcerers *could* cast spells indefinitely, the more magic they used, the more likely chaotic magic would result, affecting the spell in unknown ways. Just like Kiana practiced to grow her

Regent Tree, mages practiced to ward off Chaos. Kiana had never seen chaotic magic in action, and she wondered how close Tash had come to his threshold.

Ozmand held out an arm, which Tash clasped respectfully.

"I see you're true to your word. You've helped keep my daughter safe."

This elicited a small chuckle from the sorcerer.

"If anything, sir, I'd say it was the other way around."

"Don't sell yourself short," Aravel said, advancing. "Where in the hells did that bronze dragon come from, and why didn't *that* happen sooner?"

"Aravel," Ozmand said fondly, moving forward to embrace her. He whispered something into her hair that Kiana didn't catch.

By now, the troops from Tribali had caught up to them but maintained a respectful distance. They kept a wary eye on their surroundings in case the danger wasn't fully past. Most were Tide Hunters, armed with bladed weapons of various types and lengths, though a number of druids and mages dotted the ranks as well.

Releasing Aravel, Ozmand's focus landed on Reyan, who stood quietly ten feet away.

"I don't believe we've met." The High Druid extended a hand. "I am Ozmand Paletine of Tribali."

Aravel shifted away uncomfortably as Reyan moved to take the proffered hand.

"Reyan Thein of Estlin. I've been traveling with your daughter and her companions for some weeks." He dipped his head. "Sir."

"Then it seems I owe you a debt of gratitude as well." Ozmand's grip and words were warm, but a piercing chill entered his stare.

Reyan didn't break eye contact. Instead, he gave a slight nod.

"How they came to be in the company of a werewolf is a story I would very much like to hear."

Kiana looked at her father in surprise.

"That makes two of us," Aravel interjected.

Tash cleared his throat.

"Three," she corrected.

"You didn't know?" Ozmand asked with a lilt of surprise.

"Not until the walls were crumbling down around us and an ancient red dragon was burning a trough through the countryside," Aravel said.

Ozmand threw her a look. "Perhaps it's time I hear the full story."

Aravel hung her head and pinched the bridge of her nose.

"I wouldn't even know where to begin. There's just . . . so much."

"We'll start at the beginning, in due time." Kiana brushed a hand down her father's arm. "For now, I think it's best if we look for survivors."

"I think I know someone who will be eager to help with that." Ozmand put two fingers to his lips and whistled.

A blur of orange zigzagged through the legs of the waiting warriors. "Snow!"

Kiana opened her arms to the fox bounding toward her. She didn't put him down until they were standing atop the rubble, digging for a miracle.

Kiana found Kezrac, Shaerna, and their companions buried near the blackened corpse of an ice troll. They'd seen one last victory before the end. Tash found Nya, the druid from the observation room, who had drunk the healing potion and gone to find her brother, also still alive. A handful of others had made it to safety before the glacier collapsed, maybe twenty all told. The bodies of fallen druids lined the grass along what had once been the western edge of the glacier. They never found the yeti, and Kiana prayed it had met a swift end beneath the crushing weight of ice.

The afternoon sun had moved far beyond its peak by the time the search came to an end. Already the shadows stretched longer. This far north, as winter crept in, evening dark would be upon them soon.

After the search, Oohry thanked the elves and Reyan for their help and took her leave of them, withdrawing with the others up the nearest mountain to perform their own sacred rituals, politely declining an invitation from Ozmand to stay for a mourning feast. Watching the druids retreat, Kiana caught a glimpse of movement on a distant outcropping. Snow-white fur wafted in the breeze beside a large boulder.

Nix.

Kiana smiled, feeling the solid presence of her own furry companion against her calf.

Exhausted beyond belief, she dropped onto a stump. The physical and emotional strains of the day, of the weeks, bore down on her, and it was all she could do to keep her head aloft.

Lystrix had let them live.

Why? Kiana thought.

She let her mind go back to the encounter, replaying the interaction with a more objective eye.

Because we are absolutely, utterly insignificant to her.

The thought crashed down in a wave of mixed emotions. Relief at being spared, certainly, but fear and hopelessness commingled in no small amount.

Gradually, the area around Kiana began to change. The grass at her feet became thicker, lusher, while stumps, rocks, and bushes morphed into comfortable seats. Vines encased shorn slabs of stone, hoisting them into makeshift tables. These tables, Kiana knew, would soon be covered with the great feast Ozmand had offered Oohry. Off to the right, a small group of druids worked in unison, infusing the land with magic. They would camp here tonight. Kiana probably couldn't walk ten more steps if she tried.

As daylight waned, tiny motes of light sparked to life throughout the camp, and hundreds of fireflies took flight. One by one, Kiana's companions joined her, all now fully recovered—physically, at least—from the day's battles thanks to a generous outpouring of healing magic. Tash slipped into the smoothed cradle of a rock at Kiana's side, while Aravel cuddled with Snow at her feet. Reyan, still wary of the effect his presence now had on them, chose a plush nest of leaves across from them. The general sobriety of the group led Kiana to believe they'd come to the same conclusion about Lystrix's apparent mercy.

Ozmand found them soon after, having set up guard posts and issued any further orders to the rest of the troops. He whispered a campfire into existence, settling in beside it.

"So, it seems we have much to discuss."

"Yes, like how someone we welcomed among us as a friend turned out to be a werewolf." Aravel had clearly moved from shock to anger. The bite of her words drew a wince from Reyan.

"Indeed. Took me quite by surprise, particularly after your mind-controlled attempts to stab me to death," Kiana added.

"To be fair, I did say I wouldn't kill *our friends*." Reyan managed a half grin, but his attempt at humor fell flat. Kiana watched him stoically. He blew out a heavy sigh through his nose.

"I'm sorry. Truly. I hate myself for being too weak to keep him out of my head."

"I'm not blaming you for that," Kiana said.

Reyan smiled sheepishly and pulled the Potion of Mental Resilience from a compartment in his quiver. "Are you sure?"

Kiana glared at the potion. "I suppose I'll let it slide. But how could you not tell us you're a werewolf? How did this happen?"

He shifted in his seat under the scrutiny of so many eyes. He inhaled, long and slow. "Five years ago, I was on a hunt with my brother. We'd had a good day, bagged a couple wild boar, and we decided to celebrate with some homemade whiskey." He paused, struggling with the painful memory. "We got drunk, careless. We'd heard rumors of something attacking folks in the vicinity, but we were young and cocky, felt invincible. We let our guard down." He picked up a stick and poked at the fire. Sparks popped out from the end of a log. "At first we just thought it was a regular wolf, one that had strayed from its pack. It came into our camp, teeth bared, looking for a fight. Tried to take one of the pigs." He kept his eyes on the fire, as though the memory played out for him in the flames. "Well, we couldn't have that. Eris took a shot at the wolf with his bow, but werewolves can't be hurt by normal weapons. Arrow didn't even make the thing blink. Instead it took a snap at Eris, and I got in the way." He pulled back his sleeve, revealing a nasty scar on his forearm that had heretofore been covered by his arm guard. "Got his jaws around my arm, and I didn't think he was ever gonna let go." He pulled the sleeve back down.

"How'd you get away?" Aravel asked. She leaned forward, sucked in by the story, anger forgotten, for the moment.

"Our daggers were silvered. Gifts from our father on our sixteenth birthdays, identical. Eris flanked the beast and got a couple good stabs in. Got him to let go. When the wolf turned to get Eris, it was my turn to stab. Apparently, we were no longer worth the trouble. It took off."

"But it was too late," Aravel said softly.

Reyan nodded. "Next full moon, I shifted. Didn't really know what was happening. Scared the shit out of the villagers, but fortunately, Eris got me under control with the help of some buddies before I could hurt anyone too seriously." He sighed. "I've spent the last five years learning to fight the curse as best I can. The change can be unpredictable, happen in times of intense stress or if I'm wounded too badly." He shook his head. "It's a miracle I didn't change when that ice scorpion had me in its mouth." He shuddered at the memory. "For a long time, when I changed, I wasn't me anymore. The monster took over, and I was powerless to fight it. But then Madame Lesant came to Estlin, nearly a year ago now, and started teaching me meditation techniques from some ancient discipline once practiced by those with other blood curses. Thanks to her, I can control the curse most of the time now, even in shifted form. But during a full moon"—he glanced at Kiana—"like the one last night in Sanctuary . . ." He grimaced. "I can still be too unpredictable. I needed to get out of town, make sure I didn't do anything I'd regret."

"That doesn't explain why you didn't tell us," Tash said.

Reyan snorted. "I'd just met you. Most people don't take too kindly to werewolves. You even lied about hunting them the day we met. Then, the longer I stayed with you . . ." He sighed. "Just never seemed to be able to find the right time. I was still the outsider. And part of me was afraid that if I told you, you'd ask me to leave, and I couldn't face returning to Estlin, where—you may have noticed—I'm already an outcast. They let me stay because they're too afraid to ask me to leave, but only the kids ever interact with me beyond the most basic formalities." He looked at each of them in turn. "Please, forgive me. I should have been honest with you from the start."

Silence settled over them for a time, everyone digesting this new information. As usual, Aravel broke the silence first.

"Wait, if werewolves are immune to nonmagical attacks, silver aside, how did that fiery ice scorpion of doom almost kill you on the plateau?"

Reyan shrugged, eyebrows arched. "Surprised the fu—" He caught Ozmand's eye and cleared his throat. "—heck out of me too. Most things that bite me only feast on disappointment." He furrowed his brow. "Wouldn't be the first magical monstrosity I've come across, though."

"Magical monstrosity?" Kiana leaned forward.

"Yeah. That octopus, when Eris and I first fought it, I got clipped by one of the spikes, and it tore into me pretty good." His eyes found the ground. "It's why I couldn't save my own brother."

Kiana winced at the memory of her own encounter with those spikes. "Speaking of, we owe you a showdown with that thing."

"What thing?" Ozmand chimed in. He'd been listening closely, obviously gleaning what he could about the adventures that led them here without appearing to pry. The blitz falcon message from Kiana had talked only about the Deep Ones and the Shiver Tree.

"Reyan's village is being plagued by a mutated giant octopus that, well, almost killed me." She checked her father for a reaction. He tilted his head, looking at her through hooded eyes, but otherwise remained impassive. "I told him we'd help him get rid of it when all this was done." She gestured vaguely in the air.

"Well, if you want some help with that"—he motioned to the elves around them—"I'm sure we can scrounge up a little hunting party."

"I appreciate the offer, really," Reyan said, "but I can't endanger anyone else's life."

An enigmatic smile flickered on Ozmand's lips. "Son, battling such creatures is what these warriors do. Once they learn of this beast's existence, I would dare you to try to stop them from helping. Especially since they were unable to assist with the Deep Ones."

"Sir?"

A druid named Jerrith stood behind Ozmand, a platter filled with food in one hand.

"Ah, dinner is served."

The feast was great indeed. According to Tribali's custom, the Hero's Banquet was served in celebration of a great victory or in preparation for a great battle. Or to honor fallen comrades. In this case, they offered up a celebration of life for all the Ice Druids lost. Platters piled with magically conjured fruits, cheeses, breads, olives, and meats made the rounds alongside endless pitchers of wine and mead. Aravel nearly cried at the sight. To Kiana's immense pleasure, some of the Ice Druids trickled back down the mountain to partake in the festivities and honor their brethren.

The friends used the time when their mouths weren't stuffed with delicious things to fill Ozmand in on all that had happened. He listened, soberly rapt. Afterward, he took the floor, offering what information he could to fill in the gaps in their knowledge about the war between the Deep Ones and the Shadow Wraiths. The spark of the conflict between the two sentient races of the Realm of Eventide turned Kiana's stomach.

Deep Ones had not always resembled the beings the party had fought that day. Their species started not so unlike human mages, the most notable difference being, as Tash had asserted, that they spawned from queens—but in a wholly unique way. The Deep Queens magically fused with beings of other races, turning those beings into hybrids that adapted to the weaknesses of the chosen cross species. Unfortunately, most of the other species in the Realm of Eventide were far inferior to the queens in both intelligence and power. And then the queens discovered the Shadow Wraiths.

For a time, the only beings from the Primary Realm to see a Wraith were the gold dragons of old, who could freely travel between realms. Their stories told of beings made from cold and shadow—hence their name—who could wield darkness as a weapon and were particularly vulnerable to heat.

After fusing with a Wraith, the Deep Queens noted an exponential leap in power among their progeny, nearly surpassing their own. This fusion also produced the Deep Ones' distinctive appearance. The new progeny quickly developed proficiency with fire and lightning magic in response to the Shadow Wraiths' weakness. The Deep Queens' arrogance and lust for supremacy prompted a culling of the Wraiths, unwilling participants in the crossbreeding. Finally, the Wraiths would stand no more. So the war began.

The Wraiths eventually turned the tide of war when they ventured to the Primary Realm seeking allies. They found black dragons. Wielding their enhanced powers of persuasion, the Wraiths enticed the chaotic dragons into the fight, nearly eradicating the Deep Ones with their aid. The surviving Deep Ones fled to the Primary Realm's Shadow Core until they had repopulated enough to return and take back control of the realm. Unable to fuse with Wraiths while in exile, they relied purely on magical cloning, a much longer process that weakened their strength over time, forcing them to require greater and greater numbers. Each time they believed their numbers superior, they returned to Eventide to restart the fight. And so it went for centuries.

Had the Deep Ones taken Lystrix, would they have stopped their onslaught after victory over the Shadow Wraiths? Or would they have sought new worlds to conquer? Fortunately, no one would ever know. The Deep Ones had failed in their quest, their chances of winning the war all but lost.

As the night's revels wore on, Kiana and Tash found themselves alone at the edge of a dance circle, just far enough back so as not to get sucked into the to-do. They watched happily as the others twirled and pranced in a sort of coordinated frenzy. A celebration of life in the midst of too much death.

"I guess I have my work cut out for me." Kiana smiled as she watched Aravel, who spun merrily under Reyan's arm in a series of tight circles. It was the liveliest they'd ever seen the withdrawn ranger.

Tash stood behind Kiana, arms encircling her shoulders, cheek resting against her head. "At least you won't have to do it alone."

She tilted her face skyward, leaning her head against his chest. "You'll come with me?"

"I'd love nothing more." He hugged her shoulders and whispered, "It's not every day you find a woman who keeps one of your old buttons as a souvenir of the day you met them."

Kiana scrunched her nose. "Oh, so you caught that, huh?"

He chuckled softly in her ear.

"It might just have been the sweetest thing I've ever seen."

They held each other in the flickering firelight, basking in the still-ness. Kiana felt the tension she'd carried since Old Home begin to fade at last. Hundreds of miles from Tribali, she was home.

Approaching from the right, Ozmand cleared his throat before in-terrupting the moment.

"I suppose I don't have to tell you how proud I am of you, but I will anyway." He looked at his daughter fondly. "What you've accomplished these last couple of months . . ." He shook his head. "It's incredible, Kiana. I never should have questioned the path you wanted to take."

"Thank you, Father. I told you I'd find my way."

"You did. And you have." He hesitated. "I suppose this means you'll be going after the other Seeds."

Kiana nodded. "We will."

"I don't suppose you'd consider taking a regiment of Tide Hunters with you this time?"

Kiana laughed. "We seem to have done okay on our own. And with any luck, we won't be fighting Deep Ones for control of the others."

Ozmand let his reluctance and acceptance play out in his expression.

"When you decided to set out to restore the Orders, I never imag-ined the journey would require so much from you so soon." He smiled. "You will make a fine High Druid one day."

The words set off a memory, and Kiana felt herself sitting atop a snowy mountain, boots dangling over the precipice. She looked over her shoulder, face toward the sky. Through the darkness she could see the spot Soran had sat. She'd now walked in the druid's footsteps.

It was time to make her own path.

EPILOGUE

Books littered the table where Kiana sat tucked in a far corner of the library in Sanctuary. The words in the green leather tome propped against her knees blurred as her mind drifted.

She missed Tash already.

Tem had sent word that Laera's condition was worsening, the stasis spell failing after only a couple of months. The sigil burned out like the last ember of a dying fire, sucking away the small bit of hope that remained. On top of that, Kellen was missing. No one had seen him in weeks. Though reluctant to leave, Tash knew he had a duty to his family. Kiana assured him she'd be fine, that he could catch up to them when Laera was better and Kellen was found. Now, she wasn't so sure, and he'd only been gone two days.

She shifted, dropping her knees to the side and knocking a book to the floor in the process. As she bent over to pick it up, the book floated up to greet her.

"Uh . . ."

"Seems you've been doing your homework."

The voice that spoke was rich, silvery. It sent an inexplicable pang of nostalgia through Kiana, a familiar warmth. She turned to the source.

Standing silhouetted by sunlight from a second-floor window was a tall man, a little over six feet. His dark, well-coiffed hair had streaks of gray, and his kind, intelligent eyes burned a golden caramel. He wore maroon robes embroidered with silver. He stepped closer.

"My name is Xander Gold. I've come a long way to find you, Kiana Paletine."

"Me? Why?" She glanced around, as if maybe another Kiana Paletine had sprouted into existence when she wasn't looking, born of the books she so loved reading.

The man smiled. The strong set of his jaw reminded Kiana of her father.

"I've been hearing of your adventures. You've made quite the impression on some acquaintances of mine."

Apprehension clenched at the druid's insides. "What do you want?"

"Your help."

This stopped Kiana short. "My help?"

"Yes." He began to pace, hands clasped behind his back. "The situation in Amarra grows perilous. There are dangers unknown to most that threaten to throw the world into chaos." He paused. "The Terrors among them."

Kiana fingered the cover of the book she held. "I'm working on that."

The corners of his eyes crinkled with the lift of his lips. "Yes, I'm sure you are. And so it seems our goals are aligned. But there are other factors to consider, as well. Which brings me to the purpose of my visit here."

Kiana waited. She was comforted by this man's presence but unsure of why.

"I'm putting together an adventuring party, your sister among them."

He pulled a dagger from his belt. Kiana's breath hitched, heart fluttering. The dagger was the twin of her own.

"She said you'd know the significance of this."

Kiana smiled, nodded.

"Her work tracking down those responsible for pillaging your shores has put her rather close to the center of this tangled web of treachery. What I'm asking of her, of the others, is dangerous. It will put them in the crosshairs of some beings who wouldn't think twice before killing them in the streets. I mean for them to root out the evil that has been tightening its grip on this continent since the fall of the Tors, to put an end to the poison infiltrating the highest tiers of society. Your destiny, and that of the Seeds, is intricately intertwined with their quest." He paused, eyes boring into Kiana's, weighing the worth of her soul. "Will you join them?"

Dust drifted through a shaft of sunlight like miniature fairies at play. Kiana hesitated but a moment, eyes falling on the dagger, a hole inside her aching to be filled.

"Yes, I will."

PRONUNCIATION GUIDE

CHARACTERS

Kiana Paletine	Kee-**aw**-nuh **Pal**-uh-tine ("Ki" = Key)
Tash Ilirian	Tash Il-**leer**-ian
Aravel Zavir	**Air**-uh-vel Za-**veer** ("Ari" = Airy)
Ravaini	Ruh-**vay**-nee
Nelami	Nay-**la**-mee
Xendal	**Zen**-doll
Alsäm	All-**som**
Madame Lesant	Madam Le-**saunt**

PLACES

Tribali	Trib-**all**-ee
Amarra	Uh-**mar**-uh
Rovenia	Ro-**ven**-yuh
Akkra	**Ak**-ruh
Corval	**Cor**-vul
Estlin	**Es**-lin
Byce	Bice
Dulin	**Doo**-lin
Monjelé	Mon-zhuh-**lay**

ACKNOWLEDGMENTS

Writing a book has been a lifelong dream. I've had many stops and starts over the years, but I finally found the story I wanted to tell—and what fun I had telling it. My most profound gratitude goes to my wonderful husband, Ben, who not only inspired the world in which I ran free but also has been my biggest champion. I asked him to read this book more times than anyone should have to over the course of its writing, but his thoughts and support are always and forever invaluable. His patience should win him awards.

I also wish to thank my brother Drew Milligan and my dear friend Zeke Hudson for diving into early drafts and providing thoughtful feedback that made the final outcome all the better—and for letting me hijack their D&D characters for my own fantastical purposes. Then there is the incredible Micah Hudson, whose enthusiastic support has meant the world to me.

I owe so much to my agent, Cole Lanahan, for believing in my book from the start and for being my advocate through thick and thin. She's a rock star and deserves so much more than these few printed lines of acknowledgment. My editor, Betsy Mitchell, also deserves an ocean of gratitude for digging into the heart of my manuscript and helping me shape, hone, and rework to get that heart beating.

A million thanks to Rick Bleiweiss, Josh Stanton, Josie Woodbridge, Lysa Williams, Lydia Rogue, and the rest of the amazing Blackstone family for making my dream to publish a novel a reality. Their support and hard work have been a blessing.

Last but certainly not least, thank you to professors Edwin Battistella and Bill Gholson for helping set me on the path I'm on today. Your guidance and inspiration lit the way.